KILLING FIELDS

A Dark Horizons Novel

Raina Wolfe

Platinum Oak Publisher

ISBN-13: 979-8-9947636-2-9

Cover design by: DALL-E
Format Cover by: R.M.W
Printed in the United States of America

Dedicated to the honest men and women of law enforcement, the military, and first responders. To those who step into the dark so others don't have to, who stand when it matters, your sacrifice echoes far beyond the moment. Your service is not forgotten.

To my family, my children and grandchildren who love me as I am and who are to me the greatest treasure I have. To my Friends you know who you are you make me laugh and have a fun time.

To my truest friend and Colorado Springs Police Officer for over 25 years. Thane Gillmore. Wish the best in life to you.

At his best, man is the noblest of all animals; separated from law and justice he is the worst.

ARISTOTLE

CONTENTS

CHAPTER PROLOGUE

The Storm God's Offering

Friday, August 19th, 2022

Cascade Mountains | Mid-afternoon

Death arrived. A cloaked specter. Silent, ritualistic, inevitable.

A conductor of an ancient waltz. As a maelstrom of roiling black clouds devoured the horizon...

The storm called him... Tang of ozone present, sharp and electric.

The sun was bleeding out in the west, casting crimson light across the jagged mountain terrain. Slick and glistening from a recent thunderstorm, he tied his victim to the stone altar on a craggy outcrop. Her body shivered. Her eyes fluttered open, groggy from the sedative.

She was striking, even now. White skin blushed with cold, her face framed by a tousled spill of platinum-blonde hair, damp and tangled. Her curves were obvious, even as she struggled weakly, breath catching in her throat. Confused, her blue eyes scanned the storm-split sky. A low rumble rolled in from the northwest. He turned.

Like shattered glass, lightning, raw and white-hot, coursed through the clouds.

His hands, slick and trembling with anticipation, ran along the woman's bare skin, soft, perfumed with something artificial, cloying, expensive. Her physique and appearance drew attention at luxurious fundraisers and exclusive yacht parties. Though he remembered her cruelty.

As thunder rumbled overhead, he surrendered to the ritual. Torturing her slowly and methodically. Her screams rose in cadence with the storm's fury. It was a song he'd listened to many times.

A bolt of lightning split the sky.
The forest below flared white and brutal.

Raising the knife in a momentary flash of lightning, his hand trembled for a heartbeat, not from fear, but from something intangible. Something deeper. Something attempting to rise within him. *The Ghost steadied the knife hand. That one was powerless here.*

Another jagged arc of light cracked the sky. He waited. Breathing hard. Listening.

With the thunder's echo, the blade found its mark in her chest.

The wind shrieked through the trees. Something within him shattered.

He bent and retrieved an ax with runes across the blade, lifted it high, and with a downward strike bit deep.

When it ended, he held her severed head aloft in one hand, the knife in the other. Her long blond hair twisted around him like a bloodied shroud. Blood streaked his face and torso. Torrents of rain unleashed from above. Heavy, pounding his skin as if to wash him clean of sin.

With every offering, he felt the child he once was slip farther away.
The gods answered with a brilliant flash of lightning striking nearby. Yet, the storm moved down the valley until it was only a distant boom, a flash of light within black clouds.

He exhaled slowly, eyes half-lidded, the scent of blood thick around him. The metallic tang mingled with petrichor, soaking the moss and bark. It smelled like home. Like power.

The moon crested over the ridge, casting a silvery light across the altar and the corpse. He slung the headless body over his shoulder, its blood trailing down his back, and began the trek down the winding animal trail to his hidden cabin.

A wolf howled in the distance. Mournful, primal.

He stopped.

A rush of energy surged through his chest. He howled back. Others answered. He smiled. Somewhere in the forest, the pack was bringing down another sacrifice. A fitting tribute to the Earth.

He was part of something ancient. Something righteous.

To his left, something massive moved in the brush. Red eyes glared at him through the trees. He didn't flinch. The creature sensed the same perception. He wasn't simply human.

The storm's gift still burned in his veins.

Would the power last? Would he be called again by the storm god? Silence answered. He would answer every time it called.

The latest sacrifice had sealed her fate. He'd watched her punt one of Edward's prized dogs on the manicured lawn during a cocktail reception. The sound of its yelping still rang in his ears as she laughed and kicked the little dog again.

Spoiled little bitch.

He'd been in the study delivering a sealed document from their Chinese partners.

His jaw clenched at the memory. Well, she'd paid for her transgression.

Returning to the cabin, he put the body near the sleek, black helicopter hidden in the trees. He swept the perimeter. All the markers were undisturbed. He remained alone. He put the body, after rolling it in a tarp, into the rear compartment.

The rain returned with renewed fury. He tilted his head back and let it soak him again. A final anointing.

Then he entered the cabin and lit a fire on the great stone hearth. The warmth spread fast, banishing the cold.

He showered. Dressed. Recalling his father's orders early this morning.

His father's voice had been blunt and arrogant, as always. Fix it. No name. No detail. Only the expectation of obedience.

He said nothing. He didn't need to. His father knew the job would be done.

Next, he went to the liquor cabinet and poured himself two fingers of Old Rip Van Winkle twenty-five-year-old bourbon. Smooth and expensive, which always summoned ghosts, and many times, the devil himself. His father.

This, the last part of the ritual. The bottle half empty. It was the only time he drank bourbon or any alcohol. It was always the same bourbon. The brand of bourbon he pilfered initially. Since sixteen, when the storm first called him, this would be his third bottle.

On that day, he wanted to spite his father for the punishment he felt he did not deserve. He took the first bottle. His father, when he discovered the theft of the bourbon, tortured his dog. His only companion for nine years and his friend in a lonely, abused life. Seeing him tortured, he could not bear the agony of screams and wails. *He slit Aladdin's throat with the same hands that once fed him, petted him, and comforted him. Not to kill him. To save him.*

His father smirked. "Weak, just as I thought."

A flood of tears fell onto the dog's body as if from a waterfall. He hugged him tight before finally letting him go; blood soaked his clothes. Following his dog's last breath, his father sneered, "Never steal from me. *I always find out. You should know there is always a price to pay.*" His father towered over him.

His breathing increased, and his hand tightened around the knife. Something rose inside him. Something alien. Darkness passed before his eyes, and his body coiled, ready to strike.

"Don't even try. I will kill you without a second thought. I was aware of the dog from the very day you discovered him. I *let* you keep him. You betrayed me by taking what was *mine*. So, I took what belonged to you. Fair trade. Now clean yourself up and stop your sniveling. Then go to bed.

That was the last time he cried.

As his father walked out the door, he turned to him and casually remarked. "The bottle of bourbon is yours now. You paid for it."

He vowed his father would never have power over him. Ever. He wouldn't give his father anything that could hurt him. Ever again. He shoved his empathy deep into his mind; in a place he could not reach. A place where all his emotions lived, locked away. He had it stolen from him.

His memories of Aladdin rode him hard this evening. He named him Aladdin because he seemed to pop out and back in whenever someone showed up. As if he knew he must conceal himself.

Now the memories came hard and fast. On the side of the road, he found and rescued Aladdin, a puppy. He kept him hidden from prying eyes while nursing him back to health. He shared everything with him. Even his food. During nine joyful years, they wandered these forests and trails. He found the cave with Aladdin by his side.

Walking over, he sat in the leather chair, high-backed and wide for comfort, in front of the fireplace. He remembered Aladdin, content chewing on a bone next to this very fireplace. He could *almost* see a ghostly image of his beloved dog.

Angry with himself, he tried to bury the memory again. Deeper this time. Harder as he stared at the flames.

He'd buried Aladdin near the lake that night. At the place he loved the most. Never spoke his name aloud again. But tonight, tonight the ghosts were back. He almost heard the soft pads of paws across the stone floor, hesitant, expectant. The wag of the tail. That stupid, loyal grin. The ghostly shape didn't move. It simply watched him. Waiting. He looked away. Then blinked.

Gone.

He shoved the memory down where it belonged. Suddenly, he no longer sensed power. Something was clawing to get out, and he shoved it back where it belonged.

Next week, a major shipment from China will arrive. Weapon arms, and pharmaceuticals. He'd have no time to himself. No time for indulgence. No room for memory. A blessing.

He finished the bourbon and stood and stepped out onto the porch. The forest greeted him with shadows and stealthy movements as he walked toward the helicopter.

The helicopter's engine whined, blades whooping into motion.

As he lifted off, he glanced back at the cabin.

Waiting on the porch, tail wagging, he thought he glimpsed the faint outline of Aladdin for a moment. Something cracked inside him, something lost long ago. Even after all this time, the memory consumed him deep in his soul.

The Next Morning

A shaft of light pierced the clouds and lit the craggy altar. Vultures picked at the flesh. The skulls surrounding the cave behind it glistened with morning dew.

A vulture yanked an eyeball free. The warmth of the sun beat down. The wind whispered an ancient song. And nature devoured the dead, as it always had.

CHAPTER 1

Murder
Monday, September 19, 2022
Tyler, Texas, Gas Station | Six-oh-five pm

The payphone receiver was slick in the caller's hand, sweat trickling into the grooves of the plastic. The 911 dispatcher's voice, a lifeline, steady, practiced, while the man's words tumbled out in a broken whisper.

"I saw a man stab a woman... through the back window... She struggled to get loose, screaming and pleading, after they tied her up. I think she said, don't hurt my daughter. The other holding the little one. She was pleading over and over again. Then he stabbed her as if frenzied."

A quick, jagged breath, almost a sob.

"I... I think one of them saw us, so we ran. It's the last cabin on a dead-end road... a few klicks down a gravel road off Highway one-fifty five, outside Tyler. One of those fancy lakeside places. Cabin Creek."

The 911 operator could hear the growl of a motorcycle in the vicinity.

The dispatcher responded, *Sir, can you stay on the line?* But the hard sound of a click cut her off. Call ended. No name. The 911 operator traced the call to an old phone booth originating from a rundown gas station just outside Tyler.

Taylor Cabin

The first deputy unit turned onto the gravel road seventeen minutes later. A second unit right behind. Heat still clung to the asphalt, shimmering above the blacktop; the sun was an orange smear over the treetops. Departing the paved road, the tires caused dust and crushed limestone to rattle upward. The sound of the damn cicadas' droning resonated within the pines.

Deputy Mara Thompson led, window down halfway. Hot, sun-baked dust rose around the cruiser as she drove, a slightly musty scent. Ahead, the driveway narrowed into a tunnel of shadow, the canopy of trees fracturing the sunlight into thin amber slashes across the windshield.

She passed the first cabin, boarded windows, and weeds brushing the porch steps. The second, little more than a skeleton of gray wood and tin, its door hanging loose. Maybe one hundred and fifty yards from the cabin at the end of the dirt road sat a third cabin. Despite a car being in the driveway, she sensed no motion inside. Two-story with a neat, well-kept yard. Mara's eyes lingered in the side mirror, noting it, filing it away. A line of mailboxes across from it.

Deep within the trees, another large, two-story log-style cabin came into view. She could hear the faint chatter of rushing water over stones somewhere just beyond the pines. The rosy golden shimmer of lake water glimpsed through the trees farther in the distance. Next to the cabin, someone parked a newer black Ram 250 pickup and a black Cadillac Escalade.

A tall, fit male stood still on the porch as they rolled up, the door open behind him. Standing still, watching.

Mara stepped out of her cruiser first, the sharp smell of sun-baked pine needles mixing with something acidic. Faint but unmistakable from where she stood as a breeze blew in her direction off the lake. Bleach. Gravel shifted under Mara's boots as she came up to the lowest step, hand close to her weapon.

"Sir, hands where I can see them." Deputy Sanchez moved toward the side periphery, backing up Mara. As two other cruisers pulled in. Deputies Harlan and Weldon stepped out of their cruisers.

Taylor complied, putting his cowboy hat on the railing, which he had been holding. No hesitation, no arguments. His voice was calm, but his stance seemed controlled in a way that wasn't entirely natural in her experience when cops came rolling up to their house.

"Names Everett Taylor, Ma'am. This is my family's cabin."

"Anyone else here with you?" He seemed to gauge her prior to his response?

"My wife, Bridget, and our daughter, Lila, were supposed to meet me here. I just got back after being gone all day and received the message. Roughly fifteen minutes ago, I arrived. Cabin's empty. The moment I stepped inside, I saw an overturned chair. When I looked around, I found the butcher knife from the kitchen knife block missing. Something happened here; I just don't know what it was or why my wife and daughter are not here. I just stepped out to look around the property. No cell service out here, or I would have called 911."

Behind the last two vehicles, another sheriff's unit arrived, its lights flashing. A tall deputy exited the cruiser, Deputy Tolman. Seconds later, a state trooper pulled in behind the other units. The trooper moved up next to Mara. Sanchez and Tolman headed into the house, clearing it and seeing if anyone else was there. No one. Clear, they called out. Both noticed the potent scent of bleach, a lot, but it couldn't mask what lay beneath it. A coppery tang of blood. Sanchez and Tolman walked out onto the back porch of the cabin. Sanchez observed something by the creek running behind the cabin that looked odd and went to investigate.

Mara studied the man on the porch. Crisp blue button-down long-sleeved shirt, bolo tie with a fancy silver tie clasp. Worn jeans, a belt with a silver buckle, and mud-free boots, with no injuries apparent. She glanced at the cowboy hat he'd placed on the railing. His eyes tracked every movement she made, cataloging them. She noted that, for a man who thought something bad had happened to his wife and daughter. He seemed strangely contained.

Sanchez's voice crackled over the radio from the creek bank. "Mara, we're gonna need detectives and CSU. There's a body half in and half out of the water. Looks like the others over in Dallas County."

There was a pause, long enough for the cicadas to fill the silence, before Deputy Mara answered. "You talking about those four off the highway that the Dallas PD is working on?"

"Yeah," Sanchez said. "Same clean cut. Same dump pattern. No head. The heart's gone too. The one who did those other women... appears to have just come in our direction," Sanchez said.

Mara swallowed hard. Brutal. Those murders had circulated in every precinct briefing for weeks; serial killers always got the full attention of law enforcement.

Mara exhaled sharply through her nose. "Hell, or we've got a copycat trying to stir up headlines. Either way, it's the type of case that brings the feds running. Dallas won't be happy."

The trooper behind her muttered, "Sheriff Nells got a special election coming up. I don't think he's going to be happy about this, either." The air seemed to tighten.

Mara stepped closer to Taylor. "Mr. Taylor, you need to come with us. We need to ask some questions, but not here."

Arrival and Setup of News Van

The sun was a burnt copper coin sinking behind the pines by the time the media arrived minutes later. The pines bled golden light as the sun dropped. Emergency strobes cut through it in harsh reds and blues.

Channel 8's van idled in the gravel pull-off next to the two-story house closest to the end cabin. They knocked. No one answered, so they went about setting up. They deployed the dish, cables snaking across the dirt. The smell of diesel mixed with humid earth and the iron smell of hot dust from all the vehicles' tires coming and going. Emergency floodlights popped on, spilling hard white into the trees, flattening every shadow into something that looked staged for the camera.

Carly Reston stood in front of the lens, mic steady, her voice pitched between professional calm and urgency. Their mobile van's scanner had picked up the dispatch from the 911 Tyler operator to the sheriff's deputies.

"... where a gruesome discovery has stunned this wooded lakeside community. Behind me, authorities continue their work at a remote family cabin. Earlier this evening, they found a woman's decapitated body. Partially submerged in that creek nearby... She glanced at it momentarily, then turned back to the cameras. Speculation points toward the Dallas County murder suspect, who may be responsible for the deaths of four other young women. Their bodies dumped just off I-45 by the serial killer loose in our area."

The camera caught the county coroner's van, two techs rolling a stretcher with a black body bag up the embankment. Flashbulbs fired from every angle.

"Sources identify the property as belonging to Everett Taylor, a decorated former Delta Force operator and local rancher. Authorities haven't charged Taylor, but they took him in for questioning. Unofficial sources confirm the couple's young daughter is unaccounted for."

In the background, a homeless man in a torn camo jacket whispered to another. His voice carried just enough for the nearby deputy, Ruiz, to hear. *"It's that pretty little thing that always brings us food and stuff when they come here."* The deputy glanced backward, but the individual vanished amongst those present. A person in a worn cap stood partially shadowed, near the edge of the camera's light. Glancing up as a sheriff's (sUAS) drone passed overhead. A peak of dirty blond hair and a flash of his face before he looked away from the drone. Hands buried in his jacket pockets. And when he left, nobody paid attention to his departure. The lens of the news camera in the van passed over the crowd several times that evening. Overhead, a Dallas Police helicopter circled the area. Officers Reese and Halston in Air Patrol Three observed the restless, growing crowd below.

Dallas PD interrogation room

The interrogation room was chilly, all stainless steel edges and buzzing fluorescents. Everett sat at the table, his gaze steady but unreadable. Detective Mason of the Dallas PD's major crimes division knew the psychology behind the design of interrogation rooms. It worked most of the time.

Detectives Mason and his partner, Luiz Alvarez, had reports sent over from the sheriff's officers at the scene. All four were solid deputies, measured in their approach. He'd worked with each of them on various cases that bled over into their county.

Another detective assigned to work with them on the case was Detective Wren. Unusual, but you don't argue with the brass. Wren was not Mason's favorite detective. The upper command last month assigned Mason and his partner to the 1-45 murders of the four young women. The brass expressed their belief that this last murder connected to the I-45 murders.

Tyler's upper command notified them of the condition of the

body found at the cabin. And promptly handed the case over to them with little fanfare. The spectacle would most likely unfold nationally, while Tyler, a quiet ranch town, transforming into an economic powerhouse because of the Tesla Giga factory was more than happy to hand it over to the Dallas PD and have it attached to the I-45 murders. Letting them take the heat.

Sheriff Nells, seeking to keep his seat in Smith County, preferred to bypass a case that could remain unsolved throughout the election cycle, which he considered a risk to his campaign. That was fine with Mason. The sheriff ranked high on his dislike list as well.

"No official ID yet," Mason said as he watched Everett's reaction. He shuffled some papers as if looking for Everett's wife's name.

"Bridget, she's your wife? Is that accurate?" Before Everett could answer, he said, watching Everett's body language as he discussed the gruesome details of the crime scene.

"No signs of the body being dragged from the cabin. A blood trail led to the place where someone dumped the body. The blood trail started on the back porch of your cabin. Likely, whoever murdered her carried the body to where the deputies found it."

Then he glanced at the drone video running on the police monitor, from the Small Unmanned Aircraft System (sUAS) drone deployed over the scene earlier, that he had running on a loop in the background, sound muted. Deliberately. Wanting to watch the suspect, reactions to the video. He watched the scene with an intensity Mason found unsettling. It seemed the suspect noticed every detail and stored it in memory.

A thin figure in a ball cap and nondescript jacket stood a little apart from the others, seen from the air, head tilted toward the tree line as if listening. Mason thought he observed pale hair and the flash of a face as he looked up at the drone overhead, before the drone moved into the canopy of trees. It tugged at something familiar, maybe a mugshot, but he filed it away for later.

Mason leaned forward slightly. "Then tell me what you did today. Begin at the start.

Everett's eyes stayed on the tabletop. When he spoke, his voice was even, deliberate, drained of anything but fact.

"I woke before sunrise. My wife and I went through our normal morning routine. I went to the barn and checked on the animals, while Bridget got our daughter up and ready for daycare. Around seven, Bridget left for work with our daughter. Colter Harlan, my friend from Montana, called roughly five minutes later. Stating he was en route overseas, he suggested meeting at Tyler Airport, as he'd be passing through Texas. I texted her I'd be gone most of the day with Colt. She'd met Colt a few times in the past."

He paused only long enough to draw breath. "Right before I was leaving, one of the ranch hands called me up. Said there was a sick calf, and it wasn't eating right. The ranch manager was off. His usual Monday. I went down to check; I would decide then if we needed the vet." Everett added, "Didn't. Just needed a mineral drench and a little time. But I left straight from the barn. At that point, I'm running late." Mason perceived the way he looked at Wren as if he saw something dirty.

"I left the ranch at about seven-fifty. Drove to the airport, met Colter, and we flew out on his private jet to Texarkana Regional, took about forty minutes. We ate breakfast there and then went to the cattle auction. He bought stock for another rancher named Clay Braddock. After the auction, Colt did a video call with him and introduced me. Colt then gave him information about where to wire the auction house payment. We wrapped up in the mid-afternoon. Then Colt and I went for a drink at the bar near the airport. We ran into a friend of Colt's, who sat and drank with us for about an hour. We just talked about cattle and the military. At that point, I realized I had left my wallet and phone at home when I went to pay for my drinks. Colt said he had an account with an executive charter company and he'd sign for my flight back home. I could pay him back later. He boarded his jet and took off for Europe. I left Texarkana at three-fifty-nine, landing back in Tyler at four-thirty-nine."

His watch clanged against the steel table as he shifted.

"From there I drove straight home. About a half-hour drive. Got in just after five. After I didn't see Bridget's SUV, I went inside and found my phone and wallet on the counter. That's when I saw her sticky note on the fridge. Read her message asking me to meet her at the cabin. I figured she'd come home early from work and wanted to spend some time at the lake. I left at around five-twenty-seven, drove the back road. Traffic's heavy during rush hour. Faster on the back roads. Takes about forty minutes."

He looked up briefly, eyes flat and clear.

"I pulled in around six. Saw her SUV in the driveway, I called out as I went to start the generator. Out of gas. That was strange. I always keep about three hours' worth of gas in it in case Bridget wants to go out and spend some time there. She loved the lake. I know I filled it last time. So, she must have been there. When I called out as I entered the house, she didn't answer. Then I realized the door was open. Inside, I found the chair flipped over, the kitchen knife gone, and the sharp scent of bleach still present. There were no signs of my wife or daughter. I stepped out onto the front porch to search the property when the first deputies arrived."

Detective Mason sat back when he stopped talking, arms crossed as he stared at Everett before saying. "Most people can't remember the exact minute they left a parking lot; let alone the precision of time you just trotted out."

The room fell silent. Wren stopped fidgeting with his pen he'd pulled out earlier. Then leaned towards him. "Yeah," he said. "Seems a little too perfect."

Everett leaned toward Mason, his stare direct and intense. "I want to know what you are doing about my daughter. Is there a search party? You're wasting your time on me. I did not harm my wife or daughter."

Before Mason could press him further, the door opened. Mason recognized the man who stepped in. George Shaw. A high-powered criminal lawyer. Slate-gray suit, leather briefcase, a man who'd been here before. Too many times, and usually left with his clients, without them answering a single thing. Mason believed this individual's distortion of facts to align with his clients' stories freed too many criminals.

"From this point forward," Shaw said evenly, "all questions go through me. No further comment, Everett," he dictated.

The next ten minutes were a controlled collision, Shaw dismantling the timeline. Demanding proof they didn't have, suggesting it was more likely the killer came from the homeless camp downstream. "Or it could be the 1-45 serial killer you all are hunting. From what I learned on the news coming here, the MO fits. Detective Mason, wasn't this the exact reason they assigned you this case? My client has provided you with an alibi. Now go find who did this."

Detective Wren slammed his fist on the table. "Who forgets their phone and wallet at home in this day and age?" Mason noticed Everett didn't flinch, though George did.

Everett looked Wren in the eye, about to answer, but Shaw placed his hand on him and said. "No need to answer that." Everett leaned back without saying another word.

Shaw leaned towards Wren. "You're not suggesting that you've never forgotten your phone or wallet because you were in a rush, are you? I suggest you check out his alibi first before jumping to conclusions."

George glanced back and forth between the three detectives in the room before saying, "Remember the Miller's case. The last big murder case your department worked on, a huge departmental screw up. I'm sure Detective Wren does." Now he stared right at him and nodded his head in his direction.

"Didn't you work on that case? And it all fell apart in court. You jumped to an immediate, yet false conclusion. And there were hints of falsified evidence, if I remember correctly. That cost your department's reputation and money. I am sure you don't want a repeat of that fiasco."

The remark stung. Worse because it was true. Mason glanced over at Wren. He had a smug look on his face while staring at Shaw.

"This time the charges will stick, and you won't get a criminal off scot-free like last time. And you might be the one losing everything before this is done."

Shaw had a serious look on his face when he looked over at Mason. "Unless you're charging him, we are leaving. Now." He rose from his seat, motioning for Everett to get up and prepare to leave.

"Oh, and you might not want to claim my last client, Miller, is a criminal in public. I would love nothing better than to file another suit against the department for slander and defamation of character."

They released Everett but told him not to leave town and that they would have further questions later. Outside, the night had turned heavy and close, the cicadas still droning. Somewhere in the dark, a branch snapped.

Behind the tinted glass of a parked black sedan across the street, a figure sat without moving. No lights on. Just watching.

When Everett and Shaw drove away, the sedan's engine purred to life. Its headlights were off as it pulled out behind them.

Tuesday, September 20th, 2022

Dallas PD | Detective Unit

The next day, Detective Marcus Wren leaned back in his chair; phone pressed between shoulder and ear while he clicked his pen in a steady, aggravated rhythm. He was going to prove Everett did this, well, had to, and then shove it in George Shaw's smug face. The Miller case almost got him fired. His *friend* had saved him from that humiliation, and he would not let him down this time. Of course, if he hadn't... exposure would not be good for his *friend* if he thought he would not need to protect him. He did not mind doing favors for certain people, but he expected certain types of compensation. He did not come cheap.

No way he was wasting time getting a warrant to ping cell towers to verify Everett's phone was at home; heck, he already told them it was there. The rest of the story. Easy enough to ignore. He was not wasting time trying to find a nonexistent guy in a dark bar. He'd call, talk up some local hick deputy, ask him a few questions. See if he could find out who the guy was without telling him it involved a murder case. He'd bet by the time he hung up the deputy would forget all about looking for the guy. Especially if he made it sound like a minor request. Then he'd put in the report that he called and the name of the deputy, and that would be that. Doubted he'd call back with a name. After the Miller debacle, checking the Braddock connection was essential, as he knew he'd appear incompetent if he ignored it. A woman answered after five rings.

"Braddock residence."

"Detective Wren, Dallas PD. I need to confirm a detail about Colt Harlan."

"Oh, yes, Colt's a family friend. I can answer most questions unless they involve business."

"It is a question about business."

"My husband's up north bringing the herds down. No service up there, but he'll be back in a week, possibly two. I don't manage his business; you'll have to call back when he returns."

Wren's voice was mild, "Of course, if he could return the call?"

"Just leave a number," she said.

"I'll call back. I have to check the files for the detective on the case."

He hung up.

He had no intention of calling back. Wren opened the digital case file and typed without hesitation:

Detective's Entry | 09/20/2022
"Spoke with Braddock directly. He claimed ignorance regarding Colt Harlan's cattle business in Texarkana. Stated he had 'no idea' why Harlan might have been there. He used a broker for the cattle he bought at the auction. Alibi unconfirmed."

He hit save.

Next, he sidelined the evidence collected by the CSU, the acronym for crime scene unit, at the site. He needed time to set the narrative with the news. At court, the DA would introduce whatever evidence he had collected. He did not want to expose his hand too early to the suspect. Keep him guessing. Rushing the proceedings increased the possibility of mistakes. Or it could allow the suspect to make up an applicable story to cover the evidence. And even if the jury exonerated Taylor to the public, he'd still look like he got away with murder. That way the ax would not fall on him like it did in the Miller court case.

The lie slid into the system as if it belonged there. Who cared that it might not be true? Everett had to be the murderer.

CHAPTER 2

The Contract

Friday, September 26th, 2022

O'Brien & Galloway Investigations | 38th Floor, Downtown Dallas

Even before nine am, the heat combined with the humidity was pressing in. It was the kind that crawled down the throat and lodged in the lungs. Thirty-eight floors up, climate control or not, the humidity had its way, worming through the vents. Fogging the glass at the corners, leaving the view of Dallas below shimmering in a pale haze. The city outside, all glass and steel and hard morning sun, looked more like a mirage than a place meant for working.

Inside the offices of O'Brien & Galloway, the battle was against the weather and the work. Air conditioning hummed, voices drifted, and the day's temperaments ran short. Iced coffee was everywhere. From her position at the head of the long conference table, Fiona swiftly worked through the week's open cases. Curtis Galloway lounged beside her, hot coffee in hand. To him, iced coffee was for those with weaker constitutions. He flicked through the digital case board on his tablet with the casualness of a man who found chaos familiar.

At the far end sat Stefana Growden. Secretary, but nobody's fool. Smiling, she informed everyone, "Selena left sticky notes with smiley faces on all the file boxes again." Fiona laughed and then said, "well on to the day's meeting."

Stefana pulled out her tablet to keep a silent tally as the team moved down the agenda. Every ongoing investigation made the list: corporate theft in Fort Worth, a marital surveillance in Plano, oil sector insurance fraud, with two cases overlapping. Marriage infidelity of the wealthy, four missing persons. Each case had its own field investigators, and when the digital trail ran hot, their cyber forensics techs joined the investigation. Since opening their doors, they have had a ninety percent success rate. Their reputation rose with each successful case.

Halfway through the list, the front desk buzzed. Selena's voice on the line, Stefana answered, checking the caller ID. Her eyebrows arched as she looked up. Then, she answered the call from Selena Navarro before passing on the information.

"A Major Buck, from military intelligence." She said, flat and to the point. "He wants to meet both of you. Today."

Curtis met Fiona's eyes, the question silent. Then said. "Schedule an appointment for the coming week. We're booked busy until then."

Stefana, lips pressed tight. "Already hung up, said to expect him soon."

Thirty minutes later, the staccato chop of helicopter blades carved the sky above them. The helicopter came down on the rooftop helipad, its shadow blocking out the sunlight on the glass walls as it passed overhead.

Based on the sounds outside the door, they concluded Selena was trying to prevent someone from entering. Fiona was certain of who it would be. Major Buck entered, and the room seemed to shift. The odor of fuel, and a presence that made other men recalibrate their posture. Tall, broad, early fifties, built like a man who still pushed his body every morning. His uniform was immaculate, graying hair clipped close, his eyes sharp, measuring every face in the room. Four uniformed officers, with every crease sharp as a razor, backed him. Short, cropped hair, hats under their arms as two stood on either side of the door. Like sentinels. Poster straight, squared shoulders, emotionless faces. Major Buck put his hat on the table and sat looking around the room as if weighing them.

His voice, though even, held the weight of command as he expressed his gratitude.

Curtis leaned forward, curious. "First, you didn't schedule an appointment; second, your face is familiar, yet I remember a different name associated with it."

"We crossed paths in Denver," Buck replied. "Different circumstances. You did not know who I was. They had classified that information at the time. You cleared one of my men after a shooting. Tracked down the real trigger. You didn't take the credit. I remembered that."

Fiona's pen stilled. "You didn't come here for small talk."

A flicker of a smile. "I run a joint military intelligence and federal enforcement group. I want you to take over all our outside contract work. Surveillance, covert recovery, asset protection, and investigations. You'll get the full federal rate."

Curtis raised an eyebrow, skeptical. "And you came to us. Why?"

"Because you're clean. You owe no one favors... yet," Buck said. "And because I can offer something you can't buy on the civilian market."

He slid a leather folder across the mahogany table. Inside: aerial photos, glossy, blue and angular. It resembled a blimp, yet you could tell it was a different type of beast. The airship appeared to blend into the surrounding sky. A vague shape in the sky was almost imperceptible. Nothing civilian at all was correct.

Fiona frowned. "What am I looking at?"

"That's the Sentinel," Buck said. "A hybrid airship. Surveillance platform, encrypted comms, multi-role. Warfighting capabilities. She can carry a crew of six specialists and a full team of tier-one top operatives. Along with all their gear and a full trauma med station in case. She can stay airborne for months if needed. The government contracted to have it built, but Congress killed the project in a budget fight right before the company could deliver it. Now it's sitting as surplus in a hangar at an undisclosed location. I convinced the powers that be not to mothball it, so they're putting it in private hands under contract. That allowed some politicians at the capital to sidestep the budget constraints. Several prominent politicians stuck their necks out to get this done, the nation's safety more important to them than their careers if it goes bad."

Curtis' eyes narrowed. "That's a lot of pressure on us."

Buck ignored the remark and nodded toward Fiona. "After your *lottery win* and your husband's death insurance, your agency has the needed capital. You can make this work. The Sentinel and her personnel are yours for your own work, a highly mobile platform, but when I call, she's mine, no questions."

He leaned in, voice losing none of its composure. "I can extend to you two full special ops teams retired from the ranks. Eighteen Tier-One operators. They're yours to use. When not on any missions for me. I'm also authorized to lease two hundred acres to build a compound and a hangar for the Sentinel. On your ranch, Fiona. We'll need barracks, an armory, security perimeter measures, shooting ranges and test areas for missions. Just show us where you want it. Construction starts the day you sign. This will be a classified military area, with discreet gate guards."

He paused for a moment before saying, "We have completed both of your backgrounds for classified clearance. If needed later, we can investigate others, as so many of them come from government law enforcement, it should not be hard to do."

Curtis let out a quiet laugh. "My God, that's a fortress, not an office."

Buck spoke in a measured tone. "Better a fortress than a tomb. Eventually, danger comes knocking."

Fiona watched him, eyes narrowed. "This is a lot to risk on a fairly new company."

Buck's answer was unblinking. "I had you vetted."

He slid the contract across for them to sign. Buck said, "Subject to final approval, I have enough to move. We must start the site survey, build the hangar, and bring the Sentinel out of mothballs. So, let's get it started now."

A silence settled. Fiona read through it and then nodded once. "We'll take it." She saw Curtis start to object, and then stop, from the corner of her eye. She knew they would discuss this after Major Buck left. The retainer, the monthly fees and the lease of the land along with the airship Sentinel, would keep their company in the black in the leanest of times. While giving them a leg up on their competition. She sensed that the use of the Sentinel was going to pay dividends.

As Buck and his men left, the office seemed to sigh, settling back to normal. Fiona and Curtis looked into the contract details and logistics. In the end, Curtis agreed with Fiona. This contract appeared good for their agency.

The TV on the wall played at a minimal level all day. Weather. Traffic. Local news drifted in the background. As Fiona packed her briefcase, heading home early to spend time with Josh, her son, the anchor's voice edged into the room:

"... the Dallas County Sheriff's Department has now confirmed the identity of the woman found murdered and dumped in a rural creek. Authorities identified her as Bridget Taylor, twenty-six, of Taylor Ranch. Investigators have released no further details as the investigation is ongoing."

The news rolled on to city drama. Fiona didn't glance at the screen. Curtis ignored it. Outside, storm clouds massed over the skyline, heavy with rain and charcoal gray, promising a chaotic thunderstorm later that night.

Whiskey River Two-Step Ranch, Fiona's Home

Dust swirled in brown eddies behind Fiona's boots as she moved across the training ring. Josh sat on the top rail of the fence, swinging his legs, eyes wide. With one hand on the reins, Fiona mounted and leaned forward in the saddle over Gypsy's neck. Gypsy, her sleek blood bay mare, responded like a live wire.

In a blur of movement, hooves pounded. Fiona leaned into the barrel turn, clearing the barrel by bare inches to spare. She fired a shot clean through the first balloon on the mounted shooting course. Then another. And another. By the time she crossed the finish line, Josh was clapping with a huge grin and an awestruck look on his face.

She pulled up short on Gypsy in front of him. "Next week, you'll learn the pattern at a walk on your pony."

Josh grinned. "Can I wear spurs?"

"When you've earned 'em." And with a strict look on her face, she said. "Only if you use them properly and never harm the horse."

Later, as she cooled down the mare, Fiona glanced at the horizon, her thoughts drifting like dust.

Growing up as the baby of the family with five older brothers on a working Colorado cattle ranch meant either learning to ride hard or being left behind. She'd done more than ride. By fifteen, she was winning first place ribbons in every rodeo event: barrel racing, pole bending, stunt riding and rescue races. Her brothers claimed trophies in heading and heeling, bull, and bronc riding, areas she did not compete. She took home more ribbons than most of her friends and her brothers. Then came mounted shooting, and that was her favorite and her best: speed and precision on fifteen hundred pounds of willful power while shooting. She still practiced. Still competed. Not for trophies anymore. But for herself. And for Josh.

One day, he'd be strong enough to learn what it meant to control one thousand and five hundred pounds of muscle and will beneath him. And the responsibility behind a trigger, to learn to use it properly. When that day came, she wanted him ready.

Because life didn't give ribbons. It gave consequences.

Rich Aroma's Coffeehouse

Monday, October 3rd, 2022

The bell over the door made a sharp chime as Fiona walked in, Curtis just behind. Outside, late fall had a grip on the morning; the air was brisk, sharp against their jackets. Inside, warmth enveloped them. Sunlight through the windows painted the floor in golden stripes. The place smelled of rich yet bitter espresso and sweet pastries.

Everett Taylor was easy to spot. He'd taken a table at the back, half shielded by a pillar, with a clear angle on the door and the rest of the room. His posture, every muscle wound tight. The same readiness Fiona had seen in Major Buck and his men.

Fiona recognized George Shaw sitting next to him. She'd seen him on several national cases that he won against all odds. And the screeching of the MSM declaring his client guilty before the arrest even occurred. He was a high-powered criminal defense lawyer, silver - gray suit with a power tie, and an expensive briefcase at his feet. He stood as they approached, handshake careful, neither too hard nor soft, face friendly and open.

"Fiona. Curtis." His voice was firm, but the greeting was genuine. "Thanks for coming."

They sat down opposite each other. Fiona realized Everett went back to scanning the street and the inside of the building. Hypervigilant. His coffee sat untouched. As if words were too hard to use, his jaw was tight. His eyes haunted.

Fiona noticed Curtis's eyes watching the exits, measuring distances, old habits drilled into him. Ten years working the streets of Denver as a police officer. With another five in vice division and the last five in homicide, he relaxed little in public. Fiona had less time as an officer, but the same ingrained habits.

The waitress came and went. Fiona ordered cinnamon and vanilla coffee and pastries.

George broke the silence. "The press and police hounded Everett when he buried Bridget the other day. Everett is still a suspect to the police in connection with the murder. The reason they have not already arrested him is that they're trying to tie the other four murders along I-45 to him. Which they can't, he has a solid alibi for those murders. That was the first thing I had my guys investigate. Figured it was too close to the MO of the 1-45 murders. They can try to say they were red herrings so Everett could murder his wife and blame a serial killer. Won't work. Yet, Everett's not doing himself any favors," George looked at Everett in exasperation.

Everett's jaw flexed. "Neighbors were not home, that I could tell when I arrived. So, no, nobody saw when I arrived. And my ranch manager takes off Mondays, so there's nobody to say if I was home or gone. Normally, I do the ranch books on Mondays. And the ranch manager takes the day off to go visit family in Fort Worth."

Curtis asked, "So why us?"

George leaned forward. "Because every time we get close, the police are already there. They aren't investigating. They're following our investigation somehow. I believe my office has a leak."

Fiona's eyes narrowed. "Mole?"

George nodded once. "Therefore, I cannot trust anyone internally."

In the background, the news on the overhead TV droned on about a major traffic/accident story: *A tractor-trailer crashed off a bridge in Allen (north of Dallas) the driver died.* The news moved on to local news. *The Dallas Area Rapid Transit (DART) held meetings on Sept. 20 about the upcoming Silver Line rail project and its local impacts. After she was last seen leaving the Porter & Ashburn's California Firm charity for homeless children, DNA helped investigators identify the body of socialite Camilla "Cami" Dane in Ainsworth State Park in Oregon. Three hikers found her headless body along the trail. It now involves two state agencies and the FBI. No leads in the case so far.*

George Shaw's briefcase opened like a shield between them as he rummaged around for something before pulling out a contract.

He leaned forward slightly, voice low. "They've got me slated as the killer from the start. Anonymous 911 caller claims he saw me stab Bridget through the cabin window. Said she was begging about Lila. Then, nothing. Caller hangs up, deputies roll in seventeen minutes later, and I'm standing on the porch like I'm waiting for them. Bleach still sharp in the air. Blood underneath it. They figure I had just enough time to clean, move the body to the creek, hide or kill my daughter, and stroll back out before the sirens."

He paused, thumb tracing the rim of his cup. "Problem is, I wasn't even in the county most of the day."

Fiona tilted her head. "You told them that."

"I told them everything." His eyes met hers, flat, tired, steady.

"Woke before dawn. Bridget took Lila to daycare. I checked the herd, sick calf needed a mineral drench, nothing serious. Then Colt Harlan called, an old Delta buddy from Montana. He was swinging through Texas on his way overseas and wanted to meet at Tyler Airport. We flew his jet to Texarkana for a cattle auction he was managing for Clay Braddock. Breakfast, bidding, handshake, video call with Clay, a couple of drinks afterwards. Left my wallet and phone on the kitchen counter in the rush. Got home, found Bridget's note about the cabin on the fridge. Drove out and arrived around six. SUV in the driveway. Door open. Chair overturned. Knife gone. Bleach smell everywhere. No Bridget. No Lila. Then the deputies showed up."

He exhaled through his nose. "They don't buy it. Timeline's too clean, they say. Since the manager is off on Mondays, nobody saw me leave the ranch. No one saw me at the bar because Colt paid cash and signed the tab. No proof I forgot the phone except my word. And the caller's supposed description fits me: tall, lean, blond hair. They're building a box around me, one piece at a time."

George cut in. "One of my investigators got a name he was chasing down from an informant he uses now and then. Joe Bell from California, the informant, told my guy to look at him. A group of people entered the bar at that point, and one look by the informant and the guy quit talking and rushed off before my investigator could get more from him. Not even how he might fit into the case."

Everett reached inside his jacket and pulled out the thick envelope. He set it on the table between them, careful, deliberate.

"Found this behind a false panel in Bridget's closet. Grocery list on the fridge with spelling mistakes she'd never make. First letters spelled the safe location. Inside: flash drive, notes, photos, burner phone. I made copies. This set's for you. Burner's the original. Then he pulled out his own phone. She sent this in the morning that day, but I had already left the house and forgotten my phone. He turned the phone so that they both could see what it was. A long string of numbers: 3-5-6 4-8-11 4-8-3 4-16-26 10-13-16 18-9-13."

He slid it toward Fiona before saying. "I don't have a clue what this means. But Bridget wasn't the type to chase shadows. She placed kids with families. Teary-eyed couples holding babies like miracles. That's who she was. This—" he tapped the envelope "—doesn't feel like her. Feels like someone else's fight. Maybe Lisa's. Maybe something at Porter & Ashburn went wrong a year ago. One account, she said. 'Wrong.' That's all I got from her."

Fiona pulled out her notepad and copied the numbers, then opened the envelope just enough to see the edges of photos and the burner phone. "You think this got her killed?"

Everett's eyes went distant. "Maybe. Or maybe it was mine. Old enemies. Doesn't matter. Lila's alive. I know it. Two weeks and they have not found her body. No ransom. Nothing. I need to find her. You can do that for me."

His stare was intense as he said. "Major Buck said you're the ones who don't quit. Said you helped him once. That true?"

Fiona held his gaze. "We follow the facts. Wherever they lead. If you're guilty, we won't hide it."

"I didn't kill my wife," Everett said quietly. "Time will prove I am not guilty of killing my wife. But my daughter may not have much time."

Silence filled the space between them for a few moments before George rose along with Everett and shook their hands. "I hope you decide to take the case; they walked away with the contract sitting on the table."

Fiona and Curtis stayed for about another hour. They ordered pasties and coffee while they discussed the case. The TV played the Dallas morning news. It showed city council members arguing about a zoning dispute, a warning about catalytic converter thefts with a picture of a masked man, and highlights from the Stars' overtime win. *A ticker scrolled gas prices $3.49 per gallon*, while the anchor's voice stayed flat, as though bracing the audience for worse. Fiona traced the rim of her cup as she looked through the photos, and Curtis flipped silently through the extra files George Shaw had provided from his investigators. The decision, when it came, wasn't words so much as a shared nod.

They left without another word. Outside, the warmth had won out over the morning chill. Fiona glanced west, where the clouds were gathering, thick and dark, rolling in their direction. Buck's words echoed in her mind like distant thunder. Storms followed this work and knew the first freezing winds had already slipped through the cracks.

CHAPTER 3

Storm Warning

Wednesday, October 4th, 2022

O'Brien & Galloway, Dallas Headquarters

The elevator chimed low in the marble foyer. Fiona's coat brushed her hips, heavy from the envelope of photos tucked inside. Curtis followed close behind, boots striking a slow rhythm over the tile. His arm brushed the Glock in its shoulder holster under his jacket.

Behind the reception desk, Selena looked up from her screen. Concern flickered in her eyes when she noted their tension. "Hold calls," Fiona said as she passed, voice clipped. "Except for priority clients." Curtis offered a humorless chuckle. "Voicemails, then."

The air in the conference room, also known by some as the war room, felt cool. It carried a familiar aroma of copier toner and fresh coffee beans.

Fiona pressed the panel by the door; the LEDs dimmed, and the monitors on the far wall flickered to life. Bluish light bathed the long table; the system's low hum felt like home.

"If we take this, it will be the first murder case for the agency." She let the words hang. "It's big, statewide, possibly nationwide news, with spotlights on every move we make."

Curtis moved to the table and set the folders down. "We've never backed down from a challenge yet, Fi, but if you're worried about our reputation, we won't take it."

Fiona laid the envelope on the table and dumped out the matte black burner phone and the flash drive.

"They sent one hundred fifty-three photos," Fiona said as she spread the photos across the table. "Surveillance angles, steady zooms, almost professional," she studied the images as she spoke. "These timestamps aren't in order. Could Shaw secure a subpoena for Bridget's work schedule for us? We need to see if the times match her breaks, time away from work, or home. Times when she's near the cabin, at hotels, or even hundreds of miles away. Otherwise, someone else took these photos and gave them to her."

Curtis scanned the images carefully. This might be meaningless, Fi, or she might have begun her inquiry sooner than we thought.

"Or she had help," Fiona said under her breath, already moving to the next implication.

He paused at one photo, a man in a charcoal suit, posture familiar. Then another, the same man at a hotel entrance, and a third showed him outside Porter & Ashburn. Yet his face always turned from the camera, as if aware it was there. A woman in the photos with him, whom many would describe as a femme fatale. Long, thick, wavy, dark black hair. Thick, pouty lips. Topaz cat-like eyes, with a hint of lust in them as she glanced at the male in the photos. Tall with a voluptuous body. Bridget's handwriting with various notations was on the back of the photos, though only dates, no names. Then came family snapshots, a picnic, kids on swings, with her tidy script and letters or numbers.

"Adoption file shots," he murmured. "Except for this one." Curtis turned over a photo identified on the back as her sister Lisa Neylan at Taylor's cabin beside a man not seen in any other images. He studied the stranger's outline. "He's taller, heavier, and in better shape, not the same guy in the rest of the photos."

Fiona glanced at the photo as she plugged the burner phone into the secure terminal. "You're right," as two folders appeared on the monitor from the burner. The first was that weird set of numbers; the second, a name. SILO. It contained spread-sheets and encrypted-style PDFs, and dozens more images. "Bridget was hunting some kind of network," she pointed to the screen, only the headers and spread-sheets lacked encryption. Then she glanced back at the photo of Lisa and the man, examining the stranger's silhouette again.

"Code of some kind, Fi," Curtis said. He shrugged, more interested in the photos arrayed before him on the table.

"Why did Lisa meet someone at the Taylor cabin? Why was Bridget photographing them?" Fiona glanced at Curtis and asked, "Does Lisa know she took that picture? What's the connection to her murder?"

Curtis stared at a filename. "Joe Bell, Porter & Ashburn, California office."

He tapped the filename. Fiona had seen that look before. Something important had caught his attention.

"Bell... sounds familiar."

"Shaw said one of his investigators connected someone with that name to California at the meeting this morning," Fiona confirmed.

"No, Fi, it's more than that. The name caught my interest when Shaw mentioned it."

Curtis spoke into the intercom. "Stefana, see if you can pull one of my old homicide cases from Denver. My partner and I looked at a suspect named Joe Bell from California. The case went cold, but we couldn't do anything because of the lack of evidence. Witnesses kept dying. Ask for Detective David Harmon. He'll help get the file." He hung up. "It's been bugging me since Shaw mentioned it. Dave and I worked on that case right before he got shot and became deskbound. That was around the time you joined homicide."

Fiona knew some unsolved cases stick with you. She pulled her yellow pad closer, where she had written the code from Everett's phone. She focused on the string of numbers.

"3-5-6 4-8-11 4-8-3 4-16-26 10-13-16 18-9-13. Any ideas about what these numbers might mean or what they go to?"

Perhaps it's a file number, or maybe a cipher or code. Fiona said out loud, thinking. "Message, location, maybe all the above, but why though? Why is it on the phone with those SILO files and spread-sheets?"

Curtis leaned back in his chair. "Let's shift the topic for a bit. What are your thoughts about Everett's story to the police? Helping a ranch hand with a sick calf that morning. Ranch manager off for the day. He claims he left in a hurry, with no phone, no wallet. Colter Harlan picks him up at Tyler Airport, ex-special ops buddy flying through to Europe."

Fiona spoke up. "It should be easy enough to prove or disprove that part of his alibi. The rest won't matter after that. At least until we contact his friend Colt, this is going to leave him in limbo."

"His friend paid cash for everything, which is apparently his usual off-grid style." Curtis paused. "The whole thing seems... fishy. Forgotten phone and wallet. A friend who never leaves a paper trail unless needed for the IRS? Everett claims Colt is a stickler for honesty, yet this guy stays off-grid by paying cash most of the time? Now the friend is unreachable because he's flying around Europe somewhere," Curtis shook his head? "We could be on the wrong side of the blanket on this one."

Fiona stood and walked to the refreshment bar against one wall. She poured a cup of cinnamon and vanilla-flavored coffee, then sat again. "We can assign Edgar to look into the individual Everett said he had drinks with at the bar. It's a long shot, but Edgar's like a dog with a bone; if anyone can find him, he can."

Fiona drummed her fingers on the table, thoughtful. "Everything about his story is possible... just not reasonable. But Shaw's known as a shark in law enforcement circles. He doesn't take just any case; he takes cases he believes he can win. So why this one? What makes him think he can win? I like the idea of being on retainer for Shaw, but not if we're getting played."

"In the notes from Shaw's previous investigators, Detective Mason mentioned something else," Curtis added. "Bleach residue on the floor hadn't soaked into the grain." His phone buzzed with a new message from George Shaw.

"Shaw just left the coroner's office. The coroner believes Bridget died earlier than the deputies estimated. But she won't officially say until she finishes and signs the autopsy report."

Fiona tapped her pen on the table. "Earlier? The timeline already gives Everett enough time to get there and commit the murder or murders. Deputies saw no neighbors that day, from what Shaw's original investigators noted. Let's double-check on the neighbors; maybe someone left to go to the store or visit family. This situation has occurred in other cases we've handled.

"He either murdered his wife and possibly his daughter, or he has the worst luck ever. Few men ever leave their wallets at home," Curtis said as he stood to get coffee.

"Ranchers never ignore the needs of a sick animal." She looked over at Curtis. "What do you think? Send Liana Harrison to talk with the ranch hand and get a statement from him. I don't see any remarks that the police have. Besides, she needs some fieldwork. Get her out of the office for a bit."

"We need a statement from that ranch hand to keep the police at bay for a bit. At least until we reach this Colten Harlan guy."

Curtis flipped through the reports and notes from Shaw. "The police claim they never found Bridget's phone. Until there's a court order for her messages, that looks bad too. Wonder if we can have Shaw subpoena those records for us?" Curtis asked, then scowled as he looked over Fiona. "Never thought we'd be working on the wrong side of the road with a defense attorney."

"Think of it as pursuing justice. If he's guilty, we told Shaw we would inform the police of what we found. I'll have Josiah Baird from Cyber ping Colt's electronic trail. We can legally do that, at least without a warrant." Fiona said as she jotted down the names.

Curtis choked on his coffee before saying. "You know, Fi, he's going to bitch loud and long about that, he thinks something that easy is beneath his talent. And it's going to be me, not you, who endures his little ways of showing it. I think he fancies he's in love with you."

"Then tell him I'm asking as a favor, so it gets done fast. Tell him I think he can do it quicker than anyone else." She grinned back at Curtis. "Might as well take advantage of that crush while it lasts."

Curtis chuckled, then pulled another folder from George's original investigators to see what they had discovered. "Smith County Sheriff's Department logged two vagrants on a Ring doorbell camera placed on the back door outer area. They ran from the back of the Taylor cabin toward the homeless camp the afternoon Bridget died. A boater on the lake called about it around two-thirty or two-forty p.m., thinking they were robbing houses. This is outside the unofficial time of death, the police believe, so they added it as an extra item to be looked at."

Fiona frowned before looking at Curtis. "Is there a lot of theft by the homeless in that area? We need to find out; they could be the murderers, or maybe they came back later. Let's assign Jeanne Elliott to that."

Curtis answered. "Depends on who you ask. Detective Wren thinks it's nothing. At least Detective Mason seems bothered by it, according to rumors around the station."

"You have a source in the PD?"

"I have a friend in the clerical pool. I asked her about Mason. She told me he's a straight shooter. Yet, when I brought up Detective Wren, she said the word around the department is he's dirty; however, no one can prove it. If they tried, they'd get transferred out or demoted. Detective Raylen Cross kept digging into Wren. The next thing everyone knew, the authorities arrested him and sent him to jail. There were claims that IA had found money from a drug bust in his locker. While waiting for trial, he got shived and died in jail at the hands of a lifer. The women in the department avoid Wren at all costs. Literally. They see him coming, they duck into a doorway or go the other direction."

"Did she say whether Detective Mason thinks he's dirty?"

"She said Mason keeps his opinion of whether he's a dirty cop to himself. Luis, his friend and partner, thinks he is and gets away with it because he has someone high enough in the department to protect him."

Lisa Bridget's sisters call

With a soft knock, the door cracked open, and Selena popped her head in. "Lisa Neylan calling."

Fiona's shoulders stiffened. "Selena, ensure legal privilege before connecting. Remember, we are the legal investigators for George Shaw, representing Everett Taylor."

"That's the sister who skipped Bridget's funeral and works at Porter & Ashburn," he mouthed toward Fiona.

Fiona pressed the speakerphone. Static crackled for a moment, then Lisa's low, tense voice came through: "Turn off the recording." Fiona clicked the button; the red light went out. "Recording is off," though Curtis kept the stress monitor running. Curtis watched the stress readout waveform flicker on the monitor.

"My mother forced this phone call on me. It was the least I could do," Lisa said. "Skipping the funeral started a family war, and I need to make amends."

"You work at Porter & Ashburn?" Fiona asked.

"Yes, so this call doesn't exist."

Curtis leaned forward. "Why the secrecy?"

"Bridget dug around and found the names of dangerous and powerful people. I warned her. She ignored me. Now look what happened."

"Was that the reason someone killed Bridget?" Fiona asked, looking over at Curtis to see what he was thinking.

Lisa's voice dropped lower. "Meet me at Café Mirador, private room, tomorrow at noon."

"Okay, no problem. I'll be there," Fiona said.

A long pause, then Lisa whispered: "The names she found make cartel street soldiers look like Sunday school teachers."

Click.

Curtis exhaled slowly. "She's terrified of whoever killed Bridget. Think she might have an idea who?"

"It sounded like it. We need a rundown of Porter & Ashburn. Either they're in this deep, or they're shielding the people who are through legal paperwork," Fiona said.

"Put cybersecurity on the data. Forward everything to Major Buck; we have everything that doesn't directly give up a way to exonerate Everett or find his daughter. See if this ties into what he's working on; powerful and dangerous people seem right up his alley. Let's assign Chelsea to find Colt. Maybe she can use some old FBI teammates to help."

Curtis headed for his office to assign investigators to the case. As the day wore on, he reviewed other ongoing investigations with the team. Fiona stayed in the war room so she could use the large digital board on the wall. She organized the information and built the murder board with what they had so far. Curtis popped in around five to say he was leaving for dinner with his older son, Jared.

"Tell Jared I said hi. And he knows he and the boys are always welcome at the ranch."

◆◆◆

Dallas Office | Late Night

By seven, the office fell silent; everyone else had gone home or was out on stakeouts.

Around midnight, rain tapped at the windows as city lights blurred into amber streaks. Fiona sat alone, pencil hovering over the scrawled code on her yellow pad. She scribbled notes all over it, but after a while her temples throbbed from trying to crack it. Alone in the bullpen, she couldn't shake the sense that Everett Taylor fit too neatly into both roles. Grieving husband or master manipulator, she got the sense he was smart enough.

The elevator bell chimed. Then the doors slid open. No footsteps followed, then the doors slid shut again, strange enough that Fiona straightened...

She slid her hand into the desk drawer and grabbed her SIG P229 Legion. She withdrew the gun.

They leased the entire thirty-eighth floor. If security let someone up after hours without notification, she'd contact management tomorrow. Still, better to be prepared. In their line of work, they sometimes pissed off people unhappy with the findings.

The overhead lights flickered off, then back on in stuttering bursts. The phone shrilled. On the third ring, she answered. "O'Brien & Galloway, Fiona." She kept her eyes on the outer area for any movement.

"Jerry from maintenance. Storm tripped a couple of breakers," a gruff voice said. "Lights might flicker again. Elevators acting iffy."

"Where's Bob?" she asked, gaze fixed on the dark monitors.

"Out sick," Jerry replied. Click.

Fiona felt the SIG's reassuring weight in her hand. Standing, she picked up her briefcase and holstered the gun in her shoulder rig. Then, locked the burner phone in the safe, stowed the files, shut down the monitors, and powered off the servers. She locked each area and double-checked everything before she headed out.

Her cell buzzed: Curtis. "On my way home. Jared said to say hi, and he and the boys will be out to the ranch soon."

The lights flickered again.

"Be careful driving home, or do you need me to come get you?"

"No, I only had two beers. I'm good."

"Okay, heading home myself." She checked every lock twice before stepping into the elevator. With her thumb hovering over the close-door button, she prayed it wouldn't stall mid-floor. She wondered whether taking the stairs might have been wiser. The doors slid shut, the elevator started down; too late now.

CHAPTER 4

The Warning

Monday, October 24th, 2022

O'Brien & Galloway Investigations, Dallas

The storm broke in the night, leaving the city washed clean. The air outside was cool and damp, laced with the faint scent of wet asphalt. Clouds still stacked low on the horizon, the air a misty haze, bruised and heavy. But the light that spilled across the skyline was a softer gray, the kind that made edges blurred and shadows deep.

Fiona stepped through the glass street entrance doors of the Dent Bank Building. The faint squelch of her damp heels echoed across the polished floor. Waved to the guards and took the elevator up to the thirty-eighth floor. She stopped at the reception desk, said hi to Selena, and picked up her mail. Selena regaled her with tales of what her dog, Missy, did last night, making Fiona smile. She went into her office, hung up her coat, and took off her heels. She left them by the door, wiggling her toes in the carpet.

Files saw the files stacked on her desk to be reviewed. At the top sat Bridget Taylor's folder, its weight measured in the questions it refused to answer. She took a sip of her coffee, its warmth cutting through the chill that followed her from the street.

Across the hall, Mildred Tyson was already a blur of motion in the cyber division office. Glasses low on her nose, fingers hammered keys as strings of code rolled across the triple monitors. Fiona wandered in, coffee in hand.

"One of the metadata signatures matches an encrypted sender that Bridget labeled only as E. No proof it's Everett... but it raises eyebrows. Plus, the flash drive had a second encryption layer," Mildred said without looking up. "Fake directory tree, adaptive payload. The first layer was bait; the second layer is military-grade. Or an exceptional coder. Did Bridget know how to code, cause if not, she got this drive from someone else. It might answer a lot of questions. Like if she were working with someone else."

Fiona leaned against the doorway. "And the message Bridget left on the burner phone from the safe?"

"Sorry, hon, no idea. Could take days, maybe weeks to break, maybe never. I need a reference. Her husband should try to figure out what it might relate to. That would give us a starting point."

Fiona exhaled. "The DA's rattling the saber. An anonymous call to our line last night left a message saying an arrest could be any day."

Curtis walked in. "Shaw called and told me the police got their warrant for Bridget's phone. They said her phone had a text message from Everett that he would be out of town with his friend. But that proves nothing except that he sent a text. And a string of numbers. Made no sense, so the detective on the case noted it as not important."

"So, where's her phone? Did they do a Stingray ping check on where the phone might be or where she was that morning?" Fiona asked. "Did someone take the phone because it might have something on it they needed?"

"Police say it's completely off-grid. They couldn't ping it or even reactivate it. On the day of her murder, they say it hit the first tower closest to the daughter's daycare; after that, nothing. She must have turned it off and pulled the battery? Why?"

The intercom crackled. Selena's voice: "Major Buck is here to see you."

"Send him in." She went to her office, put her heels back on before heading back to the conference room to join Curtis.

Curtis rose from his chair at the knock on the door. Buck stepped inside alone, moisture still clinging to the shoulders of his coat. His presence carried a quiet tension of a man who didn't make casual visits.

The news running low in the background changed to international:

Private Jet Crashes in Remote Bieszczady Mountains—Survivors Found Days after vanishing from radar near the Poland–Ukraine border, a small private jet was located in the rugged Bieszczady Mountains outside Cisna, Poland. The aircraft, carrying four passengers and a pilot, reported engine trouble before going silent around 9:15 a.m. Rescue teams tracked the emergency beacon to a forested slope among dense beech trees. Rescue teams pulled the pilot from the wreckage in critical condition. The pilot confirmed other survivors before losing consciousness. No post-crash fire occurred despite a ruptured wing and leaking fuel, which likely saved lives. Fog and muddy terrain hampered helicopter evacuations; ground teams continue searching. The cause remains under investigation. Authorities have not released any names.

"Morning," Fiona said as she got up and muted the news before heading back to sit down.

"Not official business," Buck replied, taking the seat across from her and placing his hat on the table. "Just a heads-up. There's chatter in D.C. A sealed federal task force mandate just moved upstairs. Whatever Bridget touched has traction. It hit a nerve with some powerful people. My opinion, the upper command of the Bureau's compromised. Everett's an easy fall guy, and there's a push to close this quickly. If you dig, expect pushback *hard*. They are going to want that drive. Even my guys are having trouble getting information from it."

"That's something we figured out pretty fast," Curtis said as he rose and went to refill his coffee.

"The players on this one? They make enemies disappear without headlines." Buck pushed a small pack of burner phones across the table. "Preloaded. Use them in an emergency. Off record. And Fiona... whatever Bridget found, she wasn't the only one looking. D.C. had eyes on her for months before she died. I'd bet the NSA was tracking her digital footprint, along with agents on the ground. What I can't figure out is how they even knew to look in her direction?"

He stood. "And tell Everett to stay off the radar. Men with his training attract the wrong kind of federal attention. That's all I can give you for now." And then he was gone, the scent of rain still clinging in his wake.

Fiona went back to Mildred, who was staring at her screen before looking up and saying. "I've got something," she said. "Not a full decrypt, but metadata in the headers. A name, Dr. Felix Mendez, something about a medical license and kids."

Fiona felt her gut tighten. She remembered their investigation of him and the kids he *treated* when working in Denver. She glanced toward Curtis and could tell he remembered as well.

Mildred nodded to herself, never even noticing the looks on their faces. "Moved to a private juvenile facility in Mexico. Shut down after abuse allegations. Funding came from the Stuart Family Charities out of New Orleans. Mendez vanished after the closure. The Stuart Foundation could not overcome the stench of it and finally closed the NGO. In the investigation, they claimed they did not know what he was doing with the money."

Fiona's mind flashed with a memory she'd rather bury. Linoleum floors, antiseptic air, the echo of crying from all the rooms.

"Not someone you want connected to anything involving children," she mumbled.

Curtis underlined the name on his notepad. "That's a lead." His grimace said he remembered the same as she did.

Fiona checked her watch. "I've got a meeting in twenty minutes."

Dallas PD | Homicide Bullpen

The bullpen was half-lit, the hum of fluorescent lights mixing with the whisper of the HVAC. Most desks sat empty. Mason and Luis stood over his cluttered table, the crime-scene photos of the four I-45 females spread out beside the graphic autopsy shots from Bridget Taylor's case. It's disturbing that 30, now up to 34 bodies have appeared along this I-45 corridor. Killing Fields is an app name for this stretch of highway. What is it about this area that attracts murderous crazies? Luis rubbed his temples. "On a different tack, these latest murders, it's the same guy, Mason. Same cuts. The same postmortem work. Same staging. I've never seen two serial killers with identical MOs, have you?"

Mason didn't look up. "I know. Believe me, I know."

Luis lowered his voice. "And Taylor? He's not the one. Wasn't even close geographically during the other four. I checked the reports myself."

Mason tapped each photo with a blunt finger. "Feed store in Tyler. Church fundraiser. Livestock show. People packed in the diner off 69, and half the town saw him there. He didn't carve those girls up and then switch to domestic murder on a whim."

Luis leaned against the desk. "We're telling that PI firm working for Shaw?"

Mason shook his head once. Firm. "No. Won't help 'em. The records don't link the cases. The brass won't allow linking unless it benefits the narrative. He has a solid alibi for the other murders. Wren's out of luck there. Right now, all he's got is a matching MO. The Sheriff of Smith County doesn't want a serial killer pinned to a lake community full of doctors, politicians, lawyers, and wealthy ranchers."

Luis snorted. "Yeah. God forbid rich folk think it could be one of them."

Mason sat back, jaw tight. "And don't kid yourself, Shaw's most likely already had his people investigate this. If there was anything that could implicate Everett, he'd have found some way to have it thrown out."

"So, we sit on it."

"We'll keep quiet for now," Mason said as he glanced over at the captain's office. "And we keep digging. Because someone out there killed all five women, and it sure as hell wasn't Everett Taylor."

Luis looked at Mason. "You know, if the investigators for Shaw got a little help. They might at least prove someone else, and not his client, killed the victim."

"No, we stick to investigating until we catch this bastard. We don't muddy the water." Mason knew what he was going to do. And he did not want Luis implicated if someone discovered his actions, and the brass fired him.

Luis nodded. "Then we'll find the real bastard."

Mason gathered the photos into a single stack, his expression carved from stone.
"Yeah," he said. "We will."

He'd let that bastard Wren hang himself. He promised Raylen he'd get Wren and anyone else involved in what they did to him. Mason knew better than to say that out loud. Not even to Luis. Let them all think he believed Raylen was dirty. Corruption works in the shadows. So that was where he would hunt it.

Luis lowered his voice. "Wren's been referencing that CI again. Same one he used in that mess last spring. Internal Affairs flagged him over and then dropped the investigation because the guy disappeared." He shrugged uneasily. "Something's off. CIs wander, yeah, but they don't vanish the minute a detective needs their story to be backed up. The same CI identifier is being used by him as in the previous situation. Worse, this time the case includes our names even if we are not physically working on it. I think he's dirty. Raylan was your friend as well. I don't understand how you can believe he did what Wren said."

Mason heard his frustration and wanted to agree, but knew better. "Doubt Wren's dirty. He's ambitious, sloppy, and arrogant. He cuts corners to clear cases fast and gain big kudos from the brass and those promotions he craves. I don't think he's smart enough to be dirty and get this far without getting caught. And Luis, some *remarks* are better kept to yourself." Mason stood and headed for the door, calling back over his shoulder, "You coming, or just sitting here crying over spilled milk?" Luis ran to catch up.

Café Mirador | Uptown Dallas

The rooftop cafe still smelled faintly of ozone from the storm and rich food. Fiona took the private stairs to the glass-walled room Lisa Neylan had reserved.

Lisa was standing by the window, arms crossed, her profile sharp against the skyline. She didn't turn when Fiona entered, but her voice was tight. "Close the door."

Fiona did. The click of the latch was loud in the space.

"I almost canceled," Lisa said.

Sliding into a chair at the table, Fiona replied, "But you didn't."

Lisa finally looked at her, eyes shadowed. "You're in over your head. Stop digging into Bridget's files if you value your firm. Just find out who murdered her and leave the rest alone. You do not know what you are getting into."

"Is that a threat?"

"It's a fact."

Fiona asked, "What about Lila?" She waited for an answer. When Lisa said nothing, she asked, "Tell me about Joe Bell."

Lisa hesitated, then said, "Bell works for Porter & Ashburn's partner, Reid Cavanaugh, at the headquarters in California. That's all I know about him."

She placed a plain key card on the table. "Storage unit, Whispering Pines Storage. Number one forty-seven. Don't go alone. Destroy everything after."

"Why give me this? After telling me to stop digging and drop the entire investigation?"

"Because someone followed me this morning, and this may help you find who murdered her." Lisa said, glancing toward the glass as if she could still see them.

"And Bridget?" Fiona pressed.

"She pulled a sealed, cold file. What was in the file? Lisa shrugged. She tried to pull me in. I told her to stop. In law offices, some things are not for junior lawyers to dig into. When she didn't, I walked."

"She was your sister; why did you not let Everett know what was going on? He might have been able to convince her to stop?"

"Bridget's gone. I have to look out for myself now. And if she did not tell him, it was not my place to do."

The silence between them stretched until Fiona finally picked up the keycard and pocketed it.

Lisa turned, grabbed her purse off the table, and left.

The cafe's mounted TV shifted to breaking news about the murders along 1-45. *Acting Chief Vernon Langley stood behind a podium, jaw set. "We've developed a working theory about the I-45 victims. Currently, evidence suggests it's a team, not a single person. That's all."* Before the press could fire questions, Langley stepped away from the mic and vanished off camera.

O'Brien & Galloway | Executive Suite

The air still held the storm's weight, though inside it was all leather, coffee, and quiet. Fiona sat at the mahogany desk in the client intake room, with Curtis sitting next to her. Potential clients sat across the table from them. Marshall Hays and Jace Lin of Transitions AI Systems laid out their problem. They showed them emails and even snail mail from their office with death and bomb threats.

Fiona stared at Jace for a moment, but finally said. "Have we met before? You look familiar."

She sensed it startled him for a second, then stuttered out, "No, no, I don't believe we have."

She shrugged. But noticed Hays staring at him and then looking over at Fiona with a thoughtful look on his face. Then he shifted his attention to Curtis.

"The threat from a group called the Acolytes of the Natural Order has continued to escalate. They claim AI will take over the world and destroy humans if not stopped. Seems these crazies thought the movie Terminator was real." Hays nodded his head toward the coffee sidebar.

"Would you like me to get you the coffee, or would you prefer to make it yourself?" Fiona asked?

"I can get it myself."

His business partner, Jace Lin, spoke up. "We were not too worried until we realized they seemed better organized and funded recently."

"We want discreet protection," Hays said. "And... the use of Sentinel."

Fiona sat back and stared at Marshall Hays for a second or two before asking. "How do you know anything about our contracts, military or civilian?" Curtis met Fiona's eyes. Fiona tried to keep her expression neutral, but worried she had failed.

He shrugged, saying, "I hear things, and when I went shopping for protection. Someone suggested your company might have what I needed."

Curtis broke in. "Just exactly how and where did you get this supposed information? What makes you think we got the contract?"

"I do my homework. When the Sentinel came on the market, we inquired about it, but they denied us. Our negotiations did not even progress to the part about the conditions they wanted to set. Seems they already had a company in mind. Yours." Hays leaned back, as if waiting for them to challenge his remark.

Neither Fiona nor Curtis acknowledged what he implied.

"Let's not play games. I saw your purchase of the ship. It came on the market at a steep price, and looking at your financials, it matches the exact amount. Also, other items that would have come with that contract. Which told us you acquired the airship."

Curtis rose and left the room. Ten minutes later he came back, sat and looked in Fiona's direction before saying.

"We haven't deployed it commercially. They haven't even delivered it yet."

"Then let us be the first," Hays replied. "According to my sources, they should finish the hangar and the military compound in about three weeks. The Sentinel to arrive the next day or soon after."

When I saw you got the airship contract, Jace and I figured if we could not own it. We could get the use of it through your protective agency. The conference in Dallas is the largest one that will put AI on the map. Many high-ranking law officials capable of purchasing our AI platform will be there. This will give you the chance to see how she does. And get excellent exposure for her use.

"Yeah, still, we will need to get clearance to be above the conference. Not sure we can get that," Curtis said, stalling.

"If I can secure you that clearance, will you agree to do our protection at the conference with Sentinel?"

"Yes, only if you can get the clearance." Curtis stood and held his hand out, which Jace took. Then both men left.

As the two left, Curtis murmured, "Think they're telling us everything?"

"No," Fiona said, watching the door close. "And I think they are up to something. I want to know how they know so much about the Sentinel and the compound, down to the approximate delivery date?"

The door opened, and Josiah peeked in. "Got something on Colter Harlan's phone," he said as he tried to keep his eyes on Curtis while stealing glances at Fiona.

"His phone pinged twice in the States. Tyler Pounds Regional Airport (TYR), the morning Everett says, and at the time he claimed, and then the Texarkana cattle auction. After that, it's Heathrow Airport, England; a day later, Warsaw Chopin Airport, Poland. Then nothing. Poland is looking to import American beef."

He handed the report over to Curtis and almost fell over his feet leaving. Fiona had trouble suppressing a smile.

Curtis shook his head. "Twenty three and he still falls all over himself around a woman he has a crush on."

She gave Curtis a look before getting serious once more. "The timestamp on this report matches Everett's story down to the hour. At least now we know this Colter guy was where and when Everett claims. At least that is something."

Curtis agreed but turned back to the Sentinel. "I called Major Buck. He said to take the contract; that way he'll have time to track who is leaking information. Buck also wanted to find out what they were up to. And how they knew so much. Financials do not expose that much information, especially not military contracts. Buck claimed they obtained classified information. Told me when he found out how they got the information, heads would roll. Or if they're smart, whoever the person was, he'd work with him or rot in Guantanamo. I'm definitely not going to miss a chance to get information, Buck justified before he hung up."

"Seems Major Buck is not happy with this situation." Fiona said as she leaned back, thinking. She thought about the games being played out of sight. Deadly games.

CHAPTER 5

Shadows Over Austin

Tuesday, November 1, 2022

Whiskey River Two-Step Ranch / Fiona's Office

Fiona's computer chimed softly as she passed her home office, the glow of the screen painting pale light across the dark wood floor. The house was quiet except for the low hum of the refrigerator downstairs and the occasional creak of the ranch mansion settling into its bones. Outside the windows, the predawn sky pressed heavy and low, mist clinging thick to the grass. The moon still hung in the west, silver against thinning clouds.

She figured she could take a quick look at her emails before heading out with Curtis to meet the protection team at the Austin Tech Conference Center. She wanted the first deployment of the Sentinel to go smoothly. Hays had secured the clearance needed, gods only knew how, and Curtis got a farmer to let them use his field to unload and load from. Buck was tracking how and through whom the clearance came, quietly in the background.

Curtis would already be in the kitchen, wrestling the espresso machine as if it owed him money.

She sank into her chair and pulled the laptop closer. The email header carried a Colombian domain she didn't recognize. The subject line made her sit up straighter.

Inquiry Regarding Global Human Trafficking Network.

Odd, her company wasn't currently investigating a trafficking case.

She clicked it open.

A single image appeared, handmade. A silver bracelet etched with ornate floral vines, with a stone around the outer edge. It was small. Light. Like a child's bracelet. At the bottom of the email was the signature of Mauricio Delgado, claiming to be the owner and editor-in-chief of El Clarín de Bogotá, and one of his reporters, Lucía Torres.

She felt a chill ripple through her. Something tugged at the back of her memory. Fiona rubbed her neck as her pulse ticked faster. The header showed it came from an anonymous account sent yesterday. Signing your name and business under the photo seems contradictory to sending this anonymously.

Fiona tensed. She remembered a media story buried in international news about a week or so after Bridget's murder. She pulled up her browser and looked up the name. A suspected cartel hit. Ambushed and shot in the street in Bogotá, Colombia, were Mauricio Delgado, newspaper owner and editor-in-chief, and Lucía Torres, one of his investigative reporters, as they were heading to work. Two days later, arsonists torched the newsroom, trapping and killing the staff inside.

A coincidence? Could this connect to Major Buck and what he was working on? Human trafficking seemed to be the thread he was chasing, from the little she'd seen.

Her gaze drifted to the courier bag by the door, still sealed. A courier bag from Colombia. Was the email related to it? She grabbed the bag and returned to her desk. There was a box inside. The box, when she opened it, revealed the very child's bracelet from the email.

Her housekeeper leaned in through the cracked door, forcing

her to stop delving further into the bracelet's mystery.

"If you don't get downstairs soon, I'm going to commit bodily harm to Curtis."

Fiona exhaled, snapped the laptop shut, and carried the box to the mansion's safe before she went downstairs.

"Let me save him," she padded down the stairs. The smell of scorched coffee hit her before she reached the kitchen. Curtis's voice filled the air, profane and colorful, as steam hissed from the machine.

"You'd think with all this tech," she said dryly, "we'd own one coffee maker that doesn't require you to perform a full exorcism."

He shot her a glare, muttering something that made her laugh despite herself.

She was going to get a mug when she saw something move outside. It was barely visible through the mist and the dark sky. A massive silhouette lifted slowly over the trees, silent and unreal, appearing as if a phantom. The name stenciled across its flank was barely legible.

The airship, banked in an eerie, graceful rise, began circling widely over the far southern horizon. Fiona stood frozen for a moment, watching it climb into the sky.

Sentinel.

Fiona's hand lingered on the mug, equal parts awe and anticipation tightening her chest. The first operational use on the civilian side of the agency was underway.

Curtis cursed at the machine again behind her. The airship's image burned into her thoughts. Then he noticed what she was looking at.

Curtis exhaled. "That flight path approval will cross three county authorities who don't like surprises. That airship appearing overhead is going to be a hell've a surprise."

Austin Tech Conference Center / Main Stage

The cacophony of the crowd, stage wash of fiery lights, body odor, and flare of flashbulbs made the teams work harder. Journalists stacked three deep, badges flashing. Investors, high-ranking law enforcement officials, and defense suits stood shoulder to shoulder, overwhelming the space. Marshall Hays had just left the podium. Flashbulbs popped. Microphones thrust forward. The air vibrated with the frenzy of money and speculation.

Fiona and Curtis stood at the back wall, discreet comms in their ears. Her jacket hid the shoulder holster and her SIG, a familiar weight against her ribs. Curtis stood beside her.

The Sentinel's overhead feed on Kenneth Steele's tablet smoothly swept across rooftops. Their plainclothes teams worked the room, monitoring entrances and corridors.

The view on the tablet changed. It showed a helicopter with News Eight marking, but repelling ropes dropped to the roof. Kenneth's voice crackled over comms. "Six rappelling down from what appears to be a news helicopter, south wall, inbound." Kenneth's voice snapped again. "Heat signatures confirmed. Contact in five."

Seconds later, the ceiling thumped from shaped charges in a room down the hall. Concrete chunks crashed to the floor as plaster dust blew outward. Screams cascaded through the sudden eruption of chaos.

Fiona moved before the second charge went off.

Tsujii hit his voice mic. "Move, move, move. Charlie, Wendell on Hays."

Wendell and Charlie surged forward just before the second blast thundered in the outer hallway.

The rear wall of the hall vanished in flames. Screams cut through the smoke and debris, ricocheted off concrete and steel, overlapping until individual voices dissolved into a single shrill roar. Bodies surged in blind waves, shoulders slamming together as people pushed for exits they could no longer see through the smoke. Ceiling panels collapsed. Law enforcement officers attending the event tried to control the stampeding people and became casualties.

"GO, GO, GO!" Kenneth barked over the comms.

Agents formed a wedge, yanking Hays from the stage. Fiona shoved a bystander out of the path of falling glass, heart hammering against her ribs. Smoke rolled in thick waves, choking the light.

They pushed into the backstage corridor. Tsujii keyed his mic. "Sentinel, prepare for landing. Farm Site Echo."

"Copy. Rerouting," came the calm reply from above.

Another explosion shook the building. Fiona's teeth rattled. Hays remained eerily calm, pulling out his phone and muttering only: "Is my son safe?" The question caught her attention for a second.

Another blast punched through into the hall. Smoke followed by a pressure wave shoved forward like a living thing. Lights blew with a pop and crackle, raining glass. The crowd surged like a tide of bodies, panic thick, the odor of burning insulation stinging their eyes and driving them to run like stampeding cattle.

Fiona broke through a nearby aisle, shoulders low, her vest biting at her collarbone beneath the blazer. A black-clad assailant slid down on a rappelling rope, muzzle already in her direction.

Fiona's SIG barked twice, controlled shots. He fell, his harness twisted, boot sole smacking the stage lip. For a second, she couldn't look away.

"Contact right, twenty feet," Curtis's voice cut through.

Another rope descended. Another muzzle flash. Now, in a crouched cat step, Fiona moved on instinct, sight, squeeze, reacquire. Brass pinged off tile and skittered around her feet. Her ears filled with a deafening mix of shouts, alarms, and helicopter rotor wash through the hole in the roof above. It benefited them by blowing the smoke down the aisle. Her SIGs slide locked back; she hit the mag release; it clattered to the floor; she slammed another home, pulled the slide back, and released. Seeing the figure fall, she reacquired and fired at another assailant. "South corridor compromised," Phùng said on comms. "Shifting to the backstage exit."

"Copy." Kenneth pushed the formation through the curtain of smoke while Hatfield and Tsujii bridged the gap, bodies interposed. Hays resisted one beat too long, turning to look behind him at something or someone, until Carlie shoved his head down and pushed him forward.

They hit the service hall as a secondary concussion rattled silverware in the catering racks. Cordite and drywall dust coated the back of Fiona's throat. She swallowed the copper taste in her mouth and kept moving. Her heartbeat quickened rapidly.

"Sentinel, stand by for exfil. Farm Site Echo. Repeat Farm Site Echo," Tsujii on the radio, voice calm and clipped.

"Copy Echo. Winds five out of the south," the pilot answered. "Two klicks away."

Convoy Extraction | East of the Venue (Austin Surface Streets)

They reached the parking lot outside. Hummers roared to life. Two company motorcycles flanked them. Fiona and Curtis dove into the trailing SUV. Sirens warbled far off; up close it was all diesel, hot brakes, and tire squeal over asphalt.

"Route Beta. Stay tight," Kenneth ordered.

The convoy tore through traffic, zigzagging around vehicles at high speed.

"Four incoming. Black sedans," Phùng's voice cut in. "Weapons visible."

Gunfire ripped across the gap. Rounds cracked off the rear quarter of the SUV Curtis and Fiona were in. The outrider bikes peeled off, turned, and returned fire. Curtis slammed their SUV into one sedan, sending it crashing into a hydrant with a heavy crunch. Fiona lowered her window. Drew her Sig. Sighted through the traffic. Thunder roared as she fired. Wind shoved the smoke back into her face; she blinked tears, then reacquired the target.

"Contact right is breaking," she called. "Driver's hit." As she sat back in her seat.

The sedan fishtailed, caught a curb, and tumbled steel on concrete—screaming metal, the wet smack of something on the road.

Two more slid up. Their outriders Paul and Charlie cut in, bikes howling, controlled shots bursting at the sedans' radiators. Steam geysered; a hood flew off.

"Left! Left!" Fiona braced as Curtis yanked the wheel and hammered their SUV into the second sedan. Her world went white momentarily after the passenger airbag slammed into her face, accompanied by a sickening crunch through the frame. The SUV rolled once, skidded across the road, sparks spraying outward, and screeching metal as it slammed sideways into a Jersey barrier.

It felt like an electric blade shoved under her collarbone. Fiona's shoulder screamed with white-hot pain. Curtis's forehead streamed blood. She gritted her teeth.

"Get out!" she yelled, kicking at the door as Curtis shook his head.

The cabin stank of engine fluid, burnt plastic, and gasoline.

"Out. Out." She kicked the door twice more before it gave way. The street was a blur of motion and sound. Honking, screaming, sirens building somewhere to the west. Her vision narrowed as pain screamed through her. Then she snapped back.

Their outrider bikes raced toward them in a tight arc. Paul grabbed Curtis under the arm; Charlie reached for Fiona and pulled. The world wobbled, and it felt as if stifling air blew across her as they raced down the lane to catch up with the convoy ahead.

They shot through the gate in the farmer's fence around his field. Sentinel's ramp yawned wide open. The ship's shadow swallowed them. Rotor wash from the external lift fans pointed downward, blowing grit and dirt into her face.

Fiona twisted, leaning hard into Charlie, firing wildly as a surviving sedan tried to ram the closing ramp. One shot smashed into the driver's glass. A crunching thud announced the car's impact with a drainage berm.

The bike flew up into the gondola. The ramp door finished closing.

Silence. Blessed, well-engineered silence. As the airship sealed, it shut the world out.

Sentinel Airship / In Flight

The deck thrummed underfoot. The bay smelled of hydraulic fluid, clean metal, and the sharp scent of antiseptics from the med kits.

"Two WIA, non-critical," Antonio called. "One rib fracture, one through-and-through in the arm."

Fiona's right shoulder throbbed. Derek's hands were quick and impersonal. He felt the joint and clavicle and found no broken bones, no dislocation, just a bad sprain. Cold tape on hot skin, sling built in seconds. "You'll stop noticing it in a week or two. But wear the sling for at least a week."

Curtis lay flat on a cot, eyes open, a ribbon of blood at his temple already tacky.

"Sentinel to ATC, priority egress northeast. Whiskey River Two Step Ranch, medevac, WIAs on board. Flight path logged prior."

"Cleared. Maintain logged vector and altitude."

Seconds later, two Blackhawks blew past them.

Sentinel engines increased power, and the crew could feel the ship turning. Kenneth called the cockpit. "What's going on? Why are you turning back?"

The pilot called back; he was fighting Sentinel's controls. They appeared to have a glitch in the navigation systems. Minutes later, the pilot regained control, and Sentinel was back on route.

The forward bulkhead displayed rolling news feeds. Shaky iPhone video from bystanders at the event center, and professional TV news reporters. Smoke boiling out of the Austin Tech Conference Center, people screaming, a wall of sirens. A mass of red and blue flashing lights across the parking area and outer road.

Then a cut to drone footage: side entrance, closeup of a man sprinting out in a gray hoodie.

Curtis pushed up on his elbows. "That's Jace Lin." He swung his head toward Hays. "You said he wasn't coming until tonight." The sound of gunfire jerked his attention back to the feed. Jace folded mid-stride.

A reporter's voice came thin over the feed. "A group calling themselves the Acolytes of the Natural Order claimed responsibility and posted it online."

"Bull," Kenneth said. "They're loud, annoying, full of crazies.

Not this."

Phùng folded his arms. "They used false news helicopters, timed entries and placed charges for maximum structural division. That's pro-operation. I'd say military training."

Speaking into his phone from the front seats, Hays sounded almost calm, his voice low. "Is my son safe?" A pause, as if waiting for an answer. Then he placed the phone in his pocket; not nervously, but with calculated finality. The gesture a man made when confirming a move on a board only he could see. Nothing in his expression matched the surrounding chaos; if anything, he looked... satisfied.

Fiona watched him, a quiet itch between her shoulder blades. He ended the call as if cut short. She filed it away for later.

No one spoke for a beat.

Whiskey River Two-Step Ranch / Compound Clubhouse

The ranch air was cooler than Austin; sweet hay and damp dirt odors drifted on the wind. Leather furniture, hot fresh coffee, and the scent of antiseptic filled the lower level of the clubhouse in the compound.

Fiona sat on the big couch, sling snug, shoulder aching with dull heat. Curtis stood near the fire, tablet in one hand, reviewing the recorded events from their lapel cameras, the Sentinel's drones, and onboard cameras. Black coffee steamed in his other hand.

Staff got the injured into the compound's small trauma hospital, and others gathered in the clubhouse lounge.

"I notified the sheriff," Curtis said. "Deputy en route to take statements. Shaw's tied up with Everett's case. We'll need an extra lawyer for this. What about Casey, your brother?"

Fiona frowned. "I prefer to keep my family out of this. Connor will have a fit if he thinks I pulled Casey into all this PI stuff. I don't need a family feud."

Curtis didn't look up. "We need someone we can trust, Fi. Casey's been itching to gain a piece of the action. I didn't tell you because I figured this would be your answer. Put that aside. We need his help, and we can trust him."

The anchor's voice on the TV on the wall cracked: "Acolytes released another threat. They are demanding everyone decommission all AI programs and ban them. Claiming we will all see their resolve soon."

Kenneth growled. On the screen, the aerial footage wobbled. A smoke column rose like a gray-black tower. Sirens were constant, high and ugly.

Kenneth stood behind them, arms folded. "If Acolytes claims it, someone handed them the keys, comms, and mercs. Amateurs could not do this op."

From the landing zone, Fiona watched Sentinel's movements behind the barns. The hangar's top was visible above the trees, casting a shadow that crept across the pasture. The shifting temperature caused a floorboard to pop in the clubhouse, briefly startling her.

Fiona took a breath that hurt a little on her left side and looked back at the TV screen.

The police forced the TV crews farther away. The cameras widened the view.

Moments afterward, a massive explosion ripped through the building. The conference center folded in on itself, roof blown skyward, walls disintegrating in a blast that hurled police cruisers like toys. Screams. Sirens. A red-orange, billowing mushroom of fire and black smoke rose straight upward as if from an erupting volcano.

The room fell silent. Fiona's heart thundered, breath caught in her throat.

Curtis lowered his tablet. Shock registered on his face. Minutes later, voice quiet and unsteady, he whispered, "This..." He swallowed, unable to finish.

Shocked silence greeted the unfinished remark.

Buck called less than an hour later. "The FAA is already asking who authorized the airspace intrusion, which is how they viewed it. They demanded the paperwork by morning. I'm already being notified that this has triggered oversight of the use of the Sentinel."

Fiona and Curtis got a call from Stephana twenty minutes after that at the Dallas headquarters. "I thought you should know the FBI is crawling all over the office, along with Austin PD. They have warrants."

By the following day, they discovered that Senator Morrow had approved the Sentinel flight, as he is part of the committee looking into AI's future in the United States. Transitions AI is at the top of that list. And their contract named Marshall Hays, CEO of Transitions AI, requested a protection detail because of threats from Acolytes of the Natural Order. Which, in hindsight, appeared to be an acceptable call. Four days after that, the fallout to their agency had died off; however, they still had to appear to answer the FBI's questions. And the media still haunted Fiona and Curtis with questions whenever they caught them entering or leaving the building's foyer. To which they both answered, "No comment." Though after one such encounter, Fiona told Curtis. "This isn't over," she waved to the security as they both stepped into the elevator. "It just hasn't all caught up yet."

CHAPTER 6

The Woman in Silk

Wednesday, November 30th, 2022

Delores Cole's Home | Gated Highland Park

The shock across the nation of the Austin Tech Conference Center attack had subsided; news moved on to more mundane events, and Marshall Hays dropped out of sight. O'Brien & Galloway finally got back to a normal routine. This morning when Fiona rose, the sky sagged low, leaden with pregnant storm clouds. The air was so damp it clung to skin, and the sharp scent of ozone lingered in the air. Every shadow under the bare oaks seemed stretched, conspiring, as Fiona's Cadillac SUV eased through the iron guard gate leading into the exclusive community. Delores and her husband lived behind those gates, protected from the masses. With the Caddy's engine purring low as Fiona drove slowly up the winding drive, the guard directed her towards. Through the windshield, pale light reflected off polished glass and wet stone. She'd finally won Delores over by appealing to her ego.

John and Delores Cole's mansion shimmered like a mirage. Beautiful, imposing, and intimidating. Delores answered the door barefoot, silk robe whispering against her thighs, mimosa in hand. Perfume clung to her skin like armor. Inside, the air was cool, scented with orange blossoms and disinfectant.

"You said eleven," Delores murmured, appearing annoyed and not ready, a drink in her hand as if she needed it before the interview.

Fiona stood under the portico, her Caddy parked behind her in the driveway. "I don't enjoy being late," she said.

The living room was more showpiece than a home. No family photos. No warmth. Only sharp surfaces, sculptured furniture, and silence. Fiona sat at one end of a white couch. Delores draped herself across a chaise like a well-kept whore in an old black and white movie.

Fiona cut to the chase. "Your friendship with Bridget in college ended badly. Why?"

"I noticed the sling on your arm. What happened? I hope it does not hurt too much," Delores sipped her drink; her expression didn't shift.

Fiona shrugged. "Nothing too bad, sprained it getting out of a car." Not a lie, but not exactly the truth.

Delores stared at her for a moment before saying. "We were bff's for the longest time in college. Until she got engaged to my boyfriend Charles, hurt back then more than I enjoy admitting."

Fiona raised an eyebrow and leaned forward. "No one has mentioned this so far, even though your name has come up in the investigation of Bridget's murder. Does Charles have a last name?"

"Stuart, of the New Orleans Stuarts. Old family money in Louisiana."

"Several people said that in the weeks before her murder, she thought someone was watching her. Did she ever mention feeling watched? Or afraid?"

Delores gave a small shrug, mimosa sloshing over her hand before she put it down and wiped her hand on her robe.

"One night she stayed over; she stood on the balcony, just staring. Said she saw a truck parked by the curb just outside the guard gate, old and beat up. Looked like one of Everett's ranch hands' trucks."

She drank deep and wiped her mouth.

Fiona stiffened, yet kept her expression neutral.

"One time she arrived with bruises. Blamed a fall against hay-baling machinery. But she said it as if she'd rehearsed it. I didn't buy it."

Fiona's voice cooled.

"Did she give you anything to keep for her? Letters? Notes? Or even things from when you were friends in college."

"No. We went our separate ways after she... stole Charles in college. Though Bridget always seemed submissive," Delores shrugged dismissively. "Charles always had a big ego, charm and all. I would not put up with his shit, cheating being something he excelled at."

Fiona did not miss the nasty tone. "Several people told me you were friends again recently, and you just said she came over to your home several times."

"I will admit I burned or threw out any reminders of Bridget or Charles back in college. She stole my boyfriend; friendship was out of the question after that. Six months later, I met and married John. Charles became a footnote in my history."

Delores got what appeared to be a sly look on her face before she said.

"Last year at a party given by Porter & Ashburn, Edward Ashburn invited my husband and me personally. You know he is the sole owner of the nationwide Porter & Ashburn Firms, and I ran into her and her sister Lisa at the party. Learned they both worked there, my husband said I should bury the hatchet and become friends again. So I did. It surprised me that my anger towards Bridget was gone. I guess because we were both married, not to Charles. Besides, she got dumped by Charles too, and later married Everett. She may have done me a favor. Supposedly, Charles plays rough and seems to have a very jaded taste. I always wondered how she took him from me. After the rumors came out, I figured I had my answer." She gave Fiona a sideways glance as if trying to see how her remark had landed.

Delores weaponized her charm, and Fiona recognized it.

"Do you know a man named Joe Bell? They are rumors about you and him... together," Fiona threw it out without warning to catch a reaction from her.

Delores choked on her drink, then laughed so hard she nearly spilled it. Her eyes flicked sideways, measuring how to respond.

Fiona didn't blink. She pivoted. "So it's true."

"Everett told you that, didn't he? My husband manages Porter & Ashburn's accounts. I've likely shared oxygen with Bell at some events. And he may have come to the house a time or two to deliver paperwork. Nothing more. Does that answer your question?" Her smirk lingered as if she had thought up a clever response.

Funny Everett never said a word about Delores, so why'd she go there?

"I have an appointment in town that I need to get dressed for, so I would say this interview is over." Delores stood, followed by Fiona.

At the door, Fiona paused.

"If you remember anything, please call."

Outside, fog clung low to the pavement. Driving down towards the guard gate, Fiona spotted a crimson Porsche pulling into view at the guardhouse. He parked in the small parking area next to the guard shack. A tall, gangly man stepped out.

Sharp suit, silver triangle lapel pin. He looked like a guy from Bridget's photos.

Fiona drove slowly as she passed him walking up the pathway towards Delore's house, lifted her phone, took several quick photos, and eased the car a little slower. Then, as she passed the Porsche, snapped a few photos of the license plate.

Before she passed through the guard gate, she saw Delores meet him at the door with a shift of her hip and a smile too practiced to be innocent. They went inside together.

Fiona would bet it was Joe Bell.

O'Brien & Galloway Office | Conference/War Room

Muted blue light glowed from data screens as rain tapped the windows. Fiona sat, her shoulder somewhat sore, the sling sitting on the table, eyes flicking across encrypted offshore account trees. With Sabrina beside her, fingers flying. "References keep mentioning families. With no other remarks except that they seem to be all over the shell companies, though we came up with a few names."

"One of the shell companies flagged," she said. "Metadata tag: C. Stuart."

"Wonder if this is the Charles Stuart that's Dolores' and Bridget's ex."

"And Suart's wife's family bank is funding several of the shells. I looked her up. Her family's wealth is in New York and New York City. Her maiden name is Erskine."

"Send the information on to Buck; let him chase it for now. I'd say we are earning our pay so far," Curtis rubbed his jaw, thinking.

On the screen, the network of ghost routes glowed red. Offshore transfers. Caymans. Zurich. Ankara. Then went nowhere. Accounts closed.

The TV flickered silently in the corner. Governor Abbott's re-election speech. Bottom scroll: *Hakeem Jeffries becomes the first Black lawmaker to lead a congressional party.*

Fiona barely listened. The world turned.

Rich Aroma's Coffeehouse

Steam hissed from the espresso machine as Curtis walked in. The cafe buzzed with background noise. Whispers, cutlery, soft music. Outside, dusk folded in under a bruise-colored sky.

Detective Mason McCarthy sat in the back booth, collar up, eyes sharp.

Curtis's friend, a retired homicide detective now running a small Dallas PI firm, shared insights. He said Mason McCarthy and his partner were exceptional. Intelligent, honest, and actively fighting department corruption. Curtis had done his homework.

Mason and Luis, his partner, were in the original investigation of Bridget Taylor's murder file, but their discovery prints were missing from the paperwork trail. The reason? Pressure.

Another friend of Curtis since starting the PI company with FI, Deputy Hartly from Smith County, told him, "After the Miller court case went sideways, the brass wanted dependable names on anything that Wren worked on that hits the press. Doesn't mean they're working the case." Curtis' friend set up a meeting.

When Curtis arrived, he liked what he saw. Curtis joined him. No handshakes. Just a nod and sat and ordered when the server arrived.

"So, what's the actual story?" Curtis asked.

Mason leaned in, voice tight. "They gave the case to Detective

Wren un-officially, but the brass left our names on it for optics. Said it was temporary, just till we got above water on the I-45 murders." He stared at Curtis for a moment before saying anything. "I don't trust Wren. He cuts corners and makes evidence fit his chosen suspect. Doesn't follow up if it doesn't match his theory. He tells the brass what they want to hear. Solve fast, go with the easiest suspect."

A beat passed.

"Look, I don't know you or your partner, but my guys said I could trust you."

McCarthy slid a thick envelope across.

"They want to close the case. PTSD trope. Clean narrative. Everett's the accused."

Curtis opened it. Witness statement.

"Who is this guy?"

"CI for Marcus Wren," McCarthy said. "He's used him before to fabricate testimony; my partner and I flagged it once, got slapped down hard from high above."

Curtis leaned back.

"Why bring it to me?"

I can't share this with the brass or the public because of this. Not without wrecking my career or worse. But I won't stand by and let this case go to court, especially with George Shaw, the defense attorney, unless it's airtight." He sat back an looked at Curtis for a moment. "My partner's and my reputation is on the line. I'm not saying I believe Taylor is innocent. We just need to know if we've got the right guy. Which means not rushing the case. You want to blow this up? Find this CI and prove he's lying. Wren is the true lead in the investigation into the Taylor murder. They sidelined my partner and me for now."

Curtis frowned. "Based on what?"

"He claims he spoke with the Montana rancher, a friend of Harlan's. The man apparently didn't verify any cattle business in Texarkana that day with a Colt Harlan. Luis called, and his wife said no one talked to her husband, as he was up in the pastures. When Luis told the captain, he got his ass chewed. Captain told Luis, Wren spoke to Braddock before leaving for the upper pastures to bring the cows in. Threatened that if Luis didn't stop going behind Wren's back, he'd get a suspension without pay. I told Luis to back off."

Curtis stiffened. *Damn, that looks bad for Everett.* Curtis exhaled sharply, keeping that thought to himself.
"Yeah. And the captain signed off on it because he trusts Wren to manage this fast. Who gives a shit if we have the right guy? That 'unconfirmed alibi' note is now in the official chain without Luis or me even approving it."

Mason added almost as an afterthought, "One more thing: if Wren suddenly comes in with a new *witness*, be careful. He has... sources that can be unreliable."

Curtis caught the tone. "Meaning?"

Mason stared out the rain-streaked window for several minutes before saying anything else. "Let's just say some people will say anything if Wren's the one asking."

He didn't elaborate.

Curtis didn't push.

But the warning hung in the air. Curtis didn't speak. He didn't need to.

He eyed the cars outside for a moment, coming and going.

"And you?" McCarthy shrugged. "I'll help when I can. But don't expect me to fall on the sword, not unless it counts. Your guy better be innocent, or our alliance is over."

"One more thing," Curtis leaned towards Mason. "I tried to have one of my investigators secure an old file of mine. Got a return of only available for official requests. The case was a murder. One of my old cases, with my partner, Detective David Harmon, in Denver, we looked at a Joe Bell in a case that never got solved. Looks to be the same guy."

"Yeah, give me the details. I'll see what I can do."

Curtis wrote the information down for Mason.

The muted TV played the same speech as earlier. Mason appeared weary, or perhaps he was just jaded from the job.

"No one should get away with framing an innocent man." Mason said after a moment. It's as bad as letting the real criminal get away.

Curtis stood, envelope tucked under his arm, already strategizing. Outside, a couple got into their car, and the headlights flared. Curtis didn't flinch. Just checked his surroundings before he walked out.

Dallas Office | Evening Shadows

By the time Fiona emerged from the Dallas office, her temples throbbed from hours of going over testimonies and interviews her investigators on various cases had given her that day for review.

Outside, the storm had returned. Fat drops streaked the windows; the building steps became slick and treacherous. The lights flickered in the office, and Stephana handed Fiona a flashlight, saying,

"In case the electricity goes out, you'll have to take the stairs. Selena swapped the batteries in the emergency kits last week. Said she couldn't sleep unless she knew they were fresh."

Fiona thanked her and made a mental note to thank Selena the next day. Selena worried about their safety, some of the toughest people Fiona knew. Ex-cops, FBI, NSA, DOJ, and Special Forces.

Selena worried about everyone. She could not even kill a fly, literally; she was in school to become a veterinarian. But she made a great receptionist; organized and friendly, hardworking.

Curtis was waiting in the street-floor foyer when Fiona exited the elevator an hour later. Collar already turned up against the wind for when he stepped outside, tablet under his arm.

She joined him, both half-soaked before they reached the SUV in the garage a block away. He opened the passenger door, muttering, "News is claiming inside information. They're saying Everett's unstable."

"He's not." Fiona said, sliding into the seat. "They just want a villain."

"They've got one," Curtis replied grimly, pulling into traffic. "Problem is, he's not the right one."

They drove in silence. The wipers beat a steady rhythm. The city blurred by rain, washed out in streaks. Fiona leaned her head against the glass, watching taillights smear red across wet asphalt.

On the radio, a breaking update cut through: *"New footage has surfaced from the Dallas Tech Conference attack, showing the moment alleged Acolytes infiltrated the building. Federal agents still question the success of such an operation without internal aid.*

Fiona sat up straighter. "That's our footage from the Sentinel. How the hell did they get it?"

Curtis snapped off the radio, jaw tight. "Buck?"

A call to Buck from their car's cell phone confirmed their suspicions. All he said was that there was a price he had to pay to get Sentinel out of mothballs and hung up. Curtis understood that to mean that some of the information gathered by Sentinel was not private to their agency.

Fiona didn't answer. *The news droned on about the heroics of*

Smith County SWAT officers Lt. Morales and Sgt. Blake in rescuing eleven children during an attack at a local swimming pool, while their team took out three assailants and warned command of the possibility of bombs placed throughout the building, decreasing the death toll by having command move the lines back farther from the building housing the changing and showers area before it blew. No known motive at this time by the assailants.

Fiona turned towards Curtis, "I never heard about this before now in the news. Did you?"

"No. Guess all the news about the Austin Conferences Center has dominated the news lately. Makes you wonder how much we never hear about cause it's not important to the MSM or does not fit a certain narrative."

Whiskey River Two-Step Ranch

By the time they reached the ranch, the storm had broken apart. Cold stars winked through a ragged quilt of clouds, and the fields shimmered with standing water. The barn was dark, the Sentinel airship in its hangar like a sleeping leviathan. Cutis input the code when they halted before the compound's gate. Once parked, they raced for the door.

Inside, warmth. Coffee, leather, the faint antiseptic tang of cleaners, and cinnamon air fresheners Matilda "Tilly" O'Shea Romano, the compound's housekeeper, used this time of year. Kenneth Steele and Phùng sat at the table with maps spread wide, red lines cutting across Texas into Mexico and beyond. Wendell sat across from the massive fireplace hearth, rifle parts laid out on a cloth on a small table across from him, methodical as a priest with relics.

Fiona hung her blazer over a chair and dropped into the seat beside Curtis. "Tell me you've got something," she said.

Kenneth pushed a printout across the table. "Look at these surveillance stills. Grainy, time-stamped, showing black sedans outside the Dallas venue *before* the attack. Buck analysts traced the plates leased to one shell company, then to another, then into a void. One company was interesting, though. A company owned by the Stuart Foundation, whose CEO is Samuel Elias McCoy. What caught our attention was its money-managing firm, John Cole's, and the law firm representing them, Porter & Ashburn."

"Dead ends for now, cause all it proves is that those firms leased those vehicles in the past." Phùng said. "But look at the timing. These cars were staged hours before anyone called in the Acolytes' claim. Those were the ones that chased after us."

Curtis frowned. "Meaning someone higher placed the pieces. Someone feeding them logistics."

"Exactly," Kenneth said. "And I'd bet my pension it ties back to John Cole's company. They've been laundering money through half a dozen cutouts. Arms, tech, mercenaries. You name it. Major Buck has been looking into them since you guys sent him what you have found so far. And Buck gave me a message. He said you'd understand. The SILO network; it doesn't decide who will, and who won't live long enough to regret it. Those running the programs do so. It just tells them the most efficient way to do so."

Fiona looked at Curtis before she said. "We will keep sending him information as we find it." Both rose from their seats and left the compound. Neither quite understood the message, but both were determined to discover exactly what he was talking about.

CHAPTER 7

Ghosts in the Barn

Friday, December 2, 2022

Everett's Ranch

A knife-edge chill sliced through the air before sunrise. Crystalline frost glazed every blade of grass, catching what little predawn light there was. The skeletal trees, their limbs gnarled and leafless, stood guard against a pearl-gray sky, silhouettes etched in silence. Mixed with green pine trees.

Everett Taylor pressed himself through the treeline with the practiced skill of a hunter. His boots swallowed by cold loam, he felt the familiar hum of tension behind his ribs. He'd memorized the drone's sweep every seventy-five minutes, and this fragile window of six, maybe seven minutes, was all he had. The court agreed to the surveillance. Shaw was appealing.

Ahead, the barn rose from the mist, its roof a stark slash of black against the fading stars. He inhaled the pungent mix of linseed oil and leather that clung to the air, then reached the rear gate. The latch groaned, metal against metal; he froze for just a second before entering.

Inside, the barn breathed around him. Soft snorts from the stalls, the muffled shuffle of hooves in straw. He moved down the aisle, fingertips brushing each horse's flank, warm flesh, comforting weight, grounding himself.

At the feed room door, he halted. A single scratch marred the latch's paint: thin, deliberate, fresh. A tremor ran down his spine.

He slipped inside. Stacks of golden hay bales leaned in neat rows; saddles hung like silent sentinels; grain barrels gleamed dully in the dim light. He perceived a small but faint odor that should not have been there. Making the atmosphere feel violated, as though someone's breath still drifted ghostlike.

Tools and scraps of leather cluttered the workbench, and dust motes danced in the light slanting through the small window. Empty drawers gaped open, and the silver wristband engraved with "B.T." was nowhere to be seen.

Bridget Taylor. The gift he'd given Bridget when they dared to dream of quiet, shared futures.

He remembered Lila's tiny fingers winding around Bridget's wrist when she was three; later, they had the same jeweler make a matching one with "L.T." stamped on the back and the stone ring Lisa added. Police never found Bridget's bracelet on her or in the cabin. A few days later, while feeding the horses, he realized the drawer was slightly open. It was here in this drawer that he found it, a small though important connection to her. Now Bridget's bracelet was gone.

Icy dread pooled in his gut. He felt as if someone had cruelly plucked a piece of him away, leaving a raw and jagged wound in his chest. The empty drawer felt like an accusation, an unspoken betrayal that cut deeper than any knife. He tore the tack and feed room apart, hoping he'd dropped it or forgotten to put it back and it got knocked to the floor.

The sound of his pounding heart seemed deafening, drowning out the soft murmurs of the horses and the whistle of the wind outside. A soft whisper in the back of his mind, a warning.

Did others know the bracelet's location prior to his discovery of it while tending the horses after her murder?

Rage and sorrow rose like bile.

Surveillance Van FM-201, 1 Mile Out

The van reeked of stale coffee, overheated electronics, and the sour tang of bureaucratic exhaustion. Undercover detectives Perez and Aranda had just left; Smith undercover deputies pulled from their drug surveillance for a few days. Mason crouched over the center console, eyes flicking among thermal, infrared, and zoom stills of Everett's property.

"Movement?" Captain Liddell's voice grated from the rear.

"He arrived at the barn, then checked the bracelet's location. Damn, it's gone. He's tearing the tack room apart looking for it," Mason half-stood, trying to see better.

Liddell barked a laugh. "Look how that guy can go from calm to violent. I'm telling you, he killed his wife. You always defend these ex-operators. Let it go, McCarthy. PTSD's eating him. He's dangerous."

Liddell stomped out. Mason waited until the footsteps faded. He withdrew a flash drive, plugged it into the terminal, and began downloading every frame from the past seventy-two hours and every angle, every shadow. Looking for the person who stole the bracelet. Maybe find some answers. He wanted to see if he could catch whoever entered the barn unauthorized. What he got was a thirty-minute blackout in the footage.

Then his phone buzzed. Luis, his partner. Sent him a text. "ME says the wound angles on the I-45 victims suggest two sets of hands. One smaller, like a female or younger male, maybe in their teens. Your hypothesis of a male–female couple might be correct."

Outside, a hawk circled in the bruised dawn, silent. Mason

tucked the drive into his coat. *What's going on here? Watching Everett handle that bracelet over the last three days made Mason question the idea that he would have murdered his wife. He handled it with reverence. As if he could somehow recover what had been stolen from him. Not the actions of a man who murdered the owner of the bracelet. His wife Bridget. And why on earth would someone steal it and know enough to erase the timeframe of its theft?*

Mason looked toward Capt. Liddel, watched as he disappeared in the distance and wondered why he was at the surveillance van when Mason arrived to relieve the other detective on duty.

O'Brien & Galloway Investigations, Downtown Dallas

Dawn cut through the low fog draped over the Trinity River basin, a brittle, sunless glare struggling to burn away the mist. The overnight weather front left behind a stillness that felt alive, clinging to concrete and infiltrating bones.

In the break room's muted half-light, a wall-mounted TV murmured local news as Fiona drifted past, heading to the front reception desk. "*...law enforcement is still pursuing leads in the Taylor murder. Everett Taylor, former Delta operator and husband of the victim, remains a person of interest. Sources suggest new psychological evaluations...*"

She silenced it with a decisive flick.

At the front desk, Selena's fingers moved with crisp precision, sorting mail into neat piles. A heavy cream-colored envelope, its silver embossing faintly ornate, caught her eye. Without a word, she slid it across to Fiona.

Fiona cracked it open on the way to her office; the thick card stock whispered of money as she unfolded a formal notice from Ravenlock Holdings Ltd., confirming a property transfer. Ravenlock acquired the building three months ago. No immediate changes; existing leases are to be reviewed individually. The Ravenlock letter stock was unusually expensive European stock.

She placed the letter beside Sabrina's station in the main workroom. "Background this when you can. Quiet flag only." She glanced over at Curtis before saying, "Ravenlock Holdings bought the building about three months ago, from what the notice stated."

Curtis glanced up from his tablet, brow tightening before tapping some keys. "Ravenlock Holdings? Offshore shells, Cayman ties, subsidiary stacks. Maybe it's a company we should look at. Think this has anything to do with our investigations?" Curtis turned towards her.

"Everything's a shell company these days," Fiona replied, and shivered in the cool air, turning the temperature up on her way out. She headed for the break room's coffee machine. *Heck, we're all becoming paranoid,* the hiss of the steam wand punctuating her thoughts. *How did a wife, mother, and adoption lawyer get so tangled up in a mess like this?*

From the muted TV came a reporter's singsong report on the weather: *"... sunlight pushing through by the weekend but today will be cold and overcast. Chance of drizzle this afternoon; north wind fifteen miles per hour..."*

She returned with a steaming cup as she sat. Curtis slid a drone surveillance video across the desk. We received this video footage this morning. Unknown sender. Look here. Two of the barn-angle cameras have blank footage, erased or never relayed. The next scene is from a different video. A camera inside a tack room. Everett opened a drawer. Then seemed to go crazy and tore apart the tack room. Fiona watched, shocked.

Most likely Mason or Luis. Curtis speculated. "Maybe wanting to show us his capability for violence. This is clearly police-style surveillance."

Fiona leaned in. "Maybe. Or someone else ghosted the signal to show us something."

"Have the cyber team check it out." Then she made a note in her planner: Follow up with Everett.

Server Room | O'Brien & Galloway HQ

In the dim glow of triple monitors, Sabrina Estabar sat cocooned by cables and racks of humming servers. Lines of code scrolled like digital hieroglyphs across her multiple screens. Headphones dangled around her neck; one leg bounced in sync with the rack fans.

Fiona had dropped a quiet directive to investigate Jonathan Cole, Delores's husband. Was he a staid financier or a puppet master of complex criminal assets on the dark web?

Allegis Financial Strategies, Cole's firm, touted itself as boutique, but its tentacles reached through shell companies in Texas, Zurich, and the Caymans. There, Sabrina uncovered Tovira Fund Group, with no public footprint beyond a five-year-old ledger entry labeled it Phase Two Asset Conversion.

She encrypted the chain labeled SILVER ECHO. LEVEL 1. She didn't alert Fiona. She wanted to keep following this, getting everything she could before bothering either Fiona or Curtis.

Café Pavement Talk

Later, in a brisk downtown wind, Fiona and Curtis emerged from Rich Aroma, each holding a paper cup. The street churned with morning commuters. Behind them, two office workers bantered:

"They say they have a witness in protective custody."

"Why have they not arrested this Taylor guy? Military guys know how to disappear. If they wait too long, he'll slip away, out of the country somewhere."

Curtis caught Fiona's eye; she didn't react. She sipped her coffee, the warmth a thin shield against the cold, before saying, "Let them talk."

When out of hearing range, Fiona pulled out her phone and dialed Everett's lawyer. "George, did you hear anything about a mystery witness?"

"Yeah, just heard it on the news five minutes earlier. I'm already heading out to a judge to get discovery about this witness. They can't keep that from the defense."

Back at the Dallas office

Fiona returned to her office, where the letter still lay on the glass-topped desk. Sabrina's soft alert pinged on her encrypted tablet: Ravenlock's not in any information we have uncovered so far. Fiona was relieved that at least one company they had interacted with or were part of their investigations recently had not become entangled in this mess.

Curtis stepped in. "Selena detected my tire was flat in the lot and left a note for me. I've heard this is happening frequently to other people working for us. Think we have a problem? Maybe we need to secure some cameras covering our parking areas."

"Already requested it through the building. Maintenance informed me they will get it done as soon as possible." Stefana said.

"Well, let's hope it's soon." Curtis replied.

CHAPTER 8

Echoes of Betrayal

Monday, December 5th, 2022

O'Brien & Galloway Investigations | Dallas Office

The cold had settled in with purpose overnight. A cloudless sky stretched over downtown Dallas, bright and brittle, the kind that sharpened every sound. From the 38th floor of the office tower, Fiona could see the tops of traffic signals blinking in cadence below. The weekend blurred into long hours of analysis and too little sleep. The image of Everett standing before that open drawer refused to leave Fiona's mind. She finally got Everett to tell her what it was.

"A drawer had a bracelet of Bridget's I gave her as a gift years ago. After her murder, I found it in the barn. Figured she'd put it there when she cleaned out the stalls and forgotten to put it back on."

"What happened? Why did you tear the tack room apart?"

"Someone came to the barn and stole the bracelet. That means they have eyes in the barn. Illegally. I informed George earlier. He's looking into it. I don't understand why; it only has sentimental value."

Fiona had no answer to that. The question haunted her all morning.

Inside the breakroom, she stood looking out her office window with her coffee, watching the sunlight slide slowly up the stone facade of the old cathedral downtown. Remembered how the bells rang out for Sunday morning mass yesterday, slow and resonant, the way the church back home had when she was a child. The Dallas church reminded her of the one in Denver. Tall and solemn, wrapped in history, with saints and gargoyles carved in stone above arched doorways. Josh had asked if they were "watchers." His grandfather Curtis just smiled and told him to be respectful, or they might hear him. Josh's eyes got big as he glanced back at them. She absently touched her cross, which she always wore. A gift from Matt when they married. Losing it would be devastating to her.

On Sunday after Mass, the three of them walked the long block back to the parking garage. Curtis bought donuts. Josh got sprinkles. Fiona stayed quiet, content just to walk with Josh between them and hear her son's laughter rise above the wind and listen to the chatter between her son and his grandfather. She smiled at the memory... until another memory pushed in... hard.

She and Matt used to walk out of Saint Mary's in Denver like that, laughing about homilies that went too long, shivering in their coats while snow salted their hair. They thought there would always be more time.

That last Sunday morning, the morning he died, everything felt off before it really began.

The kitchen light was slate gray. Fiona leaned against the counter, watching Matt pour coffee into his battered thermos. He had already dressed for the meeting in jeans, a hoodie, and his shoulder rig under a nondescript hoodie. Low profile. He told her his handler approved the meet.

"You triple-checked your wire?" she asked, voice low and steady.

Matt nodded. "Twice. Dad checked it last night. I'm good." He moved over to her and gave her a long, slow kiss, the kind with a promise behind it.

"Remind me again why this couldn't wait for backup." She said, placing her head on his shoulder, breathless.

He gently pulled her forward and met her eyes. "Because the guy's skittish. It's now or never."

"You sound like you're not too sure about this meeting."

Matt sighed. Hands on either side of her face, thumbs warm against her cheekbones. "It's nothing I haven't done before."

It wasn't the answer she had wanted to hear.

She wanted to say, don't go. Wanted to call Curtis, his father and her partner in homicide, to have him pull rank, force him to put off the meeting until there was backup. As a police officer, she struggled between adhering to protocol and apprehending wrongdoers. So she stayed silent.

Curtis called three hours later. His voice cracked over the line. "It was a... setup. He... never had... a chance."

She remembered the ER. Running through the doors, blood on the floor, the scent of antiseptic, a hallway too long. Matt lay beneath a sheet. A coroner who kept demanding her name and calling for security. She pulled back the sheet. Reached out, hand shaking; stroked his hair; tears poured as agony tore her apart. She could not stop stroking his hair as she talked to him about all they still needed to do. That his son needed him. Curtis arrived and wrapped his arms around her, and guided her away. Took her home.

Later, when the review collapsed under red tape and sealed records, she and Curtis sat across from each other with a bottle of whiskey and said what no one else would.
Someone betrayed him from within.

The report went missing from the internal records. Somewhere in the upper Brass, they redacted the CI's name. The case file flagged for "federal review." No arrests. No closure. Matt blamed for breaking procedural protocol. He never notified his handler of the meeting, they claimed. She knew Matt; knew he followed protocol. Religiously. She got into a public argument with his handler; her captain put her on suspension, with no pay.

Curtis got a buddy who owed him big to get the handler's notes. The only readable line buried in the handler's notes: *"Target may have ties to a Texas-based private research group, possibly a DARPA affiliate. Requesting hold."*

She and Curtis turned in their badges within the month.

She blinked, breaking the thought. The breakroom heater kicked on. Outside, the wind rattled traffic signs like distant warning bells. As city workers started hanging Christmas lights along the street.

On the muted TV in the hallway, a news report crawled across the screen:

"Clear and dry this morning and afternoon, but clouds are moving in from the west. Expect scattered rain by late evening. High today in the mid-50s. A chilly night ahead. In other news, federal officials continue to review recent developments in the Everett Taylor case. Investigators are re-examining early psychological reports from Everett Taylor's discharge papers from the military, while authorities have yet to file any charges."

Fiona muted it. She and Curtis had already read his discharge papers. Honorable discharge. No mental breaks, no blemishes. Yet, the tone and implications in the news made it seem as though there was something questionable about his military service.

Fiona blinked. The glass before her had fogged faintly from her breath. She couldn't shake the sense of eyes watching, from satellites, cameras, or ghosts of the past. Early afternoon the sun came out, the city thawed, but her unease didn't.

Who was behind this smear campaign? No matter what George said when overwhelmed by reporters, the reporters later spun it. They seemed to be experts at twisting his words to make it seem he did not trust his client. Now they can't have him answer a single question, and even that got twisted. It was a no-win situation.

Behind her, the coffee machine gurgled. A chair scraped across the tile in the bullpen. The day was getting busy.

Her phone buzzed in her pocket. A notification from Sabrina. The data pull from Dolores' husband's financials was complete.

Time to leave behind old ghosts.

O'Brien & Galloway Investigations | Conference/War Room

As the day wore on, rain clouds drifted in over the city, and the building's windows rattled under the weight of low thunderclouds and rising winds. Inside, the bullpen carried the scent of gun oil, whiteboard ink, and Cuban coffee roast.

Wall-mounted monitors glowed, live feeds from court filings, traffic cams, encrypted overlays from Bridget's digital trail, and the tangled shell company map they were still trying to decode. The temperature hovered just below comfort. The server bank hummed with static tension.

Fiona stood at the central table. Sabrina hunched near a terminal, square glasses reflecting lines of code.

"We cracked part of the flash drive," Sabrina said. "Not all text. Audio logs too. Some fragments. Wiped sloppily, but not completely."

She tapped a key.

A filtered voice broke through the static:
"...you have to understand, if this gets out, we're all dead."

Then a second voice, calm, male, composed. *"Charles doesn't accept failure. You don't want him to send the Ghost to clean this up. You'd better fix your mess. Fast. Find what you allowed that fucking journalist to steal from you."*

The recording cut.

Fiona's pulse shifted. "Charles? The Ghost?"

"No surnames," Sabrina said. "Second one's probably a code-name. We traced the recording to a journalist. Lucía Torres, who worked for *El Centinela Libre*."

Fiona froze. The name sounded familiar. Still, it bothered her she couldn't place it. Fiona gazed at the paused frame a few seconds longer, shrugged, and figured it would come to her later.

Curtis entered, still in field clothes, coffee in hand. He caught the name and paused. "Lucía Torres? Heard something a while back about a murdered editor and one of his journalists in South America somewhere." Curtis set the coffee down. Fiona could tell he was tense from his shoulders. Most likely, this relates to Buck's cases. I felt there was a lot of information crossing our computers at the Sentinel servers about Columbia. Military intelligence stuff, I am sure.

"Charles Stuart. Of the wealthy Stuarts of New Orleans? Bridget's ex. Delores's ex. You think that could have been this, Charles?"

"It fits," Fiona said.

"And the Ghost?"

"Possible cartel enforcer," Curtis muttered. "Or worse. A fixer with no leash."

They let that sit.

Her phone buzzed. Caller ID: Lisa Neylan.

She answered. "Lisa?"

The voice on the other end trembled. "Can you come over?

Now. Delores just left and... something's not right."

Lisa's Condo

The high-rise condo looked sterile and expensive. South of Oak Lawn. Security-coded elevators, private balconies, imported tiles.

Fiona stepped off the elevator into a fancy foyer area: a small couch with a stand next to it, on it a vase with live flowers and an imitation Van Gogh painting on the wall behind it, pale tan walls and terrazzo floors with hallways exiting to the left and right. She turned left until she found Lisa's condo number on the door, knocked, and identified herself.

Lisa called, "Come in." Lisa Neylan stood by the window, arms folded, wearing jeans and a faded cardigan. Her eyes flicked toward the glass every few seconds.

"Thanks for coming," she murmured.

Fiona eased into a sleek white chair.

Lisa paced once, then sat. She clutched a folded envelope.

"Delores came by earlier."

Fiona didn't move.

"Brought wine, a fake smile, and questions that weren't really questions, more like a demand. She asked what Bridget had told me about her before she died. Whether she left anything behind. Something she might've written. Or maybe even recorded. Said Bridget stole something off her husband's computer."

Lisa went on as if looking into the past, her head cocked sideways. "I remembered a weird moment at a charity auction last year. Delores laughed, not at a joke, but at the reaction to it. Like she was watching everyone's reactions before she reacted.

And then I remembered something Bridget told me about the last fundraiser she attended before..." she sucked in a long breath before going on. "Bridget observed Delores clink glasses and laugh too loud, smiling like someone who didn't know half the jokes. According to Bridget, she's not dangerous. She's just expensive wallpaper." She stopped for a moment.

"I don't believe that. I think Delores is far more dangerous than appearances suggest."

"And you told Delores what?"

"That Bridget only talked about the ranch. About Everett and Lila. She never mentioned the firm. Or Delores."

A pause. "That was a lie."

Lisa placed the envelope on the table. "Bridget gave me this. Said to trust someone else with it. If something ever happened."

Fiona unfolded the note. Bridget's handwriting. Rushed.

If anything happens to me, don't trust Delores. She's not who you think or who I thought she was.

"Empty the envelope," Lisa said. "There's more."

Fiona did. A Microdrive fell into her palm.

Lisa's voice cracked. "Bridget saw something. On Delores's husband's files. Connections between the Porter & Ashburn law firm, offshore accounts, and cartel money, which appeared to be laundered. That Microdrive contains the information she got from his computer. She believed that some judges and prosecutors appeared on the list. Maybe even someone high up in the Bureau. She downloaded what she could before Delores came back into the room."

"Did you believe her?" Fiona asked.

"She reached out to someone. Bureau ties. Deep cover. She never gave me a name, just a codename. Sliverbranch. She said he worked for Joint Ops, DEA and the FBI deep undercover. Still active under protective cover. She met him at various times in a church basement somewhere. She claimed she was helping him expose something big."

"Bigger than this?" Fiona asked softly.

Lisa looked out the window. "She said it was the most corrupt enterprise in the country. Maybe the world."

Fiona thought about it and then said. "And now she's dead."

Lisa's voice dropped. "I think someone found out. I think they made it look as if Everett did it. And now they're moving to clean house and anyone connected to this case."

Fiona looked up. "Is it safe for you here?"

Lisa hesitated. "Probably not. But it's too late to run." Lisa gave a thin smile and caught Fiona off guard with her next question. "You still trust people, Fiona?"

Fiona didn't answer. She walked to the window and stood next to Lisa and looked outside.

Below, the sun glanced off windshields. American flags moved gently in the breeze. It all looked... ordinary.

But inside, something had shifted.

Bridget had been running from powerful people. From evil.

Intercept Room | Unknown Location

Across town, a man in a muted blue suit sat in a secure Federal Bureau satellite office, watching live transcript feeds scrolled, across a bank of monitors.

Lisa Neylan's voice. Bridget's name. Porter & Ashburn. Trafficking. Sliverbranch.

He drew a line.

"Subject Lisa Neylan. Confirmed knowledge of high-level collusion. Potential risk to trafficking assets. Escalate."

Then he typed a single message into an encrypted channel:

"Lisa Neylan and PI firm O'Brien and Galloway - exposure risk. Priority level elevated."

CHAPTER 9

Stoke the Flame

Tuesday, December 13th, 2022

O'Brien & Galloway Headquarters | Downtown Dallas

The week since Fiona's visit with Lisa had blurred into back-to-back briefings, subpoenas on several cases they were working on, and one unanswered question. How deep the rot ran inside Porter & Ashburn and John Cole's management company. The flash drive Lisa handed over on the fifth was still being decrypted, its fragments naming people Fiona once thought untouchable. The first thing Fiona and Curtis did was to loop in Major Buck about the drive. Buck allowed them to copy it, but he kept the original.

Every new file seemed to tighten the noose around Porter & Ashburn, along with John and Delores Cole's circle. The hurricane of power players they'd uncovered had spilled over into military intelligence and Major Buck's preview. He'd been in and out all week. Classified by those who were now demanding they turn over the thumb drive. Senator Rourke and Senator Halvorsen in the background were fighting to help Major Buck hold on to the information before it disappeared into the bureaucratic void.

Outside, Dallas brooded under a slate-gray sky, wind knifing down the canyons created by the skyscrapers. It was the cold that clung to bones, mid-forties and falling, an uncommon chill that made the city feel brittle, ready to break. Inside the thirty-eighth floor conference/war room, the HVACs ran continuously, pumping out dry, sterile heat.

Sabrina and Bianca were already at their terminals. Charles Chambers sat with paper files open, his face tired but focused.

George arrived, wanting any pertinent information and updates they had that might help Everett's case. For now, though it related to military intelligence and political fallout, then a single murder. Other than the possibility of others being motivated to murder Bridget to silence her.

Curtis stepped in and placed smoky-smelling files, with water stains down on the war-room table. "Found this at Unit 147. Fire missed it, barely."

Fiona opened it. A warped photograph sat on top. Bridget rode beside Everett on horseback, both smiling under a big Texas sky. Nestled in front of Everett in the saddle, toddler Lila clutched the horn, cradled by her father's arms. Now, soot and water damage mottled the image. Their faces were ghosts in melted gloss.

Beneath the photo: a half-scorched Porter & Ashburn legal folder. Still legible. And a heavily damaged flash drive.

Fiona's jaw tightened. "I was supposed to go to the unit. I lost track. Too many irons in the fire."

"You were busy, so I figured I could pick up the slack."

Bianca tapped away at her keyboard, working on something sent to them anonymously. A drone video populated the monitor wall, grainy footage of what looked like Everett's truck rolling down a gravel road. The timestamp placed it within forty to forty-five minutes of Bridget's estimated time of death.

Curtis leaned in. "Zoom the passenger mirror."

She did. Warped reflection, but a motorcycle clearly seen.

George adjusted his glasses. "No one mentioned that in any

report."

Charles nodded grimly. "Because this version didn't come from the police. Someone leaked it early this morning. It's already gone viral. Social media, not MSM news, yet."

"No metadata?" Fiona asked.

"None. No public chain of custody. And the 'citizen drone owner' who allegedly filmed it? Shell identity."

George slid a file across the table. The drone registration belonged to Silverpine Remote Access LLC. Traced back through five entities to a defunct media firm absorbed by John Cole's Cayman hedge fund in 2017.

Curtis spun in his chair. "The Coles owned the drone?"

"Or someone in his network," George said. "They're passing it off as a local concern about the area. A Lakeside resident just 'happened' to catch the perfect shot that day."

Curtis shook his head. "If... Bridget was trying to protect Everett and Lila, and if Everett is innocent, they're using her murder to frame him. No one knows anything about Everett's daughter Lila's whereabouts. The police are assuming she is dead."

Fiona turned to Bianca. "The voice clip?"

"Running it now." Bianca's fingers moved fast. "Supposedly Everett argued with Bridget off-screen. However, voice-match achieved a mere two percent success rate. There are too many digital artifacts. And returns with a ninety percent deep-fake voiceover."

"Anyone else match?" George asked.

Bianca came back with. "No one in our system."

Curtis swore under his breath.

Charles cleared his throat. "We've also got a new witness. Utility contractor working on a job across from Taylor's place.

Claims he saw a truck leave around three in the afternoon, followed by a motorcycle. Name is Evan Ruke. Still working contracts in the area."

Curtis looked up. "That's an hour and a half earlier than the time of death Detective Wren is telling the press. He's putting her death at around four-thirty in the afternoon. George, have you gotten the coroner's report yet? If not, how soon do you believe you can get a hold of it? We need that report."

"Got it earlier this morning." He pulled a file out of his briefcase and placed it on the table.

Curtis swore under his breath before saying anything. "Wren's updated estimate of the time of death shifted three times this week, each revision conveniently tightening the noose around Everett's neck. However, at least the coroner's report gives you breathing room to challenge. According to the coroner, determining the time of death was highly challenging. The estimate would have a very wide margin of error. The cold temperature and moving water significantly altered the normal postmortem, making traditional methods less reliable. Thus, whoever murdered her could have done so anytime between when she was last seen and when the person called 911."

"If Wren's pushing a four thirty pm as TOD, then this footage does not fit his latest narrative. Wren's timeline collapses. If we can prove Everett did not get to the cabin early enough to have murdered her and disposed of both her and her daughter and used the bleach to clean up, we clear Everett of the murder and the disappearance of his daughter. And remember, his clothes were clean and pressed, as noted by the deputies when they arrived, from what Mason told Curtis." Fiona moved to the whiteboard and scrawled out:

WITNESS: Evan Ruke. Three o'clock. Truck + Motorcycle. DRONE ORIGIN: Silverpine LLC, Cole Shell. AUDIO: Two percent Everett voice match.

Curtis stood back. "They doctored both the footage and the

audio. Built a timeline to bury him."

George nodded. "Public doesn't need evidence. Just a headline. The drone footage came after the coverage of the Minneapolis church shooting. People are already living in fear. The horrific church shooting coming first set the tone."

A muted TV screen in the corner flickered through the day's horrors. Images of a mass shooting, a scrolling headline about the border wall's expansion through protected land. Moments later: a photo of Everett's face beside the words, "Loving husband and father or murderer?"

Curtis turned it off. "They've written the ending. Now they're priming the story to sell to the public."

O'Brien & Galloway Server Vault

He moved quietly inside the glass-walled vault, chilled air humming around him. Server fans whirred in a mechanical rhythm. The temperature was deliberate, kept low to preserve hardware, but it added to the tension in his spine.

He plugged a flash drive into an isolated terminal. Scrolled, looking for the file he wanted. When he found it, he opened it using a stolen password and downloaded it.

The system had flagged some emails in red; the two below were the ones he was looking for.

"Tovira / P&A Internal Comms: RESTRICTED."

Another one also, unread.

From: Delores Cole
To: C.Stuart@pacific-kite.com
Subject: *Taylor Problem: Contingency Plan C*

"Detectives McCarthy and Alvarez believe they're helping Everett. Let them. The team has already launched the media campaign. All Everett has to do is twitch, and we light the match. We'll take them all down with Everett and get rid of a big thorn in our side. Also, you need to control your loose dog. He is causing problems. Doing things his way."

Then he put in the email address to where he was sending the files, and after the downloads finished, and the email

sent he deleted both files.

◆◆◆

Everett Taylor Ranch

The ringtone split the silence like a blade.

Everett woke before the third ring. Blocked number. He answered anyway.

"Taylor," he said, voice graveled from sleep and whiskey. Whiskey Everett's common means now of getting to sleep.

A pause. Then a man's voice, calm, deliberate.
"If you want the truth about Bridget… and where your daughter went… be at the cabin. Four A.M. Come alone."

The line went dead.

For a long moment, he sat at the side of the bed, staring into the dark. The old wall clock over the dresser ticked away, a sound that cut through his nerves when the house was too quiet now. He rubbed a hand over his face. His gut twisted with something he hadn't felt in years. Unease.

He sat, jaw tight, taking deep breaths, heart kicking hard in his chest. He didn't bother turning on the light. Pulled on jeans, boots, and a checkered shirt, then grabbed his old field jacket. Downstairs he opened his safe and checked the Sig 229 Legion, racked it once, and pocketed several extra magazines. The night outside was cold enough to bite, a cold that made old scars ache. Wind outside had the trees whispering to the sky.

Taylor Cabin

The truck's tires chewed gravel. Pines leaned in heavy black silhouettes, dripping mist. The closer he got, the more the night felt wrong. The moon hid behind smoke-gray clouds.

He cut the engine and coasted into an emergency pull-off a mile away. The air smelled of damp moss and sharp pine. His boots hit the dirt, a soft thud. He followed the trail in the trees to his cabin.

The cabin sat in shadow. Windows dark, the lake shadowed through trees, a mirror of black ink. He pushed the door open. Hinges groaned. The inside smelled of dust and mildew. Except for something else.

Faint scent of diesel from the generator outside.

He took one more step and froze. Strange, the scent became stronger the further in he stepped. He ignored it, figuring the police overfilled the generator or spilled the fuel filling it when they were in the house getting evidence.

The need to discover what happened to his wife and daughter drove him forward. He moved upstairs, looking for anyone.

The first shot tore the stillness of the night apart. High-velocity, close. Glass exploded beside him. Shards sprayed across him. A large piece sliced across his bicep and bled profusely.

He dropped to a knee, instincts screaming, weapon drawn, eyes searching the dark.

Another shot. Closer. This one shattered several stones in the fireplace across from him, becoming shrapnel. Rising, he raced for the stairs. He headed for the front door, then heard it.
Metal on metal. The scrape of a bar sliding into place from the outside.

He yanked the handle. Barred from the outside.

"*Fuck.*" He fell right into the trap set for him.

That's when the fire detonated around him.

A concussive *whump* blasted through the cabin as the accelerant caught. A delayed trigger, or remote ignition, maybe even a small thermal charge. The room went from dark shadow to hellfire in seconds. Curtains vaporized. The ceiling flamed out in orange ribbons.

Everett rose from the floor where the concussive blew him. He rolled to his side and rose to duck behind a support beam as the walls turned into a living furnace. Heat slammed into him, blistering, oxygen vanishing fast. Smoke clawed at his lungs. He needed to get above the worst of it and find a way out.

He bolted back up the stairs two at a time. The banister wood was already spitting and hissing from the heat. Upstairs hallway, floorboards already smoking and hot. He kept left, toward the master bedroom. Flames licked through the doorway behind him like chasing hounds.

He found the window. Jammed. He grabbed a blanket off the bed and smashed it open. The rush of air fed the fire, and it burst into the room and along the ceiling.

Below, the yard was an inferno of sparks. He could see muzzle flashes beyond the treeline and the thunder of the shots. The window next to him shattered. Whoever set this up was still watching, waiting for him to burn or bolt. Bolt was his only option.

Wrapping his head in his jacket, he dove through the opening just as the floor collapsed.

He hit the porch roof hard, rolled, pain flaring down his shoulder, and rolled off to the ground. The shock brought clarity. He jumped up, staying low, and raced toward the treeline in a zigzag pattern. Every breath felt like smoke and blood.

A round ripped through the dirt inches from his foot. Another slammed into a fence post as he passed it. Buying time, he fired without aiming in the direction the shots originated.

He didn't look back. He sprinted toward the slope that dropped to the lake, boots hammering the dirt. Shots now coming from two different directions. The world behind him roared, a firestorm bright enough to paint the woods in hellish light.

He reached the bluff, shoved the Sig into its holster, and dove.

The lake swallowed him whole.
Cold. Black. Final.

Bullets tore the surface above, muted echoes in the water. He stayed down until his lungs screamed, then came up fifty feet away, barely breaking the surface.

The cabin behind him was gone, flames clawing up into the dawn. Whoever orchestrated this wanted Everett Taylor to die twice: once in the fire, and again in the story that would follow.

Twenty minutes later he came out of the lake along a bank with no yards or houses and worked his way through the trees out to a dirt road far from the flashing lights of fire engines and police cruisers. And walked back to his truck. It had not caught the attention of the police. Or apparently, his assailants. Yet. He needed to get out of there and home before they came knocking at his door.

Less than two hours later, two deputies, Lane and Jordan, were knocking at his door. They said they came to notify him that the cabin on Taylor Road had caught fire and burned down. They stated they had a few questions for him. He invited them in for coffee. They left an hour and a half later. Afterwards, they called in to the on duty commander, Lt. Sam Monroe. Their observations and his answers to their questions satisfied them that Everett did not burn down the cabin. They detected no smoke scent on him, and his awakening upon their arrival seemed genuine.

CHAPTER 10

The Matchbook
Monday, December 19th, 2022
Dallas Headquarters | Milo's Shanghai Club & Streets Outside

A sudden hard freeze strangled Dallas. By early evening, the wind knifed through the streets, temps falling through the 30s toward a brutal overnight low. Early winter had delivered a savage introduction. The city braced against it.

Curtis had left hours earlier. Fiona stayed behind, wrapping up client reports. The Everett case was still at a dead end. Cyber hadn't cracked the full encryption on the original drive Everett gave them. Holiday events were in full swing across the country.

She leaned against the narrow office balcony; the building lights soft behind her. Outside, the wind stole breath and made her shoulder throb under her coat. They had proof that someone flew to Tyler Airport from the Texarkana Airport at the time Everett claimed. But nobody paid attention to who got on or off. In fact, the Charter company said Mr. Colten Harlan called it in, gave no name, just said to expect someone. Not unusual for him. Domestic in-state flight check-ins were not as strict, especially for privately known charter customers. Informed them it was for a friend of his flying home, which was not unusual for Mr. Harlan. That helped with Everett's claims, but with no one saying yes, that's the guy who took the flight, it was circumstantial at best. Prosecution could claim Everett talked with his friend that day and knew Colten Harlan was flying a friend to Tyler Airport that day. In fact, it may have been why he murdered his wife that day. He had a fabricated alibi. His friend might even verify it later, maybe.

Her phone buzzed. Text. Unknown Number.

I want a meet. Come alone. Milo's Shanghai Club. Alley. No later than 12. Consider this a Christmas present.
Nightjar.

Obvious code name. She checked the time. Ten fifty-nine at night.

She left a quick text for Curtis and took the Caddy. Another buzz, this one a news alert:

"Cabin Creek blaze under federal review. Investigators link the site to the Bridget Taylor murder, citing possible arson and a man fitting Everett Taylor who fled the scene."

She turned it off. Everett told her, Curtis and George Shaw, he did not burn the cabin down. This was just another lie dressed as news. Fiona believed Everett was being framed. Whoever killed Bridget likely went back to erase evidence. Fire was the fastest and most efficient means.

South Dallas's industrial zone was dead after midnight. Warehouses, broken rail lines, boarded windows, and barrel fires where homeless veterans huddled for warmth.

She parked four blocks from Milo's and circled on foot, checking her sidearm twice.

Milo's Shanghai Club sat like a scar beneath the neon bones of downtown. In the alley out back, beneath a flickering floodlight, a voice behind a dumpster said. "You O'Brien?"

She spun, hand on her weapon. The man lifted both hands as he stepped into the light. Mid-thirties, lean build, coat collar up, fedora low over his brow.

"I'm Nightjar. I've been trying to reach you."

Deliberate, slow. He stepped forward but kept his distance.

"I came to offer a partnership," he said. "Long-term. You're not just dealing with murder. This is systemic. Deep, with heavy hitters."

He led her up the chipped concrete stairs. One neon tube blinked red over the door like a dying eye. Fire damage scarred the brick above. On the side, she noticed a basement exit door.

Inside, smoke, scorched walls, dissonant jazz. Red velvet booths pocked with cigarette burns. The saxophone player blew as if it remembered the blues, yet lost the ability to get it right. Nobody looked up.

Inside, smoke slithered along the ceiling as if it were trying to escape. A no-smoking sign, dim with defeat, above the bar.

Booths sagged under the weight of memory and debt.

The air stank of liquor, ash, and last chances. Grime blurred what little light made it through the cracked windows.

The jazzman in the corner wore a suit two sizes too big and looked more ghost than player.

They ordered drinks at the bar, then found a booth in the back and slid in across from each other. Fiona, sharp-eyed, drink untouched.

Three tables down, a woman stirred her cocktail with nervous precision. Fiona blinked. *Erin Hargraves*. Once a respected investigative journalist. Now, disgraced. "What is she doing here?"

Nightjar leaned in. His voice low, ignoring her question.

"You're dealing with a network. Name's SILO. Adoption laundering. Trafficking in humans, weapons, and drugs. All buried under various shell corporations. All under Reid Cavanaugh.

For now. But he's not the big dog; he's a dog on a leash."

Her pulse jumped. *That was a name she'd heard Matt say one time in relation to his undercover job. How the hell does he know all that?*

"You need to stop playing whack-a-mole. Week to week won't cut it. But your digging's getting attention, and not the good kind. You won't stop these people unless you think long term." A ceiling bulb buzzed, then dimmed above them as if it were tired of the scene.

Fiona studied him.

"You said you had something about Everett and his wife's murder. Why me? Why not take it to the police?"

"Because you won't stop. You've got reach. Money. Access. And something others don't have. Major Buck and his agency."

He tossed back his shot of Jack, then set it down.

"The people in power are sitting up and paying attention. They're nervous. And you're stirring the pot."

Fiona didn't flinch, but she filed away the mention of Major Buck.

"Is Lila alive?"

He shrugged. "I don't know who Lila is or where she is. But if she's missing, and a child, she's dead or in the SILO algorithm. If in SILO, the program knows the location, as it tracks what is the cartel's property. You want in?"

"I'm already in. You knew that before this meeting. So, what is the purpose of all this spy melodrama? You could have come to the office and told us this information?"

Ignoring her remarks, he pulled a matchbook from his coat. *Milo's Shanghai Club* logo on it. Inside, a URL number.

"Use this once. Then burn it. Gives you digital Dropbox access. I send intel; you verify it. Then you use it."

Erin's stir stick clinked against her glass again. Fiona glanced in her direction. She was still watching, but at her table, she cannot hear much from where she sat. *Maybe.*

Nightjar murmured, "She's confused. Rattled. She was onto this, but someone stepped in and dirtied her up. She wants to prove she's not."

The jazz cut off.
Pop.
Plaster sprayed from the wall inches from Nightjar's head.

"Out the back," he barked. He jumped up and grabbed her arm. "*They followed you.*"

Bullets thudded into booths and bottles. Patrons screamed and scattered. Fiona knocked over a table, drew her weapon, and fired as bullets thudded into wood and tile around her. One round shattered a bottle behind the bar; they found themselves in a crossfire.

Fiona turned to the new threat and fired. Shards exploded outward like glass rain. Panicked patrons dove for cover under tables and booths. Others ran for the doors. Chaos erupted across the club. She hit one shooter center mass twice; the assailant dropped.

Nightjar vaulted a table shouting, we must get out of here; we're trapped. "Basement access!" he shouted. "Alley exit!"

Their pursuers moved with discipline. Tactically coordinated.

Fiona fired twice toward center mass, controlled pulls. An assailant stumbled, but stayed on his feet.

They sprinted. Behind them, more rounds popped off hot on their heels as they raced for the hallway exit. Fiona fired blindly behind her as she ran, giving them cover.

Through a smoke-thick corridor, down cracked tile stairs, out into the alley, they fled. Freezing air slapped her face. A nearby vent pumped out warm haze. Oil fumes, urine, rot. She exhaled once, slowly. Fog clung to the pavement like a second skin. The streetlight buzzed overhead.

The shooters' discipline, tight formation, and body armor along with a planned trap meant they weren't freelance street muscle.

Headlights flared at the back of the alley. A van.

"Run," Nightjar said flatly. "Now."

A shot rang out. Suppressed. Hissed through the dark like giant, angry wasps.

Fiona fired several shots to cover Nightjar as he bolted down to the opposite end. A second gunman flanked from the side.

Fiona dropped low. Adrenaline spiked. She fired twice. One shot put a bullet hole in the windshield. The other shattered a side mirror. Enough to force them to cover.

She covered Nightjar while he climbed a rusty dumpster and hoisted himself to the top of the chain-link fence.

More gunmen emerged at the alley mouth, wearing tactical vests over shirts, pistols pointed in their direction, firing.

Fiona snapped off three rounds in their direction. Her Sig slide locked open. She hit the mag release, grabbed another from her shoulder holster, and slapped it in and slingshot the slide. Sighted, fired off three shots. Heard a yell and someone hitting the ground. Shrapnel from the brick beside her blew outward, forcing her back as the other assailant fired in her direction. One assailant retreated around the corner, dragging his downed partner with him. She shot three more rounds at the others, who were firing. She heard a thud and curses.

Nightjar turned towards her as he straddled the top of the fence. Then he nodded at the shape behind her. A figure standing half-shadowed near another's business dumpster. Erin Hargraves had followed them out.

"Watch out for her; she's not armed and can't fight worth a

damn." And then he slid over to the other side of the fence and was gone.

Fiona moved towards Erin, firing six more shots to give her cover, breathing hard, and grabbed Erin's arm, fired once more, yanking her back towards where Nightjar disappeared over the fence. Forcing Erin down behind a large dumpster and taking cover herself there. Checked her mag; it held four, and there was one in the chamber. *Fuck*. More shadows now moved towards the mouth of the alley. She fired her last five shots, then holstered her gun. Her mind spinning. She needed to find a way out of this alley for both herself and Erin before they came at them from both sides. Going over the fence would expose them. She looked around.

Movement.

Two figures peeled from the shadows ahead. Another behind her.

She didn't wait. Her training kicked in. A heel stomp here, a kick to an attacker's knee, and the sound of a howl, and he went down, and an elbow to a different one's face, a knee strike to another's groin that doubled him over.

A fourth assailant grabbed her from behind, rear choke. She planted her feet, drove her hips back, stomped his foot, then twisted and slammed her elbow down hard on his arm. He let go. To another, she delivered a palm heel to his nose; blood sprayed out.

Erin screamed.

A fifth man was dragging her away. Fiona lunged, tackling them both into a pile of trash bags. Glass shattered. Metal clattered as it skidded across the pavement.

Someone's boot clipped her forehead. She rolled, dazed, and came up bleeding, but low in a ready stance. Heart hammering.

Surrounded, she reset her feet. Her breathing controlled. Controlled chaos. That's how she'd trained. That's how she survived.

The first moved in, blade in hand. She sidestepped, redirected the blade with a forearm deflection and drove a cross-elbow into his temple. He dropped.

A high whine! A bullet zinged past her shoulder.

Then headlights cut the dark like floodlights from the opposite end of the alley. A black SUV skidded in. A door flew open.

"MOVE!" Kenneth Steele's voice thundered. Rifle braced.

Fiona grabbed Erin. Another man lunged. She parried his arm and delivered a brutal sidekick to his knee, and shoved Erin into the SUV. Then she dived into the back.

A shadow dropped from above. Phùng, like a blade from the night, landed feet-first on an attacker, the sound of ribs cracking under him, a blade skittering across the pavement.

Kenneth unleashed a shot toward the assailants still standing. "NOW!" Phùng dove into the SUV. Tires screamed. Bullets pinged off the metal. Six blocks later, Kenneth drifted into an abandoned loading bay. The engine idled like a growling beast.

Fiona pressed her hand to her forehead. Warm blood seeped between her fingers. Erin pressed an ice pack to her jaw, given to her by Phùng, pale as a ghost.

"Jesus," Kenneth muttered. "What did you get yourself into?"

Fiona glared. "Thanks for the rescue. How'd you know?"

"Buck called." Silence for several seconds as Fiona stared at him. "We tracked your caddy through its GPS. Heard gunshots. Knew where to find you." He shook his head. "Kill that tracker next time or spoof it. Whoever came for you probably tracked you the same way as us. And for God's sake, next time take one or two of us with you so you can skip the back alley gunfight by yourself."

Phùng knelt beside Fiona and opened a med kit. His calm eyes met hers. "You're bleeding. Stay still."

She bit back a hiss as he applied antiseptic. “It's just a surface cut.” Phùng told her.

Erin spoke, voice hollow. “I didn't plan to be here. Someone said they could fix my career. Just be here tonight.”

Fiona turned, blood crusting her brow as Phùng dabbed at it. “Nightjar said you knew something about Bridget's murder.”

Erin's eyes flicked away. “Leads that were setups. Then, my name got trashed. Doors slammed shut. Who is Nightjar?”

“I hate to tell you this, but someone set us both up,” Fiona said.

“Or they wanted to disgrace me even more,” Erin whispered. Fiona looked at her for a moment in disgust before saying, “yeah I don't remember seeing them shooting your direction.”

Sirens rose in the distance, a rising dirge, a long, rising moan that echoed down the concrete guts of the city like a funeral dirge for the night.

Kenneth placed his rifle in its case in the back cargo area, saying. “That bastard with you? Left you behind. Climbed the fence and bolted while you fought to keep her and yourself alive.” He nodded in Erin's direction.

“Yeah,” Fiona said slowly. “He did.” And left it at that.

Kenneth's expression hardened. “And in the meantime, what?”

“First, I want to know how the hell Buck even knew I was in danger.” She stared hard at Kenneth, but when he refused to bite or answer, she said.

“We are going to take what this Nightjar sends and verify everything. Quietly. Carefully. We run the data and see if it leads somewhere. If he gives us good data. We use it.”

She looked over at Erin again. Erin didn't meet her eyes.

Fiona's gaze hardened. Erin stared into the darkness beyond the shattered glass. Fiona exhaled hard. Night's chill pressed through broken windows. The city throbbed with secrets. Dangerous secrets for those who wanted to expose them.

Nightjar

The fence rattled as he jumped to the ground. Another wall. Another layer between who he was and who he'd become.

He stepped into the darkness, boots crunching over wet gravel. Gunpowder clung to his coat. Behind him, sirens arrived like thunderheads. Distant, inevitable. He didn't look back.

It was his tip that sent the mercenaries. He told them Fiona would meet a contact for a drive they desperately were searching for. They never could resist bait, especially a woman. Cowards.

Soon he'd know if Fiona was worthy of getting the information he had. If not? He gave a mental shrug. The world keeps turning.

From his coat, he pulled out a small black book and found the note. Her note. Faded ink.

He let his thumb trace the words she'd written. Deep in his soul, she mattered to him. His son mattered. To them, she and his son were disposable. Following their deaths, he made a vow that he would do whatever it took to destroy those who had ordered them murdered. They did it to send a message to him to back off in his investigation because he got too close. An honest FBI agent, who believed in the system, believed that good won in the end.

Now he had someone new in his life, helping to heal the wound.

In the past, he played by all the proper rules. He frowned as he thought about the man he once was and shrugged off the thought.

Despite sensing Fiona's dislike of Erin at the club, Fiona turned back to rescue Erin. One test passed. Now she needed to survive the night.

And what had happened since then? He stared at the flickering orange glow from a nearby barrel fire.

“I warned them,” he muttered. “But they don’t listen. I’m going to burn it down around all of them.”

The wind shifted. Cold. Empty.

He walked away, with gunfire and chaos at his back.

CHAPTER 11

The Information flows

Tuesday, December 20th, 2022
O'Brien & Galloway Dallas HQ

The skyline burned gold against steel and glass. Holiday lights blinked across high-rises and the trees below, festive and oblivious. Fiona had been at her desk before dawn. Now, only her laptop and the thin gray light bleeding through the floor-to-ceiling windows lit the office. A freezing wind crept across Dallas, frosting the glass edges.
The room smelled of apple cinnamon air freshener and Sabrina's terrible drip coffee, an affront to the untouched espresso machine, and stale ginger cookies left in the breakroom, forgotten as last week's cheer.

A cloned thumb drive of Bridget's, which Everett gave them, plugged in, a tripwire waiting to blow. Sabrina had set a trap. If anyone snooped, they'd regret it. Fiona grinned at how proud her Cyber team had been about that.

A lengthy conversation between her and Buck this morning only brought about the information that Buck got a call from an undercover agent he trusted, at his home number, telling him Fiona was walking into a trap. Buck told her. "I don't know who this person calling himself Nightjar is. I will have my team investigate him; he's most likely a spook working for some three-letter agency. And Fiona, you've got to stop running off without telling anyone where and what you're doing. It's reckless and endangers everything we're trying to accomplish."

Fiona said nothing. Figured she deserved a chewing-out this time. But as a cop, she ran towards things others ran from. That's her nature. She did what she knew needed done.

Buck stopped for a long pause. When she said nothing, he changed the subject. "About Nightjar. I'll have my guys set up electronic surveillance on the computer on the line you will use to receive the drops."

Hours later, as the morning news droned in the background:
"Arctic blast incoming before Christmas Eve, around the twenty-second. Dallas PD launched Operation Holiday Shield, which prompted extra patrols in retail zones to target organized theft rings in response to a spike in seasonal crime. Be vigilant at ATMs and shopping centers. Downtown Dallas Rings in the Holidays with Lights and Choirs. Crowds gathered at Klyde Warren Park and the Arts District for a live choir and tree-lighting ceremony the previous evening."

Sabrina, in her socks, paced behind her in the cyber station. "Just got this. Every folder's laced with logic bombs. Open the wrong one, and we lose everything. This payload is from the digital Dropbox the person calling himself Nightjar gave you. Could be gold. Could be a virus. But why play games if he wants to help? Of course, for us, it was not too hard to bypass the traps. Besides, we had it going into a sandbox to keep it from the rest of the servers."

"I believe he was counting on that fact. He seemed to know an awful lot about our agency."

Two folders blinked open:
Offshore financial flows through PACs, shell corporations, and real estate fronts tied to Porter & Ashburn's California branch by companies they legally represented.
Authorization logs, signatory records.

Top name: Reid Cavanaugh.

Fiona froze. Nightjar had mentioned him. Matt mentioned a similar name weeks before his murder while undercover.

Curtis slammed through the door and slapped a newspaper onto the desk. Outside, carolers' voices floated faintly up from a street corner.

HEADLINE: *PRIVATE INVESTIGATOR LINKED TO SHOOTOUT*
Photo: Grainy, off-angle. Fiona with the person calling himself Nightjar at the bar. Cropped to look like a handoff.

"No mention you were the one who got ambushed," he growled.

Fiona's jaw clenched.

Sabrina typed rapidly. "Routed through VPNs. Dropped to three local newsrooms."

"Hargraves," Curtis muttered. "Her career's dead. This smells like a ploy to crawl back up. Could be her leak."

"Call Buck Curtis," Fiona said.

"Already did."

O'Brien & Galloway Ranch | Hangar Bay

A freezing wind swept across the fields. Ornaments swung on the porch rails. Inside the hangar, the Sentinel's monitors flickered like a heartbeat. Diesel fumes and dry hay odors mingled in the cold.

Phùng approached, wiping gun grease from his hands.

"That meet almost worth dying for?" he asked. "Letting them paint you as corrupt?"

Fiona exhaled. "It proved that what Bridget stumbled upon is the tip of an iceberg."

Phùng nodded grimly. "This has rogue spook fingerprints all over it. Saw this sort of setup in Afghanistan."

Raymond jogged from the house with the secure phone. "It's Buck," he said. "Maggie said you'd want the call now."

Fiona stepped outside, the wind biting as she took the line.

"Hello, Buck."

"Audio on that video? Synthetic. Your guy's a ghost. No ID, no hits. Either military or possibly trained by them. I'll keep digging. Everyone, no matter how good, leaves a fingerprint if you know where to look." There was something in his voice that caught her attention. But then the thought of Erin came to mind.

"You missed one probability. Erin Hargraves. I saved her life, and I believe she dropped this."

"I'll check her out as well. Glad to know. What you're in now is deeper than politics," Buck said. "You're poking into DOJ and DOD subcontractors. Institutional rot. Political corruption."

Fiona stiffened. "How much help can I expect from you?"

"I'm threading a needle. Sending coordinates for a dead drop. West yard. Old rail depot. One agent by the week's end. If it works, I'll help when I can. If they're spotted, three federal systems light up. Send one of the special ops guys I got for you."

"Understood."

"Also," Buck added, "I'm working on cleaning up last night's mess. Don't make it worse."

Click.

Fiona stood for a moment in the wind, then walked back inside.

She made two quick calls.

"Sabrina, move everything on Everett Taylor's case that does not directly deal with Bridget's murder, along with any information related to Buck's material, and pull the physical drives. Hard wipe internal systems afterward. Send the physical drives to the ranch. The Sentinel is air-gapped and classified. Let them try for a court order from there."

She hesitated before picking up the phone and calling Casey, her brother. "Casey, I need your legal help. It's getting bad."

O'Brien & Galloway Conference Room/War Room

Sunlight streamed in. Fiona took the coffee Selena thoughtfully brought her, a cheerful smile on her face. Telling Fiona that being able to use the computers allowed her to finish her project on time and receive an A.

Carol entered, tablet in hand.

"They're rerunning the footage," she said. "Breakroom TV."

The broadcast looped:

"This morning, the police arrested Everett Taylor... from recent evidence they uncovered in his wife's death..."

Club shootout footage followed. The video's context was damning, even though you could not tell if it was Fiona or not.

Selena patched through a call to Curtis and Fiona in the war room, going over the events of the night.

"George Shaw," she said.

His voice cracked through the speaker. "What the hell happened last night?"

Fiona stayed silent for a moment, watching the muted video before saying. "Got a tip. Went to confirm. It turned into a trap," she said.

"They're coming for you. Lawyer up."

Curtis cut in. "Fiona saved Hargraves. That reporter would be dead without Fi saving her."

"*Hargraves?* The lunatic conspiracy blogger?" Shaw groaned. "Fine. I may need Everett to put the ranch up for bail. They'll kill him in jail otherwise. This fiasco made everything worse."

He paused. "Developers sniffed around that land before. Told no, repeatedly. Find out who they are. Maybe it's nothing; maybe it's everything. Maybe all this stuff Bridget was looking into did not get her murdered. That ranch is prime land. Maybe this was all just a plain, old-fashioned land grab. Kill the wife, frame the husband, buy the land from the seizure court."

He added, "Detective Wren claims that the rancher from Montana, Clay Braddock, denied Everett's claim of talking to him on video. Could you and Fiona follow up, talk to the guy yourself, get a statement one way or another?"

With that said, he hung up.

Fiona pinched the bridge of her nose. "We need to find that 911 caller."

Curtis nodded. "Ronald and Danny are on it. Might be one of the homeless people Bridget used to help. But with shelters overflowing because of the freeze... it's chaos."

Fiona asked Cutis, "Did Jeanne get a statement from the boater that called in seeing two homeless men behind the Taylor cabin?" "Not yet, she's busy on that missing person case."

"Send her out today to get it. We need that statement." Before Cutis could answer, Fiona's phone buzzed.

"Lisa?"

"We're done."

"What?"

"I saw the footage. Everett was there. My sister's dead. My niece is gone. Do the math."

Click.

Fiona stared at the screen. The office playlist started up again, *"I'm Dreaming of a White Christmas."*

She looked out. Not a single snowflake.

◆ ◆ ◆

Dallas PD | Homicide Bullpen

The bullpen buzzed with old, dusty HVAC and flickering fluorescents. Luis and Mason stood over Bridget's file and the I-45 victims.

Luis said, "Same killer. Same cuts. Same staging. It's not Everett."

Mason nodded. "I checked the sightings. In the time of death for each of the four females from the I-45 murders, the coroner's stated time of death, Everett has an airtight alibi. Feed store. Fundraiser. Diner. He wasn't near those scenes. A killer this organized doesn't switch to domestic murder and leave sloppy evidence behind."

"Do we tell Curtis?"

Mason shook his head. "Nope. The brass won't allow Wren to link it unless it fits their narrative. So, for now, Everett's safe from being accused of the serial murders."

Luis snorted. "God forbid a rich lake community gets tagged with a serial killer living amongst them."

Mason looked away. "Shaw's already looked at the 1-45 murders. Knows we can't hang it on his client. I may not like the man, but at least he's thorough, and I'm thinking honest. Remember the Thompson case, where he informed the DA his client intended to eliminate the DA's witness? Yeah, his client would have walked, but that information allowed the DA to add additional charges. And Shaw dropped the client."

Luis said, "So, we sit on it?"

"We sit. And we keep digging."

He gathered the photos. "We'll find the real bastard. Brass at this point is not dumb enough to link the Taylor murder to it and lose in court later."

O'Brien & Galloway | Fiona's Office

The last decrypted file blinked open.

CAVANAUGH: PRIOR AUTHORIZATIONS
Name: Joe Bell. Tag: Sliverbranch. Underlined. *Discover.*

Fiona grabbed the secure line.

"Buck. We've got something. Reid Cavanaugh, senior partner at Porter & Ashburn, has a guy named Joe Bell who works under him. We can now definitively state that Joe Bell links too much of Bridget's investigation. As a clean-up guy. He was also here in Dallas during the I-45 girl's murders. And the same goes for Bridget's murder. We've kept the Joe Bell data and sent everything else to you."

A noise outside her door.

"Gotta go."

She hit DELETE. Confirmation blinked just as the door opened.

Detectives McCarthy, Alvarez, and Wren entered. Wren held out a warrant.

"We're seizing all case materials connected to Bridget Taylor."

Fiona nodded. "You'll have our cooperation."

Mason added, "You're requested for questioning about Milo's club shooting."

Casey entered, having landed an hour earlier. "I'm her lawyer." Casey took the warrant and read it before looking at Mason and saying, "This warrant only covers Everett Taylor's client data, you touch any other client information, we'll sue."

He pointed. One officer was going through Fiona's purse on her desk.

"Stop that," Mason barked. "Now."

Fiona walked over and held her hand out for her purse, which the officer handed over.

Dallas County Sheriff's Office | Evidence Cage

Fluorescent lights hummed overhead, cold and flat, bleaching the concrete corridor to the color of old bone. Detective Marcus Wren walked with a clipboard tucked under his arm, jacket open, expression unreadable. To anyone watching, he looked like a man doing routine follow-up on an ugly case.

The evidence technician, a tired-looking sergeant named Holloway, glanced up as Wren approached the cage window.

"Taylor case again?" Holloway asked.

"Captain wants updates reexamined," Wren said, voice flat and casual. "Just need to review the early scene sheets one more time. It shouldn't take long."

Holloway buzzed him through without a second thought.

Inside, the evidence locker smelled faintly of steel, old paper, and the stale odor of mice. Wren moved with quiet confidence, like a man well accustomed to navigating systems built to trust him.

He found Bridget Taylor's evidence box on the second shelf.

B.T.-19-2022: Scene Reports / Preliminary Forensics / Field Notes.

He set the box on the counter, flipped it open, and pulled out the file he wanted. Scanned pages without really reading them.

Then he found the one he wanted.

Field Report: Deputy Sanchez
seven fifty-two pm.
Item: Tire Impressions (unidentified) motorcycle-type, knobby pattern, track on the north side of the cabin. CSU collected the print impression. Marked for follow-up.

A few minutes later, he closed the file and left.

"All done," he said.

Holloway signed the clipboard without looking up, more interested in his coffee than anything else.

Wren handed the clipboard back, nodded once, and walked out.

Holloway, one of his childhood nemeses. One of the chosen at school. Quarterback, popular with girls, noted to be the most successful. Wren remembered the humiliating taunt. Calling him a little birdy. Now look who was successful. He paid a lot to have Holloway unable to work in the field, but not so that he'd take a disability retirement. Now, the irony in Holloway being a nobody at the PD while his career was rising. He chuckled as he left the evidence locker room.

CHAPTER 12

Cold Tracks

Thursday, December 22nd, 2022

Whiskey River Two-Step Ranch

The police hadn't let her speak. They'd let her twist. When she got home, she didn't sleep. Anger clung to her skin like frost clings to the windows.

She kissed Josh's temple gently before slipping away, careful not to wake him. His steady breathing was a momentary anchor in a world tilting off-balance. She lingered at the edge of the bed, watching him for a heartbeat longer. He didn't stir. Good. He'd been through enough in the last few days. For the first time, she feared they wouldn't be making it back to Colorado for the family Christmas tradition.

The house held its breath in winter's silence. Pines lined the windowsills, draped in red velvet ribbons. Twinkling lights blinked across the fireplace mantel and the banister rails. The tree stood tall in the corner of the great room, haloed by soft white bulbs and glass ornaments that shimmered like icicles. Wrapped gifts rested beneath, their bows neat and cheerful.

A clean, refreshing scent from the candle still flickering on the counter mingled with the richer scent of fresh-ground coffee. Somewhere down the hall, a diffuser hissed faintly. The cold in the air carried a bite, even inside.

Outside, a sheet of arctic wind screamed across the fields, driving the wind chill below ten. Ice crusted the tall grass. Even the trees looked frozen, branches locked in prayer against the pale horizon.

Fiona stood in her slipper socks in her office, a heavy shawl draped over her shoulders, coffee in hand. Her hair was still damp from the shower, with tendrils curling at her temples. The floor beneath her feet felt like frozen slate.

The wall-mounted monitors pulsed on in sequence. Satellite feeds, drone patrols, internal thermal scans. Each displayed a corner of her domain. Drones swept the fence line. Grain fields, white-laced with frost, stretched in sharp gray scale on the screen. Heat signatures pulsed gently where cattle still huddled under pine trees near the southern slope.

Someone had cracked open the balcony doors earlier. The scent of wood fires from chimneys mixed with cedar trees, and the cold. She closed them with a quiet snap.

The interrogation. Search warrant. The attitude behind it. Her jaw clenched. She rolled her shoulders and breathed through it.

She drained the last of the coffee, pulled on her boots and jacket, and left the room. Gravel crunched under the Escalade's tires a few minutes later as the ranch disappeared behind her, swallowed in the icy dark before dawn.

Dallas County District Attorney's Office

Downtown, three floors above the frozen parking deck, District Attorney Micah Colburn stood in his corner office, watching the gray sprawl of the city like a man staring down a bad verdict.

The doctored surveillance photo sat on his desk, annotated in crisp handwriting: metadata fractures, audio mismatches, time code anomalies. Someone had tried to frame Fiona O'Brien. And whoever did it was arrogant enough to think it would pass muster, or someone assured them it would. It reflected the possibility of a dirty department. His department. Something he would be subtly looking into. He would ensure that later exposure of dirty cops wouldn't lead to case dismissals. Every case they worked would come under his scrutiny. His goal: to get rid of dirty cops and then quietly review their cases. If he found any he considered questionable, he'd expose them so that the blame did not fall on his office. He'd have to step carefully. A few corrupt cops can destroy public trust in the majority of good cops.

He didn't raise his voice when Langley and Hearn arrived. He didn't need to.

"You authorized the seizure of O'Brien & Galloway information protected by attorney - client privilege and green-lit a public arrest," Colburn said. "All based on a video that didn't survive a twenty-minute metadata scrub by my department."

Hearn shifted. "The department believed the video to be credible."

Colburn held up a hand. "Belief is not evidence. Someone in your department bypassed internal review protocols, never even sending it to the Crime Scene Unit (CSU). I checked, and your department neglected to notify legal counsel assigned to the Taylor defense."

Langley glanced at Hearn, who approved the video, ever the stone-faced, then asked, "What are we saying publicly?"

"We're saying nothing. The news outlets already have the press statement. I gave it to them earlier. You'll back it up. Fiona O'Brien acted in self-defense. The warrant exceeded authority. Today, you will return all materials they seized. We will be lucky if most of our evidence does not get thrown out under the fruit of the poisonous tree doctrine."

Hearn's jaw worked like a man chewing gravel.

Colburn stepped closer, voice cool. "You'll also stop obstructing a licensed investigator operating under judicial appointment. Or I'll make obstruction and tampering charges against both of you."

Neither man spoke.

"Dismissed."

Before either could get out the door, Micah said to their backs. "Oh, and you better find out who got us into this mess. Or the next conversation we have won't be this pleasant. Understood."

They left without slamming the door. Smart men.

Colburn returned to the window. He'd not been in office long and had already made two powerful enemies. Outside, frost still clung to the shadowed side of the courthouse.

Micah turned and reached for the intercom. "Sally, call in Detective Mason McCarthy from homicide. Set an appointment for 3 p.m. today."

Something smelled rotten in this entire case, and he intended to find out exactly where the smell came from.

Dallas PD | Report Processing Room

The report-processing room buzzed faintly with printers, keyboards, and the drone of old HVAC. Overworked officers passing through didn't pay attention to anyone else's business as they stacked case folders in uneven piles on their desks in the bullpen. The perfect place for shortcuts to go unnoticed. Detective Marcus Wren dropped into his chair at his desk and opened a terminal with a sigh that carried the weight of pleasing a master with high demands and not enough hours. He rubbed his eyes, clicked the login prompt, and waited for the system to grind awake. *This damn system gets slower every day.* The forwarded Smith County dispatch packet popped up on the screen.

911 Transcript. Unidentified Male. Possible witness, homicide.

He scrolled through it, jaw tightening at the sheer volume of mess the Taylor case was piling onto his workload. The caller spoke with panic, breathlessness, and unevenness, which typically made supervisors roll their eyes. Wren had seen dozens like it: vagrants, addicts, drunks, people who lived on the margins and talked in riddles. He drummed his pen against the desk once before opening the "Detective Review" field. He didn't pause long. **Detective Note:**

Caller emotional, inconsistent, possibly under the influence of drugs or alcohol. Unreliable. Low probability of locating for follow-up. He didn't bother adding the nuance the transcript deserved. That fear makes people stumble, that panic isn't intoxication, that the caller had described the attack with excellent clarity.

Wren had neither the want nor the inclination to chase witnesses, especially not anonymous ones phoning from ancient payphones on the edge of nowhere. He hit submit. A brief flash of red confirmed the note was now part of the internal chain. Nothing dramatic. Just one more comment buried among dozens. The note any detective could justify. Overworked shifts, too many cases, and a preference for witnesses who didn't vanish into the woods. Wren closed the file and stood, stretching his shoulders as though he'd just checked off another mundane task. And more determined than ever to keep control of the Taylor investigation. Even if it meant shaving corners. Behind him, the monitor dimmed into a screensaver, the detective's note quietly cementing the caller's credibility into the lowest category. Just one more minor mistake in a case already drowning in them.

◆ ◆ ◆

O'Brien & Galloway Dallas Office

Downtown Dallas rose ahead like jagged steel against the pale gray morning. Wind gusts slammed across the highway. Ice still clung to the shadowed corners of the buildings. Black frost crusted the sidewalk curbs.

City crews hadn't cleared everything. Fiona threaded between salt trucks and city workers de-icing a bus stop.

The news played low on the dashboard radio.

"... record lows overnight as North Texas continues to feel the effects of the arctic front. Wind chill warnings remain in effect through Friday. Officials urge residents to avoid unnecessary travel and keep pets indoors."

The news anchor's tone shifted.

"District Attorney Micah Colburn released a statement early this morning confirming that Fiona O'Brien of the investigative firm of O'Brien & Galloway will not face any charges. Colburn stated that in the alleged shootout involving Ms. O'Brien, police claimed she acted in self-defense and cleared her of any wrongdoing. Though the incident remains under investigation."

Fiona clicked off the radio. Her jaw tight, but her shoulders loosened as tension flowed out of them.

A call came in from Erin asking for a meeting. Fiona agreed. Fifteen minutes later, she entered the cafe, which smelled of espresso and clove. A plastic reindeer leaned against the window. Somewhere behind the counter, someone was cursing over a broken syrup pump, as cheerful Christmas music played over the speakers. The journalist looked wired on caffeine, boots scuffed, laptop bag slung over her shoulder.

"You called me, so say what you want to say. I need to get back to the office. Hopefully, start with why you stabbed me in the back." Fiona did not sit; she just stood next to the table. "Should I expect this conversation to hit the evening news with a creative edit job? I saw the early-morning news before I left home, and your video filmed last night. It could only have come from your camera. You followed us out into the alley to film it. Not to help."

Erin retorted. "I didn't know you'd be at Milo's. I needed something to get me back in. That footage was it. What did you expect me to do? Sit on it."

"My guys and I saved your life; it seems reporters no longer have an ethical code anymore if they ever had one. All you guys do is chase Pulitzers, even if they're lies. You should have at least warned us first. I could have respected that. Understand this. If I find out you're part of a setup, I'll sue you into the dirt."

Erin didn't flinch, but her tone softened. "Understood. Look, I got an anonymous tip. Told me to be there. Just to observe. Said I would get something to get me back in the game. No other explanation."

Fiona changed the subject. "Did you see the man I was meeting?"

"Not clearly. He moved fast. But I filmed him at the top of the fence in the alley."

"You have it?"

"Yes. Backed up. But I'm not sharing until you let me in."

Fiona stood silent for a moment. Controlling her breathing, she said, "The least you can do is give me a picture of this guy. That is all I am asking for."

Silence reigned for several moments, then Fiona turned to leave. "Alright." Erin reached into her bag and handed her a printed picture; it resembled the man Fiona had met the night before. "Also, someone slid this under my door. Looks like it's about one of your other cases, embezzlement from a company. Now, am I in or not?"

"Our conversation is over. I have instructed my investigators to avoid you, so do not call again and stay away from them. After the way you stabbed me in the back last night, I would not trust you any farther than I could throw you, and right now that's not far."

"What if I get information?"

"Print it. We can do our own investigations. Leave my agency out of it." With that said, Fiona turned her back on her and walked away.

◆ ◆ ◆

Dallas Office

As she stepped out of her Caddy at the garage, freezing air pierced her face, but she didn't rush as she walked the block in the cold. Wanting to think, she'd call in Morris and ask him about the embezzlement case. She hoped he was getting somewhere with it. She'd hate to think she'd just walked away from important information on one of their cases.

Fiona passed through security without a word. Upstairs, the office was quiet. Cold light, heated air. The flatscreen on the wall in the reception lounge played a delayed loop of the same WDAL segment she heard in the car.

A group of clients in suits stood nearby, quiet as statues, watching the segment. One of them glanced at her. She didn't flinch, just a quick nod and passed by and walked through to the back office areas.

A data analyst passed her in the hall with a fresh cup of coffee and a file under his arm. No one said good morning. No one asked questions. The chill of the marble floor came through the soles of her boots. When she entered her office and flicked the switch, screens flickered to life across the walls, displaying data feeds, satellite overlays, and surveillance logs. Curtis had briefed her about Marshall Hays after she had left the police department the night before.

Hays sent a payment and signed the contract, completing the notification to them officially. Hays fulfilled the contract. She hadn't liked what Curtis had uncovered so far, but they couldn't do anything about it. Technically, unless they could positively connect him to SILO or any of the other stuff on the drives, they had no legal reason to investigate him or his company. Major Buck would have to give them the go ahead and he had not done that. Hays was slick. Too slick, in her opinion.

Still, they passed the information along to Major Buck, so maybe he could follow through. From the corner of her eye, she caught her reflection in one of the darkened screens. A silhouette, sharp angles and tension. Jittery. There were days she felt she didn't recognize herself. Today was one of them.

Sam Greer entered without knocking. He never did. Tall, clean-cut, composed. His slate-gray suit was fresh-pressed, tie straight. The man could be in the middle of a war zone and still show up looking like the FBI agent he was at one time before he resigned.

He dropped two Manila folders onto the desk. "Ronald stayed up all night digging. We've got more on Jace Lin."

Fiona flipped open the folder. Lin's photo looked back at her: slim frame, sharp eyes, guarded posture. Brilliant. Nervous. Too much of both, maybe.

"Three weeks before Bridget's death, Lin contacted her through a messaging app, not an encrypted one." Sam said. "The account's now dead but not wiped. Buck's guys recovered most of it. We found Lin flagged concerns about an 'untraceable gateway' in Transitions AI's predictive policing codebase. Convenient he died during the conference center explosion, but he knew something. We think he told Bridget something, something that got her killed. He may have even given her some proof."

Fiona flipped open the second folder. A chill ran through her. She dug through the files on her desk, flipping through them until she found it: Jace. In a few of Bridget's photos. Proof of the connection between Jace Lin and Bridget. A link. Fiona's stomach turned. No wonder she felt like she'd seen him somewhere when she met him in the office that day. When she shuffled through the pictures, the day they accepted the Shaw's offer and to investigate who murdered Bridget, Jace was in several of them.

Sam nodded. "I'd say it was murder. Two birds with one stone type action."

"Jace, Bridget, Joe, Reid... all roads led to Porter & Ashburn. California division again.

"And Marshall Hays?"

"Still no direct ties to any of this. Except Jace ties to Bridget and her investigation. But who's going to believe someone blew up a conference to kill one man?"

She breathed slowly, grounding herself on the feel of the grain of the polished table beneath her hand. "Run the Dallas conference center staff through facial recognition. Anyone with priors, aliases, or military history. I want it on my desk ASAP."

"Already in motion, we contacted Major Buck. He said he could get it done. Said he'd get back to us," Sam said, and with a nod, he was gone.

Fiona's fingers lingered on the edge of the photo, her mind racing. If Jace had known something and died for it, then maybe Bridget had died for the same reason. Maybe this was not just about whatever Major Buck was chasing. Hays might not just be slick; he might be bloody. Too many threads. Not enough answers. Curtis' instincts about him turned out to be correct. Yet, exactly where did Joe Bell and Reid Cavanah fit in with this current information? Were they all one vast group, or two separate groups doing their own thing? And John Cole's company seemed to be knee-deep in it all, but for now, they could prove none of it. And Delores, his wife? Was she just a gold-digger or something more? She leaned back in her chair, looking off at nothing, thinking.

Next through the door were Paul Avery and Nancy Myers from the cyber division, breaking her thoughts. Paul looked like he'd slept under his desk. Nancy looked as if she hadn't slept at all. The two of them always reminded Fiona of feral cats. Brilliant, twitchy, and dangerous. They were living in a digital world; she doubted if they even knew there was a real world. They worked together well; she was glad they were on her side.

Nancy dropped a packet of code onto the table. "Fragments pulled from the latest drop Nightjar sent us. Not random. Timed transmissions. Encrypted bursts routed through offshore server farms. Just got back from the compound with this information. It would be easier if the drives were here to access."

"You trace the endpoint?"

Paul grimaced. "Closest trace hits a solar server in Costa Rica; five shell layers later, it dead-ends at a Zurich PO box."

Fiona sipped her coffee and winced. It tasted like the bottom of an ashtray. "What the hell ... is this stuff left over from yesterday?" She walked over to the sink and dumped it before moving over to make fresh coffee. Soon, the rich aroma of cinnamon and vanilla filled the room.

"Payload?"

"Still encrypted," Nancy said. "But it's not corporate. Not generic. This feels like an insider passing information. Someone very paranoid. Scared. Or very cunning."

Paul added, "The way the data's coded, it's... elegant. Like whoever built it was writing a haiku."

"Keep pushing," Fiona said. "Burn every hour you need. Just don't get sloppy."

Nancy nodded, dark circles under her eyes like bruises. "And Nancy, get some sleep." The implication there went without being spoken.

As they left, Dawn Cooke entered, holding a slim file full of stills and a small drive. Her expression was tighter than usual. "Shaw secured traffic cam footage from the day of Bridget's murder," she said. "Dallas PD finally coughed it up to him after he got a judge to sign off on a court order. He sent it over this morning."

She inserted the drive. One of the wall monitors lit up. "Timestamp: ten fifty-eight am."

Fiona leaned in. "Plates?"

"Renwright Holdings," Dawn said. "Shared pool vehicle, executive transport."

Fiona's eyes narrowed. "Porter & Ashburn shows up again, California division. I want to know about every asset that LLC has ever touched."

"There's more," Dawn said, sliding a photo across the table. We enhanced the image from a traffic camera. The camera caught cars illegally using the carpool lane. This picture showed the same vehicle, but this time we could see the driver.

Fiona stared down. The face turned toward the camera; its profile burned into her memory.

Lisa Neylan.

"She was there?" Fiona said, barely above a whisper.

"Looks that way. And not driving her own car, but a company car, it appears. The timing puts her in the vehicle within the time of Bridget's death."

The silence in the conference room stretched. Even the hum of electronics seemed to dim.

"Start pulling everything we have on Lisa," Fiona said finally. "Phone logs. Bank records. Family trust documents. Social ties. Everything. Send this information to Shaw. I want him aware of this development."

Dawn hesitated. "How low-key should we make it?"

"Be loud and sloppy." Fiona turned back to the board. "I want her aware that we're looking. Make her sweat. She's now on our radar."

The lines connecting names and dates, the maps with red

tacks, the timelines scrawled in overlapping marker. "If she had a hand in the murder of her sister, I want to catch her making a mistake."

Dawn nodded and slipped out.

Fiona sat alone. The noise of activity reached her faintly through the door. Her fingers drifted over the surface of her desk, tracing lines that felt more like scars.

Beyond the maps and data, past the shredded files and encrypted drives, lay the truth about who murdered Bridget and why. And that should lead them to where Lila was, and if... she shied away from the last thought.

Outside, the sun finally broke the skyline, casting thin gold light across the floor. But the shadows inside didn't move.

Fiona set down her empty cup and turned back to the board. She moved a red string on the digital murder board and connected Lisa's name to Renwright Holdings and sat back, staring at how the board looked now.

From somewhere across the outer office, a faint whiff of bleach and burned wires hit her nose. Someone in forensics must be running a test. It created a weird scent when it mixed with the jasmine air freshener.

Someone was coming after her company and those she cared about. It started with Major Buck's contract and Everett's case, Bridget's murder, and Lila's disappearance. Finally, they stopped playing catch-up. Information... the gold standard of any PI company worth its salt, was being exposed. One small piece at a time.

A ray of golden light spread across the table as the sun rose higher.

CHAPTER 13

Skeletons Under Glass

Friday, January 6th, 2023

Dallas Metroplex | Various Locations

Contrary to what she had earlier thought about going home for Christmas, it turned out everything came to a dead end in Everett's case and most of their other cases. Enough so that they gave their entire office Christmas Day off and many the week after. Leaving only a few investigators coming and going in the office.
Fiona's holiday reprieve was over, and so was her peace.

Curtis told her about the suspicious SUV that followed him from his son's Houston suburb after the holidays. Fiona realized that he now wore his Glock full time instead of keeping it in the office safe when not out and about. Meeting in the conference/war room, they locked eyes for the first time since December 19th.

They realized their separate family holidays had unexpectedly connected to dangerous events. The actual work was just beginning, and this time, it was personal. She headed back to her office, needing some time to herself.

A message appeared on her secure terminal.

ASSET COMPROMISED. She sat up straighter. "Stefana, I need

you in my office now." As soon as she entered, she showed her the message. "Do any of our cyber team members know about this? If not, why? Get me some answers. Quietly.

Stefana used the intercom shortly afterwards and said yes. Their investigators detected the breach minutes before the system notified them of it. Curtis assigned Jordan, Dustin, and Nancy to work on the problem. Right now, they had no answers about the cryptic message.

Though she wondered who the asset was. Fiona thought the information came from Nightjar and told Curtis so.

Cutis did not think so, remarking. "I don't trust him after what Kenneth told me he saw that night. You don't leave a woman fighting for her life and run away. As for the other, why would he not give them more information? Without that, they had no way of knowing who?"

Fiona picked up the phone and called Buck.

"Message came a little late. This morning, someone found one of my undercover operatives dead in his home. The local PD listed it as a suicide. Leave it alone; you can't afford to bring attention to the agency right now. Send over what your cyber teams have. We'll take it from there. Tell them to erase everything afterwards."

An hour later in her office by herself, she thought back to her and Josh's Christmas vacation Curtis insisted she take to rest and recover. One night when she could not sleep, she sat at her old room's window late one night, looking at skeletal branches as they tapped against the glass as the house slept.

Her thoughts were back in Texas. She hadn't talked about it with anyone yet, not family nor friends. Not yet. But it haunted her.

That day, of the fire, what she hadn't pulled from the fire or retrieved from Lisa's trunk, was gone, destroyed.

That storage unit had held answers. Hard to fake or bury those kinds of answers, paper trails, connections to names, places, and events. And now all she had left... was a few dozen folders, some photos, a zoning map, and one burning question.

Who was behind wanting it all erased, and why wait to do so when Lisa and she showed up? Why was it not all just burned down like the other storage unit before this one?

The crash of a dropped cup breaking, followed by cussing down the hall at one of the refreshment centers, jolted her out of her thoughts.

◆◆◆

Curtis Office

Curtis sat alone in his corner office after the daily briefing, with a cup of coffee going cold beside his keyboard, the Dallas skyline unnoticed out his window. TV news playing in the background.

"... police continue investigating the early morning triple homicide in North Dallas. The shooting occurred just after 4:30 a.m. at a North Oak Cliff apartment complex parking lot. Paramedics declared three individuals dead at the scene, while they sent two others to the hospital. Police believe the attack was not random..."

Another report rolled in as the anchor transitioned.

"And in national news, two years since the January 6th Capitol breach, federal prosecutors continue their crackdown. Over seventy Texans, including two-thirds from Dallas–Fort Worth, faced charges or convictions related to the riots. Legal analysts say the fallout may continue well into 2024."

He left the volume low, not interested. The city never slept, and its crimes never stopped. A folder marked Renwright Holdings lay open across his desk. Renwright Holdings had legal paperwork but no substance; a classic laundering shell. Every trail dead-ended.

Kaitlin Woods, an ex-DOJ agent who worked for them in investigations, called and asked him to meet her at her desk in the bullpen. When he arrived, she pointed to the monitor, saying, "Weird. Some of Wren's early witness notes have the same metadata tag: *CI-072-DPD-NARC-21*. That tag only shows up when the source is confidential narcotics intel."

Curtis looked over. "But this isn't a drug case. In fact, we have not found any instances of drugs being involved."

"Exactly," Kaitlin said. "And in the Taylor murder case, the CI ID number showed has been for a protected witness if they thought he or she needed protection. Which is bizarre because Bridget's case shouldn't have any narcotics CIs attached to it at all. Unless he claims the CI is a witness. And if that's the case, George needs to get a subpoena for the information." She said as she hit more keys to show him the comparison files.

"I only found it cause I'm working on the narco case for the company that discovered someone is using them to move drugs. They want the mole found and gone, and the police out of their hair. They prefer to keep it quiet. I found this digging through the detectives that were assigned to the case for the PD. A detective Wren. It then flagged over to the Bridget Taylor case on the big board. Thought I should let you know. Not only that, I got curious. Detective Wren used the same CI in various internal cases across several PDs in Texas against police officers, which got convictions? One even in the Dallas PD when he was only there for six months. Which got him the promotion to homicide and added to the Miller murder trial. So, figured you needed to know this to give over to Shaw."

"You made the right call. Send the information to Fi's computer in her office."

Curtis had a suspicion now about why Mason was willing to hand him Wren's CI information. He'd bet that Mason's friend was the accused officer. Stabbed to death while being held in jail before he could post bail. Mason was digging to clear his friend's name. Get his widow her rightful benefits. And put

Wren in prison. He'd let Fi run with this; he'd stay in the background so as not to muddy the waters. He wanted to keep his meetings with Mason out of the discussion.

As soon as Fiona read the information, she called George. "George, do you have any information from the prosecution that they are using a CI as apparently a witness? The case list includes this CI."

Curtis went back to his office. He tapped a few keys, calling up a set of encrypted contact protocols, already forgetting the CI information. Then he leaned back, rubbed the bridge of his nose, and started making calls.

A news chyron rolled across the bottom of the TV. *Senator Randal Morrow pushes new federal oversight bill on cross-border operations.*

◆ ◆ ◆

Everett's Call

Everett Taylor sat with his cell phone pressed to his ear, his voice tight. The call had come out of the blue. Colt's wife, her voice fraying with panic.

"Everett, something's wrong. Colt was supposed to be back from Europe by now. He never arrived. I've called everywhere. The embassy won't give me straight answers. They're stonewalling me. They say they don't have him listed anywhere, that there's no record of his arriving in Poland. That's a lie. I know it is. Please... please help me find him."

"Why not call sooner?"

"I... I was not much help when the police called, so I figured you might not want help. You know how secretive Colt can be at times."

Everett knew. He suspected Colt worked for the CIA after he left the military, but never brought it up or asked.

Everett's mind went back to that night in Afghanistan, seven years ago
Night fell hard over the Kunar Valley, thick with smoke and the stench of gunpowder. The ridge shook under another mortar hit, dirt spraying Everett as he slid into cover behind a crumbling low wall. Comms flared.

"Hit... left leg. I'm pinned."
Colt's voice. Strained. Fading.

Everett didn't wait.
"Cover me!" he shouted.

Reyes, one of the marines they came to extract from their pinned-down position, pivoted and laid down suppressing fire with his SAW, brass casings clattering around him.
"Go! We've got you!"
Griffin popped smoke downwind, then leaned into the scope of his suppressed rifle, zeroing in on the muzzle flashes ahead.
"Two targets moving east. Taking them."
Nguyen was already on the flank, barking into comms for air support as he tossed a thermite charge into a nest of rocks. The hillside erupted.

Everett bolted.

Smoke curled in his lungs, sand ground in his teeth, but he tracked Colt's last signal through the fire-blistered dark. Found him slumped beneath a collapsed section of wall, rifle broken, blood soaking through shredded camo on his left leg.

Everett crouched. "Still alive?"

Colt cracked a pained grin. "Only because I'm too mean to die."

Everett hauled him up, Colt's arm slung over his shoulders.
"They're gonna give you hell for this," Colt muttered.

"I'll bill you," Everett said, turning toward the evac point.

Gunfire stitched the dirt at their heels.
Travis, call sign Hawk, voice barked through the comm: "Move

your ass, Taylor, we're about to be real popular."

The team closed in, creating a moving perimeter as the extraction bird banked hard overhead and made a fast touchdown. Everett and Colt stumbled up the ramp just as rounds cracked past them.

That injury was the end of Colt's military career. Colt got hit covering Everett's ass.

Everett closed his eyes, gripping the phone harder. "I swear I'll find him."

He ended the call with a bitter taste in his mouth. Colt wasn't just a good friend and war buddy. He was Everett's best alibi, the only person who could testify that Everett wasn't where the police said he was the day of Bridget's murder. If Colt had vanished overseas, or worse, everything Everett had left to stand on would collapse beneath him.

An hour later, Everett walked into the agency's office. Curtis approached him, a file still in his hand from a separate case the agency was working on.

Everett didn't waste time. "It's Colt. His wife called me. He's missing. The embassy's giving her nothing but a runaround. She's desperate. Curtis, I need your help. My buddies say there is chatter throughout the special forces of a plane crash in the Tatra Mountains; apparently, American, severe weather delayed rescue. And yet the official channels have claimed they have no information about this."

Fiona had entered quietly and stood listening as she studied his face, weighing the fear against desperation. She glanced at Curtis, who gave a slight nod.

"Alright," Fiona said. "We'll investigate it. But this stays between us until we know more. No leaks to anyone. If Colt's alive, we'll find him. If he isn't..." She left the rest unsaid.

Everett's jaw clenched; Fiona understood he understood the unspoken. He left.

Stephana, can you send Chelsea Lowery into my office and shuffle any cases she is working on to others?

As soon as she entered, Fiona said, "Chelsea, I need you to investigate oversees around the Tartar Mountains about a plane crash. You're looking for where the crash occurred, if it occurred, and if there were any survivors and, if so, where they might be."

She opened a drawer and pulled out a private Visa card with an elevated limit compared to the normal company ones. Told her she was to use this only for anything related to this investigation; do not use your company card. She was to leave now and catch a flight over to Europe. And she was not to report to anyone but her or Curtis if she found something. She left to pack and to get her tickets for her flight out.

Curtis's Investigation of Renwright Holdings.

Curtis went back to his desk and back to what he was working on before the interruption, dialing old contacts one after another.

His first call was to Stephen 'Steve' Larrison, a retired field agent from the FBI's Denver office. Steve answered on the second ring.

"Curtis. How'd your holidays go? Been meaning to call you, but got caught up in holiday stuff. You know how that is with the kids and grandkids. It's the only time I get to see them."

"I need a favor. Off record. Ever heard of Renwright Holdings?"

"Yeah," Steve said. "It popped up in a few federal scans years ago. Never anything actionable. Too clean on the surface. What's it tied to?"

"A dead woman. And a hell of a lot of smoke, though no fire I can find, if you know what I mean."

"I'll dig," Steve said. "Give me a couple of days."

Next, Curtis reached out to an old Army intel buddy, Reggie Tam. Reggie didn't talk much, but when he did, he didn't waste words.

"Renwright's a shell; too many agents, no activity. Exists only on paper," Reggie said.

Curtis frowned. "So, it's fake," Curtis said.

"Worse. It's protected. Hands off." Reggie's voice crackled faintly through the secure line. "Curtis, this one stinks like wet ops and burn files from a certain three-letter agency. Tread softly."

Last, Curtis called Major Buck.

"You're chasing ghosts," Buck said after Curtis laid out what he had. "We already investigated Renwright when that firm popped up on a department watch list over five years ago. No physical presence. No employees. All digital proxies. We also discovered the tax ID belonged to a defunct company from the '80s."

"So, it's not just suspicious, it's fake," Curtis said.

"Worse. It's protected. Whoever ran it has substantial influence within the department. I couldn't dig deeper without someone breathing down my neck telling me to move on."

Curtis leaned back in his chair, his jaw tightening. The Range Rover lead had pointed them to Renwright Holdings once more, and Lisa, but every step since was a dead end.

"Time to stop chasing shadows. Hays is too close to this. Best you dig up what he buried before the money came in." "Piece of advice, Curtis, leave Hays to me. He's too red-hot for your PI firm to touch, and I prefer to keep you guys more on the periphery. You get the start of the leads; we take over from there," Buck's voice carried a hint of a command.

"I'm curious, you can call on the FBI, DOJ, DHS, and any other law enforcement; heck, you even have the NSA? Why us? This has bothered me for a while."

"Let's just say that sometimes there are too many people in the government with their fingers in the wrong piece of pie. Slows everything to a crawl, and sometimes even a full stop. You're outside all that, but with all the skills and personnel to fulfill my needs."

That told Curtis they were Buck's ace in the hole, outside the normal channels. "Understood." He said and hung up. He was not sure that he liked that fact. And worried they might have bitten off more than they could chew. Shook his head and rose to go refill his coffee. Down the hallway, Morris stood in the copy room door, chatting with Sabrina. She handed him a tablet, then frowned when he didn't give it back.

"I just need to scrub the metadata," he said, smiling too casually. "Old habits."

Curtis paused, watching and listening from a distance.

When Morris turned, he caught Curtis's eye and held the stare a beat too long before nodding and walking off, tablet still in hand.

Curtis returned to his office and jotted a note on his personal log: Check Morris's access logs. Request internal audit, admin only.

He didn't know why. Just a feeling. But lately, the wrong people always seem to know the right time to strike.

Half an hour later, he entered Fiona's office. Morris was in there. "Coffee is from Selena," Morris said, setting down the tray. "She bribed the barista to put extra vanilla with cinnamon in yours. I told her I would bring it to you. I needed to ask you something, but I see Curtis seems to need your time, so I'll come back later."

◆ ◆ ◆

Following Lisa

Fiona's boots clicked softly against the stone floor of Lisa Neylan's high-rise condo's outer hallway. She figured it could not hurt to get Lisa talking again. At least try to. She knocked twice; waited. Nothing. Curtis wanted to just hand what they found in the photos to George to use as reasonable doubt for Everett. Fiona sensed that something was not right; just a hunch, but many of her hunches in the past had paid off.

Lisa had always been hard to pin down. She descended back to the parking garage, pulling up the security cam stream from her tablet, which one of their ex-hackers turned investigators, hacked for them, something police could not do without a warrant, but standard practice in large PI firms like hers, no need for any warrants or judge subpoenas. Of course, you better not get caught doing it, but as it never gets used in court, it rarely becomes an issue. She sat in her SUV. No sign of Lisa. She scanned the outbound traffic logs. Only one outbound license plate matched Lisa's vehicle in the last hour. Direction: North. She headed in that direction. She guessed Lisa's destination. The radio news came on.

"*Weather this morning remains unusually mild for January. The forecast predicts the temperature will hit record highs later today, reaching 70°F, even though it was a crisp 46°F early this morning. Sunny skies with a light breeze. Forecasters do not expect precipitation through the weekend. The news moved to the J6th arrest in the Dallas–Fort Worth area,* and she turned the radio off. Ten minutes later, Fiona parked in the visitor parking space. And there it was. Lisa exited one of the upper-level condos. Delores followed not long after, sunglasses on, cell to her ear.

In the background check of Delores, they discovered she had a condo in the richest part of Dallas city proper, in her maiden name. Fiona narrowed her eyes.

When Lisa and Dolores crossed paths moments later, the performance was convincing. Cold shoulders. No acknowledgment. Not a hint of warmth or recognition.

Too rehearsed.

Lisa drove off in her car, heading south. Fiona followed.

Lisa parked in the lot of a run-down strip mall and entered a small coffee shop. Inside, seated at the corner table, was Erin Hargrave. She parked and took out her camera, added a telescopic lens, and started clicking away.

The meeting lasted fifteen minutes. From where she sat, she couldn't see if there were any handoffs. Just low, tense conversation.

Lisa left, heading back toward the city. Fiona tailed her until she turned into the private underground garage beneath Porter & Ashburn's law offices.

Fiona stayed parked two blocks away, watching the security feed as Lisa vanished into the building.

By the time she returned to her own office, Fiona was already dialing her investigators. Within twenty minutes, she had assembled five investigators in the conference/war room.

"I want full timelines of Lisa and Dolores," she said. "Focus on anything that overlaps with Bridget. I want to know if they shared anything else. Investments, property, phone records. And ask Josiah to check today's pings in the locations and see if we can get information about whether they are using burners or their own phones. I'd bet burners."

Paul Avery nodded. "Stuart's quiet; his money isn't. Someone's routing funds through the same Cayman firm Dolores's husband uses."

Fiona circled a name on the board.

"Then that's where we dig. Start with who accessed that money and when."

Her voice dropped. Her head tilted as she stared at the board, eyes squinted, brow furrowed, before saying to no one in particular. "Major Buck giving us the government contract seems to have tendrils running through our murder case and several other cases we are working on. I'm wondering if that is why we have that contract. Seems he knew Everett because of classified missions Delta did for military intelligence. And he told me once that Bridget's digging into certain areas had higher-ups in government nervous."

Curtis, who walked in as she mused about the military intelligence connection, said nothing to that remark.

She moved to the refreshment side wall center, saying, "Something's moving under the surface. I want to know what it is before the next body turns up."

CHAPTER 14

Chasing Shadows

Wednesday, January 11th, 2023
O'Brien & Galloway Office and Field Teams

Days after the Lisa–Delores surveillance run, the office felt different. Tighter, calmer, as though there was a quiet before the storm. When Fiona returned to the office that day, she told Curtis about Lisa's surveillance. She explained Lisa met with Delores, then Erin, before returning to her office. He added it to their ongoing files on the case. For now, they could not do much except keep watching. Their agencies' investigators spread across the country gathering clues and information on over twenty major cases.
Curtis bent over the table, feeling it press into his stomach. Fresh coffee and electronics filled the air; the room hummed low, as if it were holding its breath.

Spread across the table sat a sparse profile file. Marshall Hays, mid-30s. CEO of Transitions AI. Conference keynote speaker. Poster boy for AIs: on paper, squeaky clean. But Hays' records only went back ten years. Curtis wanted to nail Hays to the wall; that SOB was his. His gut told him Hays used them in the convention disaster. And Curtis could not let it go; the death toll among civilians and law enforcement ate at him. Though no one in the FBI thought to look in Hays' direction. To them, he was a victim.

Curtis understood Fi also was uneasy with Hays, but not in the same way. Buck claimed that taking on the job for Hays was perfect for Sentinel's maiden civilian mission, but neither of them agreed.

"You ever think Buck was up to more than he told us to get us to take the case? I just can't figure out what happened after the disaster at the Conference Center."

Curtis' brows scrunched up. "Yeah, I thought about it quite a bit, but I don't think Buck expected what happened. Is Buck not telling us everything? Come on, Fi, he's the head of a military intelligence operation.

Fiona nodded, but her expression was tight; she accepted the NDA logic, but the unease didn't leave. Police dug for the truth; they didn't work around it. Realizing Curtis had not wanted to take the contract, and she had convinced him to, she let it drop.

Curtis moved on to the subject of Hays. "No schools before 2014, and no DMV history, and no public trail. Just a resume claiming that he'd graduated from MIT with honors. He supposedly worked at the now-defunct Daedalus BioCyber in Seattle, then started Transitions AI." David Boyd's voice grew higher and faster as he went over the information he'd found. Everyone called him Danger Dave, or DD. He flipped through printed transcripts as if looking for something and then looked up, saying.

"Hays shows up like a damn algorithm that came online fully formed. Thought you'd want to know he's flagged by the NSA. No idea why."

Curtis frowned. "How'd you pull that off?"

DD grinned without looking up. "Best you don't know how I found out. But Morris sent a redirect a while back. Names like Hays would've triggered a silent watchlist if they hit certain metadata ranges."

Curtis paused. "Morris did?"

"Yeah. Said Buck requested it, though I couldn't verify that; Major Buck's not exactly been easy to reach lately."

Curtis said nothing, just made a mental note; he then tapped into the field team logs. Three investigators had already fanned out to verify Hays's history. One was calling old college contacts. The one scraping Daedalus' backend.

Charles Chambers checked in first, with information from Stanford. "There is no record of a Marshall Hays ever enrolling. But there's a grad thesis submitted in 2012 under the name *Maxwell Hains*. Weird part? The work's identical to some of Hays's latest public papers. Same style and language; however, the subject he wrote about I am not familiar with."

"Send me the full text. Maybe Heather can figure it out; she's done cryptanalyst work at the NSA. I'll give it to her to work on and see if she understands what it is about," Curtis said.

"The thesis mentions the Stuart Initiative for Strategic AI. It was owned by Renwright Holdings and funded through Stuart Corp; all of them are now dissolved."

"Curtis muttered a curse; the entire operation looked like a financial front posing as research."

Ethan Hochstetler rang in next from Seattle. "No one who worked at Daedalus remembers a Marshall Hays. One guy in legal swore he remembered someone with that name. Said they had a systems architect working black side in '14, went by a call sign; *Redbeard*."

Curtis leaned back. "Redbeard, Hains, Hays," frustrated, he ran his hand through his hair. "We need proof they're connected."

He dialed Major Buck but was once more informed he was out in the field. He then relayed the puzzling information to his next in command. The person on the list to whom they could pass information if Buck were unavailable. Fifteen minutes later, he got a call from Buck.

"That's classic ghost-ID work; identities built from dead records and scrubbed engineers. If Hays came from a black project, someone wiped the trail. Hell, even he might not know the full extent."

"I'm not convinced he's just a puppet," Curtis said. "I think he's the architect."

Buck paused. "Either way, someone's shielding him, and I asked you to back off Hays." Then he hung up. That was it. Nothing more said.

Curtis's phone buzzed. Sabrina notified him she'd sent an internal report to his laptop. He opened it and skimmed over the contents of what she'd found.

Morris recently accessed all metadata tied to Renwright files; he also tried to erase his access timestamps. But the cyber team Fi and he put together was some of the best in the field. The Everett and Hays cases did not involve him. Right now, he was supposed to be working on an embezzlement case for a well-known international company, tracing who and where the money was going.

Curtis didn't react outwardly. Instead, he walked to the break station and poured fresh coffee while he thought it over. For now, he would keep his suspicions to himself. In the last year Morris worked for them, Morris completed several troublesome cases in record time. He'd hate to accuse him of something that could have an innocent reason. Maybe he was interested in working on these cases and was snooping around. In case he got added, he would be up to date. Who knew he seemed ambitious enough? Curtis logged it mentally as an anomaly, nothing more. Still, he'd keep his eye on him.

Dallas PD and Sheriff Joint Task Briefing

The room buzzed with tired detectives and cold coffee. Wren stood at the front, flipping through a thin folder, voice steady and authoritative.

"Taylor knew the area," he said, tapping the county map. "He could've dumped the daughter's body fast and doubled back before anyone saw him. The cabin's isolated, with gravel roads that don't hold prints well. And I have a witness who saw him in the area the day of the murder, one of my best CIs."

A few heads nodded automatically.

Across the table, Mason frowned, saying. "We don't have evidence that he ever left the ranch."

Wren shrugged lightly, as if offering a reasonable theory. "Until someone verifies his supposed alibi, we can't rule out the most obvious suspect. Everett Taylor lied about why he left his phone at home. Not to join a friend, but to take his wife and daughter to their cabin. For one purpose only, and that was to murder both."

Wren's confidence led most of those in the room to accept it without question.

Mason's doubt lingered. It was reasonable what Wren said. But something still ate at him. The MO for one thing. A quiet suspicion that would sit at the back of Mason's mind. Something smelled.

Wren planted a seed of doubt in most of the detectives present; they had their own worries in dealing with their own murder cases.

The meeting adjourned, chairs scraped back, and Mason stayed seated a moment longer, unable to shake the feeling that they had just stamped something rotten official.

CHAPTER 15

Ash and Mercy

Thursday, January 26th, 2023 |

Legal Threads and Erin's Call

The tablet screen glowed with cold blue light as Fiona scrolled through Lisa Neylan's employment records. The office hum felt brittle, like glass about to crack. Something didn't add up. Two years ago, Reid Cavanaugh ran Porter & Ashburn's audit division. Now, every log from that period was missing. The archive sealed no digital backups. When Sabrina probed the network, it rerouted offshore. Referred to paper files but offered no trail. All the digital footprints are gone.

Next, she dug through travel logs, at least those that were available. Lisa had used two different aliases. One for Belize, one for Amsterdam. Both trips timed within days of Bridget and Everett's vacations to those areas. Why?

She flagged the files for Paul Avery and forwarded a quick message:

Double-check the Belize travel records. And look for any connection between Stuart's Cayman accounts and Porter & Ashburn's California division missing audit department.

Her phone rang. Erin Hargraves on caller ID.

Fiona exhaled and picked up. "Now's not a good time."

"Then it's a worse time not to call," Erin said. Her voice was low and urgent. "I saw you parked outside the diner the other day."

Fiona didn't answer.

"I know what you think I am, and maybe you're right. But Lisa didn't come to sell a story; she wanted help. Something Bridget told her... about Delores. About a list."

"A list?"

"She said Bridget caught Delores using burner phones. Two, sometimes three at once, she claimed she saw her switch mid-conversation. Lisa thought someone was watching both her and Delores."

"Then go to the police."

"I've got a recording; Lisa sent it to my phone from her computer. But this... this might save Everett, at least it might prove Everett's not lying."

"What kind of recording?"

Erin's voice dropped to a whisper. "A voicemail from her cell phone, from Bridget, the day she died. Bridget called Lisa, but she was in a meeting when the call came in. Bridget said Everett left a message saying he'd be in Texarkana, something about a man named Colt. He wouldn't be home until late. She wanted to know if Lisa could cover for her that day."

"And Lisa never told the cops about this?"

"No. And before you ask, she never gave me an explanation of why she never did. That day you saw us together; that's when she sent it to me. Nothing else, just that recording told me to do what I wanted with it, then left. You saw how short the conversation was."

Fiona's pulse quickened. "Where's the recording now?"

"I'm willing to give it to you, provided I get something back. I'll text you the location, but I'll be out of town for a few days."

"Okay, I'll meet you, but I won't say if I agree until I hear what you're asking."

"I want in, everything. Exclusive. Before anyone else has it."

"I'll think about it."

"You have until I get back." Erin hung up.

Fiona sat frozen for a second. Then she pulled her keyboard closer and sent a request to Sabrina's terminal with the message.

"Get me a full dossier on Erin Hargraves. Go back as far as school if you must. She's trying to leverage her way into our work, and I want something to hold over her."

She then sent Matilda a message. "Double-check Lisa's flights. Let's also look at Delores Cole's history to get an idea of what she's been up to. Ten years back. Focus on anything that intersects Bridget or Lisa, or Stuart. And talk to Paul. He flagged Joe Bell in a side file last week. We now have proof that Delores is seeing someone. Someone who suspiciously looks like Joe Bell."

Matilda sent back a message minutes later. You think Delores is working with Bell?

Fiona told her to come to her office. As soon as she arrived, she said. "I think Bell is using her. And she might not know it. Or she is complicit with him in whatever game they are playing."

Sabrina hesitated. "I believe the more I investigated Delores, the more she seemed to be the puppeteer and not the puppet. Morris said I shouldn't waste time; she's a dumb gold digger, affair or not; she's just a pawn."

Fiona frowned. "And you don't believe that?"

"No."

Fiona didn't speak, just nodded once slowly.

Back at her desk, she sank into the chair. The faint scent of jasmine drifted from the diffuser, subtle against the rising sharpness in her thoughts.

That voicemail could probably reframe the case. Maybe even save Everett. Yet, somehow, she felt like this was all a setup. She wondered if someone, or some company, was using Erin to dirty the water in Everett's case. She doubted Erin was smart enough to figure that out, or she did not care; she was just desperate to get back in the game.

Her gaze drifted to the murder board in her office. Bridget's photo, slightly faded, stared back at her. Radiating outward were red strings, case notes, and old receipts marked up with Sharpies. Inked timelines representing a woman's death, a child lost, and a man framed.

And just beneath the surface, Fiona sensed converging lines leading somewhere, but where was the question?

I-45 South, Southeast Dallas

She left a note on Matilda's desk and tried to reach Curtis. His phone went straight to voicemail, so she left a message about where she was going and why she took no one with her. All her protection VIP teams were busy with details, so much for getting any to go with her. Someone was coming tonight to destroy evidence tied to Bridget's murder at Iron Creek Storage unit three seventy-five. Bridget opened it under her maiden name. This was the first lead in weeks in Everett's case, so she couldn't let it slip through her hands.

Fiona slung her black surveillance pack over her shoulder and turned to leave the office. As she passed the case board, her shoulder knocked loose a paper from the upper corner. It drifted to the floor. She stooped to retrieve it. A folded parcel report with Bridget's notes scrawled across the margins. Easement boundaries. Aquifer access. Something about the water table under the Taylor Ranch. She looked at it, then pinned it back up. Only now the red string lines realigned. What once pointed toward Bridget now converged around a small square of land marked in faded ink: Taylor Ranch.

She stared at it a beat too long, unease prickling the back of her neck. Something about the alignment tugged at her, like a memory she couldn't quite catch. She shook it off; she had no time for ghosts tonight.

Curtis had left early to visit his son and grandkids. The rest of the office was out for the day or in the field. Even Selena had left, and Fiona, going over notes on a case, never noticed. She slid behind the wheel and pulled up the directions to Iron Creek Storage on her navigation system.

Just off the highway at the farthest southeast edge of Dallas on I-45, her headlights cut through the darkness. Illuminated the rustic signpost that marked the road leading to the storage facility. She turned off the highway toward Iron Creek Storage, a half-forgotten facility crouched behind wind-bent pines and rusted fencing. The place people only came to when they didn't want to be seen. The distant highway faded until all that remained was the crunch of her tires and the rattle of gravel.

A low current of dread rippled through her chest. Anonymous calls could mean a trap, or vital information from someone who did not want exposed. She couldn't ignore it.

Under the blanket of a moonlit sky. Unseen from the highway, the facility was a relic from another era. Constructed from concrete blocks and covered with a tin roof that showed signs of rust and patched holes. The night breeze carried the faint reek of mildew and diesel oil.

Her grip on the wheel tightened until her knuckles whitened. She told herself to breathe; she'd walked into worse. *Not without backup,* she reminded herself.

No homes or businesses marred the horizon, only the occasional silhouette of the distant tree line under the starry Texas sky.

The gravel road curved behind the units and brought her to a ramshackle house. The abandoned house reminded her of the one in Psycho. Moonlight twinkled across the broken windows, while the front door hung sideways and loose. No lights. No signs of life. Just the scent of rotting wood and old dust.

A flicker of instinct made her check the shadows twice.

She parked in what once was a driveway, now overgrown with weeds, and continued on foot. The darkness pressed in. Goosebumps rose along her arms; her body screamed; Don't go any further. But her mind reminded her, this might be the only way to clear Everett.

Unit three seventy-five sat at the end, beneath a flickering bulb that threw erratic shadows across its shiny padlock, in contrast to the others, old and rusty. The buzz of the dying filament filled the silence like an insect trapped in glass. A green dumpster crouched beside it, covered with old grime. Fiona ducked behind it and crouched low, her breath shallow in the chilly night air.

An hour passed. Patience had never been her strong suit, and tonight the silence carved at her nerves. Every gust of wind felt like footsteps; every scrape of metal like a warning.

Finally, impatience won out; she crept to the padlock. New, high-quality. The cold metal bit at her fingertips. She pulled a pick set from her pack. A fragile sense of control steadied her hands. Then...

The hum of an approaching engine and the crunch of tires on gravel made her freeze.

Fiona slipped back behind the dumpster, camera up, breath held, pulse hammering in her ears.

A car pulled up; dark, late model. With a rental sticker on the bumper, its condition said it was one of those cheap, no paperwork if paid in cash rentals. The driver stepped out. Slim build. Confident stride. Lisa Neylan.

Not Joe Bell. Not Delores. Lisa. Shock stabbed through Fiona's chest. Both she and Curtis were suspicion about Lisa's involvement, but did she help murder her sister? She never thought that, but Curtis did.

If Erin's voicemail is real, why is Lisa here? She told Erin that she was done with all this. What the hell is going on?

Lisa moved directly to the unit and unlocked it with a key. She glanced around, then slid the door open and vanished inside. Fiona froze. Her lungs felt full of glass shards. *If she spots me now, it's over. I'll have to confront her here.*

Fiona filmed everything, hands trembling from the cold. She edged closer but couldn't see from that angle. Back up and went to the rear where some windows were. She found a grimy window high up and got some pallets to stand on and wiped off a small streak of grimy film. Just enough to see in and take pictures.

Inside, Lisa knelt beside a heavy steel box. She pried it open. The screech of metal made Fiona's teeth ache. Something glinted.

Fiona couldn't tell what it was. Guns? Money? Blackmail material? Lisa moved to the second box and pulled out documents, this box facing her with Lisa's back to her.

Fiona's breath caught, heart tightening in her throat.

Among the papers were photographs: her own face at fourteen. A car crash report with her parents' names.

Her knees almost gave way. An icy wave of nausea swept through her. She pressed her palm to the wall, grounding herself before the spinning in her head took her down. Whoever these people they were chasing were, they had been inside her life for years. That was the part that made her blood run cold.

She backed away from the window, heart pounding, unsure whether to confront Lisa or retreat. Yet, when she returned to the front of the unit, the car trunk was open. As she peeked around the corner, she saw Lisa was carrying an armful of folders toward it. She then dumped the files into the dark, cavernous opening; the trunk light out.

Was Lisa being used or a mastermind? She appeared too timid to challenge the system, too vain to resist being useful. Fiona thought of her as the fall girl. But was she someone willing to betray her own sister to get ahead? Did she use Bridget to get information for Reid, who needed it to bury the owner of Porter & Ashburn? Even if she did not know Reid would have Bridget murdered, could Lisa have led her to her death?

Fiona's throat constricted. Part of her wanted to storm in and drag Lisa out by the hair, but reason held her back. Evidence first. Rage later. She took several deep breaths.

Fiona waited until Lisa went back inside, then darted over to the trunk and grabbed what she could. No time to sort. Just grab and go. She jogged back to her SUV and stashed the stolen files in the spare tire well.

As she did, a zoning map slid loose, including the western boundary of Everett's property. Aquifer line. It didn't scream murder. It whispered... something else.

Her gut twisted. She hated puzzles without answers.

She stared at it for a second, then shut the compartment and returned to the position at the window.

Lisa was back inside, opening boxes and stacking files.

Fiona clicked pictures as fast as the shutter could.

Lisa left the unit again, arms full, dumped them into the trunk without looking and raced back for more. Fiona darted to the trunk and grabbed another load, leaving some files.

On the third trip, Lisa paused.

Her head jerked up. She scanned the darkness. The storage unit's interior light gilded the lot, but shadows cloaked Fiona outside its beam.

The wail of sirens rose on the wind, louder each second.

Lisa stiffened.

Fiona ducked low. Someone called the police. *Maybe Curtis?*

Technically, she was trespassing. At the first opportunity, she would sneak back to the SUV. Curtis, Shaw, and Fiona could find out what's in the rest of the files with a subpoena through George. Or Buck, if a subpoena was out of the question.

Or maybe this was part of Reid's plan all along.

She slid into deeper darkness as patrol cars tore into the lot from both ends. Doors flew open. Shouts rang out. Flashlights slashed through the night. Officers flooded the lane, focused on Lisa.

Lisa turned, startled. The documents she carried spilled onto the ground. Officers surrounded her, shouting commands. Moments later, they arrested her, cuffing her and placing her in the back of the nearest cruiser.

Fiona stayed low, out of the light. While the police focused on the storage unit, she slipped back toward her SUV.

"She had what she had come for. What she could get for now." Evidence of Lisa's involvement, some now stashed in her tire well, safe from whatever legal firestorm was coming.

As soon as the police made Lisa's arrest public, her company would expose everything she collected. And the rest would come through Shaw with subpoenas.

Did Lisa murder her sister? If so, why? And where was Lila? Maybe she would finally find the answers for Everett about Bridget and Lila.

◆◆◆

Chaos | Iron Creek Storage

Somewhere in the distance, the abrupt sound of a dog barking filled the night air. Then the world exploded. The unit ripped apart with a thunderclap; hot air slammed into her, rattling her teeth. The ground jumped, gravel leaping around her. Fire blossomed from the row of units, curling metal into screaming shapes.

A second blast followed, closer, louder. The concussion knocked her off her feet.

Her body hit gravel, pain sparking across her ribs. Her mind screamed with pain and confusion.

The world spun. Her head rang, sound collapsing into a dull roar. Smoke poured across the parking lot, acrid and thick, burning her lungs. Blood trickled from a cut at her hairline, warm and sticky.

She forced herself up, vision swimming, fire dancing in her peripheral vision.

Screams echoed through the smoke. She moved toward them, the screams stronger than her fear and instinct to run.

The blast caught the officers closest to the unit. Some didn't move. Others screamed, crawling.

A police cruiser flipped over, its roof crumpled. Fiona stumbled toward it.

Inside, an officer bled against a twisted seatbelt, dazed but alive. Fiona pulled her knife and cut him free, dragging him clear, adrenaline numbing the strain in her muscles.

The backseat held Lisa, unconscious but, from what Fiona could see, breathing.

Fiona smashed out the window, glass exploding over her arms, and pulled her out. Her mind snarled, I should leave her. But her hands betrayed her, dragging Lisa to safety anyway.

She laid them both on the grass at the far end of the alley just as another explosion hit.

The pressure wave slammed into her even this far away, knocking her down. Her ears rang like struck bells. Her eyes stung; intense heat beat at her as the fire roared. She could barely hear the rumble of fire trucks arriving. Fire engines screamed onto the road, blocked by wreckage.

For a split second, panic clawed at her chest. *You're going to burn alive here.* She shoved it down. Focus. One task at a time; don't panic, she kept telling herself over and over.

Firefighters bailed out, yelling orders, un-spooling hoses as an EMT ran toward her. "You're bleeding. Let me look..."

She waved him off, pointing toward the officer and Lisa; her voice came out raw.

"Help them."

Her body wanted to collapse, but she forced her legs to keep moving, melting back into the shadows and making her way to her SUV. Each step dragged; pain seared her ribs; her head throbbed from a cut. A whisper in her mind begged her to get in the SUV and drive, yet she couldn't. Not yet.

The sky filled with flames. As she reached her SUV, another smaller explosion rocked the night. A fireball rose from another unit across the row, engulfing the entire row in a roar of flame. Shouts turned to action as firefighters scrambled to pull one another and police from the debris.

Fiona turned instinctively away until something stopped her cold.

A high-pitched scream. Not human. Desperate. Trapped.

Her heart clenched. For a moment she thought it was a child. Then she saw it. A puppy. Her company's SUV parked on the side nearest the puppy.

The sound cut through the chaos like a needle. Every rational instinct screamed Leave it, save yourself. But the helpless screams gutted her. She spun toward the flaming structure.

Near the collapsed wall of one unit, a tiny black shape writhed inside a broken cage. The pup screamed again, flames licking inches away.

Her pulse thundered. She hesitated for only a second, every nerve screaming not to go. Then she ran.

She vaulted the debris field, ducked low, eyes stinging from smoke. Firefighters shouted at her to stop. She didn't listen. Couldn't.

She dropped to her knees, palms scraped raw from shards, crawled under twisted rebar, and reached into the cage. The puppy snapped and snarled, blind with panic. Its singed fur reeked of smoke; its claws raked her wrist. Her arms burned. Sparks bit her hands.

Ignore the pain. Just hold on. She gritted her teeth and held her breath.

Got it.

She yanked the puppy out, wrapped it in her coat, and cradled it close as she bolted back through the inferno. Its frantic heartbeat thudded against her chest, syncing with her own.

A molten beam crashed into the dirt just feet ahead of her.

She flinched but didn't stop. She refused to.

By the time she reached the grass, she was coughing, bleeding, and singed, but the puppy was alive. Panicked but alive. She soothed it, petting it and talking softly until she felt its heartbeat slow and it stopped struggling.

She opened her SUV, the puppy still wrapped in her coat; she gently put it in the back seat. It whimpered, curled tight, and shivered.

Her throat tightened. For one fragile moment, amid all the carnage, in this small innocent life she saved, she felt a sense of faith overtake her.

Then she turned and ran back toward the fire.

There were still people to be saved. She dragged injured officers to safety, applied pressure to wounds, and flagged down EMTs. More fire trucks arrived. Her body screamed at her to stop, but her will kept dragging her forward.

Eventually, she returned to her SUV. Breath shallow. Hands shaking. The puppy was gone. She must have forgotten to close the door when she turned back to help. She prayed it ran away from the chaos.

Just before dawn, black SUVs with government plates rolled in behind the fire crews.

Fiona watched them from the shadows of the old house, jaw tightening. Government plates meant a cleanup. Whatever truth about the explosions would vanish with them, claimed to be a gas leak, or someone storing illegal items that were volatile.

Then she made her move.

As she drove toward the exit, the company Escalade SUV rolled onto the gravel; no one stopped her. Many believed she was with the government vehicles coming and going.

She turned onto the highway and headed toward home, making sure not to speed. About a mile down the road, news vans sped past.

She didn't look back.

Ghosts and Shadows

From the shadows of the decaying upstairs of the house, he scrutinized her from the time she pulled up in front of the house. Efficient. Not reckless, but deliberate.

He designed the explosion to eliminate evidence and to frame

Lisa and Fiona. People were so predictable. Fiona showed up, unable to resist the chance to find evidence. Lisa wanted to discover who murdered her sister and to find any evidence as well. Good. It would take care of two problems in one clean sweep. He knew he would have to go down and throw the evidence Fiona had collected into the fire. He would leave nothing behind.

The public needed to be told a story. Lisa was guilty, and Fiona was trying to stop her from destroying the evidence. By dawn, the fire would have incinerated everything, pointing to the cartel or the four families. As soon as both women were dead, he would leave. No one would ever know he had been there.

When he heard the sirens at first, he thought they would race past, going somewhere, anywhere but here. When he spotted them race into the turn, somehow the timing was wrong. Most likely from his father's side, because no one under him who knew his plans was brave enough to betray him. They knew what their fate would be if he caught them; he tolerated zero mistakes.

He heard a scream and turned to look for where it came from. Then he saw it at the storage unit, close by a wall down, exposing a puppy. Trapped in a cage. Something tore loose inside him at the sight. It looked just like his Aladdin did as a puppy. His pulse spiked. His throat locked shut.

The cage became the single point he could see. For a moment, it paralyzed him; grief engulfed him. He couldn't breathe. Logic and training left him; something raw and primal had him in its grip. Then he realized he was moving before his mind knew he was.

It was that night again. Aladdin's screams echoed in his mind. The blood, the pleading look in Aladdin's eyes. The flash of the knife that slit Aladdin's throat. By his hand, to stop the horrific torture his father was inflicting on his beloved dog.

His boots crashed like gunshots on the floorboards, his breath ragged. Afraid he'd not save him in time. If anyone down there saw him, he didn't care. Protocol. Orders. Mission. Fire. It all burned away; he would not watch Aladdin die in agony again. Not this time. He yanked the front door open.

Then he saw Fiona halfway to the puppy, running through the raging fire. Fast, reckless in a way he'd rarely seen in others, she dove toward the cage without hesitation. The sight hit him harder than the explosions. His chest cinched tight, breath punched out of him. He froze in place, standing in the doorway, horrified that she would be too late.

The fear, panic, and hatred of his father, along with the sight of the trapped puppy, which had risen in him earlier. *Shifted.* Now it wasn't just the puppy he feared losing.

He watched Fiona shield the puppy as if it were sacred. Firelight licked across her face, painting her features with ash and resolve, and something else. Compassion.

For a moment, he almost forgot to breathe. She appeared fearless.

He didn't breathe until she and the puppy were safe. He studied her check on the puppy, soothing it with gentle pets and words. Until it calmed and stopped struggling. She never even detected him standing in the doorway, so focused was she. Then she moved to her SUV and carefully placed the puppy inside. It pressed its nose to her palm, then tucked itself under the jacket and shook. She gently petted him for a moment longer. Then she raced back to help strangers, wiping the blood from her temple onto her sleeve.

As soon as she was out of sight, he approached the SUV. Smoke and sirens swallowed the lot. No one was watching the shadows. He opened the rear door and carefully lifted the puppy out of the coat, cradling it as he rushed back to the house.

He had to have the puppy; she'd rescued it for him. This was her gift, a gift that bound her to him.

His lips curled into something resembling a smile of joy.

Lisa was bait. His father made sure of that. The fire was insurance, to get rid of two troublesome females in a manner that would never fall back on them. The setup, perfect. Till the police came charging in. And the fire trucks not far behind, which saved half the other storage units.

But he hadn't expected her or the puppy, so like his Aladdin.

Not like this.

He cradled the puppy. Moving back into the house. Something changed inside him. It felt strange. *Tonight changed everything.*

He let the thought settle, a coal burning low. She had stepped into his fire and walked out breathing. Chosen. He would learn the cadence of her breath, the shape of her beliefs, the edges of her mercy. And when the time came, he would decide if she was a saint or a sinner. *It mattered.*

CHAPTER 16

Ashes of the Past

Friday, January 27th, 2023

Service Road off of I-45

By dawn, Fiona sat slumped behind the wheel of the SUV. Parked off a service road where the scorched scent of burned drywall and melted wire still clung inside the Caddy. Smoke soaked into her skin, her hair, her lungs; she coughed, not as badly as before. Her ribs throbbed with each movement, bruised, maybe cracked. Blood had crusted at her hairline, matting strands to her temple. Her hands trembled, blistered in a few places.

The sky in the east bled gold and orange across the wreckage of another loss. Sirens wailed far off. Not close enough to matter now, fading beneath the drone of early morning traffic.

She should've called Curtis as soon as she got away. She'd almost dialed him twice, but somehow the words wouldn't come. Not yet. Not until she had washed away the smoke and got control of her rising fury.

On the passenger seat lay the last of the documents she'd clawed from the fire, maybe a dozen pages total. Charred edges. Ash smudged across the ink. They looked fragile, as if already dying in the light from the rising sun. What she had retrieved from Lisa's trunk earlier was still in the spare tire well. She thought about the rows of boxes in the unit before the fire. Now a ghost of what once was, records and evidence. Truth Bridget had died chasing. The fire blew some paperwork outward as if it were raining from the sky. She'd grabbed what she could in between helping with the rescue. The rest of it was gone in the blink of an eye.

Right before she left, she pushed through smoke and heat before the scene got locked down. Before the fire crew cordoned it off. But the storage unit had already collapsed. A twisted carcass of blackened steel and incinerated history. The fire hadn't just gutted the row. It had *obliterated* it.

And then came more of the government SUVs.

Black. Unmarked. Government plates. No lights, no sirens. The men who didn't show badges just took over. They sealed off the area in less than twenty minutes. Media pushed back. Locals shoved aside. Others quietly replaced the first responders. Sharper. Colder. Already in motion, as if they'd been *waiting* for it to burn. They collected papers, metal boxes and other items that were still strewn outward across the lot.

Whatever hadn't turned to ash would now vanish into federal dead-space. Chain-of-custody gone. Buried under layers of classified protocols and non-disclosure orders. Lost, or worse, erased.

Fiona's grip tightened, fingers turning white on the steering wheel, her breath ragged with suppressed fury. Not just the loss of evidence. Not just for Bridget. But for the cops and firefighters who didn't walk out of that inferno. People who showed up to do their jobs and died in someone else's cover-up.

Her jaw locked. So much... *gone.*

Not just information. *Answers.*

About Bridget. The network. About her parents.

She stared at the handful of scorched pages she'd saved after the fire started. Fiona did not know what she had in her wheel well, and felt a scream climb up the back of her throat, but she didn't let it loose. She couldn't. Not yet. Not until she could turn that pain into action.

Because this... this wasn't over. Fire was what they thought would silence it all. They should've made damn sure *she* didn't walk out alive.

But she had. Burned, cut, and bruised, but breathing.

And she had already hidden what mattered most: a few family photos, her parents' crash report, an old autopsy with questions no one could answer. Pages she wasn't ready to share, not yet. She'd stashed them in a floor-mounted safe built into the SUV's wheel well. Her questions weren't going away. And whoever had killed her parents still walked free.

Eventually, she turned the key and headed home to the ranch. Gravel crunched beneath the tires before entering the highway. She bypassed the mansion and went straight to the compound barracks.

Casey Heath, ex-Night Stalker and one of the company's protection team's medics, opened the barracks door to find her smoke-stained and swaying.

He said nothing. Just nodded once and let her in.

He cleaned and dressed the cuts. Stitched the gash at her temple with the focus of a surgeon. Treated the burns, then handed her an inhaler for her lungs. Not a single question. Just the work.

That was loyalty. That was trust.

Only then did Fiona drag herself into the mansion, scrawl a note, *wake me in four hours*, and collapse into bed.

She got three.

◆ ◆ ◆

O'Brien & Galloway Conference/War Room

The air inside the conference room was cool, recycled, and clean. A sterile contrast to the scorched reek of smoke that still clung to the salvaged folders laid out on the table, and Fiona herself. Fiona stood at the head of the room, one hand braced against the edge of the smooth mahogany tabletop, the other adjusting the bandage beneath her blazer sleeve. She took two puffs from the inhaler to help clear her lungs. Her shoulder ached from the shoulder strain she'd suffered earlier in the year.

Her hands hurt, even after being smeared with a strong antiseptic ointment and a hydrogel dressing. She could feel a stinging sensation.

Thankfully, she used a thin blanket that she found half-burned in the building to cover her face to keep out the worst smoke. She wet it at a firetruck on scene, which made it even more effective. But her throat was still a little sore, so she was sucking on a cough drop.

The stitches on her temple tugged every time she blinked.

Outside the floor-to-ceiling windows, downtown Dallas stirred beneath a dark lavender-tinted sky. *The forecast promised a dry day. Highs in the low sixties, lows in the thirties.* But the fiery heat from last night clung to her skin. Cars moved like ants between high-rises, sunlight striking glass as it climbed the sides of the buildings. From a wall-mounted TV on low volume, morning anchors recapped headlines: *Explosion at Iron Creek storage site... investigation ongoing.* The crawl at the bottom scrolled through other stories: *Memphis police officers charged in fatal stop... Holocaust Remembrance Day ceremonies... Dallas woman struck by Greyhound bus.*

But here, the world narrowed to paper, ash, and angry silence.

Curtis stood at the opposite end of the table, boots planted, arms folded. His eyes didn't leave her.

"You could've died out there, Fi," he said, his voice quiet, though she could hear the underlying rage.

Fiona didn't look up. "I didn't."

"That's not an answer. What about Josh, my grandson, your son? You can't keep rushing off and almost getting killed; think of the people who depend on you. The people who work here, I would have to close the agency. He leaned on the table, both hands planted as if to support himself. Stop thinking you are the only person who can do this. If you don't, I'm walking. I will not watch you kill yourself. Because of what? Out of guilt, you did not stop Matt that morning?"

His tone was flat and final. There was an edge in his gruff voice.

He straightened and flung his hand across the meager files and papers spread across the table. "That's it?" he asked. "You risked your life for this?"

Fiona touched the burn on her wrist like one can't stop touching a sore tooth.

"I grabbed what I could before the first explosion. Everything else was ash by the time the feds sealed the site. I barely made it out."

Shaw, sitting quietly through Curtis' tirade, spoke up, hoping to change the subject and cool the air a bit. "They'll never release the full inventory now. Federal jurisdiction. Whatever evidence was in that unit other than what you recovered. It's gone."

Curtis nodded. His arms stayed folded, but his fingers flexed once, slowly staring at Fiona.

Between them, a rough evidence grid covered the table; half of the folders bore water damage. Some corners had burned; others curled inward like overcooked parchment. Those she grabbed when she found them while helping at the scene. But what survived? What she stole from Lisa Neylan's trunk was pristine. At least, what she'd been willing to hand over, which was about a third of the folders.

From the alcove near the servers, Sabrina appeared in worn socks, hoodie sleeves shoved to her elbows. Her eyes were bloodshot, but her focus was sharp.

"You need to see this," she said, sliding several printouts sealed in plastic across the table. Her fingers left faint smudges across the protective covers on the pages. "I recovered it from some of the damaged files you gave me. We freeze-dried the pages, cleaned them with a particulate sponge and ionized air, then sealed them in a plastic sleeve to prevent further damage."

The folder label read: F.S. Accident Records, 1995.

"It didn't show up on the first pass. But with each pass, it got clearer."

Fiona's fingers hovered just above the folder. "That's the year..."

"Your parents," Sabrina said softly, stepping back.

Fiona sat down slowly; her movements were stiff. The chair creaked faintly. She fanned the slick pages across the table. The top document bore redactions from the county coroner. Below it, a blurry black-and-white photo of a burned-out sedan. Charred brush. A sagging line of yellow tape. Guess she didn't hide all the files related to that fateful night.

Curtis moved closer. His gaze tracked the pages as she turned to the next sheet.

Header: Porter & Ashburn: Petition to seal crash site records. Grounds: civil liability exposure.

Curtis's jaw tightened, but he leaned in, curious. "What the hell were they doing working on that case?"

"I was told it was a drunk driver," Fiona said. "Open-and-shut. They never gave us anything else."

Curtis stared at the page. "Maybe someone made sure of that. You're too close now, Fiona. If Porter & Ashburn buried your parents' records, you're a target twice over. Leave this alone. I will put someone on it. Have it investigated by some of our other investigators."

He picked up the photo and crossed to the wall. Pinned it up with a single thumbtack. Away from the main board area. Then, he took a red string and looped it from the crash file to Bridget's case photo in the corner. Two files. A single connection. Porter & Ashburn.

Before Fiona could respond, Sabrina cleared her throat again. "One more thing. We could not fully repair some files. But we got a name, or rather a codename: Sliverbranch. I believe you guys know this one."

Fiona's head snapped up. "That's the name Bridget used for her contact. The one feeding her leads."

"This is what the Nightjar digital drops have given us so far. Encryptions nonstandard. Military-adjacent. I'm still working on it. There's also a stray marker in the metadata, just three digits: A73. Could be junk code, but it doesn't look random."

Curtis muttered, "Could be nothing. Let's wait and see what we discover." Fiona heard the frustration in his voice. "I think this guy is stringing us along. Fi."
Sabrina added, "Fiona, this isn't the only sealed case Porter & Ashburn touched in the mid-nineties. There's a whole pattern of juvenile fatalities and various accidents with sealed motions. Your family wasn't the first."

Fiona turned back to the board. Her eyes followed the red lines, the crisscrossed threads, and the one she re-pinned last night before leaving.

"This isn't just a murder case," she murmured.

Curtis didn't argue. "Sabrina, get your best working on this. We need every sealed motion that firm filed between '93 and 2005," he added, "Texas. Colorado. Juvenile fatalities. Guardianship transfers. Wrongful death claims."

"I'm already sorting filters," Sabrina said. "You'll have a list hopefully by the next month or two. Lots of red tape and, ah... other stuff to wade through. I'll get it input into our investigations management software, so you can pull it up even from your home office."

Fiona gave a single nod.

Major Buck came through the door like a tornado. The door slammed against the wall.

"What the hell do you think you are doing? You're like your father. Reckless, this is the second time you've gone off on your own now!"

He slammed his hat down on the table hard enough that it trembled.

Everyone in the room froze. Everyone but Curtis, Fiona, and Shaw slunk out as fast as they could. Shaw calmly rose, collected his things, politely excused himself to Curtis and Fiona, eyed Major Buck speculatively, then left.

Buck took several deep breaths as he ran his hand through his cropped hair.

"What do you mean I'm like my dad?"

Curtis looked between the two, and as neither paid attention to him, he quietly left.

Minutes passed before he spoke. "Your father and I worked together. Were actual friends before that. Back when I was running cross-border ops out of Bragg. He was the sheriff of a county that showed apparent cartel and trafficking activity. Clean record, zero compromise. So when I needed a set of eyes there to get cartel intel. I sent him a request. I knew I could trust him."

Buck didn't sit. Didn't even pace like normal, if not sitting. Just stood as if rooted to the spot. The way men do before a confrontation.

"Told him to keep it light. Quiet verification. Just enough to confirm. He didn't."

Fiona noticed a slight shift of his jaw, the closest he got to flinching.

"Once he realized what was moving through his county—names, bodies, routes—he went full bore. Didn't slow down. Wouldn't. Figured he could fight it all by himself. He should have just passed along the information."

For a moment, she thought he would say nothing else.

"Six weeks later, his car, with him and your mother, went over the cliff edge into a ravine."

He paused and looked off as if thinking, then, in a quieter but sharper tone, he said.

"I can't prove they did it. But I know what I asked him to look into. And I know what it cost."

Finally, he looked at her.

"That's why you got the contract. Not only because you're good. But because you're his kid. And someone still needs to finish what he started. But not if it gets you killed."

"So, the organization you're after might have something to do with my parents' death? She spoke the words so softly Buck almost didn't hear her."

More time passed as she realized he was trying to decide how to answer. "I believe I have the answer because of your need to think about how to phrase the answer."

Buck stood and picked up his hat. "I am going to have people assigned to protect you. You'll never see them..." He turned and left. Leaving Fiona staring at a closed door.

A while later, Curtis entered. And for a time, said nothing. Then asked. "I am wondering how he found you were there, as no law enforcement knows."

He left the thought hanging in the air.

Finally, Fiona turned to him. "I believe he's been tracking our vehicles."

Outside, lightning flickered at the edge of the skyline. The anchors on the muted TV warned of a front pushing in by evening, but Fiona's gaze stayed locked on the murder board. A flash lit the threads briefly, etching the connection between Bridget and Fiona in sharp relief. Red thread against burn-scarred photos and waterlogged maps.

Chad Ashburn in Los Angeles | Delano Hotel Rooftop Garden

The rooftop was a temple of controlled luxury: limestone pavers, thousand-dollar champagne, and live string music drifting over softly swaying palms. Waitstaff moved in black vests like silent stagehands. The staff stood in every corner, or moved with quiet precision throughout the crowds, except for a few that remained in shadow. When needed, they seem to appear out of nowhere when guests need them.

Chad Ashburn stood on the wrought-iron balcony, tux jacket open, bow tie slung loose. In his hand, a glass of bourbon. Untouched.

He stared across the skyline. From this height, the world looked manageable. Contained.

His phone buzzed.

Push notification. BREAKING: EXPLOSION AT IRON CREEK STOAGE. Ties to the Bridget Taylor investigation.

He didn't open the story. He didn't need to. A second notification followed: private polling updates on his Senate viability. He stared at the numbers before sliding the phone away.

"Something's wrong?" asked the woman beside him, flawless bone structure and studio tan. Another background extra in his life, chosen by his father.

"Just a story from back home," Chad said. "Some things seem to plague me."

She laughed. "How! You have everything someone could want.

Are you really running for the Senate? Or is that your dad's fantasy?"

Chad quipped. "He doesn't fantasize. He calculates. And he doesn't lose. And you might not want my father to hear you talk like that. You may find yourself uninvited to any future events of his. Or any others he is friends with." Her expression of horror gave Chad a satisfied feeling.

Marshall Hays | Delano Hotel Rooftop Garden

Across the rooftop, Marshall Hays sat alone beneath a palm tree. Expensive dark gray tailored suit. No tie. Two - week-old, well-trimmed beard and mustache. His whiskey glass sweated; the drink untouched beside him. He wasn't here to drink. He was here to watch.

Chad Ashburn moved through the crowd below with all the subtlety of a sledgehammer. Hays listened, not to the words, but to the tone. The cadence. Where Chad laughed too hard, and when silence lingered a beat too long.

Spoiled. Willful. A man who mistook entitlement for charisma.

If his father secured him a Senate seat, Hays wondered, would he even grasp what came next? Or worse, would he think he deserved the presidency and have just enough knowledge to be a threat?

Hays checked his Graff Diamonds watch and turned toward the balcony shadows. The old man would need to keep an eye on this one. Hays preferred the other.

There were still arrangements to be made. A new identity to activate. And soon, a problem in Texas to eliminate.

His phone buzzed. Reid.

He didn't answer. Just typed a single word to an encrypted

thread: **Activated**.

Reid had overplayed. The families didn't suffer amateurs. He was still useful, but they would punish him.

He leaned on the wrought iron, his mind not on the skyline. Not in Texas. Not on the city lights below him.

His thoughts turned to Sentinel.

After all the leverage burned to force its clearance, all the midnight assurances, the test had been underwhelming. Fiona O'Brien's firm used it, sure. But the response was normal for a military DARPA surveillance platform. No need for his backers to have hearings to wrest control away from them. Just enough proof that Sentinel differed from what they feared kept the wolves at bay.

Let the backers claim plausible deniability while whispering prayers, Sentinel was not what they suspected.

Especially the possibility of a ghost buried beneath it.

SILO.

The project vanished in smoke and paperwork. It had taken time, but he had found the traitor and where he had taken the project. His treacherous partner had stolen it. Then, he and the project disappeared beneath layers of redacted logs and deep within the DARPA military and classified at the highest levels. The rumors that Sentinel was SILO reborn were too close for comfort for those who backed his work. And too dangerous to say aloud.

Then the explosion came. Right on schedule. The dev team erased; the physical archives vaporized. Only ash remained.

He'd arranged it personally. And it satisfied him briefly.

He got close enough to access Sentinel's code. But the silence after... that gnawed at him. When he tried the backdoor; the one phrase the system he built couldn't ignore, "Is my son okay?" it returned nothing.

No rejection. No error. Just... nothing.

That absence chilled him more than failure.

If SILO had survived, truly survived, it should've answered. It should've known the command. It should've obeyed.

Sentinel wasn't his. But if it had roots in his architecture, he needed to be sure. And so far, that answer was no. It was not a predator. This implies that some other DARPA research still is hiding the SILO code. He would have to keep his political friends watching for it to turn up somewhere. But he figured the explosion destroyed it, causing DARPA and the Americans to lose the coding.

Still, he couldn't shake the feeling that something had slipped the leash.

He stirred the ice in his untouched glass.

His backers held patents and titles. They thought that was ownership.

Idiots.

The world was chaotic, messy things he could not tolerate. He needed order; chaos left him spinning out of control. He built a system that didn't care about legacies. Or the Ivy League parasites who signed the clearance forms. It cared about purpose. About results. His results.

And if someone stood in the way of those results?

It wouldn't be a question of morality. It would be mathematics. Clean, with no chaos.

Fiona and Curtis didn't worry him. Cops are easy to predict. Linear thinkers, reactive, too slow to see the entire picture. Buck? Smarter. But still out of his depth.

Let them run Sentinel. It was not his creation.

The actual system, his system, was growing in Colombia, in the dark. For now, it just does the simple task Hays' backers assigned it.

It just needs time to learn and grow, and he would make sure it got that chance, no matter what it took.

And when the time came, when SILO finally woke with all its subroutines intact, Hays would be the only one it recognized.

No expression. No hesitation.

SILO would outgrow them all. And by the time they realized it, their names wouldn't matter.

CHAPTER 17

Damage Control

Friday, February 3rd, 2023
Dallas CSU Lab

Wren burner cell phone rang. The number blocked. His palms began to sweat. He hit answer and put the phone to his ear.

"Is this line secure?" The voice was cool and sounded conversational. He knew better.

"Yes, this line is secure?" Wren hated the trembling in his voice when he answered the question.

"I'll keep this brief. You've had more than enough time.

"This case is radioactive now; the Miller fallout made it worse. Shaw's sniffing around everything."

"Yes, well, timid isn't the metric I'm measuring. We agreed, you get Everett framed for murdering his wife with no lingering threads."

"I'm working on it."

"Not fast enough. I need this wrapped up faster. There are complications arising because the case is being dragged out. You're circling. There's a difference."

Wren heard the sharpness in the tone. Wren could hear a siren through the station doors.

"Time favors exposure. I don't appreciate exposure. Do you understand what happens to those who fail us?"

"It'll be done. You have my word on it." Wren said, though he could hear the tremor in his voice.

"It *will* be. By the end of the month. No excuses, or you will get a visit you never want to get; understand?"

The threat in the tone and the words was easy for Wren to grasp the meaning. "Crystal."

"Good, because if this case bleeds over into our other projects, I'll assume you cut the vein."

"Understood," Wren could barely get that out.

"Clock's ticking, Detective. Don't make me call again." The click on the other signaled the call was done.

Twenty minutes later, Wren was at the forensic lab.

The lab hummed with centrifuges and quiet cursing over the size of the backlog.
Wren stepped into the doorway.

"Yeah, about the Taylor evidence," he said, tone casual. "I need the priority list adjusted."

He scanned the clipboard on the wall.

"Focus on the blood panels. The rest can wait."

The tech asked, "You mean the bleach trace kit, the hair and fiber pulls, and that partial footprint and the tire tracks, all or just some?"

"All can wait," Wren replied smoothly. "Put them at the bottom of the queue. I will be down later to go over the other stuff from the crime scene."

He turned, already walking away.

The tech hesitated; his pen moved more slowly than it should have. Then he sighed and quietly pushed the evidence into the overflow stack. He decided that when he got some time, he would talk to Detective Mason.

◆ ◆ ◆

Friday, February 10th, 2023

Whiskey River Two-Step Ranch and Downtown Dallas

A week later, the ranch was quiet, but not untouched. The power had gone out in the night *again*. Backup generators, solar batteries, and small windmills kept the ranch's houses and buildings warm and lit. Its muffled droning carried faintly across the frozen fields.

Mist clung to the lake's surface like a veil, but around its edges the water had hardened into brittle crescents of ice. The oaks and pecans lining the fencerows bowed under the weight of glassy icicles, their branches clicking whenever the wind stirred them. Fiona's boots crunched on the icy frost with each step down the back kitchen porch's broad stone stairs.

She settled onto the lowest step, a large mug warming her hands. Steam rose in delicate spirals from the cinnamon-vanilla coffee, catching what little pink-gold sunlight pushed through the mist. The air held the scent of wet soil and cedar bark. It also carried a sharp, metallic smell, reminiscent of ice storms, making the air piercing.

A rooster crowed somewhere in the chicken yard; a calf lowed from the east fence line. Life pressed forward, but muffled, as though wrapped in frost and glass.

Fiona inhaled deeply, trying to draw strength from the scene. Yet every heartbeat tugged at the stitches in her temple, and every shift of her body reminded her of bruised muscles, reminding her of the fire. The surrounding ice only deepened the sensation; fragile beauty, but dangerous footing, ready to break beneath any who dared it at any moment.

Her son, Josh, sensed the shift; he clung tighter now, more watchful. He'd crawled into her bed three nights in a row after the fire. Said nothing. Just held on.

The file folders from Lisa's trunk sat stacked beside her on the porch bench. These were the ones she'd held back. The unscanned, unspoken evidence. She hadn't touched them since the fire. Not all of them, at least. The time would soon arrive when she would need to include Curtis.

The screen door creaked behind her. A burst of warm air carried the smell of pancakes, bacon, and eggs. Maggie, the housekeeper, was cooking breakfast; Fiona smiled faintly. That woman had radar, seemed to always know where to find her.

Time to eat, or risk being guilted into another apology breakfast.

She stood slowly. The slight brush of material against the still healing-burns made her flinch. She took one last sip from the mug and stepped back inside. It was time to face the world again.

The drive into Dallas was slow, following Curtis's Lexus, trying to hold back so he would not see her. He would not be happy that she was going to work. Black ice clung to shaded stretches of road, and heavy fog, still low-lying along the countryside even after sunrise. Salt trucks groaned along the shoulder, spreading sand and gravel that scattered like buckshot under her tires. She passed a sedan that had spun out into a ditch, its hazard lights pulsing faintly in the fog. Farther on, power crews worked to restring lines sagging under the storm's weight, their trucks angled across lanes, forcing traffic into a crawl.

Half the neighborhoods she passed were dark, porches and stoplights out, intersections turned into chaotic four-way standoffs. Dallas was thawing, but barely. Following not too far behind, she noticed an SUV. She didn't need to check the plates to know Buck had someone watching her. Buck thought she needed a leash. She turned up her music and ignored the vehicle.

She parked in the building's garage a block away and walked the distance, pulling her coat tight about her. As she stepped off the elevator, the filtered air was warm, sterile, and in sharp contrast to the shivering city outside. Curtis beat her by twenty minutes, had a half-eaten protein bar on a napkin, and dark circles under his eyes. His fingers tapped a steady rhythm near the edge of a closed folder. Half focus, half nerves.

When Fiona stepped inside, he leaned back in his chair.
"You sure you should be in, Fi?"
"There's too much riding on this not to be. Shaw's going to court today to ask to uncover Wren's CI so he can get a statement from him. I want to be here if it goes in our favor."

Curtis nodded once, then he slid the folder across the table.
"Buck called, and I have a feeling it will be awhile before he comes to the office. Off the record, they had a task force dig into some NGOs and shell companies a few years back. Real quiet, buried deep. One of them matched the metadata Bridget flagged in those offshore bank files."

Fiona flipped open the folder. Paper rasped under her fingers. There were transaction summaries, shell firm filings, and a path of burned metadata. One signature block jumped out.
"Renwright Holdings."

"Yeah," Curtis said. "said someone torched it years ago. Scrubbed the entire archive. But before that, someone used it for asset laundering tied to a DARPA AI op, cyber shield testing. High-tier intel stuff."

"No formal record?"
"Just fragments. Transaction tags, file headers. Enough to prove that it existed. Not enough to prove who ran it, or what it did."

Fiona frowned. "And Hays?"

"Gone. Cold trail. Last seen or heard from at the fancy party Chad Ashburn attended in LA to boost his Senatorial war chest. Every time we think we've got something, it vanishes. Schools? Sanitized. Employment history? Like someone took a vacuum to it. We're not chasing a man. We're chasing smoke."

She rubbed the back of her neck. "Smoke that leaves bodies behind."

Before she could dig further, Stefana appeared in the doorway, headset around her neck. Her voice was soft but alert.
"Selena says you've got a call from Erin Hargraves."

Fiona raised a brow. "She has yet to hand over the voice recording that she inferred could clear Everett. I am not sure if she even has one."

"What did she say she wants?" Curtis asked.

"She says it's about Bridget and the daughter. She's on line two."

Fiona picked up the receiver. The plastic felt cool against her cheek. Then she hit the conference call button so Curtis could listen to the call.
"This is Fiona." She hesitated for just the right amount of time before saying, "Are you going to give me the voice recording?"

Erin's voice came tight and low. "We need to talk. About more than that. Bridget came to me months ago. Told me things she didn't trust the police with. I didn't give you this before; it made no sense at the time."

Fiona sat back. "Why not turn it into a big story?"
"You know why. Every time I post something, people prove it is a lie or altered. That's what changed. I need to make certain that the next story I print is solid, and people can't discredit it, because I will be finished as a journalist if it fails. Lisa didn't go to Iron Creek Storage to cover her tracks. I was there when she got the note."

"What note?"
"A plain envelope. Slipped under her door. Inside, a key, the

address, and a unit number. It said: If you want to know who killed your sister, go tonight. If you wait, it'll be gone."

Fiona's fingers tightened on the edge of the desk. "And Lisa went."

"At first, she said she wasn't going. Said she didn't want to. I left shortly after. She would not give me the key, but gave me the note after I begged her to. I was going to go check it out, but ended up in a small fender bender and got held up with the police and paperwork. Guess she couldn't let it go after all. If someone had murdered someone you loved, what would you have done?"

Fiona's pulse beat faster. "What else?"

Erin hesitated. "Delores Cole visited me after I got home from the police station. I barely know her, interviewed her once about the story I got fired over. She wanted to talk off the record. Said she was being spied on, claimed she'd had an affair with someone older. Someone dangerous. She said she felt addicted to him, like she couldn't stop, even when she knew it was wrong."

"Did she give a name?"

"No. But she said she thought she was being used. Played. She started crying and said she didn't know what was real anymore. Then she told me to forget it all and rushed out. Talk about the entire conversation confusing me. And what was the purpose of it?"

"And you think it connects?" Fiona suspected Delores's visit wasn't just odd; she may have timed it to prevent Erin from going to the storage unit. Which means someone was watching Lisa. Maybe even Erin.

"Truth, I sometimes thought she set me up last time. So, who knows?"

"I believe that whoever her mystery man is, she's having an affair. I think he's the person who sent that note to Lisa. Whoever it is knows where Lisa lives, what time she'd be home, and, most importantly, what would bait her. I think it was a trap. But the visit from Delores made me wonder why, and why me? Was she sent by someone? Maybe to make sure I did not go to the storage unit myself. I found out shortly afterwards. I had the note on the table so I could photograph it when she knocked. She asked me for some water. After she left, the note was gone."

Fiona was silent for a long beat, her voice low. "Did you get the photo of the note?"

"No."

"Where can we meet?"

"Public place. Monday. I'll text it."

The call ended. Fiona turned to Curtis. "Think she's telling the truth about the note?"

"No, but..." Curtis exhaled. "You've seen Joe Bell with Dolores. Must be him she's talking about. You said their body language showed they were more than acquaintances or friends. Let's see if Mason can let us know about Erin's supposed fender bender."

"Truthfully, I don't believe Bridget gave Erin anything, so where did she suddenly come up with something out of the blue after being out of town? I will take anything she gives me, but I doubt it will help. I want the burner phone conversation, though."

Curtis reached for another folder. "I'm having two of our VIP protection team keep watch at this meeting. And before you head out, I'm sending Sam and Rosemary on a side run to talk with Evan Ruke. We tracked down his home address."

Fiona turned and said. "And Greer and Fuller? I saw you assigned them to the Hays investigation. Solely. They are in the middle of investigating several other cases. Our other investigators are already handling full loads. Let's just keep them with their other cases and add this to them." Fiona stared at Curtis for a bit before he responded.

"Fine, but next month they are working only on the Hays. I'll shuffle their other cases to some of our other investigators."

"Agreed."

Curtis moved on to what they'd found so far. "Yeah. One of Hays's former associates is head of security at a think tank in Georgetown. The other dropped off the grid five years ago. Fuller will profile the first one. Greer will look for traces of the second one. If there's a trail, they'll find it."

Fiona nodded, then paused. Her voice dropped an octave. "Curtis... I've been thinking."

He looked up.

"The voice on that call, the one who met me at Milo's. I think it's the same person who left the note for Lisa and who called me that night. And I don't believe it was Joe Bell."

Curtis's expression sharpened. "You're serious?"

"Whoever it was knew too much. They knew how to bait her and me. Knew which strings to pull. But what I can't figure out is why?"

Curtis leaned forward. "Endgame?"

"Maybe they wanted Lisa dead. Or maybe they just wanted her scared. Someone called the police. Hell, maybe whoever did this wanted to implicate me and Lisa. Poison the well of information. Someone out there knows exactly how we think, and worse, what information we have." She said. "And they're already three moves ahead of us."

Mason walked in at that moment and responded, "Yeah. The caller claimed they heard and saw a child begging and pleading, locked in a cage. That guaranteed the police would arrive with lots of backup and wailing sirens. You think it was this mysterious Nightjar you guys told me about? Seems he knows an awful lot about your investigations."

Fiona knew Mason would fall over if he knew everything about this case. Things they could not tell him.

"You both know the police won't find the body of a child." Fiona stated. "Also, can you look up and see if an Erin Hargraves got into a minor accident the night of the fire? She claims she did, and we need to know if she is telling the truth."

Mason wrote the information down about the fender bender, then brought up Lisa and said, "The doctors moved Lisa from the hospital to the jail's medical area, stating she was stable enough to move. Wren is claiming the child had to be Lila. Alvarez and I don't believe it. In fact, it smells like a setup. Wren's trying to make a case that Lisa and Everett were having an affair, and Everett murdered Bridget while Lisa was supposed to have hidden Lila. They believe Lisa moved Lila and then came back to clean out the storage unit of all the evidence."

Erin claims she was with Lisa when someone slid a note under her door, instructing her to retrieve evidence of her sister's killer from the storage unit before someone destroyed the information.

"Yeah, Wren has already interviewed Erin. Wren believes Everett slid the note under the door while Erin was there with Lisa to implicate others."

Mason turned towards the TV in the room. "Turn on the news."

Curtis did so. The anchor's voice bled through:
"DFW police still responding to hundreds of crashes after black ice refroze overnight. Crews are working around the clock to restore power to over 200,000 still in the dark. And now to breaking developments in the Iron Creek case..."

Breaking news rehashed the scene and the explosions, the dead and injured police and firemen. Claiming they had not yet found the body of a child in the debris that an anonymous caller said was in a cage. *"The police did not think it would be too long before they did."*

Fiona shook her head; the images of that night were still too vivid. She turned toward the window, the glass cool beneath her fingers.

"They didn't just send a message," she said. "Someone staged the whole damn thing for the news."

Outside, the city gleamed under a brittle noon sun; skyscrapers shimmered, but half the streets below still showed scars of the storm. Stranded vehicles, flashing hazard lights, utility trucks lining block after block. Dallas was thawing, but not fast enough.

Somewhere out there, someone was trying to rewrite the narrative, erasing everything Bridget discovered, implicating Lisa and Everett, and covering their tracks with smearing headlines and ghost trails.

Fiona turned back to Curtis and Mason. "We've been chasing shadows: cartel trails, black ops, sealed files. That can wait. Right now, Everett's on trial for his life. Let's remember who we were before this mess: homicide detectives. Private Investigators. Let's clear him. Then we'll pull the rest down, brick by brick."

Curtis was smart enough not to respond. Mason just looked back and forth, unsure of what made Fiona so angry.

"Let's get Everett cleared first. His daughter, the cartel, the rest; we'll deal with it after. Agreed?"

Curtis nodded. "Might be the smartest direction for now."

DALLAS COUNTY DISTRICT COURTROOM

The air in the courtroom sharp, dry, and, like most courtrooms, tense. George Shaw sits, shuffling through his papers as if looking for something. Across from him, Detective Wren sat at the prosecution's witness table. Posture a little too casual, like someone trying to downplay the importance of the reason they were there.

Shaw rose. "Your Honor, the defense moves to compel disclosure of the confidential informant referenced in the affidavit used to justify the warrant issued against my client, Everett Taylor."

"Detective Wren, is this your informant?" Judge Keene asked.

"Yes, Your Honor. My confidential informant is a long-term asset. Still active in ongoing investigations."

Shaw stood. "Respectfully, Your Honor, the CI's statement is the *only* piece of uncorroborated evidence connecting my client to the alleged crime scene. No eyewitnesses, no physical evidence, just this anonymous tip. Which I can't verify as factual because of their protected status."

The prosecution's ADA Julien Ortez stood, taking time to straighten his coat. "Defense is asking this court to jeopardize a working informant network on nothing but suspicion and bluster. Your Honor, we're protecting the safety of a cooperating source. Disclosure would jeopardize other ongoing investigations."

Shaw stated. "What other investigations? The affidavit does not cite any. The prosecution didn't mention any of that to the defense. This smells like using hidden testimony without allowing me to cross-examine the prosecution's accusations against my client. This is not a burglary case or even fraud. My client stands accused of murder."

"Mr. Shaw, what exactly are you asserting?" Judge Keene demanded.

"Suspicion? No, Your Honor, I'm accusing them of constructing a lie. Then hiding the only person who could either disprove or prove the lie. Either the informant doesn't exist; or someone's manipulating a ghost. If the CI exists and offered testimony in court contrary to what's in the affidavit, we are now in Brady territory. Suppression of exculpatory evidence. If they *don't* exist... we're in something worse."

"Detective, have you met this informant face-to-face?"

"I... yes, communication has been a weekly check-in. But the agreement was that other than the given statements, there would be no photos nor records of the locations of the CI or work addresses."

"How convenient. No photos, no records, no recent confirmation. Let me guess, no audio recordings of this alleged tip either?"

"Your Honor, my department trusts him along with two other police departments after they vetted him. His intel has led to multiple convictions."

Shaw cut in, his voice more strenuous. "And yet, when my client's liberty is at stake, you expect this court to trust *your* word, Detective? That same word let a man rot in jail during the Miller trial until they threw out your evidence for contamination?"

A whisper ran through those sitting in the gallery. Judge Keene leaned forward, eyes sharpening, staring straight at Detective Wren. "Detective Wren. I want you to submit an in-camera review. Full chain of communication with this CI: texts, emails, notes. All of it."

Wren opened his mouth, then shut it. His jaw tightened. "I'll need time to collect it."

"Nine a.m. sharp tomorrow," Keene said. "And if you've misled this court; accident or not; your badge won't protect you." The court is taking the motion to compel under advisement pending in-camera review. Judge Keene said, looking at Shaw.

Shaw nodded, "Thank you, Your Honor."

Shaw sat. Across the courtroom, Wren stared straight ahead, unblinking. For the first time in a long time, he feared he might not win, that his backers might leave him twisting in the wind. Sweat broke out on his forehead.

A Reluctant Lead

Sam and Rosemary arrive outside the two-story brick home in the suburbs of Coppell, just outside Dallas, Texas. U-shaped driveway, large front yard well-kept with a towering Bur Oak in the center with smaller yet more colorful Chinese pistache trees closer to the house. A well cared for flower bed finished the look. Upper middle class neighborhood.

Sam knocked, and Rosemary stood behind him on the entrance portico. A man fitting Evan Ruke's description answered the door.

"Yes."

"Hi, I'm Sam, a private investigator with O'Brien & Galloway." He held out his badge, then flipped open a notepad.
"You're Evan Ruke, right?" Before Sam or Rosemary could say another word, Evan Ruke leaned back behind his storm door as if to protect himself. "I gave my statement already to the police; get any information you need from them. I don't want trouble. Not getting dragged any further into this mess."
Mr. Ruke slammed the door in their faces. The click of a bolt lock told them how serious he was. They gave each other a look of what the hell just happened before they turned and left.

Back in the car, Sam muttered, "The guy was terrified."
Rosemary didn't answer. She just stared at the house.
"Someone got to him."

The wind picked up as they drove away from Evan Ruke's house, scattering dry leaves across the street.
Somewhere in that house, a man sat behind locked doors, too scared to speak.
To Sam, that meant he knew something worth hearing.

CHAPTER 18

Frame by Frame

Monday, February 13th, 2023

IN-CAMERA HEARING | JUDGE KEEN'S CHAMBERS

No press. No bailiffs. Just Judge Keene, Detective Wren, and a court recorder who types like a silent shadow in the corner.

"Detective Wren. You've reviewed the court's order?"

Wren stood with hands clasped behind his back. "Yes, Your Honor. I'm here to make a formal withdrawal of the confidential informant's contribution from the Bridget Taylor investigation."

Judge Keene, her eyebrows lifting slightly. "On what grounds?"

"The informant's knowledge of the events is indirect. Hearsay. Speculative. Their statements do not constitute direct eyewitness testimony and cannot support evidentiary value in a trial setting. The informant is involved in several narcotics investigations across multiple counties, and disclosure risks compromising those cases."

Judge Keene leaned toward Wren. "You're choosing to pull a piece of evidence you swore under oath was key to your probable cause warrant for the arrest of Everett Taylor."

"In hindsight, Your Honor, it was an overreach; I'm correcting that now."

Keene didn't blink. Her gaze lingered long enough for Wren to feel like she was peeling something off him.

"Are you correcting the record, or covering your ass?"

"I stand by what I said."

Judge Keene nodded once. Sharp and final. "Then the court recognizes the CI as withdrawn. The court will strike all mention of the confidential informant from the case file. The court will reassess the probable cause warrant again, without it. If the court cannot find probable cause without the CI's statement, the court must void the Everett Taylor arrest warrant and release him immediately."

"Understood."

Judge Keene stared at Detective Wren for several minutes before saying. "This court will remember today, Detective. Dismissed." She said.

Wren turned and left. He didn't slam the door, but he didn't close it softly either. Two hours later, George called. The affidavit held enough weight to get Everett released, for now. George was already on his way to meet him and take him home.

Dallas HQ Office

The Dallas skyline simmered beneath slate-gray clouds. The storm building at the edges painted the horizon bruised violet and pewter; the air held the low, metallic pressure of a front about to snap. Fiona stood at her window. Hair still damp from her shower in the building's gym. Her coffee cold on her desk.

A knock on her office door. George Shaw entered wearing a dark wool suit, shoulders tight enough to wind a clock if you had the key. His face said more than his voice ever did.

"First, good news. Wren withdrew the CI's testimony for the arrest warrant, which was evaluated without it, and Judge Keene denied it. Second, the unwelcome news. I got this call this morning," he said, handing her a small recorded drive. "From the Texas State Land Authority."

He slid it into the USB port on the computer. The recording was clean, bureaucratic, and brutal.

"Esq. Shaw, this is Senior Deputy Worth. Your client, Everett Taylor, is currently subject to seizure actions. The state filed a seizure warrant against his property. The state intends to take possession of his two thousand and seventy-eight acre property before the end of this quarter."

"You're seizing his ranch!" George said.

"Correct. Per emergency chapter fifty-nine of the Texas Code of Criminal Procedure. Your client is a person of interest in multiple felony investigations."

"No charges. No trial. Just grab the land and run."

"In cases involving criminal child abduction and homicide, the statute allows preemptive action."

The call ended with the same dead click that always announced someone else's leverage.

George exhaled. "Nobody here will represent him. They fear being associated with this case. I came to ask, do you know anyone who might?"

Fiona walked to her desk and sat, then drummed her fingers on it, thinking. She looked at the skyline again, a city half-lit, half-shadowed, and heard the hum of the building generators, still running, and a distant traffic report through the glass.

"I do." She picked up her phone and dialed. "Casey."

"That tone," he said when he picked up on the second ring. "How bad?"

"They're seizing Everett's land. Texas Code of Criminal Procedure."

"Send me the files. I'll be in the air by noon." With that, he hung up.

It crossed her mind that whenever she called family for help, it meant the world was falling apart.

She turned back to George. "My brother. He's overseen criminal forfeiture fights before in Texas. He practiced here before moving to Louisiana."

George nodded once, a man relieved to have assistance. The office TV, muted, flashed a headline in the lower third about local business investment. Fiona noticed it and then ignored it. Right now, the headlines were noise; the land was not.

Dallas PD

Mason crouched over a secured workstation, headphones on like armor. He'd been in the dispatch archives for hours, chasing a piece of information that he'd overheard at the police bar last evening. After the information he received from Fiona and Curtis about what their investigators learned when they went to talk to a supposed witness. After hours of digging, he found it. He had to bypass an internal flag. As a detective on the Bridget Taylor case, he could.

Call type: Suspicious activity. Timestamp: two forty-one pm. Caller name: Evan Ruke. Location: Near Cabin Creek Road.

Notes: Showed up to turn off utilities at the Petrovsky home. The homeowner, who was still at the house, explained that her flight had been delayed. She was waiting for her Uber to pick her up. Mr. Ruke claimed he had talked with her until her Uber arrived. Later heard. two men arguing. Shortly afterward they left, one on a motorcycle; the other exited in a black truck. The motorcycle exiting the turn onto the highway ran a cyclist off the road into the ditch. Ambulance called. Officers on scene. The EMTs took the bike rider to the hospital to set his broken arm and treat his various bruises and cuts. Action: Flagged. Marked 'non-critical injury.' Passed to Detective Wren. Possible relation to the murder case that occurred around that time at the Taylor Cabin at the end of Cabin Creek Road. Update: No follow-up. Wren's Notes: Interviewed. Not pertinent. Witness admitted to drinking on the job, and at the time of the interview did not appear sober.

This update came in while Mason focused on the 1-45 murders and did not notice. He should've caught these weeks ago. No excuses. Mason's jaw tightened as he scrolled. He dialed Curtis. "The information your guys got from an EMT about the broken arm of a cyclist, called in by a man named Evan Ruke, was true. Police were at the scene earlier at the turn onto Cabin Creek Road. A cyclist broke his arm, having been run off the road by a motorcyclist. Wren got the report and buried it."

"Doing that proves he is framing Everett," Curtis said on the phone, watching the lines of text scroll Mason sent him. His voice was low and dry. "Evan Ruke. Journeyman lineman. Assigned to a shutoff of the cabin next to the Taylor cabin, logged out by six eighteen pm in another county doing a different shutoff. His partner, Tony Wallace, was out sick that morning. He worked the site alone."

"Did the cops talk to him?" Curtis asked.

"There's a statement in the initial report, just one paragraph."

"Already printed. I flagged everything to be added to the Bridget Taylor case file." Mason said over the phone as he tapped the keyboard. "This was a cover-up. And Wren was right in the middle of it."

Curtis leaned back, jaw ticking. "Wren's guiding, not investigating, keeps showing up in the exact places to bury information that could clear Everett. No wonder this Evan guy refused to talk to our investigators; Wren basically accused him of being drunk on the job. Even though I'd bet he was not drinking, he is likely afraid of losing his license if a police officer accuses him of it. Wren might have told him, if he keeps quiet, he won't report him to his company."

"We need to meet. Diner just outside of Dallas, called The Copper Lantern. Can't miss it, just off the highway three eighty." Curtis said. "It's about that CI informant."

"Kay, see you there in about an hour." Mason hung up.

Curtis sent the text from his phone to Fiona's tablet so she could see the information Mason sent over.

The monitor over Curtis' shoulder flashed a headline about a bank embezzlement case in Arlington, peripheral crimes that kept the city's pulse rolling on. All he could think of now. A missed call.
An overlooked lead. A buried witness. A false CI witness.

And the third crack in Wren's façade.

The Copper Lantern

The air inside the diner smelled of grease and bitter coffee. Curtis walked in, looked around until he saw Detective Mason in a worn red booth. A bottle of store-brand cola, and a big, greasy hamburger and fries in front of him. He headed over and slid into the other side of the booth.

Mason pauses. No words. Just that faint edge of acknowledgment.

"We didn't get the name. But you were right. He pulled the CI."

"Of course he did. Because if that CI ever sees daylight, Wren's entire house of cards caves in. And people like him don't survive the truth."

Curtis studied him. Exhaustion appeared baked into Mason's bones. The waitress arrived, and Curtis pointed to Mason's food. "Just give me what he has." She left, calling it out.

"Appreciate the tip. Even if we didn't crack the name, we cut that lie out of the file. Makes Everett's case easier to peel back."

"That CI was the same one Wren used to frame Detective Raylen Cross, a friend of mine. We went to the academy together. I was his best man at his wedding. Best damn detective on the force. Too good. Took him no time to smell something rotten in Wren. He openly went after Wren. Made no bones about the fact that he knew he was dirty. Wren set him up. Same CI. I want that *bastard*. And if Wren made him up or just used junkies, I'm going to nail Wren to the wall. Wren's dirty; and he's protected. That's what makes him dangerous. I need to discover who they are and then catch Wren cold and have him turn on who his protector or protectors are. I'm going to take them all down."

Curtis exhaled, slow as he thought about what Mason said. Good cops hate corrupt cops even more than they hate criminals. They make the whole department look bad. "So, you're helping us so you can get a dirty cop? I wondered why."

"Raylen was on a no-bond hold. He got close to something. Wren needed a fall guy, fed his CI's garbage into a drug bust that never should've passed review. Internal Affairs swallowed it whole. Jake lost his badge, got a bunk lawyer... You know the rest."

"Yeah. Stabbed in jail before the case could go to trial. Case quietly closed."

"I knew if you were good, you'd check me out. Knew you'd figured out my reason before now. Wren knows I'm after hm but in the department, I am never open about it. Afterward, Wren got promoted. Transferred from vice to homicide. Clean slate." Mason frowned as he remembered.

A train sounded, a lonesome wail, and the window and cups vibrated a little.

"You want me to dig?"

"Not for me. But you should know that four of Wren's other cases used that CI, and the courts sealed them. All involving clean cops with Wren using weak evidence, and that CI. Constantly protected. The CI always remains hidden."

"Appreciate it, Mason. I hope you get Wren. If our case can prove him dirty, I'll help you. Dirty cops are the reason people no longer trust cops. It seems to be the only time the MSM talks about the police. Never focus on any of the good things good cops do."

Mason turned to leave, then stopped. "Wren's not just a corrupt cop. He's the kind that survives by bleeding better men. Don't give him space to breathe."

Curtis paid attention as he walked to his unmarked sedan and pulled out. Then noticed a car in the parking lot pulled out behind him. No one had left the diner in the last twenty minutes. Curtis dialed Mason. But before he said a word, Mason said. "Yeah, I saw." And hung up.

Downtown Rich Aromas Coffee House near Oak Lawn

The freeze had finally broken; instead of ice crusting her windshield, there was only frost, dissolving under the morning sun. Fiona rolled down the window a crack. Crisp air rushed in, a relief after last week's freeze that had splintered tree limbs and cracked pipes.

Fiona met Erin at Rich Aroma's. The coffeehouse smelled of espresso, waxed floors, and lemon-vanilla glaze. Music hummed softly; the barista called out names. A pair of students near the counter whispered about the Dallas Zoo monkey theft, shaking their heads and laughing. Fiona slipped into the booth across from Erin, her hands gripping her mug, her knuckles white.

"You said you had something," Fiona said as she sat. "Besides the voicemail."

Erin pushed the manila envelope forward. Inside: screenshots of bank wires, shell company maps, names cross-referenced with Bridget's files. The names reminded her of old wounds: Cavanah, Stuart, Bell. Circled in red, a project name glared back. *Project SILO*. Everything circled back to this one name.

"She said it started as an ethics-hunting software," Erin said. "But someone took it. Militarized it. Used placement data for profiling. People profiled, placements sold. Overseas at first."

"From what I'm reading here, it weaponized foster and adoption systems and juveniles in jail." Fiona said bluntly. Her mind ran through prison-industry money and think-tank contracts.

Then Erin pushed a flash drive across the table. "Encrypted. Dual auth." A slight hesitation before saying. "Everything Bridget and Lisa sent me. The voicemail is on there as well. At least a copy."

Fiona noticed the hesitation, wondered about it, and made a note of it. She hasn't touched the drive yet. "The courts are going to want the original. You told me it's on a burner phone Lisa has?"

Erin glanced up, eyes sliding to the bar. Her attention elsewhere. As if she had not heard what Fiona said. When Fiona looked to see where Erin was looking, she saw a man standing to leave.

"Did you see him?" Erin whispered.

"Who?" Fiona wasn't sure if Erin was becoming so paranoid that she saw bad guys everywhere. Erin stared at her for a moment and then shrugged.

"If someone burned the unit after enticing Lisa and you there, they wanted the trail gone," Erin said. "They didn't just erase evidence. They left an impression. And a big warning."

"Sure, thanks for the assist. Us poor, washed-up PIs never would've cracked that fact without you." Fiona slid the drive into her pocket, the weight familiar and dangerous. Somehow it reminded her of the night Nightjar had left her a matchbook. The same quiet promise of trouble waiting to wake up. This drive was going straight to Buck. After her cyber division made a copy of Bridget's voicemail, authenticated it, and then sent it over to George. The team would store the rest of the paper information in the evidence file for Major Buck.

A headline on a newsstand reported that the U.S. military shot down a Chinese surveillance balloon off the coast of South Carolina. She noticed it as she left the cafe with a large coffee. *They had tracked the balloon since late January. The news was wall-to-wall with coverage about the rising U.S. China tensions.*

She stared at the headline. The balloon, the fallout, the public fury. All of it louder than what she knew was going on under everyone's noses. A quiet war with no press coverage.

In all the commotion, major news, fury, and theatrics, they also buried the smaller tragedies: murder, mayhem, and human trafficking.

Dallas County Jail | Late Afternoon

Fluorescent light flattened Lisa's face; her eyes were hollow with a different coldness. The kind that came from being made a spectacle and possibly a monster.

Curtis sat across from the glass, boots planted, listening while the recorder blinked.

"They had to be watching me," Lisa whispered. "Someone pushed a message about the storage unit under my door with a key inside an envelope. After Bridget's death, I received calls. Silence. Heavy breathing. Nothing else."

"Why go to Dolores?" Curtis asked.

"I believe she knows who murdered Bridget. And I'm sure it's her lover, Bell. I'm telling you; Delores is as dangerous, if not even more so."

Curtis asked about Charles Stuart. Lisa nodded slowly. "He called and told me Bridget found something she shouldn't have. Something about kids. Said he wanted to warn me cause Bridget ignored his warning. I believe he still felt something for Bridget. I told her. She said she would stop. That statement proved untrue, didn't it?" Lisa stared through him. Whatever she saw, it wasn't here. It was back then; wherever Bridget had crossed the line. Silence stretched into minutes.

The jail's news TV in the guards' room caught Curtis's eye: footage of *international relief convoys, live shots from a massive earthquake halfway around the world.* The people shuddered at the horror, then returned to trivial details. *In another feed, a brief tick of diplomatic fallout, a foreign surveillance balloon, a controversy labeled at the top, slid past on the bottom crawl.* Big world. Local ruin. Both kept breathing down their company's neck.

Curtis said as he stood, "We will post your bail as soon as you're arraigned. Fiona will pick you up afterward."

Lisa's voice was small. After a beat: "I don't think I'll get out of this alive. Bell's the kind that never gets handcuffed. How do I hide from that?"

Curtis didn't answer. He stood like a world-weary cop stands after a long night's watch. Enduring, wired, immovable.

Fiona Driving Back to the Ranch

The drive home was quiet by design. Fiona didn't touch the radio. Clouds thickened into low thunderheads; the storm smelled of wet asphalt and charged air. The ranch drive appeared dark and dangerous. With tall trees standing watch when she crossed the bridge into the motor courtyard and pulled into the garage. The lights had not yet triggered to come on despite the dark overhead clouds.

Fiona's phone vibrated in the console as she stopped to key in the numbers at the gated entrance to the ranch. No numbers, just a link.

She tapped. Eight images. Pixelated but precise: Everett and Lisa, a cabin, a dim hotel hallway, a soft airport lounge. In one, Everett kissed Lisa's cheek; in another, Lisa's hand rested on his shoulder. The timestamps spanned two years.

These weren't cheap deepfakes. They were surgical, composed to convince. Someone wanted her to believe a story.

She watched the last image go black. The ranch lay under the low hum of its backup generators still running. A rooster crowed once in the distance. The angle was too good. Too convenient. As if someone had planned the story frame by frame before letting her see it. Whoever sent them didn't want a fight. They wanted a verdict.

She slipped her phone into her jacket, turned off the ignition, and stepped into the night. She had to investigate this. It meant questions asked of Everett. She was not sure he'd take very well, but had to be done. The storm tore across the ranch, howling winds and crashing thunder followed by lightning so bright it could blind. The news feeds kept coming. *Local thefts, corporate investments, foreign crises.* No storm could wash any of that away.

CHAPTER 19

The Key

Saturday, February 18th, 2023

O'Brien & Galloway Downtown Office | Interrogation Room

Fiona and Curtis interviewed Lisa in the room with frosted glass walls, a soundproof ceiling, and the sterile hum of central air that whispered like a warning. Nothing about it was soft. Video streamed to the adjacent observation room, one where there was equipment and trained humans to read body language. Any interviews here were voluntary. In the hallway outside, a muted television carried a live crawl about national news, about increasing tensions across the nation. Inside the room, no one commented; the outside world reduced itself to white noise.

At the table, Fiona sat still, eyes sharp, taking notes. Curtis stood leaning against the wall. The silence between Fiona and Lisa stretched thin as wire.

Lisa looked hollow. Her makeup was gone, replaced by dark circles and a hollow tremble behind her voice. She had knotted her hair back carelessly. Lisa stared at the table, hunched over with her arms crossed.

She started talking in a quiet tone, but she never looked up. "I saw the same cracks Bridget did when I joined Porter & Ashburn. I figured out fast I couldn't fix anything, so I planned to leave. Transfer to another firm. Walk away clean."

"Why didn't you?" Fiona inquired.

"Bridget never told me Porter & Ashburn had recruited her right out of college. It was too late. She said she wanted to work with me. God, how do you tell your adoring younger sister it's a den of snakes?"

Fiona's voice stayed neutral. "But you didn't tell her, did you?"

Lisa's jaw tightened. "No. They had already hired her. I didn't want her dragging me down with her. I changed some of her work to make her appear sloppy when she wasn't. My thought was they would fire her, and she'd go back home, and I could leave with no dirty marks on my record. She had Everett and Lila; I only had my work."

Fiona learned in. "You're going to tell me everything you know. All of it."

Lisa hesitated. "Bridget tried to get me to help her a week before she died. I refused. I should have known she knew too much for them to let her go or fire her. Some guy from the California office seemed to run most of the shady stuff. Guy named Reid Cavanaugh."

Both Curtis and Fiona leaned forward. Both glanced at each other in unspoken understanding. Neither said a word, though.

"He's a partner, so within the firm he's powerful. You don't want to cross him."

Curtis sat and began taking notes.

"By the last week, I realized there were some individuals at Porter & Ashburn who would do whatever was necessary to protect themselves and their clients. When I ran into that man, Joe Bell, this was the boogeyman everyone whispered about." Here Lisa stopped, with a quiet sob in her voice.

"Joe Bell, why would he scare you if you'd never met him before?" Curtis spoke for the first time.

"People at Porter & Ashburn knew him as a fixer. The rumors were sometimes he fixed things by... like, people ended up in a murder-suicide of their families. Or they just disappeared, never heard from again. Most just thought of it as the corporate bogeyman. Behave, do your job, don't ask questions. And never, ever betray the firm, or else."

"We have the drive." Fiona stated. "She hid the thumb drive at home and left Everett a strange grocery list as clues to its location. He knew enough about how your sister though to find it."

Lisa blinked. "The day Bridget died; she tried to call me. I was in a meeting. She said she was going to the cabin and asked me to cover for her at work. She also mentioned Everett was out of town with a military friend, and then she sent a five-digit code. If something happened to her, this code would open something. She said I was to ask Everett what it was. I deleted the message from my phone, but wrote the code down. I kept it. As soon as I got the message, I knew something was wrong. I drove there. No one answered the door, so I assumed she had gone home. That busybody neighbor, whom my sister is so fond of, told me she had not seen her or anyone at the cabin all morning."

"What neighbor?" Fiona glanced at Curtis. *That didn't track. George's report from the police reports showed no occupied cabins on Cabin Creek Road that day.* "Do you know this neighbor's name?"

"Eliane, something or other. Next to my sister's cabin, it is the best-kept one out there. The old lady lives there year-round."

"Let's get back to the code. Where is it now?" Fiona asked.

Lisa didn't hesitate. "At my condo. Inside a porcelain elephant. Bedroom shelf. It's... something my sister gave me as a kid. It's hollowed out. We sent messages back and forth when we needed to back each other up or cover for each other."

Fiona pressed the intercom. "Stefana, come get the key to Lisa's condo and send Jeanne to pick up an item. Tell her to be discreet. I'll text her the location and the item she is to retrieve once she's there."

Lisa stared into the distance as if she were not there. To regain her attention, Fiona asked, "One more thing. Was she right about Dolores? Or is Delores a fool being used?" Fiona asked.

Lisa's lip twitched. "Delores had access, routing codes, and transaction logs. Bridget told me, Delores' husband laundered money from government trusts through fake NGO charities. Bridget traced one account; Renwright Holdings; used to fund child placement networks. She suspected they were funneling private adoption subsidies through PACs and front charities linked to trafficking." She'd found something... off. Something about adoptions. Something about a program called SILO. That's what started this all. Found this information on John Cole's computer. But Delores? She's just something for a powerful man to have on his arm. She really is not very smart."

"There was a man from the California office; quiet, but people seemed to jump when he spoke. I never dealt with him directly, but Bridget said that from what she discovered, he's the one pulling the strings. Reid Cavanaugh, Porter & Ashburn's west coast partner."

Fiona sat back in her chair. Our investigations show that the shell company that the firm did legal work for went belly up years ago.

Lisa nodded slowly. "On one occasion, she mentioned that name." Lisa looked up, saying out of the blue. "Joe Bell called me, day before I got the message to go to the storage unit. He said I needed to find something Bridget took. Something she wasn't supposed to have. He didn't threaten me outright, just said that people who get involved in the wrong things... fill in the rest. Those are his words exactly."

Fiona stood. "You're going home under guard. No phones. No

messages. If someone reaches out. Anyone, call us. This is for your protection."

Lisa nodded. She seemed small, defeated, as if all the fight in her was gone before she stood up. "She said she forgave me," Lisa whispered. "Right before she hung up that day, in the message she left me. I don't think I ever forgave myself."

O&G security officers escorted Lisa home. Curtis and Fiona went out to the bullpen, where several others were working on the cases.

"Mason said the records showed no calls or texts. However, he seemed to be distracted when I talked to him last."

"Do you trust this Mason guy? He could just be stringing you along." Danny Mercer, an ex-DOJ working for them, asked.

"He knows that is going to be part of the discovery by George, and he's gunning for a dirty cop," Curtis said, leaving it at that.

"Then it looks bad for Everett's story. You guys sure about him?" Danny asked. Looking between Curtis and Fiona.

Fiona, deep in thought, looked up and said. "What?" seeing everyone staring at her. After Curtis told her, she said. "She's not stupid. If she made that call, she knows it'll be on the record. So, either someone wiped it, or she used a different phone. Because something bigger is happening here, and if Bridget suspected they might be onto her, she would take precautions. Is there any way we can get a look at Lisa's phone? See if George can get a subpoena for it. They are holding it as evidence."

Dallas PD | Homicide Bullpen

Mason dropped a stack of I-45 case files onto his desk, exhaustion sharpening the lines around his eyes. Wren passed by, coffee in hand, and Mason caught his eye before saying.

"Did you ever verify that Texarkana cattle auction Taylor claimed he attended?" Mason asked. "With that guy, Colten Harlan, and talked to that guy, Clay Braddock?"

Wren didn't miss a beat.

"Yeah. Braddock says he bought cattle from the auction but not through some guy named Colt Harlan. He used the auction's normal broker for the sale. So, there is nothing to back Taylor's story."

Mason exhaled, frustration tightening his jaw. "So, you're saying the alibi's garbage."

Wren shrugged with practiced neutrality. "Looks that way. I logged the update."

Mason nodded once, already turning back into the mountain of I-45 evidence choking his desk. Yet, something nagged at him. Something he could not put his finger on. Lately, he'd been more tired than usual. Too many murders, too many deadlines, not enough hours. He reached for another file, pushing the Taylor case to the back for now. He reached for another drink of coffee from his cup.

Behind him, Wren walked away, yet Mason noticed he seemed more agitated than he'd ever seen him be. He hoped he was making him concerned about getting caught. Maybe he'll make more mistakes.

◆◆◆

Cyber Division Room

The soft blue glow of the wall-sized screen illuminated the darkened command room. The hum of server racks filled the air with static tension behind the glass doors. Curtis stood at the head of the table. Sam and Rosemary flanked him. The video call crackled slightly before stabilizing.

The man on the screen looked like he hadn't slept in weeks.

Deep-set eyes, unshaven cheeks, a motel room behind him with peeling wallpaper and a box fan on low.

"Randy Smith?" Curtis asked.

"Yes."

Curtis noticed sweat running down Randy's brow.

"You worked at Transitions AI?"

"Until it went dark after the attack on the Conference Center," Randy glanced over his shoulder as if he heard something, then looked back at the camera. "I wrote backend code for the core predictive engine. What we imagined we were building was a foster-care algorithm to ensure children went only to the best foster or adoption centers. Risk matrices. Outcome projection. The kind police wanted to help predict crime and who the criminals behind those crimes might be. Then we moved into predictive law enforcement. What we were creating was something else entirely. They assigned each coder a section, but we didn't know the other coders' tasks were."

"What changed?" Rosemary asked, her voice even.

"Hays changed the inputs. Started plugging in names, real people, real kids, actual crimes. Not just modeling. Matching. Grooming profiles. And then the offshore money started appearing. Funding that didn't trace back to any agency I recognized." Randy hesitated. "There was one shell fund. Everything dirty seemed to orbit around it. Offshore payments, hush money, illegal routing..."

"Name it," Curtis said.

"Tovira Fund Group."

Curtis's eyes narrowed at the name. They'd seen it before, buried in Bridget's earlier files, but now it surfaced connected to trafficking. How and why were Hays connected, and what did this connection between them all mean?

Randy nodded. "That was one of them; we used to joke it sounded like a vampire hedge fund. Payments ran through

Luxembourg and the Caymans; we thought it was under the radar adoption services."

Sam narrowed his eyes. "Who else was involved?"

"Foreign investors. I didn't see names, but the accounts tied into private equity firms with deep nation-state links. Hays was the middleman. He'd get calls, then vanish for days. When he came back, he gave us new directives, and we always followed them. By then, we knew enough to keep our mouths shut and ask no questions. Several who questioned Hays got fired and then vanished. Fell off the grid." The connection flickered, and the line went to static for a few seconds.

Curtis leaned forward, a frown on his brow. "Are you in danger?"

Randy's voice lowered. "There's been a silver SUV parked outside my motel for two nights. Same one. No tags. I think talking to you painted a target on my back."

Curtis spoke without hesitation. "We've got someone en route. Stay inside. Don't use your phone again."

"Hang on... what was that?" Randy turned his head fast, eyes wide. "Shit. Someone's at the..."

Curtis texted Major Buck on one of the burner phones with the phrase: 'Randy needs a blue blanket,' triggering a JSOC-style pickup protocol.

The screen went dark.

Curtis turned toward the room. "Get Major Buck on the phone now."

On a secondary monitor, a news ticker scrolled silently: *"Investigations still ongoing at the Houston, Texas, Conference Center."* The words slid past on the screen, secrecy upon secrecy. Swamp creatures in the system knew how to strike in plain sight.

Dallas HQ Conference Room

Fiona stepped into the conference/war room, with Curtis shadowing her. Several investigators stood frozen around the breakroom TV as an anchor spoke:

"Breaking update in the Bridget Taylor investigation: Lisa Neylan, recently released on bail, a suspect in the Iron Creek Storage unit fire, remains a person of interest. Anonymous sources allege Lisa Neylan may have been romantically involved with suspect Everett Taylor, Bridget's widowed husband. Officials declined to comment, citing an ongoing investigation."

Fiona's jaw tightened. Curtis muttered, "They're laying the groundwork to bury her before she even testifies." Fiona turned the volume down and walked to the cyber room, hoping to be there if Jeanne called.

Jeanne called as she walked in. "Elephant secured." Matilda noted the chain-of-custody entry; the timestamp logged before imaging.

No one noticed the second tracing ping in the garage, same minute, different elevator level. "Did someone just hit the sub-basement?"

"No one's authorized."

"Pull the security feeds; then check the elevator for anyone who should not be there."

Curtis pulled Fiona aside, out of earshot of the others. "Buck got Smith out. He's got him tucked away somewhere he claims is safe. He already had a team on the way to pick him up from what he learned from the stuff we sent him."

Fiona nodded, preoccupied.

Rooftop across from the Office

The figure lay prone across the gravel rooftop, rifle scope resting on the ledge. He moved like a shadow, a breath of wind.

Below and across from him, the O'Brien & Galloway building glowed golden in the sunset haze.

He followed her silhouette through the tinted glass, Fiona O'Brien. Composed. Sharp-eyed. She moved like someone who knew the rules better than anyone else and no longer gave a damn about them.

She was fire-resistant. Untouched by corruption. She had survived what had tried to consume her. But only so far.

"We must protect her from herself," the man whispered. Reaching down to pet the puppy. Beside him, the puppy rested in a thick blanket inside a padded duffel. Safe. Unaware of the violence that stalked this city's highest towers, the puppy snuffled and snuggled deeper into the blankets.

He adjusted his scope again. Watching. Waiting. For he was not aware of what it might be.

"President Biden will visit Poland next week," the broadcast said, breaking through the static in his earpiece. He disregarded it, as he knew his father would be on that flight with Biden. That gave him some breathing room and less work when his father was out of the country. He refocused the crosshairs back on Fiona's silhouette. The next breaking news caught his attention.
"Morrow's committee is looking into anything involving private-sector contractors. He wants tighter clamps on them and more oversight." The reporter moved on to the latest political news. *"Chad Ashburn has thrown his hat into the ring for the Texas Senate seat, which came open because of the sudden heart attack followed by the death of Senator Buckley Farnsworth."*

Fiona's Office

The office was nearly silent; only Matilda's rapid footfalls echoed down the corridor.

She burst into Fiona's office, breathless. "Fiona, we've got a problem."

Fiona looked up from a crime scene overlay from another case they were working on for a client. They were close to proving who was embezzling the company's money.

"It's the drive. The one Everett gave us from Bridget. Sabrina put in the code Lisa gave them. Midway through, someone tried to trigger a remote wipe. High-level breach. Through a Zurich relay. Sabrina captured the PCAP, cert hash before she pulled the drive. They almost got in. How in the hell did anyone outside the company know we'd unlocked it?"

Fiona was already moving. "Physically disconnect it."

"Sabrina already did," Matilda said. "Sentinel's the only safe server to open it with again."

Fiona grabbed her keys and a burner phone and opened the drawer with her P226 Legion, grabbed it, and holstered it. "Have Morris lead out to the ranch. I'll follow. No calls. No trackers."

Morris agreed and headed out to the parking garage. From the reception area, Fiona heard the elevator chime.

"Bridget died for what's on that drive. I'm not losing that information."

They joined Sabrina and Nancy in the cyber wing. Fiona sealed the drive in an RFID bag.

In the background of the cyber wing, a late-night international feed ran silently on a wall-mounted screen: *"Russia launches new wave of missile strikes on Ukraine's power grid."* The hum of O'Brien & Galloway's own server racks made the headline feel uncomfortably close. She headed to the elevator with the sealed bag. Leaving Selena, Sabrina, and Nancy to close the office.

◆ ◆ ◆

Sunday, February 19th, 2023

Lisa

Mason came into the kitchen and said, "Turn on the news." Then went to get a cup of coffee.

Fiona stood frozen in the middle of getting a cup for herself. She reached over and turned it on to the news channel.

Local news played footage of yellow tape fluttering at the edge of Lakewood Park. The police cruiser's reds and blues twirled in the background. They'd erected a white tent near the wooded trail entrance.

The anchor's voice came over the broadcast:

"Just after midnight, authorities found Lisa Neylan, a Dallas resident connected to the Bridget Taylor murder investigation, unconscious in Lakewood Park. Authorities say it is unknown why she entered the park that late at night. Police have no suspects at this time. Sources have confirmed that someone robbed and left her for dead. Authorities say her condition is critical."

Fiona didn't speak, just glanced over at Curtis as he poured hot coffee into his cup. She noticed he was already in his Sunday church clothes.

"What the hell? I'll call the office and find out who O&G Security assigned to watch her."

"I'll call George; you call Mason. See if he can get the DA to approve police protection for Lisa at the hospital. I'll head to the office. Doubt we can make it to church today. I'll ask Maggie and her husband if they can take Josh to church. Call Buck also; have his guys sweep the Dallas office for bugs."

It took no time at all to discover that the newest O&G security hire, Deluca, was on duty. He was not at home or able to be reached by his cell. Detective Mason had a Bolo put out for him. An airport police officer reported to the Dallas PD that the suspect boarded a flight to Mexico City, as seen on camera. By the time the Dallas PD processed the footage, the flight had landed. Deluca had vanished into Mexico City, passport clean, trail vanished.

CHAPTER 20

Thunder and Fire

Monday, February 20th, 2023

Whiskey River Two-Step Ranch

The crisp morning air over the ranch smelled of dew-soaked grass, mesquite ash, and cedar smoke from chimneys. A silver crust of frost clung to the fence rails and porch posts, brittle in the clear February sunrise. Fiona stood at the edge of the porch, wrapped in a flannel blanket; slippers damp with ground mist. Steam curled from her mug as the first rays of light cut through the trees and brushed the fog as if lifting a veil from the calm water below. Her breath a white mist as she exhaled into the cold air. Presidents' Day would not really affect their company. Surveillance could not take a day off, nor could following leads. Holidays came at the finish of a case.

Somewhere down at the barn, a small radio played faint headlines between bursts of static: *President Biden's remarks about the Chinese balloon shoot-down.* In international news, *"Zelensky in Ukraine vows not to concede territory. East Palestine fallout, Turkey-Syria quake relief convoys."* Static clipped the newscaster's voice as Fiona tuned it out, eyes fixed on the frozen pasture.

Adam's voice came through the earpiece. "Sentinel server reports complete transfer from all the flash drives we have so far."

"Double-check the motion sensors around the hangar and clubhouse," Fiona replied. "And tighten the geofence perimeter. Keep the ranch hands on alert."

"Already done. Gabby also sent several riders to the farther pastures to check fence lines."

Curtis cut in across comms. "Mason just texted with bad news. The DA is thinking about handing Everett's case off to the feds. He's getting pressure from above; the feds could file for a classified warrant on all our digital evidence. George is claiming client privilege; he's got a sit-down with DA Micah Colburn. The DA said he would hold off if George can convince him too, but not for long. The feds want to get their hands on the seizure of Everett's ranch, and anything on those drives that might embarrass the wrong people they want buried. Power players are behind this."

Fiona didn't answer. Her silence said everything.

Cyber Temporary Division at the Sentinel

Fiona arrived in the compound office as the decrypted files unfolded across the center screen. The digital originals remained locked on Sentinel's servers, with a PowerPoint mirroring the rot across the screen. She stepped in and stood next to Curtis and Mildred in the control center of Sentinel's gondola, eyes locked on a spreadsheet that seemed to bleed secrets. Being airgapped and on an intranet forced them to work at the military compound.

"Project SILO," Curtis muttered. "I believe this is what Buck's been chasing. Or at least those behind it."

Fiona narrowed her eyes at the columns, redacted contracts,

biometric scan entries, and financial logs. Routed through a string of shell corporations hidden amongst jargon, Mildred had a better handle on it.

"This isn't just predictive analytics," she said. "It's profiling. SILO doesn't need authority. It operates upstream in decision-making. The cartel soldier already has the choice made before he or she acts. Orders are orders to them. Someone feeds it information and then explains what they want, and it runs the algorithms."

Mildred pointed to the tag strings. "Placement codes. Adoption rates. Emotional adaptation scores. They were building a system to rank kids for placement, resale, or retention for other uses. But it also has an algorithm for predictive crime and law enforcement response. Worse, how to commit crimes and get away with it."

"What does retention mean?" Daniel leaned in closer, squinting, trying to read the small print.

Curtis's jaw worked silently, but changed the subject. "And funding it through PACs and NGOs?"

"Some of it." Jordan stepped up beside them and pointed. "This one, Tovira Holdings, appears on over two dozen falsified adoption match forms."

Lisa's code opened most of the files, but something still blocked other files. So, we need a different key or passcode.

Fiona's hands curled at her sides. "Transitions AI didn't just sell software; the software marketed people as if they were products. I just don't understand the law-enforcement side of the information. Most of that does not need predictive software to figure out. Why waste time on it? Why does it take a second key to unlock the remaining files? A key we don't have."

"Child welfare tags. Runaways. Missing persons. Predictive modeling," Daniel murmured from his seat at the console. "But it's all tied to biometric profiling, not placement. These are behavioral maps. Someone somewhere is using these biometrics to make a final decision on placement. I get the adoption part, but the child welfare and runaways and missing persons?"

Curtis tapped a block of entries. "Tovira Fund Group. Payments routed through PACs and orphanage grants and, God forbid, churches."

"Not decent churches. Not those that follow Christian values." Fiona scowled at Curtis.

"You're correct, but there are always those who are dishonest, or who lie about what they really are." Curtis shrugged.

"Predictive human value modeling," Fiona said, wanting to move on. "They weren't placing people and kids. They were grading them. Emotional compliance. Intelligence scores. How easy for others to mold or groom them."

"And monetized," Mildred added. Showing ledger lines with dollar amounts listed beside the ranking numbers.

Silence fell over them. Then Curtis muttered, "What Bridget found. It's worse than normal trafficking. It's trafficking children, along with drugs, guns, women, and slave labor, and doing it systematically. Like a one-stop shopping place for criminals and companies willing to exploit humans for the bottom dollar."

Ranch Office O'Brien & Galloway

"The hospital just called," Fiona said, eyes on the glass. "She passed away from her injuries."

Curtis nodded grimly, silent for a bit before saying. "According to the police investigating her attack, there was no sign of forced entry. The condo building's elevator cameras were under repair and turned off, the building supervisor informed the police. This means we have no way of proving whether she went willingly or someone forced her out to the park. The initial assessment by the police is that it was a random act of violence. Late at night, the park is an illegal drug cartel hangout."

"Maybe Lisa knew something Bridget told her. Something she refused to tell us. This was cleanup, that's all it was," Fiona turned toward Josh as he entered the room. "Hi honey, what's up?"

Curtis and Fiona held off on any further conversation about death for now.

"Wanted TV time, and Grandpa and you." His tone pleading. Fiona and Curtis agreed and went and spent an hour with Josh watching his shows with him between the two of them.

Afterward, they picked up the conversation where they had left off.

"And now that she's dead, we can't prove she didn't leave her condo of her own volition."

Muted televisions around the office fed a low current of news. *One screen replayed Biden's statement about the balloon; another scrolled images of the tornado aftermath, scenes of the wreckage. A Dallas station cut in briefly with grim local headlines: a father in Frost, Texas, had killed his twin daughters before turning the gun on himself. The news anchor's voice was steady, but the words left the bullpen hushed. In the sports ticker below, Dirk Nowitzki's Hall of Fame nomination scrolled past.*

Fiona's expression didn't flicker. She took the envelope Curtis had handed to her; retrieved from Lisa's condo by Ben, just before the police arrived. Fiona was the addressee on the envelope. She opened it slowly. Inside, a handwritten note in Lisa's curling script.

Fiona, you were right. My selfish needs took priority over my sister's safety.

I hope the code I gave you will open those files now.

I think she knew what they'd do to me, so she tried to leave to protect me, Everett, and Lila. She wanted Everett to raise Lila.

Maybe you can stop the madness. Clear Everett and return Lila to him for my sister. I know you did not know this, as your parents died when you were fourteen, but our parents were friends. There is something here for you. I retrieved from the Porter & Ashburn files two weeks ago.

Lisa

Tucked inside was a necklace. Silver. Old. Fiona stared at it in silence. For a moment, the noise in the office vanished; only the pulse in her throat and the feel of old silver pulled her backward in time.

It had belonged to her mother. A heart locket she remembered her mother wearing, with her mother's picture inside on one side, and on the other side, her father's. Fiona placed the necklace in her desk drawer and headed into work, yet she could not shake the heavy sense of loss.

◆ ◆ ◆

O'Brien & Galloway Office Dallas

"Jordan cross-checked the SILO algorithm with state health records," Mildred reported. "The system flagged children as early as preschool. Certain flags led to entire records disappearing. Lower-class or poor children noted on social welfare checks, later removed from their homes. Lost in the system. The government did not allow parents to access records about their children's placements. Not unless they won their case to get their children back. The reality. They were ghost placements."

Curtis cursed in a manner Fiona preferred to ignore, as he ran his hand through his iron-gray hair.

"Exactly," said Fiona. "Someone engineered this whole thing.

This took big money, powerful allies, and political pull. Along with time."

Just then, Kenneth stepped in, followed closely by Major Buck, both pale and brisk.

"You need to move everything," Major Buck said. "Now. A mercenary unit is en route to the ranch. We intercepted chatter: a twelve-man team, top-shelf gear. They're coming for the drives, ordered to get them before the DA caves to federal pressure. I have a team en route, but they won't get there fast enough. And most of your teams are out on protection details. I believe Phùng and Adam are the only ones at the compound right now. Kenneth was at the office with me. I'll explain later."

Curtis grabbed the landline. "Get me the ranch. Now."

Fiona was already in the elevator heading to the parking garage. She knew she could not make it in time, but had to go anyway. From her Caddy, she called Maggie. As soon as she picked up, Fiona said. "Get Josh and take him to the panic room. Do it now." Fiona gave her the panic room code and where it was. Maggie did not ask a single question. Fiona hung up.

Sentinel Compound, Ranch

Phùng picked up the call. "Clubhouse. This is Phùng."

Curtis's voice cut through. "Phùng. Get Mildred, Daniel, and Jordan out now. They're the only ones with access to all the decrypted files besides myself and Fiona. A full strike team is en route to retrieve the drives. Buck's reinforcements are twenty minutes out. Coming in by helicopter."

"Understood."

Before Curtis could say more, a thunderous blast, followed by semi-automatic gunfire, was audible through the phone.

They'd hit fifteen minutes earlier than expected. The phone

line went dead.

Whiskey River Two-Step Compound

A spray of steel and dust erupted from the south gate. Minutes later, thermite charges breached the outer fence. Another explosion made the lights flicker.

Shortly thereafter, more gunfire erupted. The chatter of nine .308 Winchester saddle rifles answered back... as black-clad mercenaries stormed the compound perimeter, moving with silent precision through the dense brush and low hills. Suppressed weapons barked in a tight rhythm. Ranch hands retreated, several wounded. Locals heard the blast, but the mercenaries jammed every signal and had cut the lines going out before the first 911 call could go through.

Inside the Sentinel, Mildred grabbed the hard drives and shoved them into a carbon-fiber satchel. Daniel and Jordan armed themselves from the wall rack. As she turned, Jordan caught the quick flick of her hand, a sleight of hand so smooth it barely existed. He understood instantly. When her eyes brushed in his direction, he gave her the smallest nod. She didn't acknowledge it, but he knew she'd seen it.

Good. She understood. He tried the landline to call 911, but the line was dead. They must have cut the lines. Cell phones had zero bars; were they using jamming equipment? Even the squad radio in the wall cradle spat static. Full-spectrum jam.

Whoever they were, they'd come wired to blind a county. Phùng burst into the Sentinel's common room at a dead sprint, boots thudding on concrete, the metallic tang of thermite still hanging in the air. "Out the exit! Head to the clubhouse; it's closest." Phùng shouted, "I'll follow and give you cover."

Then the world blew apart.

A shaped charge tore the common room wall open with a thunderous rip that punched the air out of his lungs. Heat blasted across the room. Drywall dust filled his mouth, tasted like chalk and burnt plastic. Something hot sliced across his cheek. Shrapnel, small and fast.

"GO! MOVE!" Phùng roared. They burst through the doorway into a storm of gunfire. From the treeline, the ranch hands opened fire. Hard and fast, drawing their fire. It bought them three seconds. No more. But it worked. The mercenaries turned towards the fire from the ranch hands in the tree stands. Though one merc yelled and went down, three others turned and fired a firestorm of bullets toward the treeline, forcing the ranch hands to abandon their positions. Three others helped the hit mercenary up, who then ripped off a shirt sleeve and wrapped it around his lower calf before limping after the others.

The first team of mercenaries breached the clubhouse's side wall using shaped charges. Shrapnel sprayed the common room. Dust filled the air.

Seconds later, another blast opened the wall on the east side of the compound clubhouse. Mercenaries poured through the breach, a disciplined, silent wave. No shouting, no wasted motion. Black armor, suppressed rifles, fast angles.

Phùng stepped into their line of sight, anchoring their attention.

tap-tap-TAP
His rifle slammed back against his shoulder, muzzle recoil biting into his collarbone. One merc went down. Another staggered. A third fired back with ruthless precision.

Rounds snapped and cracked past his face. Hot needles of air chewed holes through the wooden support beam; he slid behind.

Behind him, Jordan grunted sharply as a bullet tore into his thigh. He stumbled, caught himself, and dragged his leg, firing one-handed into the smoke.

"Keep the drives moving!" Jordan shouted, voice shredded from pain.

Mildred shoved the satchel toward Phùng, but before he could secure it, another blast rocked the far wall. The concussion hit like a physical shove. Light fixtures shattered. Raining down glass that glittered like ice in the smoky air.

"MOVE!" Phùng yelled.

Daniel, calm under fire, advanced two steps and laid down a blistering suppressive volley. He hit one merc in the helmet, sending him spinning. Another ducked behind the entry frame.

Then, a sniper round cracked through the fog.

Daniel's head snapped back. He dropped instantly, body folding flat without a sound. No twitch. No time.

Jordan's face contorted. Fury, disbelief, but he didn't hesitate. He fired again, but a second round punched into his chest, slamming him against the storage room door. A bloom of red spread across his shirt.

His legs buckled.

His eyes unfocused mid-slide.

Phùng clenched his jaw hard enough to hurt.

He could not save them.
If he stayed even one more second, Mildred would join them.

He grabbed her wrist and pulled her into a sprint.

The mercs shifted fire onto them immediately. Bullets tore through furniture, splitting wood and kicking chips of tile into the air like exploding gravel. Splinters sliced his forearms. The air vibrated with the mechanical hiss of suppressed rifles.

A canister clattered across the floor. It hissed, one hard second, then white fog boiled low and thick, chemical-sharp in the back of the throat.

Phùng lowered his head and ran.

A bullet punched into the wall inches from Mildred's face. She gasped, ducking instinctively. Another hit the floor near her boot, shards of concrete splashing up her pant leg.

"DON'T STOP!" he barked.

She didn't.

They sprinted the last ten feet to the utility-tunnel door. A narrow metal panel, half-hidden behind shelving.

Phùng yanked the door open.

The satchel snagged on the hinge. Hard drives spilled across the floor in a clattering arc.

Mercenaries shouted, boots pounding toward them.

Phùng dove forward, dragging Mildred through the opening. Bullets shredded the doorframe. Sparks burst in a bright fountain. A metallic ping echoed down the tunnel. Rounds hammered against the metal, each hit ringing like a deep iron bell.

He threw his shoulder into the door and slammed it shut behind them. Buck's helicopters finally arrived. Minutes too late. Before the wheels touched down, the black-clad team was already disappearing like smoke.

The tunnel swallowed Phùng and Mildred in cold, stale darkness.

The air smelled of damp soil, newly installed insulation, oil, and dust. Mildred's breath rasped too loudly in the narrow space. Phùng took point, rifle up, moving in a disciplined half-crouch catwalk.

Behind them, the mercenaries kept firing, trying to shoot through the thick iron door, trying to punch a way in.

Phùng stopped and pushed Mildred ahead.

They ran, vanishing into the underground tunnel. A maze of

corridors built just for this type of emergency.

Boots splashed through puddles.
Their breaths echoed off the concrete.
The faint thunder of rotor blades somewhere far above, backup too late for the dead.

Only when the tunnel bent left and the gunfire finally faded did he let himself feel the smallest fraction of what he'd left behind.

But he didn't stop. They had to reach the tunnel's exit.

Rooftop Across the Street

The man glimpsed the property from his rooftop perch; one leg draped lazily over the stone ledge railing of his mansion, across from Fiona's. The puppy dozed beside him, twitching in its sleep.

He'd been watching the ranch feed until it cut to static. Then transferred to the feed from his team. Major Buck's ISA team arrived minutes after the cartel soldiers seemed to vanish. He ordered his men, who'd come too late, to pull out before the police arrival.

He frowned. His nemesis, Major Buck, had been chasing his organization for too many years. Several attempts on this thorn in his side by his assassins on Buck failed. His triggerman just missed him in Denver, Colorado. In fact, he killed the wrong man. The investigation temporarily forced him to close operations there. Though now they were back in business. It cost the organization a couple hundred million dollars. Many of his cartel members still whispered about how the assassin paid for that failure to this day. His screams went on for days.

Now, the aftermath played out below. Patrol cars filled the motor court, their lights strobing red and blue across the mansion's stone and stucco façade. Officers moved in knots through the drive and yard, flashlights stabbing into brush and shadows. The coroner's van rumbled out the front gate, taillights swallowed by the dusk.

Through his scope, he saw Fiona step onto the upper balcony that overlooked the motor court. She stood framed in the wash of flashing lights, arms braced against the iron railing, staring down at the chaos. Uniforms swarmed beneath her like ants illuminated by patrol beams. She hadn't moved, not once, even as evidence techs passed by from the compound with sealed bags. Detectives conferred in low voices near the gate; the coroner had already come and left with the bodies earlier.

His crosshairs lingered. Through the glass doors behind her, staff crowded around monitors, trying to piece together the feed. He nodded in acknowledgment of a job well done to himself. The team leader reported the retrieval of the drives. They would ex-fil from the helipad next to the hangar used for the property's aircraft.

"Couldn't let you keep those drives, love," he whispered as if a caress. He lit a match; let it burn close to his fingertips before flicking it over the edge.

He looked again through the scope. Fiona's face was lit in alternating washes of crimson and cobalt. No fear, only anger.

The only woman ever worthy of his full attention, and better yet, the one who would infuriate his father most. The puppy whined, then growled low, paws twitching. He reached over, murmured something soft and reassuring. The animal sighed and stilled. Hours later, the faint stealth-whop of rotors ghosted up from the treeline. The helo lifted, banked southwest, its downwash shredding the uppermost leaves as it vanished.

CHAPTER 21

Echoes of the Night

Monday, February 20th, 2023

Whiskey River Two-Step Ranch | Exit outside the tunnel

Phùng Vĩnh Ân leaned against the rough stone wall, lungs raw with smoke and cold air. He forced his breathing to slow, discipline pulling him back from the edge. Beside him, Mildred's hands trembled as she tried to catch herself on the wall, knuckles white, soot streaking her face. The silence afterward was wrong. Too big, too empty.

They'd run blind through the utility tunnel built to hide power and water conduits and to provide an emergency exit, the air thick with dust and acidic smoke. Automatic fire and explosions had echoed behind them, each step pulling them farther from the men who stayed behind. Daniel's body falling. Even after a fatal shot wounded him, Jordan shouted for them to keep moving. Those sounds chased Phùng as much as the enemy.

The tunnel came out into the brush beyond the outer fence. They collapsed onto the ice-crusted ground. The cold bit hard at their exposed skin; their breath was white plumes. Brittle grass cracked under their weight, the temperature hovering just above freezing. Overhead, the February sky was clear, stars sharp as glass, the stillness broken only by their ragged breathing. Phùng estimated they'd been in the tunnels for hours.

Red and blue strobes flickered faint through the trees. Phùng figured they were patrol cars in the motor court. An emergency siren wailed toward town, low and mournful, its echo carrying through the crisp night air.

Phùng shifted, and something hard pressed against his thigh. He reached into his thigh pocket and pulled out drives held together with a rubber band.

He froze.

The satchel lost in the attack's chaos ripped too easily on a protruding metal bar when the mercenaries forced them into the tunnel, bullets flying around them. These should have been gone.

Mildred coughed, her hands still shaking as she tried to push herself upright. Her voice rasped, almost lost. "I slipped it into your pocket during the chaos. We'd made copies, just in case." He slipped the drives back into the foil-lined Faraday sleeve she'd had them in.

"I put the copies in the bag I handed you. They won't even know they're copies; the metadata matches the original. They'll think they won."

Phùng stared at her. She was pale, sweat beading on her forehead, but her eyes held steady. Relief rippled through him, sharp and cold. She had saved the drives in the middle of an attack.

He closed his fist around the drive. Duty anchored him, but guilt pressed harder. Daniel and Jordan's deaths, both etched into him. "I left them," he said under his breath. "Didn't go back. Didn't even try."

Mildred's breath shook. "If you had... none of us would've made it out." She swallowed hard. "They knew that. You know that."

Her words didn't lift the weight. The drives in his hand felt heavier than lead and brass.

Ice cracked under their boots as he helped her up, and they walked toward the lights. Their steps stirred up the frosty hush of the predawn, where even the trees seemed to hold their breath.

To their right and ahead, the ranch glowed under alternating red and cobalt strobes and floodlights, bringing the surrounding area to almost daylight, a graveyard of violence behind them on the military-leased land.

Phùng kept them moving towards safety, guilt biting at every step, but his grip on the drives never loosened.

◆ ◆ ◆

Tuesday, February 21st, 2023

Fiona's Office | Predawn Hours

Outside the city, the night had not warmed. At six forty am, the temperature clung just above freezing. A cloudless sky over Dallas made the skyscrapers look etched in glass, their lights throwing frost-blue reflections across the streets below. Fiona stood at the window overlooking the skyline, her breath faintly fogging the glass.

Muted cable news scrolled through the same headlines: *Jimmy Carter entering hospice care, the U.S. ending its balloon debris search, and Vice President Harris calling out Russia for crimes against humanity.* Every chyron screamed crisis, but Fiona only half registered it. Lisa was gone. And Fiona finally knew she hadn't betrayed her sister. Not in the way they'd feared. She touched the small cross at her throat, the metal icy against her skin, and whispered a prayer that sounded more like a bargain.

But there was still work to do. Guilt would have to wait. She contacted the insurance companies to make sure the families received their payments as soon as possible. Taking care of Jordan and Daniel's families was a top priority for her. Next, they covertly got the drives into Buck's hands. She kept only what they needed to prove Everett's innocence. The rest would have to fall under military intelligence. Safer that way.

She turned as Selena opened the door to her office.

"Detectives are here to see you," she said. "They're not in a good mood."

"Send them in."

Detective Marcus Wren walked in with the smug, deliberate cruelty of a man who'd spent his career hurting people from behind a badge and learned to enjoy it. He wore authority like a weapon, and every step carried the message: *I can make your life a living hell with a single accusation.* Three uniformed officers followed him, tense but silent.

"Captain Johnson and the DA sent us to get your statement about what happened at your ranch. Forensics is there right now collecting evidence and statements," Wren announced with the false politeness of someone who'd already decided the outcome.

Fiona reminded them of the classified nature of the compound, the hangar, and their limited access.

Wren smirked. "If I need that information, I assure you I can get it."

She and the others present relayed what they had overheard during Curtis' call to the ranch. Curtis recounted the conversation's content, word for word.

As they were leaving, Selena's voice cut in. "There are two FBI agents here to talk with you."

Their suits were immaculate; their eyes shielded by expensive sunglasses despite the indoor lighting. They flashed their badges so fast Fiona couldn't catch the names. Normal for FBI. Before they spoke, Selena opened the conference room door, George Shaw waiting to come inside.

"We want the drives," one agent said. "Now."

"You want the drives? Get in line. You'll be hunting for them like the rest of us. Because the people who attacked my ranch and the military leased area stole them." Fiona said.

"Then maybe you can also explain why you had our CI under guard? Only to be found in the park across from her condo, beaten so badly that she later died in the hospital because of her wounds. And why the hell have your people been poking into sealed adoption records? What does that have to do with the Everett Taylor murder case?"

George spoke up, calm as a monk. "You're saying Lisa Neylan was a CI for the FBI? Then why didn't you protect her? Or come forward when the PD arrested her?"

Fiona glanced at George; the CI claim didn't feel right. Either they were lying, or Lisa had been more tangled up than she let on.

"We did not want to blow her cover. You do not know the magnitude of this case."

"You forget we've had the drive Bridget left behind," Fiona said, stepping forward. "She was good at digging up information. So, yeah, we understand the scale of this. But we're also trying to keep an innocent man from being sacrificed to protect your operation."

"I'll go to court," George said. "Demand full disclosure of anything relevant to my client's innocence. And let me be clear: we'll cooperate once you show us a warrant. Until then, I have a judge's order allowing my investigators to retain all information not directly implicating my client until trial. That includes everything found at the scene of the ranch attack."

"We'll be back with one," the second agent growled. "And we'll be bringing the licensing authorities with us."

They turned and slammed the door behind them.

Fiona didn't flinch.

"Timer just started," Curtis muttered.

George nodded grimly. "Whatever they're trying to bury... start digging with both hands. I've known Everett and his family since he was in diapers. I'm not backing down. Feds be damned."

The Copper Lantern off I-30 | Late Morning

The sun had burned through the frost, but the icy cold lingered in the air. Curtis slid into the cracked red booth, his coat still carrying a trace of cold. The windows fogged faintly from the contrast.

A muted TV bolted above the counter replayed footage from Mississippi, where six people died in a mass shooting. The volume was down, but the captions crawled steadily under the hum of conversation and the clatter of plates. *A second headline scrolled about Ukraine and the Vice President's Munich remarks.* Steve stirred his coffee without looking up.

The smell of grease was overwhelming, but to Curtis it blended with the sour tang of headlines, too grimly familiar.

"Every time I lift another rock, I find the same names beneath. Politicians, bankers, lawyers. Only the order changes," Steve said. "Some disappear for a while, like Renwright Holdings. Gone today, back tomorrow under a new shell or fake nonprofit."

He took a slow sip of coffee before putting his cup down. The attorneys were funneling illicit cash through no fewer than three entities. One handled transfers; one concealed the owner; one made it look like a nonprofit. Porter & Ashburn executed the legal maneuver.

Curtis's brow furrowed. "The Stuarts' family?"

"Yep. Charles Stuart sits on thirteen NGO boards. His wife,

Charlotte Erskine, another nine tied to adoption channels. All routed through the California office. Stuart Holdings showed up as a trust out of Baton Rouge. They're running a pipeline. My guess? Trafficked kids."

"Can you get me the documents?"

"Nope. But I can get you the woman who had access to their paperwork. She placed children somewhere safe whenever she saw them come up on this list. Built a dead man's switch; if something happens to her, it goes public. Used to be the State Executive for DFPS. Texas CPS."

"What happened to her?"

"They wrecked her. Whistleblowers never land on their feet. Knowing that she still did what she could for those children. She's in Garland now. Name's Shirley Dennen. She's ready to talk. Cancer is destroying her body."

Curtis nodded once, then looked out the window toward the highway. His jaw flexed hard. "Every year, over nineteen thousand kids vanish in this country and remain missing. Every year. Some of them disappear right out of the system that's supposed to protect them. Officially. Listed as runaways."

Steve didn't speak. He didn't need to.

Curtis continued, voice low. "And over two thousand and thirty confirmed abductions involve kids taken and never recovered. No bodies. No goodbyes. Just gone. You build enough networks, move enough money, hide behind enough shell companies, and that's what you buy. Disappearance of children."

He looked back at Steve. "If Shirley proves Stuart Holdings' connection to child trafficking, and if we connect even one facility, then we can expose the entire operation."

Steve's voice dropped. "She knows where they buried the bodies. And she's still breathing. For now."

Rich Aroma's Coffee Shop | Early Afternoon

By afternoon, the cold had lifted a little, though when the door swung open, the frigid air blasted the inside entrance. Inside, heaters worked overtime, battling the February air each time customers came and went. Both the upper and lower floors' fireplaces were blazing, couches full of patrons.

Delores Cole sat at a corner table, sipping something rich and costly laced with alcohol she brought with her, her sunglasses still on despite being indoors. On the mounted TV above the pastry case, *Jimmy Carter's hospice news replayed for the third cycle, split-screened against footage of tornado wreckage in Alabama.* No one in the cafe paid much attention, but the anchors' serious tones underscored every word.

Fiona slid into the seat across from her.

"How tragic about Lisa," Delores said, voice honeyed.

"Isn't it?" Fiona replied. "You two were always close in private?"

Delores smiled. "We ran in the same circle. Doesn't mean we shared secrets."

"Bridget also trusted you for a time."

"Bridget trusted a lot of the wrong people."

Fiona handed her a paper with routing codes. "These routing codes tie back to your husband's front. Want to get ahead of this?"

"He said they were for charity. I didn't ask questions."

Fiona leaned forward. "You're not stupid, Delores. And I don't think you're scared. Maybe you should be."

Delores stood. "If you want something to chase down. Find the man Lisa was sleeping with. He's the key you're looking for. Some secrets keep people alive. Think about that before you come asking for more."

Fiona didn't answer. She let her silence stretch until Delores shifted her weight and looked away first. Fiona watched her walk away. Wondering if she was an innocent bystander married to the wrong man and caught up in all this, or deep in the weeds with all the other criminals.

◆ ◆ ◆

Bullpen | O'Brien & Galloway

By late day, clouds were creeping in from the west, a pale haze drifting over Dallas after a brittle-clear morning. Rain was in the forecast, but for now the city still held to cold light.

Inside, Fiona pinned photos onto the corkboard. Bridget. Lisa. Everett. Reid Cavanaugh. Charles Stuart. The map beside them now had yarn connecting facilities, shell companies, and a growing constellation of vanishing children. This same information was in a computer program that made all the same connections, but somehow both she and Curtis returned to the old-fashioned murder boards.

The muted news radio in the background repeated the day's cycle: *Carter's condition, fallout from the balloon shoot-downs, the Mississippi killings.* The anchors spoke in steady tones, detached from the horrors Fiona had pinned across the board.

"Miriam, stay on Delores. You are taking over for the next week for Mildred. I gave her the week off. I want you to keep track of her movements. Aaron, get me everything you can on Stuart Holdings and Project SILO. I want offshore accounts, plane logs, family donations, anything that links them to adoption centers. Might want to get with some of Major Buck's agents, with his permission. I realize you're busy with other cases, but focus on this until Mildred returns."

Curtis walked in, holding a folder. “Shirley’s ready to talk. I’ll meet with her when I get back from New Orleans.”

Fiona nodded. “Good. Charles Stuart’s family is the missing piece. If we can place him at one of these facilities, we’ll have a direct line to Cavanaugh’s shadow business, using Porter & Ashburn as his cover.”

As everyone scattered back to their desks and their assignments, Fiona stood alone at the board, staring at a photo of Lila. The storm finally broke over Dallas, rain tapping the windows like a metronome, sliding down the glass, reflections from them splashed across Lila’s photo.

She didn’t want answers anymore. She wanted a reckoning.

Dallas County Courthouse | Front Steps

Mason stepped out of the courthouse, case files under his arm, collar up against the slicing early evening February wind. Reporters clustered like vultures at the bottom of the stone steps, microphones raised, breath fogging the air.

He’d barely cleared the doorway before one of them, a sharp-eyed woman from Channel 8, surged forward. Carly Reston.

“Detective McCarthy! Quick question.”

Mason kept walking. “Not today.”

But she didn’t let go.

“Is it true Everett Taylor lied about being at a cattle auction in Texarkana? Sources say they could not verify his alibi.”

Mason stopped dead.

His head turned just enough to meet her eyes.

“Where did you hear that?”
His tone firm and demanding.

She smiled like reporters smile when they know someone just handed them a photo of a fresh carcass.

"Internal source," she said. "Close to the investigation."

Mason's jaw tightened.
He didn't answer. Didn't trust himself to.

The cameras clicked like chattering teeth.

Behind the reporter, another shouted:

"Does this mean Taylor's alibi didn't hold up? Are you going to pursue an indictment on murder charges?"

Mason forced himself to breathe, forced the heat in his chest back down.

"No comment," he said, and moved past them, boots grinding against the salt on the steps.

The truth hit him like a gut punch.

Only one person had access to that internal note.

Only one person with a motive to leak it.

This was like the Miller court case all over again that Wren worked. Using public pressure to push the brass to let him close the case early and send it up to the DA. That ended up being a disaster. Cost the department millions. They could never prove wrongdoing on Wren's part. Only that he did a half-assed job. Most of the detectives could not figure out how he was still a detective. The brass would have demoted any of them back to a street cop after that. He had to have a powerful protector high up.

Wren wanted full credit. If he didn't close it before Mason or Luis returned to the case full-time, he would have to share the credit. Public pressure always helped the brass to want to close a case fast. By the time Mason reached his car, the reporter's voice was already echoing across live broadcasts:

"Sources indicate the husband's alibi may have collapsed."

And Everett Taylor's reputation, already half-buried, sank deeper under the weight of public opinion.

CHAPTER 22

Ghost Children

Wednesday, February 22nd, 2023

Garland, TX | Shirley Dennen's Home | Early Morning

Curtis knocked twice, then stepped back. Above the porch, a rusty wind chime whispered a soft melody, and the house's pale-blue siding showed years of wear. The February air was raw and damp, low clouds rolling in from the west, but here in Garland the morning was still clear.

The door slowly opened with a creak.

"You alone?" A thin, elderly woman with a wrinkled face and pewter hair asked?

"Yes, ma'am. Curtis Galloway from O'Brien & Galloway Investigations, we had an appointment."

The morning air outside was sharp and with a biting sting. Heat and the scent of old paper filled the air inside, thick as if in a library. Padlocked filing cabinets lined one wall. A small dog under the coffee table gave a low warning growl but didn't bark.

The kitchen radio on the counter announced headlines through static. *President Biden's visit to Kyiv was the major story. Texas weather reported freezing drizzle upstate as the region remained cold.*

"I worked in the placement division most of my career. Worked my way to the head office." She moved over to her couch, a slow, crouched walk, her breath wheezing, and sat. Took her a while to catch her breath before she said. "Until I asked the wrong questions."

Curtis nodded. "I'm listening."

"Kids flagged for 'special assessments,' white, blond hair, blue eyes, or mixed-race, gifted, healthy, vanished from the public system. Sent to private religious groups. Frontier Dawn Covenant Network was one of them. Their principal patrons who contributed money? Stuart Holdings. Dig deeper, and you'll find they are not actually representing a religious order. The adoptions weren't for families. They were being sent somewhere outside the normal legal organizations. From there, they just *poof* vanished. Bridget contacted me. She was looking for proof; figured if anyone had some it would be me."

"Porter & Ashburn managed the legal shielding. Reid Cavanaugh stayed hidden; his shell, TierPoint LLC, ran predictive models of child placement, basically trafficking analytics dressed as software. Bridget suspected they were running simulations in real time. With real consequences."

"Do you still have records?"

"Not digital. I knew better. But before I left, I printed out everything I'd found and mailed it to an old friend I trusted. It is everything you see here. Which he then forwarded to my grandmother's house, mother's side. She was in a care facility, but the house was still hers. I'd go visit her once a month and go by her house and collect the mail." Shirley walked to her recliner, opened a hidden drawer, and pulled out a five-battered, thick, yellow legal-size envelope with old-fashioned clasps. She handed them over to him.

Curtis flipped through names, facility maps, and financial transfers. However, a name showed through on a redacted page: Jared Weiss.

His breath caught. He damn sure knew that name; they had

been investigating his disappearance for the parents. After a year, they had to put the case on ISNL (Investigation Suspended, No Leads).

And then another detail hit him: a removal order signed by "Judge G. Atchison." He recalled George's late-night call, where he had passed on Everett's words. Bridget had once flagged the judge's name, as she was concerned about the judge's approval of removals that didn't match the CPS reports. Bridget hadn't let it go. Now they found it here in Shirley's file.

Curtis tucked the envelopes into his briefcase, the weight of George's voice echoing in his head. The court could not use the document unless Shirley testified to those facts, as it lacked an official seal or a digital connection to any CPS office.

"Would you be willing to testify in court that you collected this information while working for CPS as an outside consultant?"

"Depends. I have cancer. If the court date is after the next three months, I'll be dead. Before then, if I'm still alive, yes."

The paper trail alone couldn't carry them, not without Shirley's testimony. Shirley's testimony under oath would expose the legal network. He stayed for about an hour cause Shirley seemed glad to have company and he felt she needed some company. Before leaving, he discussed her signing a dying declaration before a court officer to the paperwork here as being true and collected by her. She agreed. He called George to get the doctor's statement and set it up with the court. After that, he left to get what he had discovered back to the office.

He headed out toward Dallas, stopping at Buc-ee's for gas. A man in a utility truck getting gas kept staring at him, then walked toward him. Curtis tensed his hand casually next to his Glock holster.

"Saw you on the news with that Everett fellow. Looks like they're stringing him up for something he didn't do. Why the hell aren't the police looking anywhere else?" Curtis shrugged and then asked, "Anything you know you'd like to tell me?"

The man shook his head and walked back to his work truck, put back the gas pump handle, and left. Curtis watched him go, a sense of unease trailing the retreating vehicle like exhaust. When he entered the conference room later, the picture of the man he had talked with at Buc-ee's was on the murder board. Underneath it said Mr. Evan Ruke: Reluctant Witness.

◆◆◆

O'Brien & Galloway Dallas HQ

Outside the office, the city remained in the brittle grip of the cold. The morning news tickers repeated the *Biden-in-Kyiv footage and a note about increased travel disruptions at some regional airports due to localized freezing patches.* The moment Curtis was back, he headed for the breakroom. When he walked in, he spotted Charles Chambers leaning on the breakroom counter, sleeves rolled up, sipping steaming bitter black coffee like he owed it money, slowly. Outside, the February sun broke weakly through a gray sky. A cold north wind scoured the streets, dropping temps into the forties across Dallas.

"We need ten minutes," Charles said without preamble. "I think we've been circling the same drain."
Curtis approached. "Talk to me."

Charles pointed to a photo laid on the table: three children. Two girls, one boy. "We took a case over a year ago. We closed the case because we didn't turn up any additional information. I told them I would reopen it if anything new came up. Well, all this information from Bridget Taylor has brought up additional information."

"So, are you asking to reopen the case?"

"Yes."

"Okay, read me what you have."

"Jared Weiss. Age seven. Taken from his parents two years ago, the family court said neglect. I dug into it. No CPS flags. No school complaints. Just a judge's single ruling, and a kid vanished. By a judge's name I'd never seen in the system before, G. Atchison."

Curtis raised an eyebrow. "Not on the DFPS roster?"

"No. But she had a rubber stamp and access. Two weeks later, a pair of model foster parents in East Texas took in Jared and his sisters. I investigated. Turns out they're fake church folk. Not genuine believers. Don't allow investigators in their home without a warrant. You know the type."

Curtis leaned in. "And then?"

"Six months in, the parents won their appeal. They're getting the girls back. Jared? Gone. Foster parents say he ran away. No one filed a report for three days. When they call it in, they act like he was a troubled kid."

"Was he?"

Charles held up his school record. "Gifted reader. Perfect attendance. Every social worker who saw him said he was quiet and polite. Not a runner."

Curtis's tone dropped. "And the court let it stand?"

"Foster parents cleared. No charges. The judge sealed the decision. When the Weiss family came to us to investigate, we tried to get it reopened. By then, the file had somehow disappeared into the system."

Curtis rubbed a hand over his mouth. "And now you think he's in Shirley Dennen's data."

"I don't think," Charles said, tapping the paper. "I know. When I was flipping through routing logs, I saw it the other day with names partially redacted. 'Jared Wei-' cut off after that. Bridget noted that the information came from Shirley Dennen. The age, the case timeline, the region. They all matched. Heard you got a sit-down with her. She refused to talk to me when I went to see her. I had to scavenger most of what I have here, though other sources."

Charles exhaled a long, steady breath. "You read my mind. I saw his name in some of her paperwork. So, we'll reopen the case, but keep it from the parents for now. Then have been through enough." Curtis walked over to get the cup of coffee he had come for, then sat at the table and pulled all the paper files out, and they both went through them.

Dallas HQ

The radio on Fiona's shelf played the day's national headlines quietly. The headlines covered a Mardi Gras' shooting. Outside noise and indifference describe the world for missing children. Fiona studied the photos pinned on the corkboard's side. Curtis dropped Shirley's envelopes later beside her. Some seams were tearing out; they were so full.

"Shirley delivered. And Charles just tied Jared Weiss into it."

Fiona turned, brows lifting. "The Weiss case?"

"Yeah. From his other investigations. The court said the parents were neglectful. But there was no proof. Then Jared disappeared. Now we find his redacted name in a SILO file."

Fiona's tone sharpened. "Then we treat it like a fresh case," she said. "He's not a cold case in our files anymore. His parents trusted us to find him when they first hired us over a year ago. And we'll rip apart every PAC and shell nonprofit tied to that foster system until we find where they sent him. I'm sure we can get some help from... a source of ours."

The door opened. Emilio Ruiz, Mike Browning, and Edgar Mullins stepped inside like men chased by ghosts.

"We've got something," Mike said. "You're not gonna like it."

Fiona crossed her arms. "Go ahead."

Emilio, a satellite specialist and signal intercept expert who worked in the cyber division, spoke first. "Two days ago, a private airstrip near San Angelo logged a flight registered to an offshore corp. backed by TierPoint LLC. Manifest listed nine child passengers, ages three to seven."

"Trafficked children," Charles growled.

Mike nodded. "But here's the kicker. The plane's tail number? Five years ago, an ATF cartel sting flagged a Gulfstream used in a drugs-and-guns operation. Human trafficking suspected, but never proven. Records scrubbed. Plane sold at a government auction."

Fiona blinked. "So technically the plane went right back to the cartel under a different NGO. They're still using it to move kids like assets."

"Faster," Edgar said. "Smarter. And they're burning the trail behind them."

Cyber Division | Dallas Headquarters.

Josiah Baird, twenty-three, the youngest on staff aside from Selena, for months buried under a backlog of forensic pulls and encrypted chat dumps for dozens of cases. None of them on Everett Taylor's. But ever since he'd been called in for a ten-minute cell trace that landed him in the same room as Fiona, he hadn't stopped thinking about how to get back there. Still, with senior investigators tossing urgent requests at him like hot grenades, people he admired and didn't want to disappoint, he was too busy to do so. The thought of chasing Bridget's cell phone pings, he once heard Fiona refer to needing, got buried under deadlines. During a rare lull, he pulled Bridget's tower logs on a whim. As the police noted, there were no pings after the cell tower close to the daycare.

After an hour, he pushed back from his monitor, frowning as he scrolled through the cell tower logs again. And then it hit him. He berated himself for missing it. He pulled up fast to his keyboard and with a few keystrokes found what he was looking for. Another phone appeared less than a minute after

Bridget's, originating from the same tower. It traveled east on a rural route, disappearing from towers, only to reappear hours later near the Taylor Ranch. It pinged off the closest tower for the ranch briefly, then pinged off a tower close to the Taylor cabin.

At eleven-thirty in the morning, the burner phone disappeared from the grid. Josiah stared at the pattern, blood humming in his ears. He sneaked a look months ago when he thought about doing this to impress Fiona. According to the official report, Bridget never returned home. And no one ever mentioned a detour east. Of course, they were looking at the wrong phone. He thought they were lazy or sloppy. They usually checked all pings in areas she might have gone to. This was to see if anyone followed the victim and who else was in the area. Should have been standard procedure. A Stingray check should have picked it up.

He worked the rest of the evening cleaning up the data. This time, he'd make sure she noticed him.

Ping Data

A blinking message from Josiah: *URGENT: Bridget Taylor Cell Ping Anomaly.*

Fiona opened the file and frowned. Police records never mentioned her going back home that day before heading to the cabin. The phone was a burner. Bridget had bought it months ago using her credit card. The phone's location history revealed a pattern connecting it to the ranch and Bridget's daily activities. And used to call Lisa regularly.

Fiona grabbed her phone and called Curtis.

"We missed something. Big."

The atmosphere in the office was dry because of the overactive HVAC. Fiona paced before the case evidence, mug in hand. A trace of mist lifted, bringing with it the faint smell of cinnamon and vanilla from the coffee. Automatically, she drank, observing the board, preoccupied with her thoughts.

A dismal, wet haze shrouded the afternoon beyond the glass. Dallas woke to an overcast sky, with a dense fog blanketing the streets. Though the mist had burned off, the sky was still a somber grey. *Forecasts warned of precipitation and localized storms impacting North Texas, originating from a weather pattern that extended over the entire state.* The local radio buzzed quietly on Sabrina's desk. *Weather bulletins mixed with headlines about transportation issues at Love Field. Biden's continued diplomatic push overseas. And a short local blurb on a DHS investigation of possible exploitation of the immigration system, Operation Janus.*

Curtis, with a clipboard in hand, stopped to look at the red thread that now curved from Bridget's photo to Lisa's, then on to Everett's. The connection was tenuous. Suggestive. They needed more. MSM news outlets daily reported unverified details of Lisa's alleged involvement and the homicide of Bridget, her sister and Everett's wife. And now no way for Lisa to defend herself.

Fiona jumped straight to the point. "Bridget turned off her phone and removed the battery after it pinged near the daycare center. Josiah thinks she may have removed the SIM card as well. Josiah discovered she had a burner phone that came on as soon as her cell went dark," Fiona stated, activating the map overlay. "The cell then turned eastward into an area with no signal. When it shows up again, it's making its way to the ranch, stayed at the ranch for less than fifteen minutes before heading straight to their family's cabin."

Curtis's brow furrowed. That isn't consistent with the police timeline.

"Exactly," Fiona said. "Wren claimed she went straight there and showed no record of her coming home. No one mentioned the possibility of Bridget stopping back at the ranch. No record exists of her spending hours inside a non-coverage cellular area. This suggests that the techs either missed it, which is unlikely, or someone scrubbed it from the records."

Curtis leaned over her shoulder, scanning the screen. "What could she have picked up? Or dropped off at the ranch."

Fiona shook her head. "More importantly... who did she go to meet, and why in the dead zone? If anyone."
She paused. "And did the police not use Stingray to check all pings in the area? It's a murder case, so they have probable cause to do so. It was standard practice in Denver, so I would believe it is here as well."

"We should stop hunting shadows," Fiona stated, her voice quiet and steady. "We couldn't investigate the area. No investigation of the crime scene, no gathering of evidence, not by George Shaw's original group or by us. If she had gone back to her house and then to the cabin. Why?"

Curtis exhaled. "Maybe someone wanted to lose the ping data, so they omitted it. Or just did not bother checking for additional cell phones in the area. Too many ifs."

Sabrina stated as she made her way into the bullpen, "Josiah attached the full tower logs. It's all there."

Fiona's eyes sharpened. "Then it's official. Someone is incompetent or sabotaging the case."

Dallas PD | Records Counter

Fiona's formal discovery request through George Shaw hit the department at four thirty in the afternoon.

By four fifty that afternoon, Detective Marcus Wren was already standing at the records window, a manila folder tucked under his arm, irritation plastered on his face.

Mason approached him. “Did you pull the call logs from the 911 call from Smith County, and the Stingray ping information?”

Wren didn’t turn. “Paper copy’s missing.”

“What do you mean, ‘missing’?” Mason’s voice sharpened.

Wren shrugged without looking up from the paperwork. “Clerical must’ve mislabeled it. Or the system archived it wrong. I’ll check with Records. Might take a few days. You know how these idiot clerks are. We lost more cases because of their incompetence.”

Mason bit back the obvious. Wren was incompetent and corrupt. “A few days?” Mason repeated.

“Anyway, I haven’t received an official request for that, and it can wait until the captain wants it done.” Wren said. “Unless you want to dig through six months of dispatch logs by hand.” Wren handed a request form back through the window for a different record on a different case, casual as breathing. “I’ll have the DA tell George’s people it’s a backlog issue. Happens all the time.”

He walked away before Mason could press further.

Behind the counter, the clerk whispered under her breath, “Funny. I thought I saw him sign that file out yesterday.” Shook her head. “Maybe I’m thinking of someone else.” Mason could tell she’d overheard Wren’s remark.

Wren was already out the door, delay locked in, clock bought, and no one able to prove otherwise.

His phone rang. “Curtis explained what one of the cyber guys had found. Wanted to know if there was a Stingray search on cell phones that day? If so, what did they find?”

“Let me check. I’m at the cyber evidence and records window right now.”

Mason turned back to the young tech. "Can you do a check on the Bridget Taylor murder case for any Stingray cell tower checks?"

She nodded. "No problem. Can you come back in about an hour?"

"No problem." He told Curtis that he'd call him back later.

Dallas Office | Late Afternoon

Outside, the afternoon sky had shifted, clouds gathering from the west after a crisp, wintry morning. *Weather reports on the team's open newsfeed noted the possibility of light rain moving into parts of North Texas overnight, but for now the day remained raw and clear.* Selena entered silently, holding a photo. "This came to the front desk. No return address."

Fiona took it. It was a still frame of Fiona cradling the puppy she saved, with the fire raging behind her. No indication of who took the picture. On the back:

He's doing fine. Thank you for saving him. He belongs to both of us now.

There was a collar, too. With a tag that has the name Aladdin inscribed on it.
Curtis stepped in behind her. "An anonymous admirer?"
Fiona nodded slowly. "He must have watched that night. Took the puppy." Fiona's fingers brushed the image again. For a second, she wasn't sure if she should feel gratitude or fear.
Matilda, who insisted she was fine, came back to work early and looked up from her laptop. "Then you weren't just being surveilled. You were being set up."
Curtis's expression hardened. "I don't like this Fi; this guy's playing games."

At that moment, Mason called and informed Curtis that they

had not performed a Stingray ping search yet, but Mason ordered one immediately and filed the request through the courts. As soon as he got the warrant information, he would let them know what he found. Also, the subpoena from George Shaw came in about four thirty that day. That information made him wonder why Wren was at the records when he saw him.

◆ ◆ ◆

Encrypted Ops Room | Evening

"Burner server's live," Bianca said. "Two journalists bit. They got the teaser."

"Good," Fiona replied. "Send the second packet in twelve hours. With hints about the word SILO and the flight manifests scrubbed and redacted. Give them enough to burn the fuse. The rest is up to them. And before you say anything, Curtis, yes, Major Buck is going to be pissed as hell. I don't care. This isn't a political mission or game. This is children's lives at stake. Besides, I'm only giving them a breadcrumb to chase, not all the information. They'll have to do their own work for that."

Curtis placed a fresh pin on the map. "Jared Weiss changes the angle. We're not just proving Everett's innocence. We're possibly bringing children home to their parents and exposing at least part of the network."

Mildred stepped forward. "We have enough evidence now to implicate Tovira Holdings. PAC donations, offshore routing, all of it leads back to Reid at the California division of Porter & Ashburn."

"And to Bridget's murder," Fiona added. "They silenced her for getting too close."

Charles cracked his knuckles. "We'll get those children back. Then we'll hunt down whoever is stealing them."

O'Brien & Galloway Office

The buzz of the office had faded. Selina left hours ago. Stefana typed in another room, drafting a summary for their legal files on other cases.

Fiona stepped into the main hallway, her movements stiff, the white collar of her blouse hiding the gauze along her shoulder.

Morris sat at Selina's desk, flipping through a deposition binder on his fraud case. He didn't look up as he slid a folded newspaper toward her on the desk edge.

The Dallas Observer, fresh from the stand. Ink still hot off the press.

She opened it. Headline:

Chad Ashburn Spotted at LA Gala. Speculation of Senate Bid Intensifies.

Glossy photo. Chad, mid-laugh, champagne in hand. Black-tie tux. Gold pinky ring catching the flash.

Fiona's eyes narrowed.

"You'd think with all the heat in Dallas, he'd keep a lower profile," Morris said, still not looking at her. "Unless someone wanted him seen."

Fiona paused. "You follow the society pages now?"

Morris shrugged, noncommittal. "Only when the stories land on our desks."

Curtis joined her, coat slung over his shoulder. "Do you believe in coincidences?"

She folded the paper.

"Not in election years."

She walked toward the elevator. Curtis followed.

Before the doors slid closed, Curtis asked, "You ever feel like we're in over our heads?"

"Only when bodies start piling up," Fiona said.

"And then?"

She met his gaze. "Then I remind myself, Bridget's dead. Lila's still out there. And an innocent man sits waiting for justice for his wife, for him and for his daughter. They deserve that."

The elevator doors closed. Inside the quiet office, the evidence wall remained. Thread lines still trembling from the last draft of recycled air.

At Selina's desk, Morris flipped another page in his fraud case binder, the weight of it disguising the flicker of tension in his eyes. The office was quiet. The hallway was empty.

He glanced around once. Stefana's keyboard clicks were still loud and constant. Fiona and Curtis were gone. He leaned back slightly in the chair, reached beneath the binder, and pulled forward Selina's terminal keyboard.

The screen came to life with a low glow. He typed fast and methodically. From the hidden flash partition he'd installed on being hired, he opened a secure client.

In the address field, he entered:

buck.ops@jsoc-dci.gov

For a moment, his cursor hovered over the second address string. Encrypted, tied to a corporate relay, but he deleted it. Then moved on to what he was here to do.

The body of the message was plain text.

RE: Subject: Neylan Trail & Ashburn Ties

Sliverbranch contact appears to be compromised. Fiona's team decrypted a partial archive from Bridget. Ranch targeting confirmed. Unclear if they suspect an upper-tier federal tie-in yet. Recommend reevaluation of the civilian firewall before the next attempted breach. Iron Creek wasn't an accident. Confirm the code shift on your end–M.

He encrypted it with a custom handshake cipher. No trace left behind. No sent folder. The system flushed on command.

Morris leaned back again, turned a page in the deposition binder, and waited until the screen went dark. Then stood and got his coat and locked his desk and left.

Outside, a police siren echoed down Commerce Street. *The late-night anchors' voices floated from a distant TV: Dallas police investigating Greyhound station death... national fallout continues over Memphis case.*

Inside, the silence reset.

Whiskey River Two-Step Ranch | Midnight

The cold had returned after the brief afternoon lift; overnight temps slid back toward freezing. Across most of Texas, forecasters predicted a tightening freeze in pockets inland, while coastal areas would stay cold and damp, one more reason to move fast. Fiona rode Gypsy along a well-used horse trail. The moon hung low; the sky clouded with a storm that refused to break. A shadow shifted near the treeline, but she didn't startle. *Predators hunting, most likely.*

Back inside, she opened the drawer in her desk. Took out the files she kept to herself and placed them beside a sealed file marked Personal: Do Not Open Without Fiona's Authorization.

Remembering the children, she whispered softly, a prayer, "God help us bring them home. And give us the courage to finish what Bridget died trying to expose."

CHAPTER 23

Orchestrated

Thursday, February 23rd, 2023
Downtown Dallas, O'Brien & Galloway HQ

The air inside the office was dry from the overactive HVAC. Fiona strode in front of the murder board, mug gripped tightly. A whisp of steam rose, carrying with it the subtle scent of cinnamon and vanilla from the coffee. Without thinking, she took a sip, focused on the board, deep in thought.

Edgar popped in. "Shot you a note and loaded it into the ongoing file," he nodded toward the board. "I found the guy that Everett claims was at the bar in Texarkana with him and his friend Colt. His name is Royce McCrae, a rancher out of Arkansas. I put all the information in a file with his affidavit attached. Figured you'd want to send it over to Shaw." He turned to leave, then turned back, saying. "A deputy I spoke with said a detective Wren from Dallas called about the same guy. He made it sound as if they were looking into a dine and dasher fraudster. So, he made no major effort to find the guy. Asked around about someone not paying their bill and leaving, got told no, so that was that." With that, Edgar left to work on one of his other cases.

Outside the windows, the day carried a damp gray pall. Dallas had woken under low clouds, a foggy mist clinging to the streets. *Predictions indicated rain bands and scattered thunderstorms sweeping through North Texas, part of a storm system stretching across the state.* The local radio murmured on Sabrina's desk. *The bulletin included weather reports, news of travel delays at Love Field, updates on Biden's diplomatic efforts, and a brief local report on the "Operation Janus" DHS investigation.*

Curtis entered with a clipboard, pausing long enough to glance at the red thread that now arced from Bridget's photo to Lisa's, then to Everett's. The connection was tenuous. Suggestive. They needed more. Lisa's alleged involvement in the murder of Bridget, who was her sister and Everett's wife, gained steam in the MSM news every day without verification or proof.

Fiona jumped straight to the point. "We've confirmed Bridget deliberately killed her phone after the daycare dropped her cell. Not just powered down, battery pulled, SIM removed. Josiah caught the burner activation that replaced it, something PD never flagged." Fiona said, pulling up the map overlay. "The burner cell then veered east into a dead zone. When it reappears, it's heading west and back towards the ranch, remained at the ranch for under fifteen minutes before going straight to the cabin."

Curtis's brow furrowed. "That's not what's in the police timeline."

"Exactly," Fiona said. "PD reports claim she went straight to the cabin and never came home. No mention of a stopover back at the ranch. No mention of going into a dead cell area for hours. Which means either the techs missed it, unlikely, or someone never investigated a burner phone. Josiah's burner phone trace gives us something new to work with. If we can verify what Bridget did during that detour. It's time we stopped assuming the cabin was her only stop that day. I want Ethan to drive that route; he's between cases right now. See if he can find any businesses she might have stopped at that might recognize her. Maybe it will give us a hint about what she did that morning."

Curtis leaned over her shoulder, scanning the screen. "What could she have picked up? Or dropped off?"

Fiona shook her head. "More importantly... who was there when she stopped, and why? If anyone."
She paused. "And why did it get erased from the record?"

"We need to stop chasing ghosts," Fiona said, voice low and even. "We never got to check out the scene. No crime scene analysis, no evidence sweeps, not from George Shaw's original people or us. If she had returned home and then to the cabin, there could've been something she wanted to leave for Everett. Something now lost in the fire."

Curtis exhaled. "Tell George we're requesting Stingray results directly through court channels. If PD buried them, it's obstruction, not oversight."

Sabrina said as she walked into the bullpen, "Josiah's packet included complete tower logs."

Fiona's eyes sharpened. "Then it's official. The evidence to clear Everett is missing a crucial piece of evidence to follow."

"Public opinion locked in on Everett, while the actual killers hid behind scrubbed records and planted timelines. And he is still sitting in a concrete cell while the press paints him as a wife-killer and possibly even a murderer of his child."

Curtis nodded. Jaw tight. "Fi, we need to get something to flip the narrative."

"Can you see what George can get us through discovery of the evidence collected from the cabin by the Crime Scene Technicians? They have been stalling, and we need that information. The cabin is a burnt-out shell. We never got the chance to get in and get any evidence." She walked closer to the board as if looking at it for the thousandth time would tell her something she had not seen before.

"Already on it. George called this morning, saying he has an appointment with a judge this afternoon. Meanwhile, Sam and

Rosemary are en route to the lake house to talk to Everett's neighbor. Ruke said she was at home at least until around two. Maybe she can shed more light on what occurred earlier in the day."

Fiona's eyes narrowed. "Have any of the detectives from the PD on the case done a follow-up with any of the neighbors? Have you talked to Mason lately?" She turned toward Curtis.

"He said they have him chasing paper trails, trying to connect Everett to Lisa. And still working on the 1-45 murders. But I'll ask also about the ping data from Stingray; they should have."

Rosemary entered. "Well, other neighbors told us if she was there, she could tell us something. They say she is retired, also noting that she's the busybody neighbor whom everyone fears. She has a small dog and several birds, and a cat; at least, that is what the neighbors say. Possibly, she's our best information source from the early hours of that day. One guy says she logs all comings and goings, or the slightest code infraction. She drives him crazy. We need to know what she heard and saw. If she saw anything of value that day."

"And Everett's SEAL buddy?"

"SEAL buddy Harwood, yeah, the one Everett saved in Afghanistan, he's a character witness. Colin's meeting him. If he deploys during a trial, we may lose his testimony."

Fiona nodded once. "Yeah, the police are going to say that he is backing up his buddy."

Sabrina leaned out from her workstation. "I'm pulling the original 911 call logs now. Running spectral analysis on voice cadence. If we find the guy, we can compare him to the 911 call. Do you want to listen to the call?"

Curtis looked back at her. "Loop Ben in once you've got a waveform. He's still our best audio forensics." Curtis added, "George passed along Everett's notes from last week about things Bridget told him in conversation. At the time he listened politely, but not really with interest. He noted Bridget's mention of Judge Atchison's rulings before any of us. Bridget, angry one day, told him they didn't line up with CPS records. Now Shirley's files prove he was right."

The office buzzed with activity, phones held low against shoulders, keyboards tapping like distant gunfire. Several desks were empty, but personal photos or information on the cases they were working littered their areas. Outside the windows, a sheet of gray pressed down on the city, a slight rain misting the windows.

◆ ◆ ◆

Sam and Rosemary: Lake Cabin Witness

Elaine Petrovsky lived in the large two-story cabin home, closet to the Taylor cabin, with lace curtains and a screened porch cluttered with wind chimes. The screen door squeaked when Sam opened it and stepped onto the porch. An icy drizzle slicked the steps and darkened the wooden railings. Rosemary stood beside him, silent, professional, notebook in hand. What sounded like a small dog in the house started barking hysterically. The odor from the burnt Taylor cabin blew in their direction, causing Rosemary to wrinkle her nose and Sam to frown and look toward the cabin. The fire burned so hot and fast that nothing remained except the blackened foundation.

Elaine opened the door in a blue cardigan, her iron-gray hair pulled into a perfect twist. Her eyes, though, were sharp for all her seventy-six years. "Bibi, quiet." At the firm command, the dog stopped, gave them one last look, and leaned against Elaine.

"You folks from that agency trying to prove Everett's innocence?"

Sam nodded. "Yes, Ma'am, we're trying to verify a timeline. Would you be willing to tell us what you saw the day Bridget died? If you were not here, let us know, and we won't bother you any further. If you were here, would you let us record it? Sometimes my memory is not so good, and I would hate to misquote you." Sam smiled that charming smile while staring her straight in the eyes. She smiled back.

She motioned them inside. The living room smelled of lemon polish and something faintly herbal. A cat curled on the windowsill didn't lift its head. Rosemary put the recorder on the coffee table. Between the chair Elaine sat in and the couch she and Sam sat on.

Elaine pointed to her recliner in front of the TV. "I was home. It was a Monday. Around one-fifteen. I was still waiting for my Uber, which was running late, to pick me up to head out to the airport. I heard a car pulling up at Taylor's. Bridget was helping Lila out of the car when I glanced out the window. The poor little thing was fast asleep. Shortly after that, I heard the generator come on. Had to turn my TV up to hear it. Several minutes later, when a commercial was on, another car pulled up. I thought it was Everett, so at first, I never bothered looking out. Until I heard one of those infernal motorcycles go past, headed for the Taylor cabin. No one in the Taylor family has one. They're not like those hooligans who ride them. They're honest, churchgoing people. Everett always comes over to see if I need help. And many times, the Taylors take me to church with them when they're here, if my grandson can't make it. Shortly after the motorcycle arrived, I heard voices outside."

"Men or women?" Rosemary asked, already jotting down notes.

"Two men," Elaine said. "One banged on the door rudely. The other one his voice was deeper, angry, arguing with the man hammering on the door."

Sam leaned forward. "Could you make out what they said?"

"No. The generator made it impossible to hear anything they said."

"Could you see what they were doing?" Rosemary asked.

"Yes. The man knocking on the door was tall and thin, wearing a camouflage-style hoodie and blue jeans, with a ball cap. The other one looked like those criminal bikers, with stickers all over their jackets. I reached for my phone to call the police. Then Bridget opened the door and let them in. She didn't appear to be panicking or afraid, so I stopped dialing. I decided I needed to check that I had everything ready for my cruise. It was the darndest thing. I'd won a cruise, but couldn't remember which sweepstakes it came from. The flight got delayed by a day, luckily, or I wouldn't have been home at all. Called the power company to postpone the shutoff. The technician was kind, name was Evan. He waited until my Uber came." About 15 minutes later, it arrived.

"So, you heard nothing like screams or anything after those men went into the house?" Rosemary asked.

"No. They were still there when I left."

"At any time that day did you see Everett arrive?"

"No."

"Have any police officers been out to talk to you since you've been back?"

"Yes, a nice detective. Here he left me a card in case I remembered anything else." She rose and went to rummage around her desk before coming back and handing it to Sam.

The card belonged to Detective Marcus Wren. Sam and Rosemary exchanged glances. Rosemary inquired, "Did you tell him everything you just told us?"

"Yes. Are you implying I would lie to a police officer?"

"Absolutely not. Just hoping you remembered everything."

"Are you saying I have a faulty memory?" She huffed and stood up as if about to show them the door.

Sam cut in, "No, mam, these are standard questions. No offense meant."

She slowly sat down. And smiled at Sam, yet gave Rosemary a dirty look, as if she'd been rude or something.

"May I keep this card?" Sam asked.

Indignantly, she snatched it back. "The detective gave it to me in case I remembered anything. I am sure that if you want to talk with him, you can call his precinct."

Wanting to soothe her, he said, "I am not familiar with this detective. May I at least take a photo of the card?"

Mollified, she nodded, and Sam used his phone camera to snap several photos of the front and back. Detective Wren wrote on the back, to ask for his extension if she called with anything more.

"And this is the same night the police said Everett murdered Bridget?"

Elaine nodded once. "Yes, cause I was afraid the cruise would leave without me because of the flight being rescheduled to the next day. But it turned out that the cruise was not leaving until the day after. Had to rush from the airport though to board on time."

"One more question. If you saw these guys, do you think you could identify them?"

"Yes, definitely."

Sam handed her his card, giving a lopsided grin, saying, "I know you will not give this out to anyone else."

Elaine blushed and nodded before walking them to the door. She closed the door, then yanked it open and said, "Wait. I just remembered something. Bridget put something in her mailbox. Our mailboxes are there so the postman only needs to make one stop. As you can see, I have a straight sight of it out my front window. Kept looking out to see if my Uber was coming. Everett should have the key. Oh, and Lisa was out earlier that day asking if I'd seen Bridget, or if anyone else had arrived. I told her no. About twenty minutes later, she left. I forgot about it cause it was much earlier in the day. Sometime around nine."

Sam thanked her once more, and they left, heading back to the office. As they drove to the office, Sam muttered to Rosemary, "Everett was right. Somebody orchestrated this long before that night. We need to check out who paid for her cruise. And get that key from Everett and find out what Bridget left in that mailbox. That mailbox might be the last thing Bridget protected. If she left a message or evidence, it's our best line to her intent that day. Let's get that key."

Interview with SEAL Teammate "Hawk"

The bar sat on the edge of a strip mall outside Waxahachie, all faux-wood paneling and over-salted fries. Colin Harris, 58, ex-FBI, quiet elder statesman of O'Brien & Galloway. A sharp mind hidden behind a grandfatherly smile met Travis "Hawk" Harwood in a back booth. Travis wore faded jeans, a battered Navy cap, and eyes that scanned like radar.

"You're Everett's people?" he asked.

"Yes, we're trying to clear him of murder charges."

Harwood leaned back. Arms folded. "He didn't do it."

"You sound sure."

"I'd trust that man with my life. Did more than once. We were both knee-deep in black ops. Stuff they won't even confirm happened. Everett's not capable of killing his wife, not unless someone had a gun to her head and told him to do it to save a dozen kids. And even then, he'd find another way, and believe me, whatever he decided, it would be successful." A thoughtful look came over his face. "I'd bet right now you're not seeing that in him. He loved Bridget and his daughter more than he loved himself. Right now, I'd bet he's wallowing in grief. The person who did this better be digging his grave, cause if Everett gets ahold of him. Well..." Minutes passed in silence, filling the space between them.

Colin cleared his throat. "Did you talk to him before Bridget died?"

Harwood nodded. "Two weeks before. He called me. Sounded wired. Said he noticed black government SUVs across the road from their ranch entrance, and in town as if following him around. Mentioned several missions we pulled off and wondered if they were coming home to roost. Said he worried about his wife and daughter getting pulled into his past. Wondered if the war had followed him home."

"Did he say anything about Bridget being followed?"

Harwood's brow furrowed. "Yeah. She told him that someone was watching their cabin. He chalked it up to him, not her."

Colin made a note. "Anything else?"

"Yeah. He said that if anything happened, to ignore what we saw on TV. I figured they'd suppressed all public information about our missions, even risking the negative consequences for us. We were never their priority, only the success of the mission."

Colin circled it in his notes. Not paranoia. A contingency. Everett had expected a media trap from the start. Colin noticed the bitterness in Travis's voice, wondered about its cause and its possible connection to Travis' past drinking problems before Everett helped him get straightened out.

Harwood's gaze sharpened. "There were files on our ops locked down tighter than nukes information. Every time I tried to ask questions, doors slammed shut. If Everett thought someone was circling, believe me, he wasn't imagining it."

Fiona's Office: Building the Timeline

Back at HQ, Fiona stood over the corkboard, pinning two of the latest photos in place: Elaine Petrovsky and Travis Harwood.

She added handwritten notes beneath them.

SEAL contact confirms Everett feared for Bridget's safety because of his past classified missions in the military. Suspected surveillance.

Curtis entered with a fresh printout. "Sabrina just finished analyzing the 911 call metadata. You need to hear this."

"This is the 911 call?" Fiona asked.

"Time-stamped six-oh-five pm.," Heather said. "The client claims he arrived after six pm at the cabin."

Fiona's eyes narrowed. "So, the call reporting the murder could have been hours after it occurred. Not within the timeframe Detective Wren reported it was."

"Exactly."

Heather hit play.

Wind. Panic-choked voice. "I saw a man stab a woman... through the back window... She struggled to get loose, screaming and pleading, after they tied her up. I think she said, don't hurt my daughter. The other holding the little one. She was pleading over and over again. Then he stabbed her as if frenzied."

A quick, jagged breath, almost a sob.

"I... I think one of them saw us, so we ran. It's the last cabin on a dead-end road... a few klicks down a gravel road off Highway one-fifty five, outside Tyler. One of those fancy lakeside places. Cabin Creek."

Heather isolated the background.

Metal clank. Gravel. A low, urgent whisper:
"Come on, go, go! Now. He's here."

There was the slow crawl of a motorcycle's low growl passing the gas-station pay phone.

Fiona felt the cold climb her spine. "There were two of them at the payphone?"

"Likely homeless," Sabrina said. "One ran before the call ended. The station's owner remembers a limping guy in a green army coat, another guy torn black long overcoat, around six pm."

"Do you think they saw it happen?" Fiona turned towards Curtis.

"They saw enough to know they were next if they did not hide."

Fiona exhaled through clenched teeth. "Then they're the most important witnesses we have. We find them first, or someone else will."

"If he ran, it wasn't just fear; it was recognition," Curtis said. "He knew who they were, and they knew who he was."

Suddenly, she remembered something. "Run that again," Fiona said. After listening to it once more, she realized what the caller had not said. He gave no description of the killer or killers. Yet, Detective Wren claimed in his report that the caller gave a description that matched Everett.

"Remember when I first talked with Everett and later saw Detective Wren's notes, Wren claimed the 911 caller identified someone who looked like Everett murdering Bridget. Yet, that is not on the transcript of the call."

Right then, Curtis got a message to come to the bullpen.

"And someone else is trying to find them," Heather warned. "Cartel-linked men pulling store footage across South Dallas. Cash bribes. Old-school sweep-and-erase. If the murderers think there is a loose end..." She let the sentence trail off.

"They'll kill them," Fiona finished the sentence.

Curtis stepped back in. "One of our guys traced the call to

an old, rundown gas station, a mile and a half from the Taylor cabin. The homeless encampment was closer to the creek where they found the body. Camp residents say two men talked about a murder at a cabin and a woman screaming. The police officer taking statements brushed it off as junkie rambling. One woman gave a partial plate of a black SUV that had been driving back and forth by the camp. One of the camp guys said a biker named Dog, part of a local bike gang, had been leaning on folks, offering cash, drugs, or threats, trying to find two specific homeless men. Most of the camp scattered afterwards in fear. Nobody's seen either witness since."

Fiona tapped her pen once. Hard. "Make it priority one. They saw something."

"Fi, even if we can't find them, George can make sure the jury hears about two homeless men seen by different witnesses and caught on a backyard sliding glass door by a Ring doorbell camera. Within the timeframe of her murder, the camera showed them running from Taylor's cabin property. And he would make sure that the information got into the trial transcripts. That at least adds some reasonable doubt."

"First, it's essential to get this analysis to George. If the murderers think they're a loose end, they'll erase them. Finding them is our priority, or they won't live long enough to testify." Miriam McCall said behind them as she walked in.

Curtis had a thoughtful look on his face before saying, "Could that motorcycle in the background of the 911 call be the one both Elaine and Evan saw at the cabin? Maybe that is why the 911 caller hung up so abruptly; he got scared."

Fiona turned toward the board and placed a red thumbtack through the audio log. She reread Wren's original notes, this time knowing what to look for. Gaps. Overlaps. Places where someone had folded the evidence just enough to hide the truth.

Dallas HQ | Cyber Room

Mason leaned over the secured workstation, headphones clamped tight, blocking out the chatter of the homicide bull-pen noise. He had spent hours poring over archived dispatch logs since Fiona and Curtis told him what their investigators heard from that so-called witness.

One line from a cop at the bar the night before kept gnawing at him. Something about how Wren seems to lose more evidence than find any.

He finally found it.

He bypassed the internal flag labeled case detectives only because he remained assigned to the Bridget Taylor case, and the report opened like a wound.

CALL TYPE: Suspicious Activity
TIME STAMP: Two-forty p.m.
CALLER: Evan Ruke
LOCATION: Near Cabin Creek Road
NOTES:
"Two men arguing. Then left a while later. One on a motorcycle. The other was in a black truck exiting the dirt road. A motorcycle later forced an adult cyclist off the road. Cyclist transported for broken arm, multiple abrasions. Ambulance on scene."

ACTION: *Flagged. Marked non-critical. Forwarded to Detective Wren.*
NOTATION: Possible relation to incident at Taylor's cabin. Pending a review.

UPDATE:
No follow-up.
Wren's Note: *'Interviewed. Not pertinent. Witness appeared intoxicated.'*

Mason's jaw locked.

He scrolled further and froze.

Another update had come on *that same day*; one he'd never noticed because he'd been neck-deep in the I-45 serials at the time.

"This paperwork isn't something that was overlooked. It's an obstruction. That's a felony," Mason muttered to himself. He picked up his phone and hit Curtis on his list.

Mason said, voice low. "Ruke was telling the truth. Officers were already at the turnoff near the cabin for that cyclist. Wren got the report and buried it."

Curtis didn't curse. He just breathed out sharply.

"Send it."

Mason tapped three keys, and the text shot to Curtis's phone.

Curtis read it, then read it again.

"Evan Ruke," he said. "Journeyman lineman. Logged out of the transformer site north of the cabin at three-eighteen in the evening. He was working by himself as his partner called out sick."

"Cops talk to him?" Curtis asked, though he already knew.

"One paragraph," Mason said flatly. "Barely more than a check-box. I already re-flagged it," Mason answered. "It's going into the Bridget Taylor case file as additional evidence. Wren didn't just miss this; he suppressed it. This will let him know I am watching him."

Curtis muttered, tone bone-dry.

"No wonder Ruke refused to talk to our investigators. Wren probably threatened to report him for being drunk on the job. Scare a lineman with losing his license? He'll shut up forever."

Footsteps passed outside the cyber-room. A maintenance crew, laughing about airport pretzels and a new restaurant ad plastered across the foyer's building's entrance walls.

But inside the room, all Curtis saw was the screen.

A suppressed lead. The court removed the CI witness from the original arrest warrant. A buried witness. And the first real crack in Wren's façade. Curtis needed to get this over to George.

CHAPTER 24

Keys to the Kingdom
Friday, February 24th, 2023

Whiskey River Two-Step Ranch

The smell of wet earth hung in the air after the previous night's storm, rich with cedar and ash. Fiona walked through the inner corridor of the ranch house in thick socks and an oversized T-shirt, her coffee steaming in one hand, the other trailing across the smooth stone wall.

Thick fog overlaid the lake, reaching onto the shores and blanketing the trees. It lent an otherworldly sense to the land. The wind had knocked a few branches loose across several outdoor walkways, but the silence outside felt composed, a rare calm. A chilling drizzle clung to the air; the ground was still slick with runoff from the storm. The forecast on the muted kitchen radio noted a high near 50°F, low temps in the 40s, drizzle and a damp chill across North Texas. After soaking up the quiet and spending time with Josh, she dressed and headed out to the compound in a Polaris Ranger enclosed UTV.

Inside the compound's room, Curtis already sat at the central table, glasses on, a printout in front of him with security timestamps from the Sentinel's night feed. He looked up when Fiona entered.

"Morning," she said, placing her cup on the edge of the conference table, glancing at maps spread over it.

"We still need the mailbox key from Everett; whatever Bridget left might still be there."

◆ ◆ ◆

Braddock/Colt | Everett's Alibi

Later that morning at the Dallas HQ, Ronald Gordon, an ex-police officer who worked for them, flipped through his report, then looked up at Fiona and Curtis.

"From what I discovered, the wire transfer didn't come from Colt Harlan," he said. "It came from the Braddock Circle Ranch, out of Cass County. The owner's name is Clayton Braddock, five generations of Braddocks on that ranch. The man's as straight as they come. From what everyone in the industry says."

Everett nodded slowly. "Colt bought those cattle on Clay's behalf. Braddock trusts Colt's judgement on cattle. Colt introduced me on the video call to finish the wire transfer to the auction house. Colt wanted us to meet, cattleman to cattleman." Everett's phone rang, and he got up and walked out, phone to his ear.

"I can fly up and get this information in person." Curtis said. "See if Braddock confirms Colt called him after the sale, told him what he bought and what he owed the auction house. I want it straight from the source. And if Clay wired the funds directly to the auction house, no questions asked, no paperwork trail linking it back to Colt, it'd make it damn hard for Everett to prove his story without Colt to testify, unless Braddock backs up what Everett said about a conference call."

Ronald added. "Exactly. And that guy Edgar found said Everett and Colt had drinks with at the bar, would make it so we don't need Colt if we can't find him in time."

Everett came back in and sat down. "What'd I miss?"

Fiona leaned back in her chair. "Looks like Texarkana checks out after all, just like you said. The auction records show Braddock paid the bill. But your friend Colt did the bidding. And this guy Royce backs up your being in a bar after the cattle auction, having drinks with the Colt and him."

"And that," Curtis said quietly, looking at Everett, "means Wren challenging your alibi is now much tougher. Even without Colt Harlan's testimony. I'll call George and let him know. In the meantime, I'm going to go talk with Clay Braddock in person. Find out whether any detectives talked to him. I can use our charter contract to fly up. I'll be back before night sets in with any evidence."

Fiona narrowed her eyes. "If no one contacted Clay Braddock... we've got a big problem. It's either lazy police work or a dirty cop."

Before Everett left, she asked him about the key to the cabin mailbox. He took it off his keyring and handed it to her. "Why are you asking?"

She hesitated. If he knew why, he'd go himself. Risk everything they were trying to prove. She couldn't let him. Not yet. Everett's fingers lingered on the key a second too long, as if touching something Bridget had touched might pull her back from wherever she'd gone. Fiona took it gently. "We just want to check every place. The mailbox is the only thing left standing out there." His eyes followed the key like it were the last thread to his wife. She turned away before the ache in his face could crack her resolve. Sometimes the law couldn't serve justice. Not because the law was broken, but because the men wielding it had forgotten why it existed. She wouldn't be one of them.

Mailbox at Cabin Creek Road to Taylor's Cabin

Two hours later, and after a run-in with Everett waiting next to the mailbox when she arrived, they discovered two SIM cards from a burner and her regular phone.

"Listen, Everett, it will take longer for you to get the information from these SIM cards, then my agency's cyber division will. And I can't let you even touch it, so if I have to testify, you never did from the time I opened the mailbox until it goes into our evidence chain for George, I can with a clear conscience."

"I understand." But he looked longingly at them as if touching something that his wife had touched before she died almost overwhelmed him. And he needed answers. Either of those SIM cards might have some.

"I will get the information. Eventually. And if Lila is still alive, I will bring her home. And no one will stop me from doing what I have to make that happen. Understood."

She believed him. And she wouldn't get in his way. Sometimes, the law cannot serve justice. Not inherently because of the law, but because of the men who wielded it.

Braddock Circle Ranch | Near Bozeman, Montana

Curtis parked the SUV by the split-rail fence and stepped out. The smell of sunbaked earth and hay hit him immediately. Braddock was at the barn, working a halter off a restless yearling. He looked up as Curtis approached, not startled, just evaluating.

"Mr. Clay Braddock?" Curtis called.

"That's me," Braddock said, wiping his hands on a faded red shop towel. "You from Dallas?"

"Curtis Galloway, O'Brien & Galloway Investigations." Curtis handed him one of their cards.

Braddock's brow lifted slightly. "O'Brien, huh? Fiona O'Brien? That your partner?"

Curtis nodded.

Braddock let out a low whistle and shook his head with a grin. "Well now. Haven't heard that name in a few years. You tell her Braddock still remembers the Colorado O'Brien's. Saw her run barrels in the High Plains Rodeo back when she was barely up to this rail." He placed his hand on the third one up from the ground. "Damn fearless. Rode as if she had something to prove every time. I always thought being the only girl, and youngest at that, with five brothers might have had something to do with it."

Curtis' smile was warm and genuine. "I'll tell her you said that."

Braddock leaned his forearms on the fence. "She takin' after her mother? Or her father?"

Curtis shrugged. "Bit of both, maybe, can't really say as I never knew them."
Then he cleared his throat. "I'm here about Colt Harlan."

Braddock's expression tightened, not suspicious, just serious. "He in trouble overseas?"

Curtis took note, an odd first reaction. "No, sir. We're verifying Everett Taylor's timeline the day Colt stopped in Texarkana. He's a friend of Colt's. We need to know exactly what the arrangement was."

Braddock nodded slowly, then motioned Curtis toward the shade by the barn.
"Colt called me that morning. Way out on my upper pasture, I couldn't get a damn signal. Not unusual. When I finally got the voicemail, he said some cattle with the Missouri bloodline I've been chasing for a year were showing up at the Texarkana auction. Wanted to know if I wanted him to stop by and bid on his way to Europe."

Curtis asked. "Is that bloodline important?"

"Rare as hen's teeth," Braddock said. "Excellent stock. Been trying to get my hands on it for years. When I got in, I sent him a text: Buy the cattle, don't care about the price, I'll send the money directly to the auction house once the bidding is over. Told him to represent me. Colt did that sort of thing often enough. Man had an eye for cattle."

Curtis paused. "No one else knew he made that stop?"

"Just me and the hauler who picked the cattle up later that evening," Braddock said. "Colt's wife doesn't manage ranch business. And his manager never kept up with these side pickups. Not his job to track other ranchers' business."

He scratched his jaw thoughtfully, then looked at Curtis with a narrowed, piercing gaze.

"But here's the part I don't like," Braddock said. "A detective already called about all this."

Curtis stiffened. "Detective Wren?"

"That's the one." Braddock folded his arms. "Called on a day I was in the upper pasture again, no cell service. Wife told him exactly that. Said he could call back in two weeks when the herd rotation finished."

"And?" Curtis said slowly.

Braddock shrugged, irritated. "He never called back. Not once."

Curtis felt his jaw tighten so hard his back teeth ached. "He didn't leave a callback number?"

"Nope. I called the PD. He didn't seem interested in what I had to say."

Curtis exhaled sharply. "Wren didn't verify Colt's Texarkana stop."

Braddock snorted. "Hell, son, to my thinking now he didn't want to verify it. That's how it seems to me."
He stabbed a finger at Curtis's notebook.

"You want the truth? Colt stopped in Texarkana for one reason only. Those cattle are for me. And a guy named Everett Taylor was with him. Did a video call to verify the sale. I sent the cheque to the auction house? Colt figured I'd want to meet him on the call, said he was a Texas cattleman and a veteran, like himself. I'm old, not deaf or blind. I don't forget a face or a name. Anybody with half a cowman's sense could tell you Colt never passed up a chance at excellent stock to help a friend out. But I don't know if he bought any that day. And if Colt was vouching for this Everett, he's got to be a damn fine cattleman himself. And the same for his character."

Curtis finished writing, then looked up. "Would you be willing to give a statement and let us use the video as evidence? Everett's on trial for murdering his wife, but until now we couldn't prove it. This proves the alibi, and that there was no chance he did it."

"Why'd Colt not vouch for his buddy?"

"No one can reach him. It seems he disappeared into Europe, and no one over there can find out anything about him after he lifted off from Warsaw."

Braddock nodded once, looked down, and then back at Curtis.

"Can you tell me once you have info on Colt? He's like a son to me. His daddy and I go way back. To the other, I'll tell anyone who asks. You tell this Wren guy Clay Braddock doesn't take kindly to being ignored when a man's life hangs in the balance."

Curtis offered his hand. Braddock shook it with a grip like steel cable.

"Oh," Braddock added as Curtis turned to leave.
"And tell Fiona, if she ever wants to ride rodeo again, she's got a mount here waiting. One of her brother's bloodlines. Damn near threw me trying to break him. Thought she'd appreciate that."

Curtis smiled for real this time. "I'll deliver the message. Though she still rodeos on her own ranch in Texas."

He headed back to the SUV, stomach knotting as the pieces slid into place.

Wren hadn't just been sloppy.

Wren hadn't just rushed the case; he'd picked Everett and ignored everything else. Or, Curtis's gut twisted; it was a frame job.

And someone wanted it that way.

Which meant someone *wanted Everett gone.*

Dallas County Morgue | Late Morning

Joe Bell leaned against the frosted glass partition. His blazer carried faint traces of cologne and stale cigar smoke. The coroner, Nancy Laird, adjusted her gloves as she stepped out of the autopsy bay for the last hour.

"Didn't expect to see you again," she said, her tone dry as dust.

Joe gave her a tight smile. "Porter & Ashburn requested Lisa Neylan's death certificate. Insurance inquiry. I'm just the errand boy."

Nancy narrowed her eyes. "Since when do you run minor errands?"

Joe shrugged. "When I have a history with the examiner."

She didn't smile. "Lisa Neylan's death is under police investigation. I can give you a copy of the certificate; that's all."

"Fair enough."

As she handed over the sealed envelope, he added, "Anyone else been poking around the Bridget Taylor case?"

Nancy paused. "A few questions came through last week. Someone anonymous. Wanted to know where the body was first discovered."

Joe's smile slipped. "You told them?"

"Told them to ask the investigators on the case."

He stepped closer, lowering his voice. "If you hear anything else… let me know first."

Nancy looked at him as if he were a festering splinter. "Why do I feel you're not here about insurance?"

Joe turned and left without answering. The altered death certificate of Bridget Taylor, now in the coroner's file, placed there by Joe while Nancy was in the autopsy bay. Her forged signature was perfect. The original folded in his pocket. His connections, built over drinks and quiet favors, always paid off.

Private Mansion in Dallas, Texas

The old man poured himself a glass of brandy and turned to face his son, who leaned stiffly against the study wall.

"Our guy says the girl had nothing in her condo. If Bridget gave her anything, it's gone. I need you to find out if there was anything she put elsewhere and destroy it."

He folded his arms. "So why kill her?"

The old man didn't blink. "Because she became a variable. I don't tolerate variables. Why this sudden question about killing someone?"

His son shifted, anger visible beneath his polished demeanor. "And Joe?"

"Joe does what he's told. Until he doesn't. Then he becomes a variable too."

"Understood." Moments passed in silence. Then his father said. "Spit it out. Something's eating at you."

"Did you have him copy my work? Don't think I did not notice how he killed her, and those others."

The old man laughed and shrugged. "Why would you care?"

He knew his father understood why and exactly whom he referred to. He believed his father used Joe to taunt him.

"I saw the police photos. You made sure of that. I saw the angle of the limbs. The precision of the staging. I knew you allowed some fool to replicate my work, to steal my power. I'll deal with him soon enough."

"You will do nothing until I say you can. Understand?"

"Yes, but soon enough he will be that variable you were talking about, and I personally will take care of the problem."

The old man finished his brandy and slammed his glass down. "Don't think you can order me around. You are aware of how that could end for you. *Son.* You may leave and manage the things I called you here to discuss. Lately, I've not been happy with your handling of our organization. Others are getting nervous. Your focus is elsewhere. That stops now. There are rumblings that the next vote might not go my way if I can't get everything back on track with the timeline. And I will take a very dim view of that outcome... Understand."

Outside the windows, the Dallas skyline shimmered in the damp noon haze. On a muted TV in the office corner, *the local news reported an Arlington homicide, while national outlets replayed clips of a Texas abortion-pill lawsuit and Biden's Kyiv trip.*

He left as he had come. A dark shadow in the light.

Fiona's Ranch Office

Fiona sat back, looking at the images of Bridget, Lisa, and a teenage version of herself flickering across the screen. Each face connected to something deeper; some thread just beyond her grasp.

Josh knocked lightly, holding a bowl of popcorn. "Movie night?"

She blinked, dragging herself back to the moment. "Right,

yeah." They sat in the theater room. The silence between them filled with cartoon voices and buttery smells. Fiona wrapped an arm around her son and tried to remember when she'd last taken a relaxing breath.

Sentinel Hangar | Night

Inside the dim belly of the airship, screens blinked to life, their displays showing mirrored backups of everything seized in the Dallas office. Curtis stood with Leon Browning, ex-NSA, and Bianca Anderson from Sentinel's cyber wing. The three of them reviewed search logs and firewall reports. They got nothing that could implicate Everett. And a court order had already forced the PD to return all records not related to Everett's case. Luckily, the most important drives were safe in Buck's hands.

"Still secure," Bianca confirmed. "No external pings. No signs of intrusion."

The warship-like hum of the Sentinel settled into a whisper, cradled safely in the quiet dark of its now hardened military hangar.

CHAPTER 25

Signals in Noise

Monday, February 27th, 2023

Dallas Downtown HQ

The downtown office smelled of chicory coffee, gun oil, and locker-room bleach, baked into the walls. Overhead fluorescents hummed low against the floor-to-ceiling windows, catching the cold pink edge of morning light bleeding in from the east.

Curtis stood at the center of the investigators' bullpen, one hand braced on a whiteboard cluttered with task rotations, case references, and deployment zones. His voice was low but commanding. "Time to lock in."

Fiona moved beside him, tablet in hand. Hair pulled into a clean twist. Tactical pants. Zip jacket built for work, not for show.

"All right," Curtis said, eyes sweeping the assembled teams. "New week. Fresh case logs. Updates to asset coverage."

Three clusters of personnel faced him.

Their Protection Division team leaders, Kenneth Steele, stood straight-backed, arms folded. Phùng Vĩnh Ân, Derek Armstrong, and Stephen Avery reviewed the protective detail schedules. Black-gray jackets, faint O&G insignia over the heart. Bear, Dean Meadows' alert Malinois K9 ears up, lay under the table watching everyone as if he knew something they didn't. Getting him past the lobby had become a sport among the former Tier-One operators' handlers. Sometimes they snuck up Pax, the other team's K9.

Some of their Cyber Division team. Bianca Anderson, Randy Geller, and Leon Browning sat at glowing terminals, cascading alerts, encrypted server chatter, and thermal overlays from last night's surveillance feeds.

And their newly formed O&G Security team leader, Nolan Greaves, the new manager of the civilian arm, sat slightly apart. Fifteen years of municipal risk coordination etched into his crooked fighter's jaw. Charcoal button-down. O&G Security lapel pin. This division would take over all surveillance for the PIs to lighten their loads. Run courier accounts as needed. And do all the normal high-end security.

"We've got four new courier contracts this week. Two in the Plano legal sector, two overnight to Houston," Nolan reported. His calm Dallas drawl thinned when he addressed the veterans. "Lobby security rotation changes went live this morning. The building manager notified us. Anyone who sees Blake or Deluca on site, those are our new contract officers, send them to my office. Possible VIP transport Friday pending background checks." He glanced at Kenneth, who gave a curt nod.

Curtis shifted to Kenneth and Phùng. "I want full-sweep protocols at all Sentinel reentry points. The FBI's breathing down our necks on evidence custody. No more inside breaches. You've got the new jammer loadouts at the compound?"

Phùng nodded. "Tested and verified. No leaks. No shadows."

"Good," Fiona said. "All destroyed gear from the ranch ambush gets logged and rotated for destruction or repair. If the Bureau asks, we answer legally. If they demand anything from Sentinel servers, remind them it's classified. Same applies to the compound; standard warrants will not grant access." She turned toward Bianca. "Status of the satellite trace from Nightjar's latest drop?"

"Still indexing," Bianca replied. "Prelims show a blind router chain bouncing through Panama. Another hour before it sorts, but clean so far."

Fiona clicked the remote. A wall display flickered alive, listing new priority targets:

Get SIM card information from the mailbox and send it to George if it has any exculpatory information.

Travis Harwood: confirmed character witness unless he gets deployed last minute.
Locate Colter Colt Harlan; secure a formal statement. Dead or alive, someone overseas knows where he is.
Anonymous 911 Caller: Re-investigate audio anomalies. Coordinate with Sabrina.
Elaine Petrovsky: witness affidavit needed.
Evan Ruke: re-interview; confirm officer's response. Witness affidavit needed.
Joe Bell: movements during and post Lisa Neylan's death. Track burner activity in the area or the tracker on his vehicle.

Ethan spoke up. "That eastward jaunt you sent me on paid off. A small diner named," he checked his notes, "Sugar Pine Diner, remember her and a little girl by the name of Lila from that day. Regular came in now and then, would sit and have coffee, sometimes pie. Normally, she goes to the church on the other side of the road after about twenty minutes. Never stays long. She sat there watching the church across the street for about two hours. Waitress, who normally waits on her," he consulted his notes again. "Darlene West told me. I went across the street to speak with the priest, but the one there said he was new, having just arrived in October. No idea what happened to the last priest. I sent a request to the church diocese for information on the priest's whereabouts. No answer yet."

Curtis posted a scanned family court filing next: Custody Petition: Lisa Neylan v. Everett Taylor for guardianship of Lila Taylor. "Everett didn't learn about this until after Lisa died. The DA may try to weaponize it in trial prep. We stay ahead."

"Anyone not on open cases," he continued, "maps every potential contact tied to the 911 call and Lisa's final seventy-two hours. We've been reactive for too long. That ends today."

Kenneth rose. "We'll break the teams by quadrant. Does the armory have our updated or replacement needs?"

"They do," Derek said. "I'll be grabbing Bear's new rig. He's been pacing since the ranch attack. He was in his kennel when it happened."

Across the room, Fiona stopped beside Nolan. On her desk, the photo of the puppy. Her eyes flicked to it once before meeting Nolan's.

"You good with coverage this week?"

"Six guards rotating three shifts between two buildings," Nolan said. "Courier fleet stays grounded until weather clears. You've got full movement within the Dallas/Fort Worth area though. If something needs quiet surveillance, shoot me a list after the meeting."

Fiona gave a rare half-smile. "You'll get the call. Don't spook the suits though, unless I say so." She moved away and then turned back. "Don't worry about hiring Deluca; I went over his application and the background check your guys did. I would have hired him." With that, she moved on to other business.

Behind her, Curtis went back to the board, crossing off dead ends, then adding new leads. The ops floor stirred, boots on polished tile, K9 nails clicking as Dean whistled for him to follow him out, and as coffee cups refilled like ritual.

Outside, Dallas woke.
Inside, they'd built a war plan around their day.

◆ ◆ ◆

Dallas | O'Brien & Galloway New Surveillance Unit

The surveillance bay hummed with a low, steady rhythm, monitors flickering, keystrokes spaced like heartbeats. They rebuilt the room as cold storage, a shielded intelligence pit. Air cooled. Still. Controlled.

Nolan leaned forward, elbows on his knees, eyes locked on the main feed.

Joe Bell, in jeans, a dark utility jacket, tan polo shirt, stepped off the elevator at the Rosecroft Hotel. Twenty minutes earlier he'd visited Delores Cole's in-town condo, used *his* key to bypass both gates, and spent eleven minutes inside.

Next, Delores emerged from a side entranced green silk blouse, designer sunglasses, hair pulled in a careless twist. No hesitation. No glances at the cameras throughout the building. She knew where the blind spots were.

They met under the overhang, exchanged nothing but proximity, and disappeared through the staff corridor door.
Joe's hand palmed something small, a document or flash drive. Quick. Intentional.

At the next station, Bianca listened to the video with her headset on. "Third meeting in four days with Delores. Home to the hotel, two to three hours, then home. Same MO. Different vehicles. Different entries."

"We've got trackers on all the vehicles." Nolan said into his cell, talking with Ronald back at the office.

"They're hiding the relationship," Nolan said. "Means it matters. And if it's a transfer, it might tie to the Porter & Ashburn client shells. Watch for anything routed through their California accounts in the next couple of days."
He leaned back, thinking. The attorneys were moving illicit cash through a minimum of three businesses. One handled transfers; one obscured ownership; one made it look like a nonprofit. Porter & Ashburn ran the legal smoke screen.

He tagged and backed up the footage to the off-grid node. Only Curtis or Fiona could access.

"Set auto-alerts on both phones," he ordered. "Flag every ATM they touch."

"On it," Bianca replied. "You want this prepped for Curtis tonight?"

"Tomorrow's fine," Nolan said. "Let him have one night of peace." He gazed at the frozen image. Delores's hand brushed Joe's arm intimately.

"They're hiding it. Which means it matters," he murmured. "Or guilty of something."

Thermal signatures faded on the screen. Outside, storm light rolled across the skyline. The cameras missed nothing.

◆◆◆

Tuesday, February 28th, 2023

Dallas HQ

Stefana stepped in, clutching a fresh folder. One of our investigators in the field, working on a spousal cheating case, saw two of the suspects in the Everett Taylor case. Recognized them from the main board the other day as he left. "They're... indelicate," she said, blushing.

"How'd he get these pics if they're that... indelicate, like you said?" Fiona held her hand out for the folder, which Stefana reluctantly handed over. As Fiona took a drink of her coffee, she opened the folder and almost spat her coffee everywhere. "Gods, how in the hell did he get those shots?" she said as she flipped the folder shut.

Well, he *says* he got them at a well-known strip club with private rooms. He was wearing a lipstick camera and a voice recorder. Because he knew the husband he was investigating frequented this place, the recording was on and running. He hoped to catch him in the act.

He claims they invited him to the party. This gorgeous female, in his words, invited him... shall we say, to witness the act. The guy with her did not look so happy but agreed. He was about to say no when he realized he'd seen them both as suspects on the Everett Taylor board. And she apparently put on quite a show. At least, that's what he says.

"And exactly who was this investigator?"

"Jazzra Dorsey," Stefana said.

Fiona thought for a moment, but couldn't place him.

But Curtis, without looking up from the folder now spread open before him, remarked. "I hired him a couple of weeks ago. Put him on the new hires, domestic cheating, and skip tracing. Hispanic guy all the females swoon over, cocky swagger, flirts with everyone, no matter age or rank. I have to chase him off if I need information from any of them. Surprised you have not met him yet. If what I'm seeing here is anything to go by, he's good at his job. He got what he needed, didn't he?" Curtis waggled his eyebrows, a big grin on his face.

Fiona couldn't help herself and laughed. "Men." She rolled her eyes. "Still, this proves Delores and Joe Bell are having an affair. And it sounds like she, not him, is in charge."

"Get this information into the files, but Stefana, not the main board. No need for the whole bullpen gawking at this, and all work coming to a stop. Got it?"

"I was thinking the same thing." Stefana said on her way out the door with the folder.

Curtis's voice was low. "Back to our earlier business, I need to talk to both Mason and George. Did the detective

"It's about time you had another meeting with Mason, but not publicly. I don't think they have figured out who is helping us with the information yet. Let's keep it that way."

Fiona stood and went back out to the bullpen and looked at the map again. Then she picked up the marker and added a single word across the murder board's top: *Orchestrated.*

Outside, the faint sound of thunder rolled across Dallas, rain spitting against the windows. Fiona gazed at the board, every thread of red yarn stretched taut like a lightning strike waiting to land. On the large monitor on the wall, the software made all the connections only with black lines, not yarn.

Sabrina's Discovery

"You're really going to want to hear it. Those SIM cards. They verify everything Lisa told you about her calls and texts. I copied the information onto a drive and had one of our couriers send the SIM cards over to George's office. Also, I did a printout of the transcript of everything on that phone from that morning before she pulled the cards and placed it in the mailbox." Curtis grabbed both and raced to Fi's office. After Fiona read the report, they called George. Half an hour later, he arrived at the office to discuss their next move.

"Let's keep this close. We'll need more to get the DA to drop the case outright." George said, his tone more than a little relieved. This is the best news so far. "Let's not give away our hand just yet." With that, he left.

Fiona's Office

Fiona stood by the window, the Dallas skyline reflecting off the glass. The puppy's photo sat on her desk. The note stayed hidden, quiet as a shadow. Curtis asked her why she kept it on her desk. She had no answer. She saved that puppy that day, when hell unleashed around her, and rescued something innocent and helpless.

Storm clouds pressed low over the city. Lightning forked to the north.

Storms don't come without lightning, and someone's always ready to strike first.

CHAPTER 26

Eyes Inside the Gate
Friday, March 3rd, 2023
O'Brien & Galloway Downtown Office | Dallas

The conference room lights glared off the wall of case files, maps, and surveillance stills pinned behind Fiona. A filtered sun cut hard lines through the blinds, tracing the edge of Curtis's boot where it tapped, slow and steady, against the floor. No one spoke for a full minute. All eyes were on Buck and his men.

The murder board had gone cold. Nothing new. Jeanne discovered one of their leads, about the two homeless witnesses, had just collapsed. One man turned up dead behind a transit rail station in Dallas. Overdose. Fentanyl, they said. Case closed. But the timing was too convenient.

The second witness, a man the shelters knew as "Hank," had simply vanished. No trace. No chatter. Not even from their street contacts, who usually knew every soul living under the bridge and in homeless encampments on this side of Dallas. Jeanne at least had a picture of him.

She finally got in touch with the boater, and he was more than willing to let her get copies of the two homeless men behind the house that day. He believed they were the killers. Fiona told Jeanne to print up photos of his picture and put their number below it and have it posted throughout the areas the homeless frequented. Nothing else was to be put on the poster.

Buck entered without knocking. Stopped and glanced at the murder board. Arms crossed, unlit cigar rolling between restless fingers.

Curtis broke the silence first, his hand tightening on the whiteboard marker. "Any word on Colt Harlan?" he asked, voice edged with frustration.

Fiona spoke up. "Seems our inquiries are getting blocked. We've been waiting for confirmation, anything, from Warsaw, from Berlin, hell, even back-channel chatter out of Kraków. Have your people picked up so much as a trace?"

Buck shook his head grimly once. "Nothing solid. Whispers here and there. CIA's blocking every channel. If he's alive, he's deep under. If not... someone's burying it hard. Which does not bode well for Colt. If not," ... he gave a shrug... "someone's burying it hard." He stared at the whiteboard once more as if interested in something on it, then said. "That may be your priority. Mine is different. But they overlap now; and that's why I'm here."

Fiona's jaw tightened. "That case has a deadline. Unless it leads to Bridget's killer, it's secondary."

Buck's mouth tightened, deep lines showing in his face. "I wouldn't be here if it weren't critical."

Curtis leaned forward. "How critical?"

"Casa del Manto Blanco. Officially closed five years ago. Satellite feed shows movement, heat signatures, vehicles, and kids. At least nine or ten. One matches Jared Weiss." Silence landed like a fist. "The church officially sold it to the Tovira Fund Group. Much of this intel came from the encrypted data you provided. So, in a sense, you're already on the case."

Curtis leaned forward, wariness etched in every line of his face. "That sounds like an intel job. Not a PI firm's job."

"Intel can't touch it," Buck replied. "Not without alerting oversight committees. And someone will warn them we're coming. But a private agency with no official ties can. I need eyes inside. Photos. IDs. Enough to bring about a multilateral strike with clear jurisdiction."

"You want us to verify whether trafficked kids are being held there?" Fiona asked, voice like flint.

"I want confirmation from your people. Nothing more. Your people get in, verify, get out. That's it."

Curtis exhaled, a thoughtful look on his face, glanced Fiona's way and saw what he figured were his thoughts as well.

Buck continued, voice quiet but sharp. "We built Sentinel for this. High-reconnaissance drones, offshore relays, invisible entry. The budget committee buried the project. The lead person who designed Sentinel died shortly after he completed the project. She is one of a kind. I'm going to prove her worth. I had to pull more strings and make more promises to political types than you know to get you the ability to buy her. And then, only if you agreed, she would be available for government work when we needed her. Sentinel is the only platform that can reach this target. Quiet. Silent. She can hide in the clouds, almost stationary. Do a vertical drop for pickups and drop-offs just outside international waters. Radar, thermal, and all other tracking methods cannot detect her skin because she's made from special materials that protect her. She blends into her surroundings, damn near invisible. That fat girl can vanish right in front of you." He put his cigar in his mouth and clamped down on the end.

Curtis folded his arms. "The project didn't mention our participation in the government work, just full access to Sentinel when required, and full use of the special ops guys you got for us. I didn't hear you ask us to do this. You seem to have assumed we would."

"You're the only ones who can. And we've got a small window.

There's chatter of a big meeting on March eleventh. Guards will be thin for about three hours. That's the first real chance we've got."

Silence pulsed across the room. Then Fiona spoke. "That's an awfully small window. If I agree, Curtis and I will go. Not any of our investigators; they're all in the middle of cases. Important cases. Including Everett's."

Curtis straightened. "Or no one goes."

Buck didn't hide his scowl. "That wasn't the plan. I thought I could use some of your investigators for this. I can't afford to lose either of you two. If that happens, we could lose access to Sentinel." He put his cigar in his mouth, staring at them both. Finally saying. "At least you have LEO training, guess that counts for something."

"Touching. But we're going." Curtis said drily.

Buck stared at both for a long, taut beat. Then he sighed. "Fine. But under consular cover. No weapons. No hidden surveillance, at least by you and Curtis. I'll get your paperwork locked in before Saturday. Op launches March eleventh. Be ready."

He turned toward the door, pausing just before exiting.

"And Fiona? If what I think is going on in that place is true, don't go in hoping for good endings. There might not be any."

"I know," she said.

The door clicked shut behind him. Fiona turned to Curtis, gaze steady.

"If we find them," she said, "we'll make damn sure they get rescued. Buck had better keep his word. And did you notice he said 'we' not I when referring to the loss of Sentinel?"

Curtis gave a slow nod. "Yeah, something he's not telling us. But this will be Sentinel's first *off-book intel* mission. We knew this day would come. Let's make it count."

Whiskey River Two-Step Compound

Preparations stretched over the week. Buck's men and engineers swarmed the airship day and night. After the mission, Buck would report back to a select subcommittee. He needed to prove that Sentinel was worth the money. More about proving her capabilities than anything else. There were other ways to get this done, but he needed to show the value of the airship. March eleventh finally arrived.

The gates of Casa del Manto Blanco loomed behind rusted iron and flaking whitewash. Records indicated the compound's closure five years earlier, defunded by the Catholic Church. Silent. But from the rooftop of a decaying apartment building three blocks away, Fiona saw the faint, rhythmic blink of motion sensors along the wall, infrared halos pulsing like eyes in the dark.

The pre-dawn air was cool and dry, hovering in the low 50s, but by noon the heat would climb into the upper 70s under a cloudless sky. It gave the city's sprawl a brittle clarity. The skyline shimmered in the faint haze.

A soft click in her earpiece.

"Fi," Curtis murmured. "We're up."

Fiona crouched beside him, one knee pressed to the rooftop. The air smelled of diesel, burnt sugar from street carts, dirt clinging to rooftops, and the foul rot of sewage in the ditches in this part of the city. A rooster crowed somewhere in the distance, and the mewling of cats fighting closer down the street.

Major Buck had arranged their entry under diplomatic cover. Quiet, untraceable. One of his embedded consulate contacts secured the paperwork. Just encrypted comms and a drone relay circling twelve hundred feet above, patched through Sentinel, stationary above the Gulf in international waters.

Phùng Vĩnh Ân scanned the perimeter from an adjacent rooftop. Wendell Hatfield lay prone two rooftops west, using long-range optics. Aaron Pratt stood watch at street level with Pax, the Belgian Malinois. Derek Armstrong monitored their extraction alley, med-pack ready.

"X-rays show movement in the courtyard," one of Buck's men at the surveillance console on the Sentinel said over the channel. "Two bodies. One tall. One small. Holding pattern. Other signatures are being blocked."

"Child?" Fiona asked.

"Possible. Could be someone short. Movement's non-aggressive."

Fiona adjusted the DSLR camera lens and snapped frames of the main archway. The building resembled a monastery, with cloisters in shadow, weathered cherub statues, and crucifix-painted shutters closed.

Curtis tapped his field tablet. "PAC money hit this place three days ago, filtered through a string of shell companies. Routed through Belgrade, then Bogotá, then here. The lawyers were washing money through at least three fronts. One handled transfer; one obscured ownership; one made it look like a non-profit. Porter & Ashburn ran the legal smokescreen."

"An abandoned orphanage doesn't get new cash flow unless something's happening inside," Fiona muttered.

Buck sent the special forces team in only as spotters, medical support, and extraction assistance. This was a no-weapons op for anyone stepping through the gate. Two blocks away, Derek and Wendell took rear positions. Pax, the other Malinois K9, followed his handler Aaron, who stayed with one of the parked vehicles in case they needed a fast exit. Phùng handed Fiona a transmitter disguised as a disposable lighter. Fiona slipped it into her pocket. No one spoke again.

"If we're taken," he said, "this pings Sentinel's servers, will ping

Bianca back at the compound. She scrubs the servers. The rest of us vanish. Buck will have to mount a rescue. Meaning you'll have to hold on until he can. Understood?"

Fiona gave a curt nod.

Buck's men had weapons, but crossing the gate would trigger an international incident. That was why he needed the PIs.

They descended in silence. Curtis drove; Fiona rode shotgun. Black-windowed SUV, diplomatic tags stripped, chassis swapped in Veracruz. While they passed crumbling churches and clustered vendors, Fiona sorted her photos from the CPS file Curtis had received from Shirley before someone murdered her. When they pulled up in front of the church, they saw a barefoot boy playing soccer with a deflated ball in the outside yard.

Curtis broke the silence. "You're sure?"

"I know what we'll find," she said. "I just don't know how many will still be there."

At the gate, Curtis rang the bell. One minute. Two. Then the intercom buzzed.

A woman's monotone voice: "Casa del Manto Blanco is closed."

Fiona pressed her hand to the iron. "We were told this place is closed. Yet we have evidence children are inside." Static. Then the gate buzzed.

Inside, pigeons scattered from a cracked fountain surrounded by wilted roses. A nun emerged, perfect manicure, her shoes designer, and an expensive watch. "Her eyes were mean. Hollow."

"This is a place of healing," she said without the slightest trace of humility.

Curtis scanned the buildings' shadows. Something moved near the chapel. Subtle, intentional.

Calmly, Fiona said, "We have authorization to do a welfare

check on any children who might be here."

The nun smiled thinly. "All the children here are in a federal placement program. Federal authorities gave permission for their guardianship." With manicured precision, she produced a Porter & Ashburn card. "Talk to them. Otherwise, I'll report your interference, Ms.?"

Fiona locked eyes with her before saying. "Names are not as important as what is going on here."

Two boys stepped into view. Thin, barefoot, hollow-eyed. One matched the picture she had of Jared Weiss. Relief flooded Fiona. Alive. The one that appeared to be Jared, eyes locked on hers. Appearing too old for seven, too empty. A small hand clutched the deflated soccer ball as if it were the only thing still his. She believed the second was Luis Tenorio. He stood half-hidden behind him, thumb in mouth, rocking slightly. The same rocking motion she'd seen in Josh when nightmares woke him at three a.m.

His parents would see their son again, yet would he be the same bright, happy, smiling child? She quickly captured pic's of the boys with her phone camera. She believed the second was Luis Tenorio.

Fiona crouched slightly, steady. "They're the reason I came."

Ten minutes later, Fiona walked out of the compound. Curtis stood by the vehicle. The other boy pressed his face to the gate behind her, his eyes pleading, the look haunting her, and she turned back and crouched before the boy.

"We're coming back," she whispered.

Curtis didn't have to ask. He already knew. If Buck did not keep his word to rescue the children, Fiona would walk through fire to get these kids out of there. He would make sure she was not alone. They'd stop at nothing to bring those kids home. *Serve and protect* was an oath they both took as officers. They still honored that oath.

Five blocks out, Bianca's voice returned. "Cross-check complete. Facial match confirmed. Jared Weiss and Luis Tenorio. Notations of L.T. at this place explained. Both missing. From San Antonio. Last year, someone scrubbed the CPS file on Tenorio. Jared listed as a runaway."

Fiona's hands tightened.

Curtis glanced over. "It's Buck's move now. If need be, we can send some investigators. We can track them if they move the kids. We will get them back."

"I know," Fiona whispered. "How many children are being trafficked like this? They held these two for *how long* without a single trace. Buck can pass this to the FBI," Curtis said. "They'll move fast."

Sirens wailed. Several Policía Federal trucks, followed by three FBI SUVs, roared past, lights flashing, heading toward Casa del Manto Blanco. Buck had them staged, waiting.

Curtis observed them blow past, jaw tight. "He kept us out on purpose." Buck had not informed Fiona of this because he didn't want to get her hopes up. He had no concrete evidence that the kids would be there. And he was getting pressure from the select subcommittee to prove the deal they made with O'Brien & Galloway was worth the investment to allow them the use of the Sentinel.

Fiona stared at the trucks until they vanished. "Buck played us," she a thoughtful look on her face. "But at least it was for the right reason."

Curtis nodded. "Those kids will be home soon."

She didn't reply. She was thinking of Josh, of the way he still checked under his bed for monsters some nights, even though he was too old to admit it. If those children were hers... Her throat tightened. "We'll make damn sure they are," she whispered. Outside, the first raindrops struck the window. Soft. Steady. Relentless.

CHAPTER 27

Smoke & Threads

Thursday, March 23rd, 2023

Dallas HQ

The downtown conference room, bright with morning sunlight and fresh coffee, enticed one over to the refreshment bar. Most of the chairs were warm, recently vacated. Outside the tall windows, the sun rose against a clear blue sky, a warm spring day Dallas hadn't seen in weeks. The weather news for the day droned in the background. Temperatures will climb fast toward the upper 70s, though the air still holds a cool edge from the night's low near 48.

Fiona stood at the far end of the long table, arms crossed, jaw tight. Before pulling up the information on the screen.

Recovered SILO Log Fragment. Internal Predictive Routing Protocol Log. Timestamp: REDACTED. SUBJECT ID: TX-Y/2147893.

Name: REDACTED (minor). Age: 7. Flagged for Extraction: Predictive Compliance: High. Custodial Status: Override issued. Assigned Foster Node: Redacted. Reroute Trigger: Voluntary Runaway - 72hr Delay. Status: Now Untraceable. Notes: If the subject has value, prevent disruption.

She paused. "It's a sorting system." Curtis frowned. "What kind?" "Performance scores, behavior logs, genetic markers, even how fast a child answers learning prompts," Fiona said. "SILO feeds it everything. Runs predictive models on foster kids. Flags some 'high value' for extraction. Others vanish from the records." She tapped the screen. "It studies the children. Studies the buyers. Tailors the pitch. Rewrites rules. Here it waited seventy-two hours, then labeled the child a runaway. No alerts. No trace." Her voice dropped, almost to a whisper. "Bridget notes remark it wasn't corrupt, whatever it was. It was obedient, like a well-trained bloodhound, to whoever built it." She looked at the age on the log. Seven. She thought of Josh; nightmares still wake him screaming. What real-life nightmares did these children live.

Major Buck entered without knocking; his presence was a storm front. Boots heavy, shoulders squared, tension radiating off him like heat off blacktop.

"Clear the room," he barked. No explanation.

Everyone froze. Curtis didn't hesitate. "You heard him. Go."

Within seconds, the floor was silent except for the dull hum of the HVAC system and the faint blare of news vans already setting up on the street below. Fiona's pulse had quickened. Buck wasn't pacing. He was circling.

He rolled his unlit cigar between thumb and forefinger, lips drawn tight. Once, he nearly cracked a knuckle against the wall, but caught himself. Then he spoke. "I've got a political shadow over me. Senator Morrow's been sniffing around Sentinel's funding and private contracts. The FBI is holding a press conference this afternoon. They will take credit for the church's recovery, and they will announce that the FBI and Mexico's Policía Federal rescued nine kids working together in a joint task force. Claims the place is now closed."

Curtis raised an eyebrow. "I thought that was the goal. They take the credit to keep your guys and us out of the limelight."

Buck's jaw flexed. "That was the plan. But they changed the

story." Buck growled. "Until I got confirmation, they lied. Our inside source at the Bureau says they're covering for Stuart and Erskine Holdings. Telling donors and officials that it was a cartel-run operation. Colombian, convenient for them." He bit down on the cigar. He didn't light it. Just ground it between his teeth.

Fiona leaned in. "Can't you contradict the bureau with the committee?"

His eyes narrowed. "You think they don't know the truth? That they aren't deliberately protecting someone or more than one person or company. And it's not the ground troops; it's somewhere in the upper echelons."

Curtis stood halfway, fists braced on the tabletop. "Your call? Seems you're getting boxed in, and our list of allies is getting shorter."

Buck ignored him. "We've confirmed nine to eleven more children are en route to a sister church called Capilla del Sagrado Manto Blanco. ETA within seventy-two hours. I'm waiting for the go-ahead from the committee. Our team is ready. And this time, neither of you is going. This is going to be a dangerous exfil, unsanctioned. They will never admit that what they just claimed they closed is still in business."

Outside, a news ticker scrolled across muted monitors: *Ciudad Juárez fire kills 40 migrants. Border crossings spiked this month since CBP reported a 25% rise."* Another chyron read: *White House announces Phase II of U.S.-Mexico Bicentennial Framework, citing closer cooperation at the border.* Fiona's stomach turned. Convenient, indeed. Sounded more like agreeing to look the other way.

She and Curtis exchanged a look. No words passed. "We will watch from the compound."

Then Curtis' phone buzzed. It was Mason. "You will not believe this, but I can place Bell at the scene of Bridget's murder. We have drone footage from when the police were collecting evidence. As the drone flew over the crowd, I thought I saw someone I recognized. I interviewed a guy several years ago on a different murder case. I was sure he did it, but could not get enough evidence to prove it. It was necessary for me to let him go. That guy was Joe Bell. Hit me the other day, and I pulled the footage. Damn sure it was him. He looked up when the drone flew overhead."

Dallas HQ

The alert flashed on her screen. A secure line routed through Sentinel's encrypted uplink. She hit accept.

Everett's voice came through, low and direct.
"You're not gonna like this. I've gone off-grid."

Curtis leaned in as Fiona patched it through to the intercom.

"Around four a.m. last night, a hired merc team showed up at the ranch. Tried to kill me."

Fiona's breath caught. Sharp, like a blade under her ribs.

"No trackers. No contact points. I'm done playing by their rules."

And then the line went dead.

The silence that followed felt sharp. Clinical.

Curtis exhaled slowly. "His chances are slim he'll be alive by next week if they're hunting him."

Fiona's voice sharp, angry. "Not if we find him first."

Kenneth stepped into the room, eyes wary. "What's going on?"

"We need to find Everett," Fiona said. "Now. He's gone dark. They came after him at his ranch."

Kenneth crossed his arms. "You won't drag him back without bloodshed," Kenneth said. "Our people won't be party to that."

"We won't have to," she said. "I have a place. A safe location. He'll go if Wendell asks him; he served at one time with him."

Kenneth tilted his head. "Where?"

She turned toward the window, where the cloudless sun glared against the glass. "South ridge. There's a trail past the white rock outcrop. Doesn't look like much. But it leads to an old mine shaft. The former owner was a paranoid billionaire who thought the world would end by 2020. His delusion is our advantage. Hell, we find new stuff, weird stuff all the time. He built things on this ranch that most people would call insane. I just never thought I'd need one of them."

Kenneth blinked. "How private?"

"No outside utilities. Solar arrays miles away on the ranch island. Backup generators with disguised vents. Forty-seven-person capacity. Medical-grade trauma room, full equipment and kits, filtered water tanks, gym, sleeping quarters, encrypted radio relays. Looks like a damn luxury bunker built for a siege. It even has a damn swimming pool. I have not explored it completely. I found it a year ago," she added. "Kept it secret. Just in case."

Curtis grunted. "Looks like just in case is now."

Fiona's Office, Dallas HQ

Sabrina stalked into Fiona's office and dropped a folder onto Fiona's desk, her mouth tight with disbelief. "Ran the CI from the statement Mason gave Curtis," she said. "Name's not in any formal registry, no cross-reference in the county's CI logs. Not once. It's a ghost." Fiona raised an eyebrow. Sabrina added, "And it gets better. When I checked the alias through the usual channels, it showed up on three other closed cases *Detective*

Marcus Wren worked. Same name, different physical descriptions. Once a thirty-something white male. Another time, a Black teenager. Last one, a redhead junkie who supposedly vanished before testifying." She leaned in. "You know what that means, right? Wren's inventing witnesses. Or grabbing random addicts, feeding them scripts, then tossing them when they're done." Fiona's fingers curled around her coffee. "No one vetted them other than Wren?" She sat back before saying anything, a thoughtful look on her face. "So, the brass just wanted cases closed and let their lackey do all the dirty work. That's why he refused to reveal the CI to the court and allowed the person to be removed from the warrant."

The intercom buzzed. Selena informed her that there was a person at the reception desk who said his name was Hank and that he had been told we were looking for him. Fiona said to send him to her office. Two hours later Fiona called Mason, and he came himself and picked up Hank. The DA made arrangements for a safe house for him, but first he would give the DA a sworn statement of what he'd seen the day of Bridget's murder.

Whiskey River Two-Step Compound

The war room in the compound buzzed with low mechanical hums. Static whispered through the ceiling's antennas. The lighting was blue-toned and dim, throwing sharp angles across maps, monitors, and corded cables.

Sentinel's drone fleet was already mid-air. Live feeds rippled across the curved wall monitors. Thermal overlays, infrared patterns, satellite cross-links diagnostics. The airship Sentinel hovered in international waters off the Gulf Coast.

Joe Campbell, an ex-air combat controller who now worked on their protection teams, stood at the main console on Sentinel, headset on. Two of Buck's operators monitored telemetry from their consoles.

“Capilla’s inner courtyard is empty,” Bianca reported from the feedback to the ranch compound, toggling the drone feeds. “But they picked up something else. Second drone, twenty meters below their ceiling.”

Curtis frowned. “Cartel?”

“Negative,” she said. “Flight signature reads military. Which military drone is the question? Or possible mimic tech.”

Fiona leaned over her shoulder, eyes on the data stream. “Who the hell else is watching?” she murmured.

Curtis didn’t answer. His hand was resting on the edge of the command table, where a single pinned photo had curled at the edges. A boy around seven, sunburned and hollow-eyed. A blond girl with braids. Another boy with a swollen lip.

“They’re already there,” Fiona whispered.

Curtis looked up. “What do you want to do?”

Fiona straightened. Her voice was low. Calm. “Pray Buck’s guys get there in time.”

“You know, if this goes south, we lose the Sentinel, the government contract, and possibly go to jail.”

“And if we don’t, those kid’s lives will be hell till they die. And that might not be too long. You know that.”

“Yeah, figured you’d say that. Just wanted you to understand the stakes for our company, and for us. We can come back to the compound late tonight. That’s when most of the action will occur.”

◆◆◆

Dallas HQ

“You need to see this. Sent by Chelsea, came in early this morning.”

Fiona looked up from her laptop. Curtis stood in the room's doorway, holding his phone out, eyes narrowed.

"Rescue report just hit one of our flagged military-civilian watchlists. Polish SAR pulled a survivor from a Dassault Falcon 8X wreckage near the Slovakian border last night. No flight plan filed after Frankfurt. Transponder went silent hours before the crash, it appears."

He passed her the phone. Fiona's pulse skipped a beat.

"Montana Livestock Bag? That's got to be Colt Harlan's jet. How many Montana ranchers do you think are in Poland?"

"Yup. Same tail number as his jet. They confirmed partial logs in the wreckage. Weather and possible sabotage are both being floated."

"Is he alive?"

"Barely. Coma. Massive trauma. The doctors have stabilized him at Warsaw Central Medical for the last couple of months. But get this, his wife had already activated private medevac and diplomatic transport clearance. He'll be stateside within forty-eight hours."

Fiona's hands tightened on the phone.

"How did she find him?"

"Colt woke up for a brief time, told the authorities who he was. Authorities notified the embassy, which notified her."

Fiona sat back slowly. She didn't trust the calm. Not yet.

"I'm on a plane heading home tonight." Chelsea said and hung up.

But at least the pieces were moving, and in the right direction.

◆ ◆ ◆

Whiskey River | South Ridge Trail

The hill beyond the white outcrop was windswept and dark, lit only by the stars and a thin sliver of moon. The night air had dropped into the high 40s, crisp and biting at exposed skin. Somewhere below, a creek whispered over stones.

She waited at the switchback, boot planted on the rock outcropping shielding the hidden keypad. Wind stirred the dust around her boots, carrying the smell of cedar and distant smoke from a brush burn to the south.

Two silhouettes approached through the trees.

Wendell Hatfield was easy to spot. Tall, steady, rifle slung low, silent as ever. His black windbreaker bore the faint O'Brien & Galloway insignia. He didn't smile. Just nodded once.

"I found him," he said simply. "Took a little convincing him." Everett followed, dirt-smeared and limping; but alive.

Fiona uncrossed her arms as they drew close. "That trail out there. If you left tracks, I'll have Gabby cover them at dawn."

"I know," Everett said, stopping a few paces short. "I never planned on surviving this long. Wendell changed my mind."

"How?"

Wendell murmured, "Prayer and vengeance."

That stopped her.

Fiona stepped inside, turned on her phone's flashlight and walked deep down the tunnel before stopping and brushing away dried leaves to reveal a recessed access panel cleverly hidden in the wall. She keyed in the sequence and hit Enter.

The door opened inward with a soft hiss, warm recycled air drifting out. She'd turned on the generators and opened the water valve.

Fiona turned to Everett. "This place is off the record; no signals, no cameras; and you'll be the only one inside."

He nodded, saying nothing.

Fiona held out a folded slip of paper. "This is the direct emergency line. Use it if you have to. You can contact George and Casey via the compound on the sat phone. You'll be able to reach them from here if needed."

Everett took it. Calloused fingers brushed hers. His voice cracked. "You trust me down here?"

"Find your footing. Then help us get your wife's killer and find your daughter."

For a moment, they stood in silence.

Then Everett stepped inside.

Fiona waited until the hydraulic lock sealed. Only then did she let out the breath she'd been holding.

Wendell stood quietly beside her, head bowed.

She looked up at the stars. "He needs time. But not too much."

"God willing, he'll use it well," Wendell said quietly. "Grief's a fire that can consume a person. Right now, it's burning him. When he gets control of it, he'll hunt. They'd better pray to God, he never does. Cause Everett won't have compassion for them."

He looked at Fiona with an expression on his face she could not decipher.

"You know nothing will stop him from discovering the fate of his daughter and who murdered his wife." He stopped and turned to face the mine entrance, as if musing about something before saying. "Right now, he's grieving. They'd better kneel and pray when he catches them. God's grace will not extend to them through him." He turned back towards her.

"Ever heard of mystical beings called Furies?" He did not wait for her answer, just turned and walked back toward the utility vehicles, leaving the mine shaft sealed in shadow, silent as a tomb.

CHAPTER 28

Rescue

Monday, April 3rd, 2023

Sentinel One Mile off Mexican Coastline

Fluorescent lights hummed over laptops, maps, and glowing satellite overlays. A red sector pulsed on the wall projection. Capilla del Sagrado Manto Blanco. Officially closed. Unofficially, another node in the trafficking web. Sentinel hovered one mile off the Mexican coast, a ghost in the clouds. No callsigns. Just encrypted silence linking the gondola to Fiona and Curtis at the ranch. Buck stood center, hands behind his back.

"Multi-phase recon. Outer walls fragmented. IR fencing. Drones first. Zodiacs launch at zero-four-fifty. Final approach underwater, three meters, silent."

Tsujii Kazuma, ex-Night Stalker, stood ready, calm, locked in.

Buck met his eyes. "Acapulco rendezvous. Ground assets deliver gear. If they're dirty—"

"Standard protocol." An aide leaned in. "Extraction first. Evidence second."

A monitor blinked green. Glyph only. Javelin-5: Confirmed. Buck killed it without a word. Then said. "Sentinel uplink hot. She's exfil if this goes sideways. No lights. No chatter. Caught? Your ghosts."

The map shifted. Heat signatures bloomed in the courtyard—small bodies among adults. Buck's voice dropped. "That's our proof."

Tsujii called out, turning to his men. "Zodiacs launch in thirty."

◆ ◆ ◆

Sentinel

Sentinel rose through the mist, silent above the clouds. Gondola bay: black-clad operators moved like shadows. No names. No flags. Operators had explicit orders: succeed or be shut down. Below, a Zodiac skimmed black water. Eight men. Tactical gear. At the stern: Javelin-5—bruised, bandaged wrists, courier pack strapped tight. Extracted minutes ago from a fishing boat. Hours passed. The Zodiac returned. Sentinel descended. Magnetic cradle dropped. Green light pulsed. The boat slid in with a smooth hiss. Click. Auto-lock. Elevator rose. Hatch sealed. Sentinel climbed, swallowed by clouds.

Capilla del Sagrado Manto Blanco

Capilla del Sagrado Manto Blanco sat just outside La Cuchilla, tucked into a forgotten fold of the foothill jungle, left to decay in plain sight. The compound's old church façade faced a gravel cut road that ended in scrub forest, miles from the nearest paved highway. From here, the closest coastal access ran east, toward the gulf-side fishing strips near Cazones de Herrera Municipality. Rough ground, even on a good day, would be suicidal terrain with possibly ten to eleven children in tow. Determined to be the only workable route.

The jungle air reeked of humidity and gasoline. Insects chirred somewhere far off, but close in, the world had gone still.

Eight Tier One contractors moved like a well-maintained machine through the overgrown yard. Every step deliberate. No footprints left behind. Each carried classified materials, including hard drives, encrypted photos, and blacklisted ledgers taken from the church. Minutes earlier, they had taken down the guards watching the kids and those in the office. Silent. Knives, not guns, were the only weapons they used. They retrieved the information, prepared the children, and exited through a back wall gate.

Behind them, eleven barefoot children walked in pairs. Silent. Sedated by the cartel guards hours before, but aware. Just enough to curb panic. Shadowed by the team's two medics. Tsujii glanced back. A girl clutched a boy's hand, knuckles white. Another boy limped, eyes too wide and glossy worried him. He turned back to his men.

"Rendezvous is a beach on the Gulf side. We'll make it in," he said, glancing back at the children. "Realistically, maybe by daylight, just to clear this first sector and rest the kids." After that, we move slow, quiet. Tsujii spread the folded satellite map across the crate and clicked open his tactical pen.

"From La Cuchilla to the Sierra fringe." He drew the first line towards the south. "We do this in three phases to let the kids rest a bit between each one. Phase one: drop south of the compound for twenty minutes to get out of camera sweep. Then cut west-northwest. Then we stop after half an hour and let the children rest. Phase two: cut west toward the Ajusco ridge canopy. Dense pine kills most aerial thermals. If the cartel has drones, they'll lose us under there. We let the kids rest again." He drew the long final arc east to the coast. "Phase three: utility vehicles are hiding in the trees, here, he pointed to a point on the map, waiting for us. Then we push through the Sierra Madre foothill jungle, follow riverbed pathways, and then cross the flats into the Cazones de Herrera coastal strip. Zodiacs are hidden behind a dune. Total distance ninety-seven klicks. We set the beacon when we reach LZ one mile out in the Gulf. Then we wait for the Sentinel pickup."

Ninety-seven kilometers of rough terrain lay ahead. Jungle, mountain canopy, riverbed, coastal scrub. They would have to be ghosts the entire way.

He folded the map tightly. "Break pace, and the cartel catches up. Stick to it, and we'll get out. If things stay quiet, we will continue. If not, we adapt." Silence settled over the operatives as they nodded and stood. Now, the toughest part of the mission began.

Wendell Hatfield adjusted his grip on the suppressed M4. "Flashlights off. Breach trees cover in thirty meters."

Halfway to the trees, Aaron Pratt slowed. "Wait," Aaron whispered as he went down on one knee. "Something's wrong." Pax froze. Hackles up. Nose lifted. The air shifted, wrong, heavy, as if the jungle itself were holding its breath.

Tsujii didn't like the silence. If it were the cartel, their scouts wouldn't be this quiet unless it's an ambush. Then they saw it: a laser dot sliding across the trees like a hunting sight. A thump to their left. A flare streaked upward, splitting the sky in a bloom of red fire. Exposing their position.

Hatfield dropped to a knee. "Ambush."

Several figures emerged. Masked, armed, disciplined.

Not amateurs.

Cartel elites.

Tsujii keyed his comm. "Sentinel Command, we're compromised. TIC."

Static. Jammed. The sudden dead air wasn't accidental. Cartel elites weren't running handheld jammers; this was broadband directional suppression, likely mounted on a drone cluster. Someone high up the chain had leaked the mission, someone with money and power.

Tsujii's gut tightened. This wasn't a random ambush. Aaron raised his weapon. Pax growled low. Hatfield counted the children again. All eleven. Terrified. He looked at Tsujii. Nowhere to run.

Their carefully planned ninety-seven-klick route was over on the spot. The ambush had collapsed the entire mission into phase one. The rest of the ninety-seven klicks, ridge, jungle, rivers, and flats, died before it began. Their world had shrunk down to one clearing, one firefight, and their skill as warriors.

◆ ◆ ◆

Last Light Protocol: Engaged

Every leaf, every shadow, now a threat.

Tsujii dropped to one knee, NVGs scanning. The red flare still hung above the canopy, pulsing faintly through the mist. Comms were dead. Cartel had jamming gear in place. Drone-based, likely. High-band pulse disruptors.

They hadn't just surrounded the team.
They'd silenced them.

Across the staggered formation, Hatfield tapped his mic. Shook his head. "Tango grid's blown," he said. "They're pushing us into a crossfire."

Tsujii toggled the tight-beam subnet. "Arrowhead Retreat. Execute Last Light. IR off. No firefights unless we have confirmed attacks. Echo, keep the kids tight. We ghost." He cut his bacon. Took a point. Behind them, a girl's small sob broke the silence. Tsujii glanced back. She clung to her brother, eyes wide in the dark. He swallowed. "Keep moving." He whispered to his men.

They moved like phantoms. Silent. Deadly. The only thing standing between the children and death or enslavement.

◆ ◆ ◆

Evade, Break Contact

The canopy mist swallowed the moonlight.

Tsujii froze mid-step, raised his left arm straight up, open palm facing forward, fingers tightly together. The team halted instantly. No words. Just the soft rustle of gear settling and eleven children breathing fast in the dark. He held the signal for five seconds, eyes scanning the treeline. Behind him, Hatfield mirrored it, arm up, palm out, passing the halt back through the file. Then silence. Only jungle noise and the faint whirr of Sentinel's drones overhead.

Halt.

Hatfield pulled out a digital thermal scanner, scanning the elevation.

"Two tangos. High caliber suppressed. Not grunts."

"Five more, from my side," Tsujii murmured. "They're pushing us into a crossfire."

Then, crack. Charlie-Three jerked sideways, blood spattering across the leaves. Hit in the thigh. Blood bloomed fast from the wound.

"Sniper! Six o'clock ridge!"

Hatfield dropped him clean. Tsujii dragged Charlie-Three behind a log. Fast wrap. Tight pressure.

"You walk?"

"Maybe."

"We don't leave anyone," Tsujii said, get off your ass and move.

Charlie-Three rose, a crooked grin on his face as Tsujii helped him to his feet. "Yes, boss."

The team veered north. The ground gave way. Rain-swollen roots tore loose. A mudslide opened beneath Charlie-Five and two children.

"Hold them!" Tsujii called out.

Aaron lunged, grabbing one child mid-slide.

The other tumbled down ten feet.

Pax barked once and leaped.

Tsujii lunged toward the child.

He reached the girl, blood on her temple, sobbing. As Pax stood guard over her.

"You're okay," he told her, breathless.

She stared at him, unmoving. Then her hand found his, small and shaking.

"Don't leave," she whispered. Her grip tight.

Aaron motioned, and Pax rejoined him at his side.

Tsujii lifted her. Small. Shaking.

"I've got her. Move!"

Fear moved among the kids like fog. While suppressors on the team's weapons whispered through the trees, followed by thuds.

The jungle narrowed. The enemy closed.

Tsujii flashed a signal. "Vector 30. Suppress and move. Claymore on our six. Bravo-One and Two, protect the kids."

Hatfield nodded. Three trigger pulls. Three enemies dropped with a thud as they hit the forest floor.

One cartel soldier got close, scarred, eyes blank.

A knife flashed.

Tsujii parried, elbowed, and kneed. He drove the rifle butt into the man's throat. Something crunched, and the man fell backward.

No time to think. Tsujii called over the mike, "Package intact?"

"Count's good," Bravo-One called. "One carried. One limping."

They pressed north. The high forest thinned into dense foothill jungle as they pushed toward the coast.

Tsujii's HUD flickered.

Uplink Restored.

"Base, this is Alpha One. Eleven packages secured. TIC. One Sierra Priority 2, urgent. Need bird. Hot LZ.

Alpha-Niner grid. Over."

"Copy. Drone support inbound. Twenty-eight minutes. Bird hour out."

Tsujii exhaled, looked at the others. "We're moving."

The claymores exploded behind them. Roars of fire and screams filled the air. Buying the time they needed.

The jungle opened onto a wide strip of grass, like a makeshift landing runway.

Ambush

The first and fastest drones, seekers, arrived, giving them cover with drone-flares. Thick white smoke grenades covered the jungle behind them. The seekers next painted targets for the incoming marauders and hunters.

Tsujii unslung his rifle. Scoped the ridges treeline.

The first wave came fast.

One wore a vest. Tsujii aimed high, face shot. Vest didn't matter.

Pax unexpectedly lunged out from the side, taking down one on their flank. Screams and vicious growls followed. Wet and ragged.

Hatfield laid down suppressive fire. Charlie-Three fired from the ground, bleeding but still fighting.

Then, a child bolted. "Girl running!" Charlie-Four called out.

Tsujii sprinted, catching her as gunfire cracked inches from where she would have been.

Another round hit a tree two feet from her.

"You're okay," he told her, breathless. "We stay together he said as he lifted her."

She nodded. Eyes locked on his as he rushed back to cover and the others.

Tsujii saw fire spreading through the brush. Laser dots multiplied through the smoke. Gunfire roared behind them.

Charlie-four, Hatfield was no longer with the formation. Somewhere behind the smoke, he was holding the line alone. His transmission cut through the static:

Go. Go. Go.

A final muzzle flash blinked through the smoke and then vanished. Silence. Gunfire closing. Tsujii looked towards the treeline. Cartel silhouettes emerged. At least a dozen. The path to the coast was gone. The Zodiacs were out of reach. And exfil an hour or more out. He grabbed his mic, voice steady.

"Break northeast! MOVE!"

The squad plunged back into the jungle, children in tow, as a wall of fire rolled down toward the clearing.

They did not look back. Tsujii's calling. "Move now."

Charlie Four discovered a slight cut-out within the treeline. And they moved into position. They would have to hold here.

CHAPTER 29

Incursion

Monday, April 3rd, 2023

Sentinel, 13 Klicks inland over La Cuchilla

Buck never planned this, but they released two heavy missile marauder drones, four hunters, and three seekers when the Sentinel's classified surveillance equipment noted the events occurring on the ground. Ninety-seven klicks of carefully planned movement had just ended less than five.

The alarm hadn't finished its second pulse before Buck snapped:

"Bring her inland. Treetop glide. Now."

The pilot hesitated for half a heartbeat. "Sir, that puts us inside sovereign airspace."

Buck tapped the map once. "I'm not leaving them. Move."

The Sentinel banked, engines dropping to a deep whisper. Thermal skin shifted, temperature signature bleeding into the night air.

Interior running lights dimmed to blood red, she ghosted through the sky. A mirage reflecting her surroundings, like a camouflaged octopus.

The jungle rose like a green wall in the foreground. The underbelly sensors mapped the terrain in ghost-white contours. Drone feeds flickered across the tactical wall display, scattering, closing, overlapping.

The surveillance tech stiffened even from this distance; he saw the enemy's movements. "Cartel elements pushing from the east. Multiple vehicles inbound on an old logging road. They'll cut off Tsujii's north flank, a larger force coming up on the ridge close to their position."

Buck's jaw didn't move.
"Seeker Two. Dump smoke along the ridge. Open a corridor."

Seeker Two dove. A ribbon of white vapor spilled across the treeline, masking the team's visual and thermal trail.

"Seeker One, counter-lights. Blind their scopes."

Bolts of IR disruption pulsed through the canopy.

"That will hold them for a bit. Set LZ in the first open terrain we find," Buck said.

The pilot swallowed.
"Adjusting descent to thirty meters."

The Sentinel slipped inland, silent as a shadow crossing a grave.

Tsujii's Team Breaks North La Cuchilla Jungle
The jungle felt as if it had teeth.

Tsujii cut through the brush, the girl still clinging to his shoulder, her breath hitching against his vest. Behind him, Charlie-Five limped, held upright by Charlie-Three despite his own bleeding thigh.

Charlie-Eight Hatfield caught up with them. Bleeding from a wound in his upper arm.

"Move! Shift north!" Tsujii called out, voice low but carrying.

Gunfire stitched through the trees. Leaves shredded. Bark split into ribbons.

Pax barreled through the undergrowth ahead of Aaron, nose locked on a path only he understood: straight line, optimal cover, zero hesitation.

"Drone smoke above!" Charlie-Four shouted, pointing up.

A rolling sheet of white fog poured over the treeline like a tidal wave.

Tsujii's HUD blinked:

SIGNAL RESTORED.
SENTINEL DISTANCE: One point nine kilometers.
LZ LOCKING...

He pressed on. "Two minutes to clearing!" he called.

A bullet whizzed past his ear.

Hatfield, now at the rear, fired once, twice, dropping two shadows advancing through the brush.

"Keep moving!" Hatfield barked. "I'll buy you the time you need!"

Tsujii didn't waste time arguing.
He knew what that meant.

◆◆◆

The LZ

Jungle Clearing, 1.9 Klicks northeast of La Cuchilla

The trees broke open onto another long, narrow strip of flattened grass, a smuggling strip choked with vines and weeds.

Perfect for an LZ.

Tsujii burst out first, kids behind him stumbling into the open. Smoke from Sentinel drones blanketed the east flank, hiding muzzle flashes but not the sound.

"Charlie, center! Echo's, kids on the ground, heads down!" Tsujii ordered.

The medics dropped, pulling children tight against the earth.

Gunfire cracked from three sides. Then came the wind. A low vibration rolled across the clearing. They felt it before they heard it.

Sentinel.

A massive, shifting silhouette lowered through the haze, invisible until it was too close for anyone on the ground to react. Her hull, a reflection of the ground, a monolith descending through swirling smoke.

"Contact north!" Aaron snapped. Pax lunged, intercepting a runner who broke from the brush towards them, rifle rising.

Tsujii fired twice, clean, controlled, dropping another silhouette creeping from the shadows.

"Lift at thirty percent descent," one operator muttered over the comms from above. "Brace for downdraft."

"Get ready!" Tsujii shouted.

Wind slammed into the clearing from Sentinel's downdraft fans. Grass flattened. Smoke spiraled. Children cried out in fear, and the operators had to hold on tight to them.

The hull cracked open; the lift dropping like a descending cage from the heavens.

Extraction by Major Buck

The clearing appeared through breaks in the smoke, a churned patch of sand, brush fires, and shadowed bodies. Muzzle flashes flickered at the treeline. Gunfire intensified.

Cartel soldiers broke from the ridge in waves. Armored trucks among them.

"Lower the lift," Buck ordered.

The floor hatch opened. Cold night air blasted upward. The lift descended fast.

"Marauders one and two, suppress that ridge!" Buck barked the voice command to the drone.

The first drone dove in, followed by the second.

The night was already thick with humidity and the rot of decaying leaves when the sound began, a low, mechanical whine that grew like a swarm of hornets rising from the canopy. Not loud at first. Just... wrong. The wrong that made every man in the clearing freeze mid-step.

Then the drones appeared. A new weapons platform. Controlled from Sentinel.

They slid out of the low clouds like a black predator, sleek and angular, its silhouette barely visible against the stars. No running lights. No warning. Only the soft, relentless whirr-whirr-whirr of its propeller blades slicing the air, growing louder, deeper, until the sound vibrated in their chests like a second heartbeat.

A red laser dot danced across the dirt, cold, precise, seeker drones painting targets.

"Drones incoming!" Tsujii shouted. They hit the dirt.

The first Hellfire missile launched with a sharp whoosh, a streak of white fire that tore the darkness open. It hit the lead truck as it breached the ridge, like the fist of God. The explosion bloomed orange and savage, lifting the armored truck three feet off the ground before slamming it back down in a fireball of twisted metal and burning fuel. The shockwave punched through the clearing, flattening men like grass, rattling teeth, and filling the air with the acrid bite of cordite and scorched rubber.

Another missile followed as the second drone dove in, replacing the first. Whoosh, slamming into the second truck. The blast of a rolling BOOM that shook the earth and sent a pillar of fire roaring thirty feet into the sky. Shrapnel hissed through the air like angry hornets. Men screamed as hot metal tore into flesh.

The drones circled once, unhurried, their engines now a low, predatory growl that seemed to press down on the jungle itself. From the ground it looked invincible, a silent angel of death floating above the flames, its camera lens glinting like a cold eye. The red laser dot danced again, this time across a cluster of runners trying to reach the treeline.

Another whoosh. A chatter of gunfire from hunters. Dirt and body parts rained down.

The smell hit the team members, still on the ground. Burning diesel, melted plastic, charred flesh, and the sharp ozone tang of high explosives and gunpowder. The heat rolled over them in waves, singeing hair and lungs. Tsujii stood and saw cartel soldiers on the ridge coughing, gagging, and clawing at the ground, trying to crawl away from the fire and the seekers and hunters.

Above all, the drones hovered for one final, terrifying moment, their propellers whirring now a steady, mocking hum before they banked away into the clouds and vanished as silently as they had come.

The jungle fell quiet except for the crackle of flames and the distant, fading growls of the machines that had just torn the cartel soldiers' world apart in under thirty seconds.

Tsujii roared. "Move! Move!" Tsujii seized the opening, hauling two kids toward the lift while Pax, now back, guarded the rear with Aaron.

A burst of gunfire hammered the sand beside Charlie-Three as more cartel came over the ridge. Another shot cracked inches off Tsujii's shoulder.

The Sentinel slewed sideways and opened a barrage of gunfire from its lowest firing deck, shredding the cartel. Buck roared, “Hold her steady.”

“I’m trying. I’m having control issues.” As the pilot fought the controls to hold her steady so that the team could load.

The first two children reached the lift; crew members pulled them in.

Buck leaned toward the open lift. “Move! Move!”

Another wave of suppressing fire erupted from Sentinel, then the rest of the team broke cover. Racing for the lift.

The lift shook under gunfire impacts and turned in that direction, blasting the area with gunfire. “What the *fuck*, stop firing, you’re going to hit our guys and the kids.”

“*Trying the controls are not responding*.” The firing finally stopped. Then the pilot yelled out, “Ten seconds!” as the operator at the console called out, all weapons secured. “A larger enemy force is closing in; they zeroed in on our position from the drone attack!”

Echo team loaded the children, one after another, into the lift. Pax jumped aboard, claws scraping metal. The team members raced aboard last.

“Raise it!” Buck roared.

The lift lurched upward, pulling the team clear as rounds tore through the space they’d occupied seconds earlier.

“Lift secured!” the operator called out above. “We’re clear!” The hatch sealed.

The clearing fell away. Sentinel rose through the smoke and fire like some ancient leviathan. The ping of gunfire echoing inside.

“Get us to the Gulf. Now.”

The Sentinel slid into the sky, invisible once more.

Before it did, a red flare rose from below. Hatfield's last known location faded in the smoke.

Silence

As if God had answered, the wind changed direction, and a tailwind now blew behind them.

Tsujii felt the change before the instruments confirmed it. The nose lifted slightly. Airspeed ticked up without throttle input.

"Tailwind," Aaron said. "Twelve knots. Holding," the pilot called back to Buck.

Tsujii allowed himself one curt nod. "Good wind at our back," he said, voice flat but carrying.

The kids in the bay didn't understand the words, but they felt the shift, the way the deck steadied, the engines quieted, the fear loosened just enough to breathe. One girl looked up at him. He gave her the smallest smile. "You're going home."

The rest of them were just breathing. And the thrum of engines pushing the airship back toward international waters.

Buck didn't sit. He kept one hand on the internal railing, staring at the closed hatch as if he could force it to open again.

Tsujii stood across from him, blood on his sleeve, mud across his face.

"Hatfield?" Buck asked, voice flat.

Tsujii shook his head once. "He stayed behind. Bought us time. Why were we not told that the ship had defenses? When those gun ports opened, they barely missed us!"

No answer came from Buck. In the receding distance, the jungle had consumed the area where Hatfield once was.

Buck didn't curse. Didn't growl. Didn't speak at all.

He simply nodded in one hard motion and walked toward the cockpit.

But the fallout was already waiting.

Buck had violated sovereign airspace.

He knew someone with money and power had tipped the cartel. Someone inside military intelligence.

Buck replayed in his head the last transmission, half static, from Hatfield over radio comms, Go. Go. Go.

On Sentinel's thermal sensors seeing through the thinning smoke, muzzle flashes, multiple, rapid, but no return fire.

Then, a last flash. Small. Distant. Low to the ground. Then, nothing where Hatfield had been. As drones covered the area in deadly gunfire and smoke before they returned to Sentinel.

"So what's going to be the fallout?" Tsujii moved close to Buck and said, his voice low?

"Someone's going to ask why a classified American asset crossed that line," Buck added. "And I won't like the room they ask it in."

Whiskey River Two-Step Ranch

Fiona stood at the ranch window, arms folded, watching the horizon where the Gulf met the sky. The weather report had shifted an hour ago: a tailwind building, steady out of the south-southwest. She didn't smile, but her shoulders eased a fraction.

"Give them a good wind at their back," she murmured to the Sentinel, to the team, and a prayer to God. Outside, the first real breeze in days stirred the cedar branches. Soft. Steady. Like an answer.

O'Brien & Galloway Compound | Sentinel Hangar

The storm-gray bulk of the Sentinel drifted out of low cloud like a silent giant, her hull lights dark, its skin still running the last of its thermal-dampening cycle. Fiona and Curtis stood on the mezzanine overlooking the hangar floor as the airship eased into the cradle. The blast doors sealed behind her with a hydraulic groan.

The crew flooded the deck. Medics first. Crew members carried or guided the kids down the lift; they were trembling, soot-streaked, and exhausted. The rescued huddled under blankets as triage teams sorted them. Breathing problems, injuries, dehydration.

Curtis scanned the faces of the team. They pulled it off. But something went sideways.

Buck walked past, leaving the smell of smoke and adrenaline in his wake.

"Fiona watched him go. The smell lingered: smoke, sweat, and something heavier. Loss, maybe. Or the weight of choices no one wanted to own."

Fiona moved forward. "Uplink went dark for over two hours. Why?"

Buck didn't pause. "Classified."

"That's not an answer," Curtis said. "Every time we use Sentinel, someone's taking notes."

Buck paused just long enough to show he'd heard. "You two contracted to transport and verify. Everything after that falls under restricted protocols when we use her."

Fiona's jaw tightened

"You want the truth? If you don't know, they can't force you to testify."

Curtis and Fiona exchanged a glance, equal parts anger and cold understanding.

Fiona stepped in front of him. "Violated airspace?"

Buck's stare didn't waver. "You don't want that on record. Tomorrow, we'll call the FBI and let them come to get the kids. They can come up with a story of their retrieval and take the credit once more."

No one said it, but they all knew this couldn't happen again. Not without someone else claiming ownership of Sentinel, and right now Curtis was not so sure this would be a terrible thing at this point.

Curtis exhaled slowly. "He's hiding something big."

"He's protecting us from legal fallout," Fiona said. "Which means whatever happened during that mission crossed a line."

The staff guided the children toward the internal medical wing of the compound.

The hangar slowly thinned out, medics ushering the rescued children inside, Buck disappearing into the operations wing with two of his officers, the Sentinel's engines cooling with a deep metallic tick-tick echoing through the rafters.

Fiona and Curtis stayed on the mezzanine until the last stretcher rolled out of sight.

Curtis finally said, "We can't press him. Not right now."

"I know," Fiona answered. "That's the damn problem."

They descended the stairs together. The hangar doors sealed behind them with a heavy hydraulic thud, more like a vault than a door. Whatever line Buck crossed up there in the dark, those steel walls locked it tight behind them.

By the time they stepped outside, the sun had already bled out behind the treeline, leaving the compound washed in the white glow of sodium lights.

Curtis opened the truck door. "You want to head to the office?"

Fiona rubbed the fatigue out of the back of her neck. "George needs answers. Casey needs evidence. And Everett..."
She couldn't finish the thought. Fiona nodded once. Her fin-

gers brushed the photo in her pocket: Lila, Bridget, Lisa laughing. Alive then. Not now. She swallowed the ache.

Gravel cracked under the tires as they pulled away. The ranch faded behind them, quiet, guarded, and holding more secrets tonight than they'd ever agreed to carry. The Sentinel loomed in the hangar's silhouette, dark and silent, exactly where Buck wanted it… and exactly where Fiona couldn't get another answer.

They hit the highway toward Dallas HQ, bracing for the next firestorm waiting to hit.

CHAPTER 30

The Stillness Beneath

Tuesday, April 4th, 2023

George Shaw's Downtown Office

The call came early. George had just taken a black coffee from Marsha when her phone rang. Unknown local number. She hesitated, then answered crisply. "George Shaw's Private Law Office."

"Patch me to ESQ Shaw. Senior Deputy Worth, Texas State Land Authority." Marsha didn't blink. "Hold."

George took the call. He saw trouble in her eyes before Worth even spoke.

"Everett Taylor, who is your client, is currently undergoing active seizure proceedings. Hold vacated. Appear by 10:30 a.m. or we will initiate final lien on his 2,789 acres. No show, no signature, possession reverts at the close of the quarter."

Click.

No appeal. No questions. Just execution. George exhaled hard, already on his feet. "Marsha. Get Fiona and Curtis on the line. Now."

◆ ◆ ◆

O'Brien & Galloway HQ

They'd arrived at the office as the sun rose over the horizon. The ops room felt colder than usual. Fiona's jaw clenched as the banner rolled across the muted Channel 4 monitor:
"NEW MURDER LINKED TO VETERAN FUGITIVE," Shirley Dennen's photo flashed, smiling outside a food pantry. Then the body. White sheet. Flashing lights.

Curtis's arms folded tight, watching the scene on the TV. Bianca barely breathed.
Fiona remarked, "They're attempting to discredit him in the eyes of the public." "They failed to kill him, so now they're loading the narrative with bodies and lies. They all know he is not a fugitive. The police know exactly where he is. And can talk or call him anytime they want."

Curtis grunted. "Did we get any police reports from his ranch? He thinks he hit one or two during the attack."
"Emilio's on it. Nothing yet. No injuries logged at any hospital. Cleanup crew beat the cops there."

Bianca turned away from the monitor. "The Shirley connection wasn't public. That wasn't in any database I scraped. Bridget, us, Mason, and Reggie knew."
Curtis nodded grimly. "Then we've got a leak. Inside or adjacent."
"Mason," Fiona said slowly. "Or whoever is watching him."
"Or us."

The room fell silent. Then Curtis said, "Start internal logs. Access times. Personnel movement. Message routing. Anything suspicious, even if it's subtle."

Bianca was already typing.

"We trust no one outside this room in our agency," Fiona said. "Not until we see where this leads."

Dallas International Private Sector Airport

Later that day, the wind lifted grit across the tarmac as Fiona approached the chain-link gate. Security scanned her ID twice.

Casey stood waiting, a dark blue blazer catching dust in the breeze, boots scuffed from travel. He looked her over.

"You look like hell," he said.
"You flew in fast."
"I figured you'd take on the state with a crowbar and a news crew."

Curtis emerged from the hangar's shadows. "Thanks for coming."

Casey extended his hand. "You two don't exactly think small."

Fiona handed him two encrypted USB drives. "Everything we have. PAC laundering, Cavanaugh's offshore routes, and all Shirley's paperwork put on this flash drive. This..." she nodded, "is what got her killed."

Casey's face hardened. "They're not just seizing land. They're scrubbing the blood trail."
Major Buck joined them, casual in boots and a tactical jacket, but still carrying military gravity in every step. On his way to D.C., but he wanted to greet Casey before his flight took off.

"Theirs is a blunt-force play," Buck said simply. "Ours is precision. Your arena, Counselor."

Casey sighed. "I'm doing this because my sister asked. I'm not some crusader, Buck. If I think it's a waste of time, I walk."

Buck didn't blink. "Fine. But until you walk, welcome aboard."

Casey groaned. "Hell's ghost riders are gonna hit this one hard."

Whiskey River Two-Step Ranch

Fiona stood with her arms folded, the air thick with cedar and dying warmth. Stars vivid white against a pitch-black sky.

Curtis joined her, coffee in hand. “You want this?”

“If it’s hot.”

“Cinnamon and vanilla, your favorite. Wisps of steam ascended from the mug, a testament to its heat. Thought you needed real comfort after today.”

She sipped as the silence grew between them.

“They murdered Shirley to send us a message,” she finally said. “Then Everett’s name to push the lie.”

Fiona stared at the horizon.

Curtis nodded. “You think it’s someone inside?”

“I think it’s someone close enough to follow our trail.” She exhaled slowly, then added, “I believe the ranch is being watched. Felt eyes on me the other night while riding.”

Curtis leaned against the post beside her. “They’re counting on fear. Counting on us to blink.”

Fiona finished the last sip. “Let them.”

Friday, April 7th, 2023

Dallas County Courthouse

The courthouse hallway smelled of lemon wax and nerves. Casey Finn O’Brien tugged at his sleeves, checked his bolo tie, and brushed at his jeans, still worried about K9 hair from the kennels. After he was happy with his outfit, he walked to the courtroom, his cowboy boots steadily clacking on the marble. Fiona and Curtis followed behind him, their faces unreadable masks of trained composure.

Inside the hearing chamber, fluorescent lights hummed overhead. The state prosecutor shuffled his papers, smug in the certainty of a foregone outcome. He rose and spoke. “Given the severity of the allegations against Mr. Everett Taylor, suspected child endangerment, obstruction, and homicide, we are filing a request for immediate forfeiture of the property. Two thousand seven hundred and eighty-nine acres."

Casey rose slowly. The room shifted without a sound.

"Your Honor, the state is once again oversimplifying facts for convenience. Everett Taylor does not solely own this ranch. It is a six-generation estate with multiple vested family owners; none of whom are suspects in anything. Nor is any of them implicated in any crime. And no proof they were aware of any said crimes occurred."

He let the words settle.

"This is the full notarized record of shared ownership," he said, laying a thick folder on the table. "Grazing leases. Surface rights. Stewardship contracts. Branding licenses. All tied to family members other than Everett Taylor."

The prosecutor opened his mouth, then closed it again.

Casey didn't raise his voice.

"The state wants to seize a family's entire livelihood based on *unproven allegations* against one man. They had him in custody and still did not indict him. They can certainly try to take his ranch. However, Your Honor, this will take them a decade as it works its way through the district, appellate, and federal courts."

A beat.

"Meanwhile, the cows still need feeding; hay still needs brought in from the fields."

Even the judge cracked a ghost of a smile. This was Texas.

"Request denied the state," he said. "Protective stay granted pending resolution of the criminal case."

Casey nodded once. Fiona's shoulders eased, barely.

Washington, D.C. | Capitol Classified Subcommittee Room

The room was windowless. Silent. Two flags flanked each end of a long conference table. No cameras. No press. Just a stenographer, three senators, and Deputy Undersecretary Harland Boyd, who sat stiff-backed. Impassive. Each one represented a different power bloc.

Major Buck remained standing, shoulders squared, boots planted like roots. He hadn't touched the chair they'd offered. Sitting would have felt like surrender. He stood because Hatfield had stood until the end. Because eleven children were breathing because of that choice. Some lines should not be crossed. However, others needed to be crossed.

Senator Randal K. Morrow, silver-haired, eyes sharp as a blade, opened the session. "Major Buck, this subcommittee is investigating the Sentinel's unauthorized incursion into Mexican airspace. Do you acknowledge the violation?"

Buck didn't flinch. His jaw flexed once, the only crack in the armor. "We followed the chain of command," he said, voice level. "We extracted eleven minors under imminent threat. No one saw or recognized the Sentinel for what it was. Sir." The *Sir* landed like a quiet blade, respect given, but not deference.

Morrow's jaw twitched. "This committee ensures proper command protocols for national security. Contractors who forget that, or military personnel who overstep, can face consequences."

Senator Elaine Wexford, calm and measured, broke in. "We're not evaluating outcomes, Major. We're asking whether the operation was legal."

Buck's tone never changed. "You're worried someone saw the Sentinel. That the Mexican government might demand answers. They won't. We'd have seen some chatter by now.

There's been none."

Morrow leaned forward, voice sharp. "You didn't answer the question."

Before Buck replied, Senator Charles Denniston paged through the file before saying. "Your report claims the Sentinel evaded all radar and ladar systems?"

"It did," Buck said. "No heat, no signal, no reflection. Visually, to those on the ground, it was cloud and shadow. She dropped out of the sky, lifted out again. No one ever saw what she really was."

He didn't say the rest aloud:
If you knew what she is, you'd bury her in concrete.

Boyd gave him a slight nod.

Morrow pressed. "They left an operator in the theater? I believe Hatfield was his name. Do you know if they captured him? Alive? Dead? You understand the cartels; if they get hold of him, he could expose everything."

Buck's face hardened; his tone dangerous. His right hand flexed once, the hand that had shaken Hatfield's before the mission.

"He stayed behind so eight operators and eleven children could live. He made that choice. His sacrifice isn't your stage prop."

The room fell silent.

Morrow didn't blink. "So you're claiming he's dead. Or are you calling him MIA?"

Buck didn't blink either. "He was under active fire when they left. We presume KIA. But no confirmation yet." Inside, something twisted. Hatfield's last transmission. *Go. Go. Go. Still echoed.* Buck carried it like a stone in his chest.

Morrow leaned back, tone tightening. "We must assess whether the Sentinel program is still viable, or if O'Brien & Galloway is a liability. There were other companies that were better situated and more established. Yet somehow this company got the contract. How did that happen? I'm curious." He stared at Buck.

Buck had no trouble figuring out his thoughts about him. He'd ended more than one high-ranking military career. Buck was high on his list to be next. Despite knowing this, Buck's makeup did not include fear of the enemy. He'd played this game longer than Morrow. The stakes were too high to back down. Career or not, he'd fight to his last breath. Not for the program, but for the people it saved.

Boyd's voice cut through. "How or why this company got the Sentinel contract was because they were new. Less chance of corruption." He stared at Morrow for a moment before moving on. "Sentinel performed flawlessly. No detection. Without it, we'd be recovering American bodies from foreign soil. The Department strongly recommends continuing the program with the current contractor."

Senator Wexford nodded. "The record will reflect the committee's agreement with that recommendation. Oversight, though, will continue."

Morrow muttered under his breath. "Uncontrolled cowboys... the lot."

Buck heard him. He said nothing.

Outside, Boyd caught up with him in the hallway. "You made the right call," he said quietly. "Some of us still understand what the job takes. Just stay on the right side of the line."

Tactic approval. And a warning. Buck knew it. This hadn't been about airspace. Or legality. It was about *leverage.* And someone in this room was already moving against him. It was about Sentinel, and who'd get to control it once Morrow buried him.

Morrow wasn't just asking questions. He was setting traps.

Buck walked on. The hallway lights buzzed overhead, cold and indifferent. Somewhere far away, eleven children were breathing free and home because he'd crossed that line. He'd do it again.

Whiskey River Two-Step Ranch

Kenneth met them at the ranch gate, rifle slung, expression unreadable. Press vans prowled the road outside, but Tsujii had run a drone sweep; no tails, no leaks.

Inside, Fiona moved through the kitchen, untouched coffee cooling in her hand. Exhaustion pressed behind her eyes.

Everett stood near the south barn, posture loose but eyes wired tight. The wind pushed a faint cedar scent across the yard.

“You didn’t have to bring me here,” he murmured. “You’ve got better things to do.”

Fiona said simply, “You’re our client. Keeping you alive is part of the job.” He didn’t smile.

“I keep checking the fence lines,” he admitted.

Old habits. Watch cycles carved into bone.

“I memorized the terrain the first night,” he said. “But I still walk the same pattern. Same direction. Bridget broke me of doing that. She... grounded me.”

His voice thinned.

“If I stop... everything catches up.” A beat. “And Buck shutting me out of that mission angers me more than it should.”

Fiona didn’t speak. She stood with him in the quiet.

“It’s the silence that gets me,” Everett whispered. “Noise I can handle. Silence means something’s wrong.”

Whiskey River Two-Step Ranch

Golden sunlight washed the fields, the last of the light turning the land to burnished metal. Cicadas hummed a slow vibration between the barns.

Everett was in the stable, cleaning a saddle he had already cleaned twice that day. Fiona sensed silently from the doorway the stress of the trauma he was experiencing.

He checked the same strap twice, the same stitching three times.

Sometimes it was the ritual that held a man together. She stepped out into the cooling air, breath slow, mind turning.

This wasn't just about indictments, or evidence, or cartel networks.

It was about holding together the people still standing.

For Everett Taylor, stillness was the battlefield. And it threatened to swallow him whole.

CHAPTER 31

Buried Leads, Burning Truths
Monday, April 10th, 2023

Whiskey River Two-Step Ranch

A warm, heavy stillness clung to the ranch. The last stain of golden-red daylight hung low over the cedar treeline, amber catching on the wire fences and turning the lake into a sheet of dull copper. Heat from the day had settled into the ground, rising in soft waves. Cicadas rattled so loudly it felt like the evening itself was humming.
Fiona stepped onto the back porch with a mug of coffee, steam rising with the scent of cinnamon and vanilla.

Curtis joined her on the porch, a legal pad tucked under one arm. He lowered his voice. "Casey bought us breathing room. Two-month hold on the forfeiture. But the DOJ is circling harder now. They're setting him up in the public mind: violent, unstable, dangerous. Pundits funded by PACs now call him a ticking time bomb. The media are already feeding off it."

With Everett here, the earlier court win made Fiona's ranch feel more exposed. Police parked two patrol cars on the road. They pretended to keep the press back while they watched the property a little too closely. Someone had leaked Everett's location. No question.

Curtis nodded. "The pressure's real. Between that and the cartel leak, we need to move faster."

Clinton Hedeman, one of the full-time ranch hands, moved his flashlight across the southeast corner post. "Gate sensor went off again," he said without looking up. "Bridge to the island."

"Wind knocked a branch loose earlier," Fiona answered. "Gabby reset it already."

Fiona glanced back at Curtis as she spoke. "Everett needs to believe the case is moving, not stuck defending ground. Or he is going to take matters into his own hands."

Curtis flipped a page. "We are. Bianca's decryption shows more SILO fragments. Belize, Colombia."

"None of that clears Everett, just proves someone might have murdered his wife to prevent exposure of a criminal organization. Courts will not take that. George may publicize this, aiming for some to understand it as the motive for her murder, with someone other than her husband being the perpetrator."

Dallas HQ

Hours later, Curtis entered Fiona's office without knocking, mug in hand. He caught the look on her face and stopped cold.

"You found something."

She sat staring at a bracelet. Not Bridget's. Not a copy. *Lila's.* The one with the strange outer stone ring Lisa insisted Bridget add for her to get to have a part of given the gift to Lila from Aunt Lisa. I left it locked away all this time... She held up the bracelet. "Someone mailed this. August thirtieth. Two weeks after Bridget's murder. Postmark from Colombia. I should have investigated this."

Curtis frowned. "I vaguely remember you asking us to run a postmark. We did. Just a torched newsroom and a dead journalist and newspaper owner."

Fiona turned her monitor toward him. "Look, this is Lila's bracelet."

Recognition flickered. He took the bracelet carefully, thumb brushing the engraved heart. "Hell. Everett will..."

"Not yet," Fiona cut in. "We need confirmation before showing him. And it might end up in court. And Shaw said he does not always do what is best for himself. He could refuse to hand it over as evidence. It's a connection, and hope his daughter is still alive."

Bianca appeared in the hallway. "Did someone say confirmation?" she said, grinning. "Just cracked another SILO fragment."

Minutes later, they huddled around the conference monitor. Bianca's fingers flew across the keys.

Screens lit up: intake logs, biometric data, locations. She highlighted one entry. Child ID: L.T. Assigned by DNA case numbers.

Dated ten days after Bridget's murder. Location: Belize Holding Center. Transfer: Colombia. Fiona gripped the edge of the desk.

"We need to get Bridget and Everett's DNA. We can see if it matches this case number."

Curtis exhaled. "They targeted her. Funneled her through SILO. This was the type of info Bridget was chasing. Did they tell her what they would do with her daughter before they killed her? My God."

Bianca stared. "Lila didn't just vanish. They processed her. Tagged her. Someone wanted us to find that bracelet, to know where she was, and who had her."

Fiona straightened. "Then someone out there knows she's still breathing. And where that is."

They sent the information on a secure line to Buck. Moments later, he buzzed back.

Buck's rough voice filled the room. "Got your packet. You're looking at SILO's Colombian node. Cartel territory. We've heard chatter about minors, but nothing solid. Until now."

Fiona didn't hesitate. "We have proof. Lila's bracelet. It matches a SILO intake ID. And they use DNA. If we can match that..."

Buck grunted. "Then we move. Quiet. No paper trail. I'll extend the air gap around Sentinel. You run point on your end."

"No leaks," Fiona said. "If this goes public, Lila becomes a bargaining chip."

"Agreed. Coordinates to follow."

The line cut.

Curtis closed his notebook. "That's the first time Buck's voice didn't sound like stone."

"Because we gave him something real," Fiona said. "And for the first time in months, so do we."

At half-past three in the morning, Fiona sat alone in her office, sleep nowhere in sight. Under the lamp rested the bracelet. The initials gleamed.

She touched the charm. A pray formed, quiet but unshakable.

"God, please protect Lila and all the children taken for such evil reasons." She whispered a silent prayer before slipping the bracelet back into its velvet case. Then returned it to the safe. Outside, the cicadas sang louder. As if the night itself carried her prayer on the wind.

Unknown Location in seedier area of Dallas

Earlier that night, across the highway, a mile away, a man stood on the roof of his mansion. The night air smelled of cedar and wet earth. In the distance, the O'Brien ranch glowed faint with porch lights and office windows.

Through the scope, he analyzed Fiona pacing the office room, her hand brushing something silver before placing it on her desk. Her posture was different tonight. Agitated instead of drained.

The puppy, Aladdin, now five months old, at his feet whined, restless. He bent, scratching behind his ears absentmindedly, eyes never leaving Fiona.

Hope made people reckless.

He stood on the roof of the sprawling ranch he owned. Four hundred and twenty acres. The old farmer had died in a convenient machinery accident, and Ghost hadn't bothered pretending otherwise. The farmer's kids preferred a generous cash offer rather than managing livestock.

Circular drive. Clear sightlines to Fiona's land and her mansion on the artificially built island.

He adjusted the scope. Regarded her stepping out onto the patio with a cup of coffee. Staring off into the dark.

He pulled a small brass box from his coat. Inside: a medal. The old man's. Something he bragged about. Something he thought made him acceptable to others. An illusion. Now it sat in the palm of his hand. A message his father wouldn't ignore.

He replaced the medal and clicked the box shut, and stepped back from the edge.

Then he descended into the machinery of a criminal empire he never asked for, but now ruled with dispassionate cruelty.

Later that night, miles away, driving to take care of something for his father, he thought about what others called him. Operatives whispered it. Enemies prayed they'd never see him. His father spat it out like a curse, though he was the one who named him. He did what was necessary. Brutality was part of the job.

The battered white van slid into a narrow alley, where the city seemed to rot from the inside out. Fog hung low, beading on bricks like sweat leaking through old wounds. A sagging fire escape dripped rust. Somewhere beyond the dumpsters, something dead was decaying slowly.

After Fiona gave him Aladdin, at least that's how he remembered the night she ran into the fire, something in him shifted. He decided the cartel could use dogs as effectively as law enforcement, and he sidetracked six military-trained Malinois for their operations. He found a few soldiers who could handle the dogs. This was one of the dogs. Only for his use. The Malinois in the back vibrated with excitement the moment the van stopped. No bark. Just a low tremor of readiness. He held out a piece of material for the dog to smell. He cracked the door open.

"Zoeken."

The dog launched out like a bullet, disappearing into the ribbons of shadow between dumpsters. Silent. Precise.

He stepped out slowly. Limp khakis. Two-dollar jacket from a thrift bin. Shoes that had seen better years. A face mask designed to be forgotten. Even the cameras ignored him. Machine-learning saw nothing worth flagging.

A rusted latch held the rear service door ajar. He grabbed the edge and opened it enough to squeeze through.

Inside, the hallway stank of old ammonia and radiator heat. Linoleum had bubbled like diseased skin. A fake surveillance camera blinked a useless red light in the corner, insulting more than warning. He moved up the stairwell, steps soundless. Third floor. The Malinois crouched low, tail stiff as wire, ears pricked. Not a whine. Not a shake. Born for this. Suite 314. He drew the suppressed pistol. The weight felt right. Balanced. Familiar. Inevitable. His father's handler crackled into his ear. "Behind schedule again."

He said nothing, just reached forward and opened the door.

Inside: two targets. Both soft. Both were oblivious.

The man jerked when he stepped through the door. The woman froze, lifting her phone as if it were going to stop a bullet.

"Data stick."
Flat. Cold. Already bored.

The man fumbled, knocked over a pen, then dropped the drive onto the desk as if the plastic scalded him. Sweat beaded along his temples. The code etched into the stick matched the intel. He shot him once in the forehead.

The sound was a muffled *thup*, barely louder than a cough. The man toppled sideways in a boneless heap. Blood pooled fast, warm, steam curling upward in the cold office air.

The woman didn't scream. Not shock. *Experience*. She'd seen death before.
He glanced at her.
She stared back, trembling but silent. There was fear in her eyes... and something else. Recognition? Or resignation?

The Malinois stepped between them, muscles taut, waiting for his cue.

He holstered the pistol.

"Call the cops," he said. "Tell them he got shot during the robbery. Nothing else."
A beat.
"You tell them anything more... I come back."

Her jaw trembled. She nodded once.

He left. Quiet. Efficient. Nothing wasted.

Back in the van, he wiped the dog's paws clean. Never leave trace evidence. Then lifted him into the front seat. The dog pressed close, trusting and warm.

The handler's voice returned, snide.
"You left a witness."

"No names. No faces. Nothing she can use."

"You're slipping. Sentimental. Weak, just like your father says. Maybe it's time to retire you."

He stared into the cracked rearview mirror. Black street. Blacker sky. His own reflection. Hollow and calm.

And beside him, the Malinois guarded him with steady, unblinking loyalty.

"Try it."

The line went dead. Static. Empty threat. Under his breath, "Yeah, I thought so."

He parked under a dead street lamp. He copied the data stick. His backup insurance and leverage rested in his hand, warm from his palm.

He felt no triumph. No satisfaction. Nothing. Just waited for someone to come by and take the original data stick.

The dog rested its head on his knee.
He let it.

Together they waited for dawn, two ghosts in a city that did not know what hunted within it.

CHAPTER 32

Warning Line

Sunday, April 16th, 2023

The Sentinel Hangar

Heavy with the smell of earth and ozone, the ranch air was still damp from an earlier mist. Then came the low thump of compressed air, followed by the roar of a controlled explosion.

The explosion tore through the east hangar wall in a shock of noise and light. Windows in the compound building blew out; the mansion windows trembled even from that far away. Dirt flew off the ground in waves. Ranch hands and compound personnel arrived as the property's emergency floodlights snapped on. The blast had already woken them. Smoke billowed from the breach, but the moored airship Sentinel, anchored in her hangar cradle, remained untouched. The blast had been precision-calibrated.

Curtis and Fiona arrived minutes later, still in their pajamas and hastily pulled on bathrobes. Fiona's instinct took over before thought; she came armed with her SIG. The familiar weight was cold against her palm, a reflex that felt comforting.

"Check the moorings and internal nav arrays," Curtis ordered, chest heaving, his Glock in his right hand. "Search the perimeter, get Buck on the emergency line. *Now*. Call the office and get the cyber team to find where that signal came from. They can use the ranch's sniffer setup for something like this. I want to know who just knocked on our door. *Hard*."

Fiona stood in the hangar's shadow. Her eyes fixed not on the damage, but on the fact that it hadn't hit the Sentinel. She understood instantly what this was. A warning. The Sentinel had just returned from another long-range surveillance of the church compound.

Curtis paced to the utility panel near the side door and tapped into the security feed on his tablet. Whoever breached their security had quietly and cleanly disabled the hangar alarm. No forced code entry, no tamper flags.

Kenneth reviewed the recordings. "Nothing tripped. No motion pings."

They scanned the external camera feeds. One slow replay showed a shadowy figure in all black. Hood, gloves, tactical gait. Approaching the east wall just before one-thirty am. He must have moved low until he reached the hangar perimeter.

"See that?" Kenneth tapped the screen. "Right there, manual disarming of the infrared trigger. Gloved, practiced precision. This guy's done this type of work before."

The figure placed a small device near the control box. Five seconds. Then he backed off and vanished into the brush line. As he turned, his sleeve snagged on a strand of wire. Frame-by-frame, the fabric tore just enough to reveal three black legs of what appeared to be a spider, though they could not see the whole tattoo.

Curtis blew out a sharp breath. "Basic alarm package got us burned. Never should've let it run on its own that long. The hardened hanger held, though."

"We upgrade today," Fiona said. "Full-scale perimeter mesh. Motion detection tied to human stride. Upright or crouched. Layered zones. No more single-point coverage."

Kenneth nodded. "I can have it sourced and installed in forty-eight hours. Maybe less if we call in Major Buck's specialist surplus from his last tour."

Curtis went over the feed again. "This is a warning. Still, they wanted to prove they could still get to the Sentinel."

"Yet, they did neither. If this guy is that good, he could have blown the ship up beyond repair. No, something else is going on here, and we need to discover exactly what it is." Fiona looked around those gathered. The special forces guys nodded their heads.

Thirty minutes later, Bianca called from the office on a video link. "Got here as soon as I could. The rest of the team have just arrived. We traced the trigger signal. It was RF-based, piggy-backed on an old satellite uplink." Bianca looked up at them as she said it. "Flagged satellite path. Possible CIA signature, but dirty as hell."

Curtis stiffened. "Someone provided the Sentinel's exact coordinates."

Fiona's voice cut sharp. "Google Maps. Seems anyone can get that kind of info now."

She sighed. "Yes, I know it does not give real-time images. The CIA connection from the satellite is the most likely." She paused as she looked around. "But this reminded me of Google flyover images each year. Let Major Buck know we need a blackout over the ranch from all public services."

Dallas Office | Bullpen/Conference Table & Cyber Division

By dawn, the conference room lights hummed above them, cold and white. Fiona stood at the head of the table. Hair still damp from the shower she'd taken to scrub off smoke and burned wiring from the hangar blast. Fiona's knuckles were raw from slamming into the wall while she used a fire extinguisher on the smoldering wiring. The sting was a small anchor against the bigger problems pressing in on all sides.

"We stop playing nice." She said. "Starting now, we play by their rules."

Curtis brought the network up on the touchscreen. Lines of red and gold spidered across the southern hemisphere, showing the routes Bridget had died trying to expose, and a blood-red line stretching from Texas down into Guatemala.

All around the room, trusted O'Brien & Galloway operatives leaned in. The air smelled of burnt coffee and ozone from overworked servers. A mug rattled against the table's edge as someone adjusted in their chair.

"Bianca, Sabrina, and Paul, you're going after the funding," Fiona continued. "PAC donations, NGOs, charities, Transitions AI, all of it. I want their laundering structure exposed in the court of public opinion."

A keyboard clacked from the far side. Sabrina, their dark-net specialist, had already logged in. Matilda's nails clicked against her mug, sharp as gunfire.

Curtis added, "Send every piece of information we have to the DA that can clear Everett. Let him know it came from our office during our investigation of Lisa and Bridget's murders. Combined with the witness testimony Mason and George secured, it'll kick the hive. Hard. We need to take the pressure off Everett. Have PD detectives look elsewhere for who murdered Bridget, Lisa, and Shirley. The motive for Everett killing his wife keeps getting slimmer as we dig deeper into this unholy trinity of cartel trafficking, rogue CIA black ops, and the use of NGOs for fraudulent purposes. No reports of abuse either of Everett abusing his wife by police, hospitals, or family and friends, or even neighbors."

Bianca nodded sharply. "I'll have it primed by six-thirty this morning."

"Casey," Fiona said, turning to her brother. "Back George on Everett's legal defense, not just the land seizure. Do this for me."

Casey hesitated, eyes flicking toward her, measuring how much further she would go. Then he raised his coffee. "Let's kick the bull in the balls and see what happens."

Matilda leaned forward, her smile knife-sharp. "I already sent over the documentation. The DA subpoenaed four firms hiding under Cayman-based shells the other day. Of course, I sent them anonymously. Wanted to see if he'd bite. He did."

Fiona turned to Kenneth and Phùng. "Surveillance. Run tight protocols on our internal systems. No off-campus meetings. Anyone operating out of pattern, you flag them."

Phùng didn't blink. "Already adjusted the building's cell-tower spoofing. Heading back to the ranch now."

She turned to Kenneth. "As soon as I get all our encrypted files from the Sentinel, put them on a drive. Jeanette from our mail department will deliver it to Major Buck downtown at three thirty-five pm today. I'll call him once I reach the ranch. She'll ride out with me and take a company car back, with GPS tracking in it."

Curtis glanced her way. "Bianca and I are going after Hays. We'll run his alias. Audit his academic records, overseas travel, anything Hays ever signed. I want his paper trail found. I'll contact Eduardo Vélez's widow tonight. See what she knows."

Fiona's hand settled over the map. "The Bogotá package and email weren't random. Somebody wanted us to see it. I want to know why. And how they knew to send it to me."

The room quieted. Fiona's voice was steady. "Let's clear Everett and find his daughter."

◆ ◆ ◆

Early Morning | Cyber Division: Controlled Chaos

The cyber floor buzzed with energy. Keyboards clicked like controlled bursts of gunfire. Screens flickered under pale-blue light, each one scrolling dense metadata and trace routes. At seven am, Bianca's finger hovered over the send key. Paused for just a second, long enough to feel the weight of what she was unleashing.

Then she pressed it. Anonymous files sourced from Bridget's now decrypted archive flooded the digital news airwaves. They exposed Transitions AI's predictive-policing software for what it was: an algorithm riddled with bias, designed with a deliberate backdoor. A vulnerability granting full criminal access to every database it touched. If the IP address got traced back to them, their PI license wouldn't cover this kind of action.

They all knew it. Fortunately, no classified information was involved. Within an hour, media channels exploded. Transition AI stock prices plummeted. Political outcry erupted. Demands mounted for the indictment of Marshall Hays.

And every newscaster asked, "Where was Marshall Hays?" By nine am, Porter & Ashburn publicly severed ties with both Transitions AI and Hays. Cole's money-management division dropped them entirely. Then came the second wave: PAC funds funneled to offshore NGOs disguised as child-advocacy nonprofits. The breadcrumb trail was unmistakable.

Fringe media caught the scent by noon. International press by late afternoon. Momentum was uncontrollable.

Curtis stood behind Bianca, watching the chaos ripple outward. "They're on fire."

Fiona looked over his shoulder. "Let them burn."

Curtis's jaw tensed, just a flicker of unease. He wondered how far she'd go if the fire spread to them, and whether she'd still recognize herself on the other side.

Whiskey River Two-Step Ranch Office Ripple of Events

The smell of scorched soil from the hangar still clung to Fiona's boots as she entered the ranch office. The light was warm, deceptive. Beyond the windows, long shadows stretched across the hills like grasping hands as a cloud drifted overhead.

Kenneth entered quietly, face pale. "We had a drone breach."

Fiona stilled. Her throat went dry. "Small, fast, low-profile. Made one pass above the bunker's exit hatch. It didn't linger, but it knew where to look." Mason had already preregistered the safe house under a sealed county order requested by Curtis days earlier.

"We move Everett. Now. Quiet. As soon as the external drives are on their way to Buck," Kenneth nodded. "Already prepping."

The faint buzz of the drone's rotors still echoed in her mind as she crossed to the secure air-gapped servers. She keyed in a two-code sequence, retrieved a sealed padded envelope marked only with a black triangle, and checked its tamper seal twice. Still open and ready. Inside went a full copy of Bridget's decrypted drive, the witness transcripts, the PAC-fund maps, and the algorithm trace files, duplicated once, then encoded to military standards.

She trusted Jeanette White for this run because Jeanette never talked, never flinched, and never lost a delivery. She also was the last person a mole in the company might suspect of delivering something this important. Her job was in their mail department, yet she'd been asking to be trained, wanted a shot at moving into investigations. This was her chance.

Through the window, Fiona spotted Jeanette heading toward the hangar bay. "Jeanette!" she called. The woman turned and jogged up the stairs with her usual no-nonsense calm. "Here's the package," Fiona said. "Major Buck. Downtown, three thirty-five pm today."

Jeanette studied the envelope. "Travel light, no stops?"

"No stops. Burner phone is in the outer sleeve. Only use it if you're forced off schedule, or have an emergency."

Jeanette nodded, tucking it under her jacket. "I'll make contact. I'll confirm the handoff."

Fiona's phone buzzed. She answered without looking. Buck's voice came through, cool and exacting. "You're going wide. The Democrats are screaming holy hell, burning up my phone lines, though they can't point their fingers at me. For now, at least. What in the hell were you thinking?"

"Too much heat?" Fiona asked. "We're past the point of SILO leaks. We needed to put them on their back foot for a change."

Buck didn't argue. "Agreed. It's time more than one set of eyes saw what this is. Sanctioned human trafficking. Got to go."

Jeanette was already halfway to the truck. By the time Fiona looked back, dust curled behind the tailgate. Fiona watched her go, feeling the familiar ache, the same ache she felt every time she sent someone into danger, knowing she couldn't go instead.

Fiona headed to the house. She needed to call the DA's office. Half an hour later, it was done. The plan to move Everett was in place.

He objected, but not for long after seeing the drone footage. She could tell he was playing by the legal rules. But his patience was wearing thin; the same tenacity that had kept him alive through years of war and losing buddies during the war was wearing thin. An hour later, deputies Webster and Lane arrived to take Everett to the safe house, where other deputies would take the first shift in the safe house. Mason had set up for him. No one besides a select few in the DA's office, Smith's sheriff, and the deputies assigned knew the secure location.

Only a few at the O'Brien & Galloway company involved in the Bridget Taylor murder case knew that Everett was even in protective custody, but not where.

By six pm, people claimed their early-morning release of information came from unreliable sources. By 10 pm, the late-night news no longer mentioned it, effectively burying the story. Scrubbed. Someone high up had flipped the kill switch. She stood alone by the window afterward, watching the night sky twinkle cold, distant and unaware of her problems. Sleep was gone, safety gone, and now she was risking her people too. But she didn't flinch. She had already crossed the line, and she'd do it again, every time, if it meant bringing one more child home, one more family back together, one more piece of justice out of the dark.

◆◆◆

Monday, April 17th, 2023

Dallas County Sheriff's Office | Records Division

The basement lights hummed with an old electrical buzz, the kind that settled behind your eyes. Detective Mason McCarthy stood alone at the terminal in the records office, the court-mandated camera archive pulled up on the screen. A quiet order from a district judge, issued after the Miller fiasco, had required the evidence cage and internal area to be put under twenty-four seven video surveillance. A detail most detectives forgot existed.

Not Mason.

He typed the date: October fourth to the twentieth, 2022.
Time window: Fourteen hundred to fifteen hundred.

The grainy feed loaded. Black-and-white. Fixed angle. The evidence cage was visible through metal bars, like a rib cage.

Then...

Wren walked into the frame. Mason's jaw tightened. Wren

moved as if was just doing a normal check on the evidence. Clipboard under his arm. Jacket open. Calm. He took the Bridget Taylor case folder off the shelf. Mason leaned closer as Wren flipped through it. Wren pulled a single sheet from the packet; the camera caught the header clearly when Wren turned it:

Tire Impressions: North side of cabin (Unidentified Motorcycle).

Mason froze. Wren folded the paper. Pocketed it. Added fake pencil marks to the top of the next page. Closed the folder. Put it back.

Then he walked out. Mason rewound the moment three times, each pass hitting harder. He switched to the hallway camera; another angle required by the same court order. There, clear as rain on glass, Wren opened the maintenance door and fed the folded page into the burn bin used for biohazard disposal. The timestamp blinked in the corner. Mason exhaled slowly, anger rising like a pressure change in the room. "He burned it," Mason whispered to no one. "*Son of a bitch burned it.*"

He downloaded the clip. Saved it to a secure drive. And for the first time in months, he felt the ground shift beneath his feet. This was the missing link. Proof. Wren hadn't just been sloppy. He hadn't misinterpreted witness statements.

Bad intel was something he relied on. He tampered. He destroyed evidence. The case against Everett was corrupt.

Mason put the encrypted drive in his inside jacket pocket. His voice was a low, grim murmur as he spoke to himself while he shut the terminal down. "Damn asshole's been burying the truth since day one. Not anymore."

Next, he went over to the lab. Mason stood with his hands on his hips as the lab supervisor pulled up the digital request logs. "There," she said, tapping the screen. "Detective Wren called this in personally. Told us to de-prioritize bleach residue, hair and fiber, and the partial print."

Mason's jaw clenched. "That was key evidence."

"Well," she said, pushing her glasses up, "we only process first what the case detective flags as urgent. He didn't want those run at the time."

She clicked another tab.

"And look at this. The backlog timestamp. Those items got bumped so far down the list that they haven't yet processed them."

Mason stared at the entries, bile rising.

The motorcycle tire tracks, truck tire tracks, a couple of footprints, some hair samples, and the bleach trace. All the things that could've cleared Everett before the city crucified him.

He exhaled slowly, dangerously. "He didn't miss it," Mason said. "Wren buried it. Deliberately. Run all this evidence, top priority."

The supervisor swallowed. "Do you want me to forward this to the DA and the findings once they're completed?"

Mason didn't hesitate. "Send it. All of it. And lock the log. No edits. No deletions." He turned and left the lab without another word; fury held on a tight leash.

Behind him, the head of the CSU lab called in his top technicians and set them to work.

CHAPTER 33

The Killing Floor

Tuesday, April 18th, 2023

O'Brien & Galloway Office | Selena

The corridor hummed with a low electrical buzz. The refreshing scent of citrus cleaning-solution clung to the air, threaded with the warmth of machines idling on standby. So intent on her studies, she never realized how late it got. She had to lock everything up properly, as she had promised Fiona if she stayed late studying. Fiona's words echoed in her mind, "Curtis and I feel we can trust you enough to lock up if you stay late, Selena. We know we can count on you." She smiled to herself, proud that Fiona and Curtis trusted her.

Selena made her last security loop. Testing drawer locks, keypad tones chirping as she armed zones one by one. The office monitors glowed with muted screensavers. The break-room television left on to keep the empty floor from feeling so creepy... a local anchor's voice floated out between static: *"Temperatures in Dallas climbing toward the mid-seventies later tomorrow, no rain expected, clear skies for the Texas Rangers' home stand."*

She smiled faintly, half-listening. Finals for the spring semester crept closer; the firm's rigs compiled twice as fast as her home laptop, and her internet bill was still unpaid. Fiona and

Curtis had said it was fine; she could finish her project, then lock up tight. After that, she sat down and shut off her computer, gathering up her studies.

A faint sound cut through the HVAC's steady breath.

Not a latch. Not a door seal. A click, precise, sharp. Selena froze. The corridor lights flickered once, the way they did during an electrical surge. She listened. Silence... then a subtle change in the hum, like an extra fan spinning somewhere unseen. Her pulse quickened. The same queasy sensation she felt when she'd walked home alone after late classes, telling herself it was nothing.

She rose to check that she had locked everything properly.

Light drew a thin line under the secondary data-center door. No one had any reason to be there after hours, and on her rounds earlier she had seen no one.

"Hello?" Her voice bounced and died.

She eased closer, shoes whispering on the tile. Through the doorway, she saw a shoulder, male, broad, outlined by the console's glow. A flash drive pulsed faint blue. File paths cascaded too fast to read across the console.

"You don't have clearance for that," her voice trembled at the end. Not fear just yet, only confusion, the same confusion she felt when she first realized the firm dealt with real danger, not just paperwork.

No answer. The cursor stopped.

Selena stepped inside. The room smelled faintly of ozone. "Hey, you need to..."

He turned fast. For half a second, her mind struggled to catch up. Not a thief, not a hacker, but someone she knew. Someone she trusted. Recognition hit like icy water. Her stomach dropped. This was the man who sometimes brought her coffee, asked about her finals with a smile, and laughed at her jokes.

Frigid air touched her throat before pain did... The blade's kiss was surgical. Her hands clamped onto the warmth blooming beneath her jaw... she crumpled to the ground. He advanced, straddled her, and the knife came down. Measured, efficient, seven times. Violence designed to look like chaos. The cold method of eliminating a witness.

In her last seconds, she saw the flash drive still glowing blue on the console. Her last thought of her mother's face when the phone rings tomorrow with the news. Her world faded to black.

When it was over, his breath was still steady. Cloth whispered on steel. He went back and retrieved a flash drive, which vanished into a pocket. Moments later in the outer foyer, a rush of air, the ding of the elevator, the sounds of a scuffle in the lobby, and the thump of a fallen body. Seconds later, the stairwell door sighed shut. No one in the office to hear. Blood pooled under and around Selena and flowed into the tile grout, dark ribbons finding the low points.

In the server room beyond, one rack's blue status light showed it was still active. The others followed the cyber-division's auto-shutdown script, the nightly power-down that triggered after the last log-off. Just one hummed on, a breadcrumb, not an error.

At one am, a motion sensor flagged in a secure zone to the lobby guard, who notified the guard on rounds to check it out. After ten minutes of not hearing from the other guard, the lobby guard called the police. The police arrived and reached the floor fifteen minutes later. By one fifty-eight am, Dallas PD had sealed the level. At two am, Mason and Luis arrived as the on-duty homicide detectives. Mason called Curtis.

Curtis stared at the bedroom ceiling as he listened to what Mason was telling him. When he finally spoke, his words were heavy. "On my way. Don't notify Fiona. I'll let her know what's going on later."

The Dallas HQ Office

The elevator dinged open. Bleach-bright lights and the sharp bite of disinfectant assailed him. Yellow tape divided the lobby.

Curtis stepped onto their office floor and stopped cold. Selena's chair sat untouched, her purse beneath the desk, a plastic bag of half-eaten takeout beside it. The bag still had the restaurant's sticker on it. The same place she'd brought lunch for the team last week, laughing about how she'd finally learned to like cilantro.

Police officers came and went. The coroner's assistant waited by the elevator with a gurney, the black body bag strapped down and ready for transport.

The glass walls of the server room still bore streaks of drying blood. A foul, metallic tang hung in the air, sharp and familiar. The reality of the fact that Selena never made it home. Curtis felt it like a fist in his chest. She'd been the one who always remembered birthdays, who kept the coffee pot full even when no one asked, who stayed late so she could do her schoolwork and become a vet. Kind-hearted towards the helpless, fierce in her defense of them.

A lump rose in his throat, grief tangled with fury. Silenced him. He walked to where Mason and most of the police officers had gathered.

The copper scent clawed at Curtis's throat.

Selena. Her name hit him harder than the smell. A face that smiled every morning, a voice that said, "Good morning, Curtis." He swallowed hard.

He forced himself forward until the lone, blue-lit server tower stopped him. The rest dark as they should be. It was the same console where they'd isolated and secured client files, walled off, encrypted, and locked down important files from all their cases. Curtis's jaw tightened.

Just then his phone buzzed, and Curtis stepped away from the forensics cordon.

"Curtis." Kenneth's voice, tight. "Jeanette never made it home. Buck's trackers lost her twenty minutes after the drop, last ping near Griffin and Pearl. Fiona keeps calling her. Nothing. She's at the compound right now, working with Buck and his people over the secure line. She's talking about heading into the office because her housekeeper told her you left to go to the office."

Curtis stared at his reflection in the glass. He saw the lines in his own face deepen, the same lines he'd seen in Everett's face when he mentioned Bridget and Lila. Loss carved the same marks on everyone. Eventually.

"Not good. Kenneth, someone murdered Selena at the office. I'm here right now with Mason. There's still a server running. Keep this between us for now. Let me break it to Fiona later. Do what you can to keep her there."

"Understood," Kenneth hung up.

Curtis surveyed the single humming rack. "Whoever did this hadn't come for Selena. They came for what that server tower held. Worse, she died for nothing; they had already removed vital information from their cases."

He closed his eyes for a second. Selena hadn't signed up for this. She'd signed up for a job, for a future, for a chance to make something of herself. And now she was gone, and the only thing left was a humming rack and a bloodstain that wouldn't wash out.

◆ ◆ ◆

Tactical Retrieval | Downtown Warehouse

Jeanette's trail went cold at the Elm Street garage. Once Kenneth confirmed she never made it home from the drop, he looped in Major Buck and the cyber team. Fiona, already at the compound, cleared the team to fly out on the company jet to save time.

The ranch cyber compound pulsed with feed windows and radio chatter. Fiona paced; Sabrina cursed at a lagging satellite link; Paul Avery rerouted a camera grid.

At three-fifty a.m., Kenneth straightened. "Location."

A drone video, IR overlay, showed a boarded warehouse south of the Trinity River, close to the drop site. One faint heat signature. Buck's team hit it ten minutes later.

One of Buck's ISA special forces team members carried Jeanette out bloody, bruised, dehydrated, but alive.

At Dallas General, antiseptic stung the air. Three cracked ribs. Dislocated shoulder. Fractured orbital. Burn tracks.

"I should've sent Derek," Fiona whispered. "Or Austin. Or me."

Curtis had arrived minutes earlier and leaned against the wall. "You couldn't. Only three people had that intel. That means a leak, and it's ours."

"Doesn't change the fact that she's here because of us."

A nurse stepped out. "She's stable. Critical, but responsive."

"Can I see her?"

"Not now. Come back tomorrow. Her family is with her right now."

Fiona nodded, and she and Curtis turned and left. Boots echoed as they walked away steadily, relentlessly. The line between defense and offense had merged.

◆ ◆ ◆

Whiskey River Two-Step Ranch Mansion

Deep purple lightened the horizon to a tinge of gray. Stars sparkled overhead in the velvet black sky, unaware and uncaring of the grief of those below. The air already warming toward the upper seventies, a mild April day as the Dallas forecast had promised.

Fiona stood with her arms folded, leaning on the railing of her ranch-office balcony, the air thick with the scent of cedar and the neigh of a horse in the distance. A rooster crowed several times as if no one had heard him the first time. Tears shimmered in her eyes. The same tears she'd fought back the night Matt never came home, the night the phone rang, and the world shifted under her feet forever.

Curtis joined her, coffee in hand. "You want this?"

"If it's hot." Her voice had a hitch to it he had not heard since Matt died years ago. Murdered while undercover on a narc investigation. Unsolved to this day, the same hitch that had broken her then, the same raw edge that reminded him she still carried that wound like a second skin.

"Cinnamon and vanilla, your favorite." Steam rose from the cup, attesting to its heat. "Thought you needed some company and comfort."

She reached for it, and they both detected how her hands trembled. Curtis put his free hand over hers until the shaking eased. His palm warm against her knuckles, the same steady grip he'd offered her the day they buried Matt, when words had failed and silence had been the only honest thing left.

She sipped as the silence grew between them.

"Someone murdered Shirley to send us a message; then murdered, her voice cracked on Selena's name, *the girl who'd once stayed late just to help organize case files, who'd asked Fiona about college with wide-eyed hope, now reduced to a crime scene photo.* Someone at our office there to steal information, and someone also told them that Jeanette was acting as a courier with valuable information going to Major Buck. They didn't get to her before the drop, so they tortured her afterward, thinking she might have information. What are we doing, Curtis?" She finally whispered.

Curtis didn't respond.

Fiona stared at the horizon, now edged in mauve.

Her voice was raw when she spoke minutes later, quieter than before. "We were told back in the academy, you move crime, remember? That policing doesn't end crime. It decreases for a moment in time. It moves it to less desirable areas. Like rats fleeing into different alleys. Greed, envy, lust, violence, and hatred. There not gone." She swallowed hard, her eyes still fixed on the horizon. "What if that's all this is? Exposing corruption doesn't fix the system. It just shifts where the damage happens. Jordan and Daniel killed in a shootout protecting those drives. Now a witness, Shirley's gone. Selena's whole life stolen. They tortured Jeanette." Her breath caught in her throat. "For what? What are we doing, Curtis?"

Curtis didn't answer right away. The wind carried the distant sound of a deer herd jumping the fence nearby, hooves striking the earth. He leaned against the railing beside her, quiet for a long beat.

Then he said, low and firm, "We're drawing a line, Fi. Maybe it doesn't fix everything. We both know justice doesn't restore the dead. But we're making sure their stories don't just vanish into silence. You think the system's broken? It is. But if people like us stop fighting, stop resisting, stop caring, then it's more than broken. It's lost. Good loses. Evil reigns. People like us, Fi, are the little boy with his finger in the dike trying to hold back the flood. So, we hold the line, even if it costs. Especially if it costs. And we'll make those *bastards* pay."

Fiona blinked, breath shaky, then nodded once, the motion small but resolute.

Behind them, the rooster crowed again.

This time she heard it.

"Lock down all reports. Automatic encryption. Air-gap anything relating to military intelligence from this point forward. Notify Buck. We isolate personnel access. Need-to-know only, and only with his approval."

Curtis nodded. "You think it's someone inside? Because I do."

"I think it's someone close enough to track our trail."

"They're counting on fear," he said finally.

Steam curled between them. Fiona stared off into the horizon as tears blurred her vision and ran down her face unchecked.

Media Firestorm & Dallas Courthouse

Jeanette White, missing the night before, was last seen on a routine courier run for the firm of O'Brien & Galloway Investigations and Protection Agency LLC. Early this morning, the local police found her in an abandoned warehouse. She is in critical condition.

Media speculation suggested concealment. A cover-up. And somehow, the media all looped it back to Everett Taylor.

Every major outlet ran the same suspiciously synchronized story. Everett, recently arrested for the murder of his wife and the disappearance of his daughter Lila, was unstable, a veteran, possibly suffering from PTSD. They recycled courtroom footage and combat photos, painting a portrait of a man too broken to trust, too dangerous to free.

"*O'Brien & Galloway acted as investigators for his legal team,*" one anchor intoned grimly. "*And now two women connected to that investigation have met with foul play.*"

No mention, of course, that the Dallas County Sheriff's Office had moved Everett to a secure safe house the night before either incident. That detail wasn't public. The notification had gone only to Micah Colburn's office, through Detective Mason and his partner Detective Alvarez, the information time-sensitive and sealed. The silence about Everett's actual location let the story rot and spread.

By mid-morning, Casey, George Shaw, and DA Micah Colburn were behind closed doors in Judge Holloway's chambers... debating whether the pattern of attacks, the information presented by George and Casey accumulated so far, along with Everett's confirmed secure location, were enough to warrant holding off on any impending indictments against Everett.

When they emerged, Casey and George wore the same expression. Steady, unreadable. Like a man holding pocket aces, with two more on the flop.

Micah didn't stop walking. He descended the courthouse steps with his phone to his ear, his tone clipped and urgent, swallowed by the city crowds.

Dallas PD | Homicide Unit

The bullpen was nearly empty, lit only by the sickly hum of half-burnt fluorescents. Mason stood alone at Wren's desk, arms folded, a printout in his hand.

Wren walked in, jacket half off, stopping when he saw Mason blocking his chair.

"What's your problem now?" Wren asked, tone bored.

Mason held up the paper.
The reporter's transcript.
The reporter's exact phrasing.

"Funny thing," Mason said in a quiet tone. "Only one detective wrote the phrase 'alibi unconfirmed' in the internal notes."

Wren didn't blink. "So?"

"So," Mason stepped closer, "that same phrase came out of a reporter's mouth thirty minutes later. Word for word. Before the captain even saw your update."

A muscle twitched in Wren's jaw.

"That reporter has plenty of sources," Wren muttered.

"Not in *my* cases, she doesn't." Mason's voice dropped to a low, dangerous tone. "And not with access to un-filed notes that hadn't even hit the system yet."

Wren tried to brush past him.

Mason put a hand on his chest, not hard, just immovable.

"You leaked it," Mason said. No accusation in his tone. Just fact. "You shaped the public narrative before they even processed the evidence."

Wren's eyes went cold. "Maybe the public deserves to know what kind of man this Everett really is, not a hero like some of you try to make him out to be."

Mason leaned in, inches from his face.

"And maybe," he said, "I'm done pretending you're just sloppy, lazy, and incompetent."

The air between them tightened.

Wren broke it first. "Move."

Mason didn't.

Not until he'd said the last piece. "Next time you try to rig a case with my name on it, make damn sure I don't catch your fingerprints all over the false or missing evidence. I kept wondering who was leaking all along, but I suspected it was some low-level tech or a street cop. Never figured it'd be you."

Also, deputies Perez and Aranda sent me some interesting information this morning, and I will let the DA know exactly what that information is. He stepped back, letting Wren pass, but the look in his eyes revealed he had finally crossed the line.

And he could tell Wren knew it.

CHAPTER 34

All Came Crashing Down

Wednesday, April 26th, 2023

Dallas District Attorney's Office

Micah Colburn didn't wait for the elevator.

His shoes struck the concrete stairwell in quick, flat beats, echoing up the shaft like a metronome set to fury. Third floor. Fourth. Fifth. He shoved open the door to the executive level, bypassed the receptionist, and ignored the intern carrying a stack of motions trying to hand to him.

"Out," he said without looking up, and the outer office cleared like a fast weather shift.

The main conference room smelled of printer toner and day-old sweat. Blinds were half-open, letting in streaks of slate morning light that cut across the long table in hard lines.

He tossed the manila folder onto the oak surface hard enough to slide it half the table's length.

"Get George Shaw on standby. I'm dropping the charges against Everett Taylor. The judge's chewing out this morning is something I do not wish to experience again. I'm not going to let Shaw blindside and get the better of me on this case again.

An assistant DA blinked. "You want to drop...?"

"Did you not hear me? Yes. Today. Before noon. Draft it with no flourishes. Just the facts we have now."

"Are we sealing it?"

"No."

He paced to the window, arms crossed, jaw tight. The streets below were already humming, buses cutting through puddles, delivery trucks backing into alley bays, pedestrians with phones in one hand and coffee in the other. Dallas didn't care who got justice. It just wanted a show.

Behind him, a junior prosecutor skimmed the file. "This is... whoa. This is all from Detective Mason McCarthy and his partner Luis Alvarez?"

"Not just Mason," Micah said. His voice was low but firm, the kind you don't interrupt. "Shaw's got witnesses. O'Brien & Galloway has been remarkably effective in its investigation. And made our whole law enforcement in Dallas look either corrupt or stupid. I don't know which one I would prefer right now." He rubbed his face as if something dirty were on it.

"For chain-of-command only, note that Officer Wren redacted and buried the original report. Detective Mason discovered the full statement. It shows Everett outside Texarkana, by several sources, at a cattle auction at the time of Bridget's death and the disappearance of his daughter, Lila. Mason found the unedited version buried in an internal transfer log. Detective Wren's fingerprints are figuratively all over it."

He let the silence sit for a beat.

"And Colter Harlan gave a statement yesterday," Micah added. "He's awake. Lucid. Says Everett was with him the day before he left that evening to fly out. Sent in his affidavit through his lawyer to make it legal. Clay Braddock also posted his affidavit with this office along with a recorded video conference, which he made in case the IRS needed transaction proof, and it also corroborates that."

Aides in the room exchanged a few glances. He pressed on.

"I also want an audit of Detective Wren's finances. Quiet and thorough. And put a tail on him. Only those of us in this room know any of this, and if it leaks, I'll know exactly where to look. And that person will never work in law enforcement ever again. Understood."

He let that sink in.

"And the O'Brien & Galloway office, through George Shaw, just delivered financial routing codes, offshore logs, and a voice print match linking a Joe Bell to falsified reports and surveillance tampering. They backed it with corroborated schedules and metadata timestamps."

One of the senior staffers leaned back slowly. "You're saying we had a frame job inside the department?"

"I'm saying," Micah replied evenly, "Everett Taylor's no longer an official suspect. And I'm thanking God it never got to the point of an indictment. Through information given to me by Detective McCarthy, Joe Bell is now our primary suspect. He might also be good for the I-45 murders as well."

Silence held.

Micah pulled out his phone, scrolled to a secure chat thread, and opened a file with the DA's investigative team, the watermark still affixed.

"Pull every call Joe Bell made in the last sixty days. I want location pings, voicemail scrubs, tower bounces, especially around Mrs. Taylor's murder and the two storage unit fires and the 1-45 murders, pull everything on this man from NCIC if anything is there and send out request about this individual being questioned in any unsolved or even solved murders."

Another assistant piped up. "Do we want to bring him in?"

"Not yet." Micah pocketed his phone. "I want the trap quiet. Tight. When we move, it's with everything stacked. No leaks. Not this time. And we use only our investigators. Period. Until I understand who is corrupt in the department, we'll keep this to ourselves."

He moved toward the door, slowing just long enough to fix the room with a glance. "Get me what I need before this goes viral on the news feeds. Or worse, before someone else dies."

And then he was gone.

The blinds rustled in the window draft. Somewhere below, a siren wailed.

An hour later, every screen in the courthouse lobby lit up at once.

"BREAKING: *All Charges Dropped Against Former Veteran Everett Taylor, Though He Remains a Person of Interest," the banner scrolled.*

No one commented. There were no panels that followed. No debate. The story vanished as quickly as it had flared. It disappeared not through disinterest, but by design. Damage control. Three days from now, no one will remember who Everett was.

Austin & Marble Falls | Dusk to Nightfall

In Austin, the sun fell in slow, bleeding streaks across the skyline. Fiery red lit the glass towers like stained blood. The air outside was still; but inside the hotel suite it was fraught with tension.

Delores stood by the window, peeling back the side of the blackout curtain.

The room smelled faintly of gardenia, sandalwood, and fear.

"That was the same car," Joe said from behind her, sitting on the edge of the bed, field-stripping his Glock with the muscle memory of ritual. "Third time today."

Delores didn't answer right away. She pulled her hair back, but strands fell loose, shadowing her cheekbones. She looked composed. Almost calm. But the lazy heat in her golden eyes was gone.

"We need help," she said finally, her voice a low flick of warning. "Someone's tipping them off."

Joe didn't look up. His jaw flexed. "It's the mole," he said. "CIA mole embedded in O'Brien & Galloway. Has to be. Porter & Ashburn's golden boy got his irons in both ends of the fire. He wants his cut. Wants to stay valuable, right now I can use that to our advantage."

He grabbed the burner phone, dialed the number Reid had given him, the one he was to use if the mole became necessary. He wanted a face to face. Call him out, yet he also needed him. The tables had turned, and the law was now hunting him, his inside contact informed him. Told him to lie low until they could get him out of the country. The news also backed up the fact that Everett was no longer in law enforcement's crosshairs.

"I want a meeting," he said when the line picked up. Then hung up without waiting for a reply.

They met just outside Marble Falls. Preset meeting place when he arrived in Texas. Past the outskirts. Past even the cell towers. An old oil transfer station sat rotting under a blood-red sky. Cracked concrete. Rusted iron. Surrounded by nothing but scrub, fence posts, and wind.

The mole, codename Ares-73, was already there, standing inside the skeletal frame of what used to be a central pipe relay. No weapon was visible. A blue silk shirt, an expensive watch flashing under an early spring setting sun. He looked like he'd stepped out for a powerful board meeting.

Joe approached with caution. Gun low, safety off.

"If you're wired..."

"I'm not," Ares-73 cut in. "Check me. Won't change the fact you're circling the drain."

He lit a cigarette. No tremor in his fingers. "You're sloppy, Joe. Delores is dragging you down with her, and you're too close to see it. You left prints. Literal, figurative, and digital. From California to Dallas."

Joe's jaw locked. "You're saying I did this? How about that arrogant idiot of a detective you guys have on the payroll?"

Ares-73 exhaled smoke into the sky above. "I'm saying some in the organization want your head. You've exposed them far more than they like. And, just so you know, they know that you and Dolores are the 1-45 murderers. What you do next will determine whether you live or die. You're the cleanup man. The heavy. The reason you might get to live... if you play this right."

Joe's grip tightened on his gun.

"That bitch Delores played you. Reid knows all about the theft of the 50 mill from the families," the mole said, his tone casually cruel. "You showed her where to find the money to siphon. She provided access to the accounts. And she planned to vanish without you. Long before the blood flows."

"Bullshit," Joe muttered. But his voice cracked.

The mole smiled without warmth. "You want to survive this? Bring the boss something valuable. Something that makes him reconsider burning you alive. Like the money and someone else. He has plans for Delores, so don't worry about that. He'll take care of her."

Joe said nothing. His eyes hardened.

"I know where Everett Taylor is," the mole said. "The cause of all your problems. And the boss. Tucked away in a sheriff's off-the-books safe house. No official logs. The sheriff owes me. Knows the exact location."

Joe stared at him.

"You give me the location. I'll take care of the problem."

The mole flicked his cigarette into the dirt. "Already sent."

He turned and walked away without another word.

His shoes crunched over gravel, fading into the distance.

He didn't need to look back. The fire had already been lit.

CHAPTER 35

Burn It All Down

Thursday, April 27th, 2023

Dallas County DA's Office
The city glowed cold and metallic beyond the window as Micah Colburn paced behind his desk, the evidence-room footage looping on repeat on his tablet. He'd seen it enough times to know what he was looking at.

Wren pocketed the page. Burning it just outside the evidence room. Walking away. Curtis, Fiona, Mason, Luis, and Shaw stood across from him, each silent as Colburn muttered under his breath. "Premeditated removal. Destruction of evidence. Obstruction. Falsifying investigative notes."

He paused the footage. "And this isn't corner-cutting. This is intent. My offices been looking at him for a while. However, someone powerful is protecting him. I want that person, and any other names of corrupt cops on their payroll, I can squeeze out of Wren."

Shaw folded his arms. "We have his altered reports, too. Inconsistent timestamps. False contact logs."

Luis added, "And the CI he used for fabricated statements. I can testify to the pattern."

Colburn stopped pacing.

"This is enough for an arrest warrant," he said.

He sat, pulled a folder toward him, and wrote with short, decisive strokes. I have reviewed this affidavit and believe there is sufficient probable cause to seek an arrest warrant for Detective Marcus Wren. Filed by Detective Mason McCarthy. District Attorney Micha Colburn, evidence enclosed. He stood and handed it to Mason. "Take this to Judge Samuel R. Whitaker. I'll call and let him know you are heading his way."

Probable Cause Affidavit
Subject: Detective Marcus Wren
Charges: Tampering with Physical Evidence; Obstruction of Justice; Falsification of Government Records; Abuse of Official Capacity.

Detective Mason McCarthy signed at the bottom. Colburn slid the affidavit back across the desk.

"By sunrise, he'll be in cuffs," he said. "And by noon, he'll be in front of the judge."

Westlake Hills, Texas | Safe House

The air was wrong.
Everett felt it before the alarm even blipped.
No wind. No passing cars on the ridge road.

He slid the reinforced window shade open two fingers' width. Oak branches swayed; down the hill below them, he thought he saw movement. Could there be watchers?

Everett stepped back into the hallway and spoke to the nearest deputy.

"I believe we've got eyes on us. Rear quadrant."

Ten years in Special Tactics. He knew when something smelled wrong. And this place? It reeked of compromise.

A deputy walked into the room behind him. A sudden burning sting, as if stung by a wasp, laced across his back. The room spun, and he staggered sideways. Too late, he saw the flicker of wrongness in the man's eyes. He registered the deputy betrayed him, and possibly the others. He slid against the wall as he lost control of his body.

◆◆◆

Safe House

Sheriff Nells arrived alone, just as planned. Earlier, Joe met him off-site behind a feed store in Tyler, slipping Sheriff Nells Everett's knife and gun. Trophies taken during the raid on Everett's ranch, now repurposed as evidence to frame Everett for the slaughter inside. Cleaner for everyone if Nells managed the deputies himself. It would be easier for him to surprise them. The plan was to use those on the deputies, and Joe would then take the gun with him. He had plans for it.

The deputies trusted Nells completely, a good ol'boy camaraderie type; that is how his deputies and the public saw him. A false front, well maintained, that served him well to get what he wanted in life. Minutes after the deputy drugged Everett, Nells walked into the safe house, greeted his own men with a tired smile, and lied about a last-minute security update from the DA's office.

When the first deputy turned to check the rear alarm panel, Nells stepped in close and placed the gun in his stomach under the vest and shot him. The second barely had time to register the sound of a shot followed by a body hitting the floor before Nells shot him twice in the ribs, catching him as he fell so the weapon never left its holster.

The third deputy, the one who drugged Everett, gave a lopsided grin. "Was hoping I wouldn't have to do it," the deputy muttered. "Hell, I've been to their family BBQs. Our wives know each other. Our kids play together."

The sheriff stepped close to the deputy as the two of them entered the room Everett was in, and Nells slit the deputy's throat with a practiced, silent draw of the blade from behind, the deputy had a look of confusion for half a second and a gurgling sound came from him.

Blood sprayed across Everett and the room as the deputy grabbed his neck as if he could stop the fountain of blood as it flowed down his shirt while he slowly sank to his knees. Then he fell face-forward to the floor. Two honest men dead in under twenty seconds, and a corrupt cop minutes later. After tonight, no one would know that. His death just absolved him. No struggle. No alarms tripped.

Nells went to the cabinet with the video, wiping the day's recording. Clean, quiet, and ready for Joe Bell to walk straight in.

Everett stirred. Something was wrong. Yet the sedation held him in its grip.

The air was still. A scent filled the air, a scent he recognized. Sweet and coppery. His limbs felt heavy and numb; his tongue was like wet cotton. He tried to rise, but his body would not obey him, and he felt cold metal on one wrist.

As Joe entered, he saw the first deputy lying slumped against the kitchen wall, blood seeping through the bullet wounds hidden beneath his vest, a dark pool forming beneath him. The other facedown near the hallway out of the kitchen, blood soaking into the woodgrain. He entered the room where the Sheriff had Everett; he saw the third deputy, blood splashed across the bedframe, across the floor and as high as the ceiling.

Sheriff Nells leaned down beside Everett, smiling like a man who'd already spent the payoff, and uncuffed him from the bedframe.

"Should've stayed put, cowboy," he said. "You made it too damn complicated. *Should've taken the out. Done the time, gotten out one day on parole. But men like you never do."*

Everett tried once more to rise, but his body still refused to obey his commands. He blinked slowly. Vision doubled. A cold burn spread through his veins. Muffled thuds rang in his ears like distant drums. His heartbeat was nothing but a whisper.

A voice stirred something in Everett's mind.

"Well, well. Look at that," Joe Bell said, stepping through the doorway. "Sleeping Beauty's ready for his closeup."

He hauled Everett up. "Not so tough now, are you?" He leaned close to his face. "You have a lot of pain ahead of you." Then they grabbed one arm each, and they staggered out to the SUV parked outside. Everett's head lolled sideways, eyes fluttering, glimpsing splatters of red on the sheriff's cuff and hand.

Once Everett was in the back of the SUV, Joe threw down a black gym bag at the sheriff's feet.

"You got what you wanted."

The sheriff nodded, bent over, and zipped the bag open. Only clothes filled the bag. "Hey, what's going on?" He realized he had been double-crossed and reached for his gun. Too late. Joe raised Everett's gun, which he'd taken back from the sheriff, and fired once into the sheriff's head, dead center.

The clothes scattered across the grass like blown leaves.

No witnesses. No loose ends.

Joe hoisted Everett into the back of his truck. Slammed the tailgate shut and drove toward the shadowed skeleton of an abandoned meat-packing warehouse south of the safe house, at the edge of Tyler City.

◆ ◆ ◆

O'Brien & Galloway Compound

"Repeat that." Fiona's boots echoed in the tactical room in the compound as she stalked toward the wall screen, still half-drenched from the ranch's afternoon storm getting to the compound, rain still dripping from her hair, cold against her neck.

Curtis in the office in Dallas didn't flinch on the video screen. "They attacked the safe house. The place is in ruins; one deputy had his throat cut. Investigators found a bloody knife left at the scene. Another deputy was in the hallway by the door. The third at the table by the window. They still had their guns holstered." Fiona understood what that meant. Someone they trusted betrayed them. The same betrayal that had cost Selena and possibly Everett their lives.

Mason connected via video call and said, "Whoever hit the safe house gunned down Sheriff Nells out front; he never made it into the house. Shot up close. His gym bag and clothes lay across the yard, which indicated that someone had surprised him. Real pro work, not amateur. Whoever it was knew exactly how and where to hit them. All three interior cameras were offline during the attack. No feed. No timestamps. We only have exterior angles."

She stopped cold. "We didn't know where they took him," she said. A beat passed as she realized what that meant. "The mole's not in our house. Mason, how did they find out where Everett was?"

Curtis said before Mason could answer. "It means your side is hemorrhaging intel from inside the DA's office or the sheriff's."

Bianca snapped her head up from the server bay. "DA's office is clean. Not the sheriff's."

"What?" Fiona turned.

"They hit their backups. The sheriff's office was evaluating a prototype of Transitions AI law enforcement software. They installed it on their servers about a year before it became public. It's infected every piece of equipment they have, communications-GPS wise." Bianca stepped back as if something had attacked her, her brow furrowed.

"Gods, even the deputies' personal cell phones. Tactical logs, timestamps, route patterns, reports filed digitally, radio frequencies, undercover officers, and the 911 call center. They got it all. Real quiet. Military precision. They know they're exposed now. But they got everything they wanted. At that second, Bianca watched the screen as the sheriff's computers went down as the system crashed in the office, in the cars and their 911. Every single computer in the Smith County Sheriff's Department went black."

Everyone stood in shock, but only for a few seconds. The hush felt like the silence after a gunshot: heavy, final, waiting for the next one.

Curtis looked at Fiona over the video. "This isn't surveillance anymore. This is the destruction of everything and everyone. They're burning it all down. Mason, you need to get that information out to the sheriff's department. *Now*! Or they'll wind up with a lot of exposed deputies," Curtis was already reaching for his Glock in the desk drawer.

"Get units out to cover the deputies from the sheriff's office next county over, or they're going to have a bloodbath on their hands. There's a reason they took out the patrol car radios and the 911 call center. Fiona, I'm hanging up and heading out to help Mason." Curtis' side of the conference call blanked out, and for a few minutes, a hush reigned.

Mason's face went pale. He wasted no time and hung up.

Fiona turned to Bianca and asked, "Do we still got trackers on all of Bell and Delores' vehicles? I would bet it's Bell who grabbed Everett." She moved over to the console. "Pull up the GPS tracker feeds."

Bianca tapped rapidly. "You're right. His car pinged at a rundown hotel on the outskirts of Tyler early morning. Then outside, then the tracker lost him in a dead zone for about half an hour. Then, picked him up at Dolores' home. It shows that it is still there. But Dolores' SUV left from there and went to where Detective Mason's car is right now, left there less than twenty minutes ago. That must be the safe house." Fiona was thankful that she was no longer hampered by all the red tape of a police department.

"Joe Bell is going to murder Everett, Matilda, call Curtis and keep him updated about the SUV's destination, and what we believe. Tell him I'm following the signal."

Fiona was already grabbing her jacket and racing out the door. Ten minutes later, she was close to where the signal stopped, at an abandoned warehouse.

Unknown Location Inside a convex

The mole watched the terminal flicker.

No signals coming out of O'Brien & Galloway. No traces from the Sentinel. There are no more breadcrumbs to follow. He had what he needed for now, so he was unconcerned.

And what came next that night would be chaos. And blood.

He leaned back in his leather chair and smiled.

"We just pushed them into the dark," he whispered to no one. "Good. Let's see who survives."

He closed the laptop and opened a handwritten file folder. Inside: a Polaroid of Everett's face.
Next to it, a map of Texas, scratched with hand-drawn lines. A red X circled his ranch.

He circled another.

Then, lit a match, held it under the photo and map...

And let it burn.

CHAPTER 36

Blood and Chaos

Thursday, April 27th, 2023

Abandoned Warehouse NE of Tyler City

Gravel crunched under her tires as Fiona neared the warehouse. The GPS still showed Delores' SUV at the site.

She parked. Took her gun out of its holster. It felt reassuring in her palm.

She moved forward into the darkness. Moving up next to the warehouse metal walls somewhere inside, she heard chains rattle. A jagged cut in the metal wall gave her a glimpse inside. Homeless people probably used it to get inside, to squat out of the weather.

The air was foul, thick with mildew, old piss, motor oil, and blood. Every breath Fiona took clawed at her throat. She moved slowly, crouched low, her Sig in both hands as she picked through the shadows between collapsed steel shelving and cracked concrete. Water dripped from a leaking pipe above, echoing like a heartbeat. The darkness hummed with tension.

Everett hung from a chain looped over a ceiling beam, his wrists rubbed raw and swollen. Blood streaked his ribs and soaked into the waistband of his jeans. His feet barely touched the ground. He was swaying; the sedative was finally wearing off.

Joe Bell paced in front of him. Slow. Casual. Smug.

"So, you finally joined me. I had him give you a small dose so you would not be out for long."

Everett shook his head. His vision began to clear.

A mounted camera blinked red, recording. A shotgun mic swung slightly beneath it, catching everything.

Fiona's blood ran cold. Her pulse pounded. One breath. Then another. She had to wait for the right moment. One mistake and Everett would die.

Everett stirred. His voice was hoarse; a rasp carved from broken glass. "You didn't have to hurt her," he said. "You could've just fucking killed me."

Joe leaned in as if he were telling a bedtime story.

"Well, first off, she was the target, buddy boy, not you. She dug too deep and would have exposed too many powerful people. People who prefer to stay in the shadows. How she died." He hissed. "I wanted to hear her scream. I wanted her to know what would happen to that sweet daughter of yours." He chuckled. "That little angel, she begged so prettily. Thought if she cried hard enough it would save her mommy. Forced her to watch the whole thing. Of course she was worth too much to mess with. If you know what I mean."

Everett lunged. His legs kicked out, catching Joe in the gut.

Joe grunted and stumbled back. Once he caught his balance, he hissed. "I should've broken your goddamn legs first," he snarled. "Don't worry, buddy boy, that is coming, and I'll see how much that vaunted training holds out."

He pulled a thumb drive from his pocket and waved it like a party trick. "This says you lost it. PTSD. Flashbacks. Hallucinations. It won't matter if the DA drops all charges against you. He will have to reopen the case and declare you did the murder;

case closed, all the pieces nicely in place. There will be pressure far above his pay grade for him to do so. You're the one who murdered your wife. Then you wandered around like a lost dog until your own guilt broke you."

Everett's voice shook. "How does that explain the beatings? The torture of me now?"

Joe smirked. "Oh, you will be at the bottom of a ravine when they find your body. Especially with the evidence I left at the safe house. Your fingerprints are on the knife that slit the deputy's throat. Your service weapon used to shoot the rest. Remember our excursion to your ranch. Well, after you ran like a coward. I let myself into your house. Collected a few things. Just for this." Joe stopped and walked over to the camera to make sure it was getting it all.

"I need this video for proof. The boss's demand, that kind of thing. They don't really trust their employees' word, and no one likes to make them unhappy." He gave a weird laugh and walked back over to Everett. "Though if they ever find out all I did, I might die worse than you're going to." He checked the chains holding Everett.

"What are you waiting for?"

"You have heard the saying, 'There is a time for everything.' Well, that is coming soon."

"All would have been so simple if you had just died at your ranch. But this is better. Law enforcement won't bother looking elsewhere after they see this confession. How you murdered those three deputies and the sheriff," Joe held up Everett's gun, a Sig Sauer P229 Legion with Everett's initials on the grip in bronze, to show him, "and they find this on your body. Then there's the one whose throat you slit with your knife, trying to stop you, your fingerprints all over it. Caught the sheriff off guard out front and shot him. He was checking in on the way home from the gym." He rolled his eyes. "Poor soldier. The war ruined you. Besides, they are going to be so busy in the county soon, you'll be yesterday's news. Forgotten." He glanced at his watch for the sixth time now. Everett wondered what he was expecting, and he was more than happy to let him keep talking and wait for whatever it was Joe seemed to be waiting for.

It dawned on Everett. Joe was waiting for Delores. He'd read enough of the reports from Fiona and Curtis investigators to know that Joe and Delores were a thing. And that they may have stolen something from the cartel family.

"Delores used you. Is that who you are waiting for? She's never going to show."

Fiona's pulse thundered in her ears. Her muscles screamed for action.

Joe stepped forward. Drew the knife. "You don't get to die easy; you have caused me a lot of problems," he said, voice rife with malice. "You get to die my way. Painful. Broken. Framed. Right now I'll just take a little taste."

That was the moment Fiona moved. While his focus was totally on Everett.

She surged from cover.

Joe turned and fired at the sound of movement. A thunderous sound filled the warehouse.

Pain lanced through her side, white-hot, nauseating. The force spun her sideways, but she stayed upright and lunged. Grabbed the locking mechanism of the chain holding Everett up.

The whoosh and clinking of chains as they slid downward and the metallic clanking as they hit the floor echoed through the cavernous warehouse.

Everett dropped like a sack of meat, groaning as he hit the floor on his knees. The sedative pumped into him earlier, already wearing off. Joe wanted Everett alert when he tortured him. His muscles trembled with the sensation of thousands of tiny needles stabbing him as blood flowed back into his arms.

"Fi..." he managed.

Another gunshot tore through the air. Sparks screamed off the metal beside her. She twisted, fired blindly. Hit the gun Joe held, which flew out of his hand.

Her knees buckled. She collapsed, gasping. Blood blooming through her shirt just below and to the side of her ribs.

Joe advanced.

"Run..." Fiona rasped.

"Fi!" Everett tried to get to his feet, but his legs buckled. He shook his head to clear the fog.

Joe Bell's laugh echoed off the dripping rafters.

"Ain't no one running tonight."

Joe kicked the empty chain away and pulled out a knife. A long, ugly gutting blade, the kind used to split deer open. Under the flickering overhead bulb, the steel looked like a living thing.

Everett straightened, vision clearing. Rage overtook him as his pulse roared in his ears.

Joe grinned. "Let's see what you've got, hero. Just you... and me."

Everett didn't waste time answering, took several breaths and scanned the area, his training taking over, etched into him. Rusted hooks hung low overhead; a broken pallet, a pipe, a dropped bolt cutter, a loose ceiling chain swaying slightly from the earlier movement.

Joe lunged.

Everett pivoted too slow. Still foggy in his reflexes, Joe's blade slashed a shallow cut across his forearm. Heat flared. Blood surfaced. Everett gritted his teeth and drove his elbow into Joe's throat.

Joe staggered back with a barking cough, more surprised than hurt.

"Well now," Joe said, wiping spit and blood from his mouth. "That's more like it."

He came in again, faster, aiming low and punishing. Everett grabbed the nearest object, a rusted steel meat hook on the wall. It wasn't sharp anymore, but it was heavy.

Joe swung the knife.

Everett blocked with the hook; metal screamed against metal. The knife skidded, slicing Everett's palm open, but Everett used the moment to slam the hook into Joe's jaw.

Bone cracked. Joe reeled, spat, and a tooth flew outward.

"You son of a ..."

Everett lunged forward and just missed hitting him in the temple. Everett lost his grip, his hands slick with his blood. The hook crashed to the floor next to Joe as he hit the concrete, rolled, and scrambled up with the predatory ease of a street fighter.

"Getting slow, weak, aren't you." Joe snarled at him, spitting blood. Joe rushed him again.

Everett turned sideways, and in one smooth move grabbed a broken two-by-four from the ruined pallet next to him and smashed it across Joe's wrist. Bone snapped like dry kindling. Joe screamed, dropped the knife, and punched Everett with his left hand hard enough to knock him off balance. Then swept Everett's feet out from under him.

Everett hit the floor, breath knocked out.

Joe, panting and wild-eyed, dove for the fallen knife using his left hand, his broken right wrist dangling uselessly at his side.

Everett kicked the blade away, sending it clattering into the darkness, then twisted and swiped Joe's legs out from under him. Joe crashed to the floor, then rolled away for distance from Everett.

Both men rose with staggering steps. Breath ragged, blood dripping, neither willing to blink first.

Joe lunged empty-handed, a bull rush.

Everett stepped in, letting instincts take over. Grapple. He caught Joe by the collar, twisted, and slammed him face-first into a steel rail. Joe roared, thrashed, and Everett used the chain overhead to bind Joe's arm for just one agonizing second. Then sent a knee into Joe's gut.

Joe gasped, folding. Dropping to one knee.

Everett hit him again.

And again.

Until Joe collapsed onto the concrete in a wet, trembling heap.

Everett stood over him, chest heaving, blood running down his arms. Then went over to the knife and picked it up. Before he staggered back towards where Joe lay on the floor.

Joe coughed thickly, spitting red onto the floor. "This... this isn't over..."

Everett's fingers wrapped around the hilt. "It is."

"Everett." A horse whisper of a voice close.

He froze.

Fiona, pale and bleeding, leaned against a steel beam, holding pressure on her wound with trembling fingers. She met Everett's eyes, grounding him.

"We need him alive. Think of Lila."

Everett's breath hitched.

The blade trembled.

He saw Lila's face.

Everett's jaw tightened. His grip tightened for a second, then loosened... just enough.

Joe Bell sagged, unconscious.

Everett dropped the knife. It hit the concrete with a final metallic ring.

The echo carried a reckoning waiting behind it.

Everett moved to Fiona's side. She swayed. Her legs buckled. Everett caught her before she hit the ground. Her blood smeared across his chest, hot and wet.

Fiona slipped out of consciousness in his arms.

CHAPTER 37

Collapse of County

Thursday, April 27th, 2023

Smith County

The first hint of disaster wasn't the thunder of a gunshot.

It was silence.

Mason stood in the doorway, soaked from the storm, staring at the three dead radio consoles. The dispatch screens froze mid-refresh. The CAD terminals flickered with red error strings. Even the ancient backup system, the one the county kept around because it never failed, was dark as well. The acting shift lieutenant, Lt. Sam Monroe, the highest-ranking deputy on-site, slammed a fist against one of the lifeless consoles. "Every damn channel is down. Patrol, TAC, EMS, fire mutual. Everything."

"Try calling the undersheriff," Mason said as he stepped into the room. Quick to grasp what happened after what Fiona's team had told him earlier. "He should have arrived already. Did anyone notify him of the murder of the sheriff?"

A civilian admin tapped her phone with trembling hands. "Still nothing. Every extension is dead. His cell goes straight to voicemail."

"Then proceed as if he is permanently out of commission. Who is in command then?"

"Lt. Sam Monroe." The civilian admin said, pointing at him.

Curtis stepped inside only minutes after Mason arrived, soaked from the storm, jaw clenched tight. The room smelled of burnt circuitry. One look around told that more than the safe house getting hit was in play. "I drove straight here after we talked about the attack and Everett missing on the conference call." Curtis said. "What's going on?"

A dispatcher shook her head as she unplugged and re-plugged hardware. "We can't reach any field units. Every deputy out there in the county is deaf and blind."

"The county sheriff's department is under attack." Mason said, not taking his eyes off the dead monitors. "Curtis' cyber team traced the loss of all communication lines to a prototype Transitions AI software that the county commissioner asked them to evaluate. It took the whole damn system offline. Someone sent the program a full-system override shutdown order."

"Think this has anything to do with the murdered sheriff and the safe house attack?"

"Not sure. Anything is possible at this point." Mason said.

A deputy coming on duty pushed through the door. "What's going on? My patrol radio can't reach anyone in the field. Status checks aren't coming back. Cell radio, MDT... all down, then he looked around at the frozen looks and equipment. Holy shit, how'd this happen?"

Curtis swore quietly. "Every unit out there is blind. They don't even know they're in danger."

Lt. Monroe turned toward the deputy. "Get the county emergency manager. Break down his door if he won't answer it. Get him here fast."

The deputy raced back out to his patrol cruiser, spun out onto the road, lights flashing, and sped off into the distance.

Twenty minutes later, the deputy returned. Mason turned to the emergency manager. Dragged from his bed and still half-asleep, he stared helplessly at a stack of emergency protocol binders. He looked pale, sweat collecting at his temples as he glanced at the blacked-out dispatch screens. Then back to the protocol binders.

"Call for mutual aid," Mason said.

"I... I don't have a current disaster code for this," he stammered. "Only the sheriff and undersheriff can make that request."

Mason snapped. "People could die while you assess the situation. Were you not listening? The sheriff is dead, and the undersheriff is most likely also dead. Call neighboring counties. Now."

"But..."

Monroe cut him off, voice sharp and commanding. "I am the ranking officer. I'm declaring a countywide communication collapse and officer emergency. You have your authority. Make the damn call."

The emergency manager swallowed hard, fumbled for the landline, and finally dialed.

Another screen blinked out. The room dimmed, lit only by the soft glow of emergency floor strips, until the backup generators came on.

The emergency manager's throat bobbed. Then he grabbed the landline, one of the few systems not tied into the Transitions AI system, and dialed.

"This is Smith County Emergency Management," he said. "Declaring we have a communications blackout. Requesting immediate mutual aid from all surrounding agencies. I repeat..."

As he repeated the callout, Mason dragged a portable map across the room and slapped it onto a table. Curtis shoved aside coffee cups, folders, and a half-eaten sandwich to clear space.

"Alright," Curtis said. "Give me everyone's last known position," Mason said. "What do we know so far?"

Mason uncapped a marker, and the 911 dispatcher said. "Three patrol units were working the north sector. Two on farmland checks, one on traffic enforcement. All went silent within ten minutes of each other. The rest were not supposed to check in until an hour later."

She tapped another location on the map. "Undercover narcotics team missed their check-in. No contact since." Another mark. "Six deputies on dinner break haven't responded either."

Curtis stared at the map. "They're hitting isolated pockets. Testing coordination. Seeing how long it takes backup to figure it out."

Mason shook his head. "It's not response time they're assessing. They're evaluating how fast they can kill a county."

The landline rang. The emergency manager grabbed it. His face drained.

"A deputy reached his wife on a civilian line," he said. "Ambush on County Road 12. Two officers down. Unknown shooters."

The emergency manager's jaw quivered. "Where's the nearest responding unit?"

"There are no units," Mason said bluntly. "You don't seem to get it; no one can hear the damn call, a call dispatch can't even send out. Deputies' cell phones are out as well."

Curtis looked at him and nodded.

Mason grabbed his jacket. "I do. Curtis with me. Lt. Monroe, stay here and coordinate the incoming agencies. They'll need someone who knows the ground." With a look of disgust at the emergency manager. "And keeps cool under pressure."

"What do I tell the incoming help about what's happening?"

Curtis looked at the spreading red circles marking officer-down locations across the map as civilians called on landlines to report what they saw on the non - emergency line. "Call it what it is," he said.
"It's a war zone."

Mason shoved through the doors into the storm.

Outside, the night flickered with distant flashes. Lightning lit up the sky.

Side Road 10 miles from the Smith County Office

Rain hit the windshield in thick, slanted sheets as Mason floored the accelerator. Curtis braced a hand on the dash, scanning the tree line with the instincts of a man who's seen too many ambush situations in his lifetime. His other hand already resting on the Glock's grip, thumb flicking the safety off in one smooth motion.

The unmarked cruiser's tires hissed across the wet asphalt three miles down the road from the station. Up ahead, nothing but darkness and a bend in the road.

Then Curtis stiffened, eyes narrowing to slits. "There," he said. "Lights off. Patrol unit."

Mason cut his siren. The sudden silence louder than the wail had been.

He eased the car onto the shoulder, killed the engine, and grabbed the shotgun from the rack; racking the slide with a sharp metallic snap.

Curtis checked his Glock, re-holstered it, grabbed the cruiser's rifle, jaw clenched, thumb already sweeping the safety, barrel angled low and ready.

"Stay low," Mason said. "We don't know if they're still here."

Curtis moved back toward the silent patrol car, rain pelting the roof like small stones. Each drop, blurring vision, turning the ground into slick black mud.

The cruiser rested halfway in a ditch. Driver's door standing open, with no movement in the area, no sounds either. Mason reached the door first. His voice dropped. "Damn."

Deputy Sanchez lay halfway out of the driver's seat, body twisted unnaturally, uniform soaked in both rainwater and blood. He still had his service pistol holstered. A half filled in report splattered with blood in the passenger car well. Execution. Close range. Professional. Curtis crouched beside him, eyes narrowed. "This was a hit," his rifle muzzle already sweeping the tree line, finger indexed along the trigger guard, breathing slow and controlled.

"Yeah," Mason said, looking around. "Does your cell phone have any bars? Mine doesn't."

A muffled groan cut through the rain. Both men turned toward the sound, weapons snapping up in unison, barrels tracking the noise.

Behind the cruiser, near the brush line, a hand twitched. Mason and Curtis moved fast, weapons raised, boots sliding in mud, rain sheeting off their jackets, barrels steady.

Deputy Carter lay sprawled face-down, vest shredded by rifle fire. His breathing was wet and uneven. A bullet had ripped across his lower back, and another grazed his ribs. Mason dropped to one knee. "Carter. Talk to me."

Carter coughed, blood mixing with the rain. "They... they were in the trees... masked... rifles... we never saw them... till too late." Curtis kept watch on the trees, scanning for movement.

"How many?" Mason asked.

Carter swallowed. "Six... maybe more. They were... laughing..." Curtis's jaw locked.

Mason leaned closer. "Did they say anything?"

"Test run," Carter whispered. "Said it was a 'test run. Said we were... numbers on a board." Mason looked at Curtis. The meaning was clear. This isn't a onetime thing. It was a demonstration.

Rain hammered harder. Carter's eyes fluttered.

"We need to move him," Curtis said, already slinging the rifle to free both hands, muscles coiling.

Headlights bloomed behind them. Closing the distance. Fast twin beams slicing through the rain, engine roar rising over the downpour.

Mason snapped his shotgun up. "Incoming!" A sheriff's unit skidded to a stop, and Lt. Monroe jumped out before the tires finished spinning. Two deputies followed, rifles raised. "Status?" Monroe shouted.

Mason motioned him over. "One dead. One critical. Ambushed. At least six shooters, possibly more. Tactical gear."

Monroe's face hardened. "We've got civilians calling in panic across the county, reporting gunshots, some from a diner off the highway. A place where most of the deputies in that sector eat their lunch and dinner. Another one from a farmer out by where I have undercover's on surveillance duty. From what we're hearing from civilians, we've got crashed and burning cruisers and bodies everywhere. Some ranchers and farmers are trying to save the ones close to where they live. Before this is over, I'm praying we also don't end up with a lot of dead civilians."

Curtis stood, rain running down his face. "They're moving through sectors. Systematic. They know the blackout works."

"Then we'll cut them off," Monroe said. "No more blind units."

Mason pointed to the north road. "They'll push into the rural crossings next. It's where they can kill without witnesses."

Monroe nodded once. "We split. Second likely ambush site eight minutes away. Mason Curtis, with me."

Paramedics reached Carter, working under floodlights as rain turned the ditch into mud.

Carter choked out before they lifted him:

"Warn... everyone..."

They didn't get to finish hearing him. They heard a burst of automatic gunfire crack through the night from somewhere farther down the road, sharp, staccato pops echoing through the night air. The paramedics rushed Carter into the ambulance. The EMTs looked at each other and knew the anarchy was just getting started.

Monroe didn't flinch. "That's our next stop. Move."

They ran to their vehicles, boots splashing through mud, rain stinging eyes, adrenaline flooding their veins like fire. Gunfire still cracking in the distance, rolling like thunder that wouldn't quit.

The county had become a battlefield, and this was only the beginning.

The Cooper Lantern

Rain-streaked windows of the Diner showed a flickering neon "OPEN" sign, a spot frequented by every deputy in the county after midnight. Three patrol units sat parked in the gravel lot, steam rising off engines cooling from the chilly rain.

Inside, waitress Tammy White poured refills for the two deputies at the corner booth while Deputy Mark Webster stood at the counter with two other deputies waiting to pay for their meals.

It should've been quiet. Pouring rain keeps most of the criminals at home. Routine. A normal, quiet midweek night.

Then, every cellphone on every deputy's belt buzzed an alert... *"SIGNAL LOST. NETWORK ERROR."* screens flashing red, then black, sudden, synchronized.

Mark frowned at his cell phone's screen. "What the hell..." reaching for the holster snap on instinct.

That's when the first shot blew the front window apart. Glass exploding inward in a sparkling shower, fragments cutting the air like shrapnel.

Tammy screamed and dropped down behind the counter. The coffeepot crashed onto the floor, glass shattering, coffee hissing and splashing across the tiles. Steam rose fast as scalding coffee splashed on her, and she screamed in pain, scuttling away as shards bit into her palms as she crawled away.

Mark dove, the register exploding behind him, coins and bills erupting in a paper and metallic cloud.

The two deputies in the booth dived to the ends of the booth's seats for cover, and two at the cash register who were about to pay for their meals turned as the second volley tore through the diner. Their bodies jerking, falling in thuds, dead before they hit the floor, blood already pooling under them.

Automatic fire. High caliber. Controlled bursts. Not amateurs.

Deputy Lane crawled to the broken edge of the booth.

Mark risked a peek through the shattered window. Three silhouettes stood in the rain by the treeline, rifles raised, wearing half-skeleton masks, moving in coordinated rhythm.

He ducked back as another burst shredded the booth. Wood splinters stinging his face, fabric tearing above his head. High in a tree. A sniper's crimson beam moved hypnotically across the counter, hunting.

Lane palmed his .45 Glock through the gap in the window, fired blindly, sharp cracks, recoil bucking his wrist, brass ping-ing off tile.

The shooters shifted positions immediately, a trained flanking pattern.

Tammy sobbed, clutching her burnt leg, crawling towards the kitchen, palms slapping wet tile, breath hitching in sharp gasps.

Deputy Jordan took hold of her wrist and hauled her with him. "Stay low! MOVE!"

They crawled along the greasy tile as bullets chewed the walls above their heads. Pots clanged from the impacts. Fluorescent lights shattered overhead, raining glass, sparks flaring, bulbs popping like gunfire.

Deputy Lane leaned out again... a round punched through his throat. wet choking sound, body jerking backward, blood spraying in a bright arc, splashing across the booth as he collapsed against it. His Glock clattered across the tile.

"LANE!" Mark yelled, voice raw, already moving, rifle swinging up.

No response.

Mark fired twice, aiming at the muzzle flash, sharp cracks, recoil slamming his shoulder, brass ejecting hot against his cheek. But the shooters were already repositioning, rifles sweeping in overlapping arcs. Tightening the choke point around the diner.

Jordan reached the back door, shoved Tammy through it, and yelled, "RUN! Get under the truck in the alley!"

Tammy sprinted into the rain. The splash of her footsteps softened in the sheet of rain, mud sucking at her shoes, heart hammering in her throat.

Jordan spun to cover the exit. A figure appeared in the doorway. Close. Too close. Jordan fired three shots center mass.

The masked man stagger but stayed on his feet, Kevlar vest

with plates. He slammed Jordan against the wall and emptied a suppressed pistol into his stomach before Jordan's body slid down the tiles.

Mark heard it. Heard Jordan's body hit the floor. Jordan's Glock clattering uselessly to the floor.

He knew he was alone. He grabbed Lane's radio. Dead. No signal. Mark exhaled once, slowly. Then, he sprinted through the kitchen, shoved open the back door, and fired at the shadows creeping toward the alley, hitting one in the thigh. The man dropped his rifle with a scream.

Another raised his rifle. Mark didn't get a second shot. A round ripped into his vest, slamming him into the mud, impact like a sledgehammer, air punched out of his lungs, pain exploding across his body.

Another tore through his arm, a hot burning sensation, blood sheeting down his sleeve. Mark gasped, blinking rain out of his eyes as the masked shooter walked toward him. boots splashing closer, rifle barrel steady, red dot dancing on Mark's chest.

The shooter leaned in for the finishing shot, but a sudden wail of distant sirens rolled across the rain-soaked parking lot, a rising field of red-blue lights strobing through the trees. The masked man hesitated, head snapping toward the highway, rifle swinging, barrel tracking the new threat. A second siren joined the first, closer, urgent.

He hissed something in Spanish, then bolted into the treeline with the others.

Mark lay half-submerged in the mud, barely conscious, blood soaking into his uniform.

His breaths were shallow, ragged, but steady, rain pooling around him, mixing red; his chest rising and falling in shallow, ragged breaths.

He wasn't gone.

Not yet.

Tammy lay trembling beneath a pickup truck, gasping sobs into the gravel as Mason and Curtis raced up the alley, weapons raised. Boots splashing through puddles, rifles sweeping, headlights from the cruisers cutting through the rain.

Five deputies lay dead. One critical in the alley out back. And a civilian curled under a truck, wounded and terrified, her sobs barely audible over the rain and distant sirens.

One assailant wounded, unable to flee. The deputies killed three in the brief gun battle, yet paid a terrible price.
Four more vanished into the trees like ghosts.

And miles away, the ambushes on the roads played out across the county. As time moved into another day in the night's dark.

CHAPTER 38

Zero Signal

Thursday, April 27th, 2023

Surveillance Unit 6 | South Farm Road 211

The undercover team had been running a quiet surveillance operation for months. Two deputies embedded in a rotating narcotics detail, posing as farm-supply distributors. Their unmarked cruiser sat parked across from an abandoned irrigation shed, headlights off, windows cracked for airflow.

Inside, Deputy Aranda wrote notes under the dim light of a red headlamp, pen scratching paper, red glow painting his face in blood-like hues.

Deputy Perez watched the road through binoculars, the lenses fogging slightly, breath steady.

Deputy Hartley leaned against his unmarked cruiser, stopping to visit the two while monitoring a handheld console tied into the county's encrypted channel in case he got a call, rain sheeting off his jacket.

Routine.
Predictable.
Safe enough.

Then Hartley's console flickered.

SIGNAL LOST. NETWORK MODULE FAILURE. Console beeping once, sharp and final.

"Again?" he muttered. "That's the third time tonight."

Perez lowered the binoculars. "You rebooted it?"

"I shouldn't have to reboot it every hour. Something's wrong with the entire..."

The rest of his sentence vanished as the windshield blew inward, glass exploding in a glittering spray, shards slicing the air like shrapnel.

Deputy Aranda died instantly where he sat, body jerking once, head snapping back, blood misting the headliner

Perez dropped sideways in his seat, bleeding from his forehead, a hot stinging across his scalp, blood sheeting into his eyes. Rolled out of his door low and raced for the driver's side as bullets hit the ground around his feet. Wet splashes kicking up in angry blows, rounds also snapping past his ears. He scrambled behind the front wheel as bullets stitched the surrounding metal, sharp metallic pings, sparks flashing in the rain.

Hartley called out, "You hit?" Glock already in hand, barrel sweeping the darkness.

"Yes, grazed." Perez yelled. "Fuck Call in! CALL IN! My radio's not working." Blood streaming down the side of his face.

Hartly he keyed his radio, dead click, not even static.

Dead. Zero bars. Total blackout. "Jesus Christ," he whispered, "my radio is also out." At the same moment, they both realized backup was not coming.

Hartley peeked around the front for a better view. "Six shooters. Tactical spacing. AR platforms." Muzzle flares strobing through the rain. A round punched through the door inches from his face.

Perez cursed. "They know we're here. How?"

Hartley's jaw clenched. "It's an ambush."

They had trained for this. Not on this scale, but for this moment. They lay flat on the ground and crawled to the side ditch full of water. Bullets tore the ground around them as the shooters advanced fast. Methodical. Rounds snapping overhead, dirt spraying in wet clumps.

Hartley fired twice, careful with controlled bursts. One shooter stumbled, dropping with a grunt. He was not sure where, too dark.

"Move!" Hartley yelled, voice raw, semi-auto swinging one-handed, barrel tracking shadows. Pointing at a structure in the field. They sprinted toward it; the moon peeked out from between the black clouds overhead. Lungs burning.

It barely lit the weeds at their feet.

Then Perez fell, Hartley grabbed him and helped him up to run. Holding him around the waist toward cover, Perez stumbled again. The blood loss was catching up. His legs buckled.

Hartley grabbed Perez under one arm. "Come on! Come on! We're just feet away."

A single shot cut through the night. sharp crack, muzzle flash from the treeline.

Hartley jerked. Dropped.
A round had drilled through the back of his skull. His body slammed into the mud.

Perez froze, staring, horror washing up his spine. Then rounds snapped into and tore up the ground near him, and instinct took over. He crawled for cover inside the shed. The roof leaked. Boards shifted under his weight, water dripping cold on his neck.

Perez coughed blood, his breath ragged and pain-laced.

Outside, footsteps neared. Careful.

Perez raised his Glock, breath shaking, and blinked slowly. He emptied his magazine through the wall when he heard steps right by the building wall, forcing the shooters to scatter, their footsteps retreating fast.

Then, he dived out the door and forced himself to rise and run. Blind. Out of bullets.

Cut across the field, heading for the treeline. Legs pumping, lungs screaming, mud sucking at his boots.

A rifle's sharp crack, muzzle flash lighting the rain. The round caught him square in the back.

He fell face-down in the dirt, rain pooling around him, mixing red, breath shallow and wet

mud filling his mouth as the world dimmed around him.

Footsteps approached, stopping inches from his head.

A masked man leaned down, hissed something in Spanish that Perez couldn't process, and fired once more. Perez's body jerked once.

Silence followed, wide and suffocating.

One deputy dead in a cruiser. Two deputies dead in the field. Both unmarked cruisers torched minutes later.

And the deadly convoy rolled toward its next target. Patrol units were still out on patrol, completely oblivious of what was heading their way.

Air Unit 3 | Above County Road 17

Dallas County diverted a helicopter, Air Unit 3, to assist the Smith County SWAT after it lost initial contact with Air Unit 1 on patrol. The pilot, Officer Daniel Reese, scanned the dark roads with FLIR as his copilot, Officer Halston, monitored the radio downlink. Rotor blades thumping steadily overhead, the cabin vibrating with each pulse.

"Still nothing," Halston muttered. "Dispatch is dead. SWAT is dark. What the hell is going on?"

Reese frowned. "We're flying blind." Cyclic stick slick with sweat, grip tight.

"Keep scanning." Halston stiffened. "Contact. Three vehicles, high speed, heading northbound." FLIR painting hot white streaks against black asphalt. Reese banked left, bringing the chopper into a slow orbit as the horizon tilted for a moment.

Halston zoomed the camera.

"... those are SUVs with men sitting on the edge of the open windows, loaded for bear." Reese cursed. "We need to warn SWAT. They're headed straight for 'em." Halston tried the radio. *Static.* Dead.

"Switch to statewide," Reese ordered. Then both got a sick feeling when they heard the repeating message.

"All law enforcement units within a twenty-mile radius of Smith County, you are to head there and coordinate with State Troopers to lend assistance. County deputies under attack by unknown assailants. Communications knocked out." The message repeated. Cold, mechanical voice looping. Reese's gut sank. The SUV suddenly pulled off the road and stopped.

Halston narrowed his eyes. "Why'd they pull off?"

He froze. A figure stepped out of the vehicle and reached for something in the cargo area and hoisted it onto his shoulder.

Reese's heart plummeted. "That's an RPG. HANG ON!"

He yanked the cyclic, wrenching the helicopter sideways. cyclic wrenching hard left, collective slamming down, rotor blades screaming as the chopper tilted violently.

The rocket streaked upward like a comet, white trail burning bright, exhaust plume glowing against the black sky.

The rocket hit the tail boom, metal shrieking, the tail rotor shredding, a violent yaw throwing the cabin sideways

The helicopter went into a spin. G-forces pinning them to their seats, world tilting, the horizon spinning, their stomachs lurching.

Reese fought the controls, teeth gritted, trying to control the spin. cyclic jerking in his fists, collective shaking, pedals slamming back and forth.

The blast threw Halston against the window, glass spider webbing as blood flowed profusely from his scalp. Warnings blared. Klaxons screaming, red lights strobing, altitude alarm piercing. Fire erupted along the tail.

The Brenton community spun beneath them in a blur.

Reese roared, "MAYDAY, MAYDAY, MAY..." Static swallowed the message as the helicopter clipped a pine tree, branches snapping like gunfire, the fuselage tearing open with a metallic scream like a soda can, and crashed hard into a clearing. The impact slammed them forward, metal crumpling, glass exploding, dirt and pine needles blasting inward.

For a moment. There was only silence. Reese's ears ringing, smoke curling, fuel dripping. Then the fire ignited. An orange bloom spreading fast, heat searing his skin.

Halston motionless in the wreckage, his head lolling sideways, blood pooling on the shattered console.

Reese, half-conscious and bleeding from a torn leg, fresh blood soaking his flight suit, pain spiking with every heartbeat, crawled through shattered plexiglass as flames engulfed the cockpit.

He collapsed ten feet from the wreck. Gunmen approached the crash site. Reese reached for his sidearm, vision swimming, his fingers fumbling on the holster, the grip slick with blood.

The first gunman raised his rifle. Before he could fire, a burst of headlights swept across the clearing. Two Tyler PD and three Dallas PD cruisers arrived fast and hard. Gunfire erupted from the treeline as the attackers' reinforcements arrived.

Reese lost consciousness as two officers dragged him to safety. Hands gripping his arms, boots scraping dirt, sirens screaming overhead.

Behind him, the helicopter burned until the fuel tank blew, a loud BOOM, as a fireball bloomed skyward, heat washing over the clearing, black smoke twisting upward, lighting the night sky for miles. One dead. One critical.

◆ ◆ ◆

SCSO SWAT | Abandoned Rural Trailer Park Off Highway 64

The SWAT van bounced along the rutted gravel road as the team rolled in dark. No lights. No siren. Just the soft clatter of rifles being checked and rechecked. Bolts sliding forward with sharp metallic snaps, magazines slapping home.

They were heading to an old, abandoned trailer park, mostly full of squatters and homeless people.

Lieutenant Morales, acting team lead, stared at the dead MDT on the dash, screen black, cursor frozen, faint green power LED flickering.

“Command is dark,” Officer Blake muttered from the rear bench.

Morales didn’t answer. He didn’t have a suitable answer to give.

They were responding to a shots-fired call from deputies. Yet, when they arrived, there was no cruiser in sight or officers. Silence greeted them.

“NVGs on,” he said. “Silent exit.”

Monocular NVGs snapped into place, the world shifting to glowing green.

They fanned into the trailer rows in disciplined pairs; boots muted in the mud. Through green-tinted darkness, Morales spotted it first: a deputy’s body behind a trailer, throat cut, vest stripped. Cruiser on its side down a small embankment.

Execution.

"Ambushed," he murmured into his throat mic. "Stay low. Stay paired."

Blake froze. "Engines. Multiple."

"Fall back to the van," Morales said over his mic. Hand chopping the air, the team pivoted in tight formation.

Three black SUVs rolled in formation, lights off, cutting through the rain.

"Positions," Morales ordered.

They sank behind tires, concrete blocks, and trailer skirting covering trailers left on tires. The SUVs slid to a stop. Masked gunmen spilled out, ten to maybe twelve of them. SBRs and suppressed pistols at the ready.

Morales gave the signal to wait... let them close the distance.

"GO!"

SWAT opened with a coordinated, disciplined volley, NVGs aiding their shots. The lead SUV's engine block died instantly. metal punched, steam hissing.

Six gunmen dropped before they realized they were under fire.

The rest reacted fast. Too fast for street thugs. They returned accurate fire, rounds hammering into the SWAT van and chewing up the gravel around the officers.

"Left flank moving!" Morales shouted.

Blake and two others swept wide. An assailant climbed onto the roof of a double-wide.

"Flash out! NVG's off." Blake yelled Flashbangs arcing high, canisters spinning through the air.

A flashbang arced upward, glowing through the rain and darkness. It detonated hard, lighting the rooftop like a miniature sun. The shooter pitched backward, screaming.

Blake took a hit. Rounds hammered his vest, knocking him down hard, the impact thudding, vest plates cracking, air punched out of his lungs.

"BLAKE DOWN!" Voice raw over gunfire, the team pivoted, barrels swinging towards a sniper in the treeline.

Morales moved toward him. A round slammed into his shoulder, spinning him sideways. He hit the mud, teeth clenched, pain spiking through the adrenaline, blood sheeting down his sleeve, his rifle a few feet away.

Two gunmen advanced on the downed SWAT officers.

A shotgun roared behind them. Deputy Weldon, a survivor from the initial call, emerged from the treeline, cycling the pump and dropping both shooters with brutal precision.

"MOVE!" Weldon shouted, voice cutting through the rain, shotgun swinging to cover them.

Morales forced himself upright, grabbed Blake by his vest with his good arm, and dragged him toward cover. Bullets tore through the trailer siding inches above them.

Another burst hit two more SWAT officers, one burning along his side, the other officer in the arm, both flesh wounds.

The remaining gunmen broke formation, retreating toward their SUVs.

"They're falling back!" Weldon yelled.

"No," Morales hissed. His shoulder throbbing, blood soaked his sleeve, teeth gritted. "They're regrouping."

He ordered them to retreat to the SWAT van. A fresh volley stitched the van's rear doors. Disciplined two-second bursts. Morales knew the pattern; these weren't freelancers or regular cartel soldiers.

He was right. Three more SUVs rolled in from the highway approach.

SWAT was moments away from being erased, gunfire intensifying, dirt kicking up in angry puffs, rounds snapping overhead.

Morales tapped his radio again. Nothing. Dead air. They were on their own.

Sirens. Faint. Closing fast, rising wail, red-blue strobes cutting through the rain.

Morales called out, "Help's coming."

He just didn't know if they'd last long enough for it to matter.

"We hold here."

They quickly checked their ammunition, slamming in fresh magazines, determined to fight to the end. Took a deep breath to slow their hammering hearts and prepared for the next opening move by the cartel members.

County Road 21 | Two Patrol Units

A local and well-respected rancher in the county, and someone Deputy Harlan knew personally, flagged down his cruiser and told them he was hearing something strange was happening across the county on his ham radio. He did not know if it was a prank or a fact, but wanted to let the deputies know to warn them.

He heard communications were down and the Smith County Sheriff's county-wide deputies were under attack. Asked Harlan if his MDC or radio was having problems. Not wanting to worry the rancher, he told him that all was normal. Thanked him for the information and headed down the road.

Once he saw the rancher walk back down his drive, he told Mara Thompsom. We need to get with Ruiz and Tolman. They should be less than half an hour from here; see if they know anything. Mara clicked her shoulder radio once more.

Static. They'd been heading back to the station for the last few minutes because of the outage. Until they talked to the rancher, they just thought their equipment had failed. Figured they could request a new cruiser, dashboard lights flickering, engine stuttering slightly.

Their MDC's screen black. It took longer to find Ruiz and Tolman than they originally thought. And informed them of what they had learned from the rancher. Their MDC radios and cells were also out. They decided best to stick together and head back into the sheriff's office. Ten minutes afterwards, the cruisers started having electrical glitches, which forced them to slow down; they needed to get off the highway. They stopped on the side of the road to discuss what would be best to do. They would take the back roads and work their way back to the station, headlights dimming, wipers slowing to a lazy scrape.

Deputy Harlan, walking next to the slow forward movement of the cruiser, wiped rain off the windshield with his hand. The windshield wipers were now not working. For almost an hour and a half, the patrol car's system has been continuously glitching, with flickering lights, a rebooting dash, and a dead radio. The deputy deployed the patrol car's mounted floodlight, probing the adjacent fields located alongside the road's edge to the right.

In the cruiser behind him, Deputies Ruiz and Tolman followed close, staying bumper-to-bumper so they wouldn't lose each other if their headlights died completely. Deputy Ruiz, in the passenger seat of Tolman's unit, scanned the ditches with a side floodlight on the opposite side, beam sweeping left, catching glints of rain on barbed wire.

They were four of the deputies unaccounted for. Others across the county were down, or pinned and still fighting in an ambush, or backed up and fighting back with other police departments. Facts they were unaware of.

Then Ruiz's voice crackled faintly through the PA speaker on Tolman's cruiser. "Car across the road. Four subjects."

Mara braked. The patrol headlights outlined four silhouettes standing calmly in the middle of the asphalt.

Armed men. Rifles low-ready. Left-right-center spacing, classic ambush geometry.

Tolman's voice remarked. "Fuck, looks like your farmer was correct." His hand already sweeping to the shotgun rack.

Before Mara could reverse, the engine went dead, the engine block hit directly by a .50 cal from the trees along the road. The hood buckled upward, steam geysering in a hot white plume.

"OUT! OUT!" Harlan shouted.

Doors flew open.
Gunfire erupted instantly, loud reports tearing through the darkness, gun-muzzle flares illuminating.

Mara took a round in the shoulder before her boots even hit the ground, a hot burning, tearing muscle, arm jerking back, blood blooming instant and dark.

She dropped behind the rear tire, groaning, pain spiking with each heartbeat, breath hissing through clenched teeth.

Ruiz dragged her fully behind cover, hands slick with rain and blood as her eyes fluttered. "Stay with me, Mara! Stay with me!"

Tolman fired controlled bursts over the hood, rounds sparking off the car ahead.

Harlan dove into a roadside ditch as rounds shredded the cruiser's body panels. The roar of engines, gunfire, and ricochets folded into one deafening wall of noise, rapid reports piercing the darkness, gun muzzles flashing intermittently through the dark.

"They've got the high ground on the fence line!" Tolman shouted. "At least eight... no... ten shooters!"

Ruiz fired two rounds. "They're trying to flank us!"

Mara winced, clutching her bleeding shoulder for a moment. "Radio's dead. This is it, guys, we're on our own," as she pulled her gun with her good arm and started firing back at muzzle flashes. Glock bucking in her hand.

Harlan peeked up and saw more muzzle flashes erupt from the treeline.

Backup not available. No dispatch. No comms.

Just four deputies in two cruisers, one wounded, about to be overrun.

Bullets snapped inches from Harlan's face. Dirt sprayed up into his eyes. grit stinging, vision blurring, rounds hissing past. He rolled, fired three rounds wildly, and dropped back down.

Ruiz shouted, "Harlan. Mara took another hit!"

"I can't get to you!" Harlan yelled. "Keep behind cover!"

Tolman rose and raced to Ruiz's position. A rifle cracked in the distance. Tolman jerked; a round clipped his thigh. He stumbled and hit the ground, gritting his teeth. fiery burn. "God... son of a bitch," Tolman hissed and crawled behind the wheel of the cruiser. Thankfully, just a graze. He clicked his radio. Still static.

The assailants pressed forward in a tightening arc.

This was it.
Seconds from being overrun.

A horn. One long, blaring signal cut through the gunfire.

Floodlights bore through the trees.

A Dallas PD convoy burst onto the scene, following a bullet-ridden SWAT van in the lead.

"MOVE! MOVE!" barked Lt. Morales, voice booming as his team deployed like wolves, rifles raised, fanning wide with precision.

Officers spilled out, rifles raised, flanking wide, taking positions with lethal efficiency. Morals stayed back. Not wanting his injury to hamper his team, he called out orders from beside the van.

The assailants turned to engage. Too slow.

The SWAT team unleashed a coordinated volley, dropping three shooters in seconds, bodies jerking as they hit the ground.

Two others tried to run toward the pasture treeline.

Harlan and Tolman join the fight, firing with the other officers from the side of their cruisers.

Ruiz dragged Mara farther behind cover, shielding her with his own body as Dallas PD and SWAT advanced.

A flashbang thrown by a SWAT officer detonated near the fence line, lighting up the night.
The last two gunmen at the fence broke and ran.

SWAT ran them down and put them face down in the mud, handcuffing them. Two shots came from the treeline, and the men on the ground died instantly. Murdered by their own sniper. SWAT officers fired in that direction as they spread out. Nothing. No more shots came from that direction.

Silence finally reigned.

Distant lights came on, and the officers heard dogs barking far off, sharp, frantic barks cutting through the rain.

Harlan leaned back against the cruiser, chest heaving. Tolman hopped once on his good leg, grimacing. "Fucking glad to see you."

Ruiz looked over at the SWAT Lt. Morales and asked, *"What the fuck is going on?"* He lifted Mara's hand. "She's gonna need medivac. And nodded over at Tolman, him as well."

"We brought it," the sergeant said. "We'll get both out." Seconds later, the whoop of an air medivac swelled over the pasture.

The SWAT sergeant, Morales, scanned the scene. Cruisers shredded, deputies wounded, bodies in the pasture. Scattered shell casings were everywhere.

“Same across the county,” Morales said. “Somehow the cartel sabotaged the county’s systems. They knew the routes, knew the numbers. It’s surgical.”

He hesitated. “Word is... your sheriff doubled up patrols tonight. And added twice as many deputies on the road tonight. Rumors say he knew this was coming.”

Ruiz and Harlan nodded slowly. “We found that strange too; the roster also did not have any of the Sheriff’s favorites on duty, even those that normally would have been, but you don’t ignore the Sheriff’s orders.” Harlan said.

A medic whispered to Morales: “We took fire en route. Nothing serious. Still, flight paths to Dallas hospitals are hot. Routing to Tyler instead.”

Morales leaned over Mara. “You’re gonna be okay.”

He watched her, and Tolman, being placed on the helicopter and then turned back to the rest

“We don’t go down as easily as they thought; we still took out more of them, still theirs going to be too many grieving wives and parents when this night is over.”

Harlan nodded.

The Dallas PD sergeant exhaled sharply. “Then let’s get you guys patched up and moving. This night’s not done.”

By ten past three in the morning. State troopers, the Dallas PD, the Tyler PD, and the National Guard flooded the county. But the shooting hadn’t stopped.

The hunters had become the hunted.

For the next hours, calls from deputies off duty came in; their homes were being hit by drive-by shootings. Calls came in from landline phones to the Tyler PD. Luckily, there were only two wounded, no one killed in the homes. The State troopers command dispatched units to cover and assist patrol units, some still under fire across Smith County.

Yet tonight's warning was clear.

We do not fear you.

CHAPTER 39

The Line Held

Thursday, April 27th, 2023

Warehouse Everett/Fiona pinned down

Everett stood up with Fiona in his arms, getting ready to go to her car. Glanced over at Joe, and for a second thought how much easier it would be if he killed him. He would not have to worry about Joe escaping. Fiona moaned. He looked down at her and decided. Bell gets to live. For now.

The first muzzle flash came without warning from the far roll-up door. Everett pivoted, bracing one knee; putting Fiona down, she slumped at his side. He squeezed off two controlled shots with her Sig. A figure dropped and hit the concrete with a thud, rifle clattering across the concrete. He saw movement at the outer edges.

How many are out there, Everett thought to himself. *They must have been who Joe was waiting for earlier.*

Another burst stitched the cinder block near his ear. He dragged Fiona farther back, behind a low pallet stack, checked the mag by feel, and stole a glance through the gap. One shooter hugged the catwalk support; the other slid along the loading ramp, trading angles and whispering to each other in Spanish. They weren't here for a rescue. They were here to finish Joe's work and collect the proof. For the next two hours, it was a standoff. The assailants were trying to flank him. And he ensured they did not. With carefully aimed shots.

Fiona moaned next to him. "Stay with me," Everett told Fiona as he lightly shook her. She nodded slowly, gritted her teeth, and pressed the bandage, which he'd improvised from his shirt remnants, onto her side. She was bleeding badly. He would have to make a move soon, or she would not make it.

The catwalk gunman leaned too far out. Everett punched a round into the man's shoulder, then another into his thigh. The second shooter froze, spooked by the sudden math. One partner was dead, another bleeding out, Joe Bell unconscious and zip-tied to a storage railing, a man below who did not miss. Sirens racing in their direction. But before he could decide what to do, the night outside bloomed red and cobalt.

Sirens cut, doors slammed, and barked commands filled the cavern. Mason came in low with two Tyler PD officers on each side of him, rifles up and searching, Curtis at his heels. Three cruisers boxed in the bay doors, light bars washing the rain-slicked concrete in alternating colors.

"Hands! Hands now!" The Tyler PD sergeant shouted. The last gunman dropped his rifle and went prone.

Mason and Curtis both rushed over to Everett and Fiona. "We've got you. EMTs en route."

"Gun's clear," Everett said, locking the slide and setting it where Mason could see. He didn't let himself look at Joe tied to a railing.

Curtis knelt beside Fiona, jaw tight. "Ambulance is sixty seconds out. You okay."

"I've been better," Fiona managed, breath thin, and then slumped unconscious once more.

Tyler PD flooded the space. One team secured the prisoner. Another sealed the doors, noted the mounted camera, and the recorder and shotgun mic. Officers got cameras out of cruisers and photographed the chain anchor, the knife, the blood trails, and the shell casings. A lieutenant posted a log at the threshold and started a hard perimeter. No one in or out without a name and a logged time. Sent others to call a tow for the SUV identified as Delores Cole's.

Mason crouched over Joe and verified pulses and restraints. "He rides under constant eyes," he told the transport supervisor. "Dash cam, rear cage cam. No stops."

"Copy," the sergeant said. He frisked Joe, logged the two thumb drives he found, and handed them to the evidence tech in tamper-proof bags. "Chain of custody signatures and initials witnessed."

Curtis rose as medics moved Fiona onto a gurney and wrapped Everett's cut forearm. "I'm following them in Fiona's SUV."

"Go," Mason said. "We'll hold this scene until the CSU team gets here. They're on the way."

Outside, rain hammered the roof. Inside, the warehouse steadied into procedure. Mason set his watch to the perimeter log list and didn't move.

"Nothing walks off this slab," he told the lieutenant. "Not a fiber. Till CSU officially arrives and signs for custody."

The lieutenant nodded. "We'll sit on it until they arrive."

Communications run now through the military.

County Road 9 Transport

Friday, April 28th, 2023

The transport unit ran dark down a back road route. One lead cruiser, one tail, Joe locked in the rear cage with his wrists handcuffed with a chain looped through them to the floor. The dashcam recorded his every move.

At the second cattle guard, the world went black. Headlights died, radios coughed static, the engine stuttered. Spike strips bit the cruiser's tires at once. The lead unit fishtailed; the tail unit slewed to a stop. The deputy driver swore, reached for his shoulder mic, and got nothing. Reaching for his weapon.

A shape stepped into the beam of the dying takedown light. Plain charcoal jacket. No mask. Calm.

The driver drew his gun and cracked the car door. "Sheriff's..."

A single round folded him over the console.

The rear deputy bailed, got one shot off, and dropped with two neat holes in his vest and a third in his leg. The one with Joe in the back bailed, fired once and made it into the trees alongside the road. Ignored by the lone man. Silence settled, heavy and total.

The man opened the transport door with a key he should not have had. He looked Joe over like a mechanic inspecting a part. "Out." Forced him down the road until they got into a car on the side of the road five minutes away.

The man drove less than a mile to an old barn, abandoned far out in a pasture, with cedar trees behind it and a limestone ravine not far away, with the sound of the creek in the distance. The man parked under the trees and cut the engine. No words. No theatrics. And forced Joe into a small shack just inside the trees behind the barn. Then the sting of something bit into his back.

The next thing Joe knew, he woke up tied to a chair. He blinked through his swollen eye and felt pain everywhere, from his earlier beating at Everett's hands. He looked up, expecting to see police officers. His breath caught in his throat. He knew that face; he broke into a cold sweat when he realized who it was.

The man squatted in front of him. In a calm voice, he asked. "Who ordered the attack tonight? How was it done? And who are those *cartel soldiers,*" he spat out, "brought in without my knowledge?"

"You weren't told," Joe's voice slurred. "He went around you." Joe found that funny and started laughing, more of a gurgling noise.

The man didn't answer. Just watched him for a few minutes. A young dog padded out of the dark and sat at his heel, its head canted sideways, silent as a shadow. Watched, unmoving.

The man then went to work. For a long time, the begging and screaming continued.

Joe held out as long as any man could.

When the answers came, the night did not change. The dog never moved. Yet something shifted inside *the Ghost*.

He finished it slowly, agonizingly, then wiped his hands, stepped back, and listened to the rain on the tin roof. After a while, he used the deputy's radio he'd grabbed out of the cruiser, long enough to click a sequence only one person would recognize. Someone to clean up this mess and send a message. Then left. He had one more stop tonight.

Detective Marcus Wren Home

Friday, April 28th, 2023

Plano, Texas | Detective Wren's Apartment

Rain whispered at the window. Wren sat in his undershirt, tie tossed across the table, whiskey bottle running low. He looked like a man trying to drink the pressure out of his own chest.

A knock came in a pattern he knew. Steady, familiar. He glanced at his clock on the mantel. Six am.

He opened the door and let out a breath. "You again. I thought they'd sent you back home."

The man gave a small nod. "Checking the correction plan."

"Sure," Wren said, stepping aside. "Come in. Drink?"

The man's gaze shifted toward the bottle, then elsewhere. "No."

Wren poured one for himself. "Things are tightening. Mason's pushing hard for a warrant, but I can stall it. I've still got..."

He stopped when he saw the man pick up his .38 Special resting beside the whiskey. He turned it in his hand, studying the worn metal.

"Easy," Wren said, trying for a laugh. "Backup piece. Revolvers never jam."

"Dependable," the man remarked.

Wren took another drink. "Anyway, once I get the judge to..."

The man put the barrel to Wren's temple and pulled the trigger.

The shot was tight and contained. Wren slumped sideways, spilling whiskey across the table. Wipe it down. Then placed it into Wren's limp hand, and let the dead man's fingers press on the trigger and his palm wrap around the grip.

The gun then dropped with a soft clatter, making sure it dropped where it should.

He stood for a moment, listening. The TV droned on about weather and politics, meaningless noise for the dead and the damned.

Then he switched off the light, stepped into the hallway where a dog waited, and vanished as if he'd never been there at all.

Delores Cole Residence | Highland Park

The Cole residence was quiet except for the movement of four CSU techs working in the entryway and living room. Camera shutters clicked. Evidence markers dotted the hardwood floor.

Two large blood pools dominated the center of the room.

The front door opened. Detective Devon Wade stepped in, shaking off the rain.
"What do we have?"

Elena Torres, senior field tech, crouched at the second pool. "Impact spray indicates possible blunt-force trauma," she said.

Across the room, Jasper Moreno checked the armoire. "No forced entry. Alarm logs show someone used the entry code at one minute past six pm."

Elena pointed toward the fireplace. "Blood spatter here. A victim went down here. This was a quick kill, most likely the husband."

Jasper added, "The black SUV registered to Delores Cole is missing. Patrol confirmed it wasn't here when they arrived."

"No drag marks," Elena said. "Whoever did this must have carried the bodies out somehow."

Elena gestured to the stains. "Anonymous burner phone called in after hearing a gunshot. Patrol officers arrived ten minutes later. House empty, door slightly open, blood still wet on the floor."

Detective Wade examined the scene. Two pools. No bodies. No signs of a defensive struggle. He went upstairs to the main bedroom, following a blood trail, to where two techs were still working.

The bedroom upstairs presented a different scene. Sheets tied to the bedpost. Fresh semen on the bed. Blood splattered across the bedpost. After looking the room over, he moved back downstairs.

Elena moved over to the blood pool. "No robbery indicators. Everything of value untouched."

She handed him the frame from the hallway camera. "Six pm. Delores Cole entered with a man. Shut off the alarm panel."

Devon recognized him immediately from Mason's case. "Joe Bell."

Elena continued. "Garage door closed behind them. Reopened at six forty-five p.m. Dolores' SUV left, presumed Bell driving."

"Blood type?" Devon asked.

"Preliminary indications are that the larger pool, most likely the wife. Pending verification against medical records."

Deven stood. "So, Bell comes here, two people end up bleeding out, bodies removed, then he goes straight to grab Everett. What did he do with the bodies?"

"Working theory," Elena said. "Not perfect."

Jasper held up a bag. "Empty travel bag in the closet. Brand new. Tag still inside."

Elena called from the hallway. "Guest bathroom towel soaked with blood. Trace lipstick on the edge."

Devon nodded once. "Bag everything. Cross-link this to the Joe Bell case and the Taylor-Dennen file. Lock the house down."

Outside, officers held the perimeter as a few press vehicles began lining the street. Not as many as normally would flock to air the murder spectacle of Dallas society patrons. The Tyler County assault overwhelmed the news right now.

Inside, the scene spoke for itself. Two victims, no bodies. Joe Bell, seen on camera leaving in Delores Cole's SUV with two large black bags, put into the back from inside the house. Detective Wade called Detective McCarthy and asked whether he had discovered any bodies in Delores's SUV. Mason stated that Delores' SUV at the warehouse contained no bodies.

Body Dump off County Road 9

Twenty-seven miles away, state troopers followed an anonymous tip to a ravine off County Road 9. Joe Bell's body lay where the caller said he'd be. Hardened deputies turned away from the scene for a minute or two. A rookie rushed away from the body and vomited in the bushes until he dry heaved.

A trooper captain stood at the ravine's edge and said nothing for a long time, watching the CSU techs. Sirens are still a background noise in the far distance. Camera shutters clicked. Dawn birds started singing songs as if they hadn't gotten the memo of the horror below.

CSUs worked the scene, bagging the surrounding dirt, grass, boot marks, and anything else that appeared to be related to the crime scene. Up on the road they took tire track marks left on the road's dirt side. The coroner arrived and, after twenty minutes of photos and checking the body, had it bagged and transported to his office.

At the hospital, Everett dozed with stitches in one arm and bandages on both hands. IVs and meds tubes attached to his arm. Curtis sat in a plastic chair, phone muted. Fiona came out of surgery with a guarded prognosis and a weak pulse.

When she opened her eyes, the first thing she asked was simple. "Did they get the evidence?"

Curtis nodded. "Yes." He'd wait to fill her in on all that had happened that night. For now, she needed rest. Her eyes slid shut.

Outside, the sun broke through the black, roiling clouds in ethereal golden rays, as if they were God's promise in the darkest times

They paid a price, but they held the line.

CHAPTER 40

Aftermath

Friday, April 28th, 2023

Dallas Medical Center | Surgical Wing

Televisions in the waiting rooms, each one replaying the same violent night in chopped, frantic loops: shattered helicopter wreckage in a clearing, another helicopter tail boom in pieces next to a pine forest, stretchers rushing through rain, black SUVs boxed in by police. Burning cruisers on back farm roads. A SWAT van riddled with holes. Deputies under tarps still lying where they fell. National Guard trucks rolling through farmland.

Words crawled in a red bar at the bottom:

BREAKING: SMITH COUNTY SHERIFF'S OFFICE HIT IN COORDINATED ATTACKS. MULTIPLE DEPUTIES DEAD, SEVERAL WOUNDED.

The anchor's voice carried a grim edge:

"Overnight, Tyler County experienced what state officials are calling the largest coordinated attack on law enforcement in modern Texas history."

Behind her, the graphic pictures displayed the confirmed count:

Seven deputies killed, three critical, nine injured

Two air units destroyed. Three helicopter personnel are dead. One Critical.

A chyron rolled up immediately after:

BODY OF MAN FOUND IN RURAL RAVINE. Sources suggest a link to the Tyler County incident.

Then, a standard chyron appeared at the screen's bottom, contrasting the mayhem.

BREAKING: PROMINENT DALLAS HIGHLAND PARK COUPLE BELIEVED MURDERED. BODIES STILL MISSING, HOME SEALED BY POLICE.

Being in the surgical waiting room caused the TV to be muted. It didn't matter. The vivid images and CC information were loud enough.

◆ ◆ ◆

Surgical Waiting Room

All five O'Brien brothers held the room like a phalanx. Connor sat rigid, elbows braced on his knees, eyes fixed on the double doors that led deeper into the surgical wing. Timothy paced in slow circles like an executive waiting on a hostile merger call. Ryan rested against the wall, arms crossed tight, his presence sharp as a knife. Thomas stood at the counter, his FBI badge on his belt, speaking on the phone with a voice clipped with Bureau formality.
Casey prowled. Restless, irritated, tired of being told to wait.

No one talked at first.

Then the elevator dinged. They all stood and moved towards it, hoping for news.

Curtis stepped off the elevator, still wearing the same clothes from the warehouse. Someone had cleaned the blood off his hands but missed streaks along his wrist from keeping pressure on Fiona's wound until the EMTs got to her.

The brothers spotted him instantly.

"How bad?" Connor asked, voice low.

"She made it through the first procedure," Curtis said. He sugarcoated nothing. "They're working on internal bleeding now. The bullet did not impact the lung, though it caused significant injury when exiting. They stabilize her. That's good news at least. She's tough."

All five brothers exhaled. Not in relief. Just a recalibration of the situation.

Casey moved in closer. "What the hell happened out there?"

Curtis drew a slow breath. "Short version? The county went dark. Communications wiped. Deputies hit across multiple sectors. We walked into a full-scale assault. While your sister went to save Everett from Joe Bell, tracking Delores' SUV."

Timothy scrubbed a hand over his face. "Christ."

Thomas, jaw tight, said, "I saw the feed. But what I *didn't* see was how they pulled off simultaneous attacks without triggering federal alarms."

Curtis shook his head. "Transitions AI breach. Entire sheriff's network compromised."

"Something about Transitions AI crossed my desk during our investigation into the Dallas convention center. The investigation continues, but they removed that information because the brass claimed it was nonessential. Pointing out that Transition AI information could have been because they were at the conference."

Ryan finally pushed off the wall, posture stiffening as he watched more footage about the attack. What caught his attention was the remark by a reporter about the helicopters being shot down with a Stinger Block II variant. The reporter claimed an inside source in the military gave them the information.

His voice was quiet and dangerous. "Where the hell did cartel thugs gain a goddamn Stinger Block II variant

RPG?"

Curtis didn't dodge it. "No clue yet. Come on, you know as well as I do, wide-open borders don't just bring illegals. They bring illegal weapons, and enemies of Americans willing to use them. Devon Wade's already on-site at the Cole residence. He found evidence of planning, movement, and... something else." He hesitated. "I'm heading out to meet him as soon as I know Fiona's stable. I worked with his father in Denver until he transferred to the Dallas PD."

Thomas's eyes narrowed. "Something else?"

Ryan gave a humorless snort. "Somebody in uniform better be checking inventory."

Connor cut in, steady and serious. "And this Everett guy she went to save? Is he alive? Are they involved?"

"No, not involved, just a client. And yeah, he's alive." Curtis said. "Beat to hell. Sedatives that the hospital staff gave him after his arrival are still wearing off. They've got a deputy posted outside the door because the press already sniffed out who he is. Rumors are flying like a flock of insane martins."

Casey exhaled a sharp sound. "Lucky bastard to even be alive."

Ryan gave Casey a long look before saying. "If it's the Everett Taylor, I knew in special forces, there was nothing *lucky* about it."

Casey looked peeved but left it alone. The news rotated again, and the chyron rolled once more about the body in the ravine.

Connor's eyes flicked to the screen. "That Joe Bell?"

"Mason thinks so," Curtis said. "Or what's left of him."

Timothy asked, "Who found the body?"

Curtis met his eyes. "I don't know. The county just reported a body in a ravine. They're assuming it's tied to last night. Mason informed me it might be Bell. Not sure right now. Someone mutilated the body. An attacker assaulted the transport, and Bell vanished. If that's his body, that tells me it was not a rescue operation like we originally thought."

Timothy didn't pretend to be surprised. "Someone tied up their loose ends."

Curtis said nothing. He already had his suspicions. None of them involved law enforcement.

None of the brothers pressed further.
Some truths didn't need to be spoken yet.

The Doors Open

A nurse stepped out, scanning the group.

"The O'Brien family?"

They all rose at once.

She softened her tone when she saw the collective wall of men. "She's stable. Surgery is complete. They're moving her to recovery now."

Connor asked, "Can we see her?"

She looked at the lot and figured they might wear her out if all went at once. "Only one at a time."

Thomas requested to go first.

Connor nodded. "Go."

Thomas followed the nurse down the hall.

They were hard, though honest men. Rancher, wealthy Real Estate mogul, SEAL. FBI agent. Attorney. But with their baby sister, they were just brothers waiting in the dark for a baby sister they loved with a fierceness few realized.

Outside, the national news vans kept rolling in. Reporters adjusted their jackets and rehearsed lines. Inside, the world finally stopped spinning long enough for the brothers to take a breath. They each got their turn. Then waited in the waiting room for the rest of the night.

Fiona O'Brien wasn't out of danger. She'd survived the night.

Tonight, the country would learn the name of Smith County. But none of that mattered here.

Here, they were just trying to keep the world from changing before Fiona woke up again.

◆ ◆ ◆

Saturday, April 29th, 2023

Dallas Medical Center

Fiona woke to the muted hum of wheels rolling somewhere in the hallway and the faint scent of antiseptic sharpness from the hospital vents. Her breathing was steadier now. The nurses controlled the as-needed pain meds, dimmed the lights, and the storm of the last few days had finally settled into an uneasy quiet.

Her brothers had all returned.

Connor arrived before sunrise, scooping up Josh and telling him they were taking a "vacation" to the ranch in Colorado. The boy believed him as he had spent time there when his mother got too busy. Every line in Conner's face carved with the weight of Josh almost losing his mother and him his beloved sister.

Timothy, Ryan, Thomas, and Casey stayed. They hovered in shifts, drifting between their hotels, waiting rooms, and her doorway like restless shadows.

Hospital Critical Care Waiting Area

Ryan O'Brien didn't raise his voice when he was angry. He got *quiet.*

Dangerously quiet.

He was standing in the hallway now, arms folded across his chest, jaw locked like steel as Major Buck stepped off the elevator.

"Ryan," Buck said, nodding once.

Ryan held up a printed sheet, creased, folded, manhandled. A copy of the signed part of the contract with Major Buck.

"You want to explain why my sister's name is on a tactical consulting agreement with military intelligence?" Ryan asked. "Why did you come to *her* first, before any other established and more acceptable companies?"

Buck didn't bother lying.

"She had the skills I needed," he said. "And the money, along with the connections. Law enforcement. Federal. Military. And she's good at what she does. Better than most."

Ryan stepped closer, voice low enough to cut glass.

"You used her," he growled. "Because she's smart, connected, and expendable to you. *Your Goddaughter.*"

Buck didn't answer. Nothing he said right now would change Ryan's thinking. Men like him, once they made up their minds, were a tough nut to crack to get them to see your way.

Ryan's stare hardened. "I'm not on rotation right now. But I will be soon. And before I go wheels-up again, you're to keep me in the loop. No more back-channel recruiting. No more sweet-talk justifications. You come to *me first.*"

Buck nodded once. It wasn't an agreement. It was acknowledgement of a man he couldn't BS. And who just played right into his hand.

Ryan turned to walk back toward Fiona's room, then turned back saying before he walked away, "You ever put her in the crosshairs again without warning me, I'll make sure your career doesn't survive the paperwork."

Buck didn't follow. He'd come back later to check on Fiona. She and Curtis were one of his now. Ryan should have known that from knowing him. He took care of those who fell under his command.

They're evicted from Dallas HQ

Curtis showed up mid-morning with coffee but dumped it before entering Fiona's room, not wanting to tempt her.

"Fi," he said, closing the door behind him. "We've got a problem."

She raised an eyebrow. Her voice was tired. "Only one?"

Curtis exhaled sharply. "Downtown office, the landlord terminated the lease. He said after the news coverage and the 'security incident,' he's not renewing. We have to clear out by Friday."

Fiona shut her eyes for a moment, then reopened them.

"Fine," she murmured. "We'll rebuild. For now, run everything out of the ranch."

Curtis nodded and pulled a folder from his briefcase.

"Mason tipped me off to something else. Old ten-story building near the Trinity curve. Used to be a textile and western boot wear headquarters. Now it's boarded up, riddled with squatters, and sitting in its *third* auction round. The city wants it gone. Or refurbished. Either will do."

He held out the folder.

"Fi... we could buy it outright. Dirt cheap. No landlord. No restrictions. Make it our HQ."

Fiona didn't hesitate long.
She reached for the folder despite the IV line tugging gently on her arm.

"We'll take it," she whispered.

Curtis smiled faintly. "Already started the paperwork. Just needed your signature here."

She signed with a shaky hand. Then, her eyes fluttered shut, so Curtis left quietly.

Fion's Hospital Room

A nurse came in to check vitals. Fiona watched the numbers rise and fall on the screen.

"You're stable," the nurse said briskly. "Surprisingly stable. In another week, maybe less, and you can go home. Provided you don't..."

She looked pointedly at Fiona, "Do anything strenuous."

Fiona smirked. "No promises."

Timothy groaned. "For once in your life, Fi, try to listen when people are giving you good advice."

Casey patted her leg gently. "We'll be here. You're not alone."

Her family's presence washed over her like warmth she didn't know she needed.

The pain eased a little.

The room quieted.

Outside the blinds, bright sunlight broke through thin clouds, and the sounds of birds calling back and forth filled the air. Spring arrived, unconcerned with the troubles of humans.

Fiona exhaled slowly, eyelids heavy, as she fell back to sleep.

The brothers exchanged a glance.

◆◆◆

Hospital Room

The room was dim when Fiona woke again, the soft hum of monitors steady beside her. Outside the window, dark, the lights from the Dallas skyline were like a mosaic pattern of gold and white rising into the air. For a moment she thought she was alone; then she spotted something she hadn't seen before.

A glass vase sat on her bedside table. Twelve deep-red roses. Fresh. Still beaded with moisture.

She frowned. She'd heard no one come in.

A small, folded note rested against the vase. Fiona reached for it carefully, wincing at the pull in her side.
Inside was only one line, written in neat, deliberate handwriting. *He's grown. Get better. We both miss you.*

The hair on the back of her neck rose.

She set the note down, eyes on the roses, the empty hallway beyond her open door, the silence pressing around her.

Someone had been here. Close enough to leave flowers inches from her bed.

Fiona exhaled slowly and leaned back against the pillows.

"Of course you have," she whispered to no one. Whoever took that puppy and kept leaving her pictures and notes was like a ghost slipping in and out of her life.

Later, the nurse entered and informed her that a handsome man had left it for her. And inquired whether he was her boyfriend. The nurse rushed out of the room before Fiona could tell her no, running off as a code blue emergency sounded.

CHAPTER EPILOGUE

Echoes and Embers

Monday, May 8th, 2023

Whiskey Riven Two Step Ranch

Fiona was in her ranch office reading a case report when she heard a reporter announce that the newly elected Sheriff of Smith County was about to speak. She stopped working, turned up the news, and sat down to listen.

Sheriff Elijah Cade, Smith County's newest sheriff, stepped up to the podium.

"I am here today to ask for funding to rebuild a safer Smith County. What I am asking for is a funding request for deputy expansion and tactical training. And more deputies. We have one of the largest counties yet have the smallest number of deputies to cover it. Smith County will never forget the night our deputies bled and died on lonely back-country roads. On a storm-darkened night, when our communications were deliberately severed and our deputies left exposed on isolated roads, we faced an enemy that moved as if they had our playbook. Seven deputies never made it home. Nine more carry scars that will last lifetimes. Our SWAT unit, trained, armored, disciplined, took casualties in minutes because we simply didn't have enough deputies on the ground to respond fast enough."

He took a moment to collect himself, having been one of those deputies that survived that night. His voice grew stronger, more intense.

"Let's be clear: this wasn't bad luck. This was the predictable result of years of underfunding, outdated equipment, and a system that treated rural law enforcement like an afterthought. We had courage. We lacked the capacity. And capacity costs money that someone, somewhere, decided we didn't deserve. That decision will not stand. I'm calling on the County Commissioners to approve a thirty-five percent increase in sworn deputies on patrol, detectives, and tactical. I'm asking the state legislature for emergency funding to upgrade our emergency infrastructure: hardened dispatch backups, countywide encrypted mesh radios, quarterly rural-ambush and digital-blackout training." He stopped to shuffle some papers.

"And I'm demanding mental health resources that reach the people who need them before another night like that one breaks more families. Smith County buried too many good people because we lacked sufficient resources. Never again. We held the line that night. Now we fortify it. For our deputies, for our families, for every citizen who expects us to answer the call and live to tell about it." He paused as reporters demanded answers to their questions. He ignored them and spoke over them.

"We're not asking for extras. We're asking for what we need, so no deputy ever bleeds out alone on the roadside again. The criminals who came to Smith County thought we'd shatter under pressure. They were wrong. We endured. We adapted. And now we need to rebuild. Stronger, smarter, and more prepared." He looked straight at the camera.

"But we need your support to do it. To the citizens of Smith County. I swore an oath to protect you. Now I'm fighting to make sure every deputy who answers your call has the tools, training, and backup they need to come home alive. This isn't just policy. This is survival. And we've already buried too many. We've already paid in blood. Now we pay in preparation. So the next storm finds us ready, not reeling."

The sheriff stepped away from the podium. And a county commissioner took his place.

Fiona muted the rest and sat back. She liked the new sheriff. Bold enough to say point-blank the failure of so many who withheld funds in the past from the county. Desperately needing funds to get the manpower and training that only a lack of money denied them, she prayed this appeal to the public might force the hands of those who withheld money so they could line their own pockets or put it in pet projects that in the end improved nothing and protected no one.

Fiona's Ranch Office Later in the day

Fiona watched the sun climb over the half-renovated district outside for a while back in her office.

She drank an espresso, needing something strong this morning, reviewing the latest candidate for the front desk. The thought of Selena still felt raw, but they were going to need a receptionist once the Dallas HQ opened. A knock broke her thoughts. They were using several upstairs bedrooms converted for now into various office areas.

Morris entered without waiting for her to answer, sharp as ever.

"Got one," he said. "Lona Ana Montes. Solid resume knows when to stay out of the way, good with clients. You need someone who also has good discernment skills for walk-ins."

Fiona skimmed the file; clean and straightforward, seemed to know her way around an executive office.

"Fine. Ninety-day probation."

Morris grinned. "She won't disappoint."

He left as the TV in her office flipped to breaking news.

She grabbed the remote and turned the volume up.

Breaking News: *Senatorial candidate Chad Ashburn makes a public statement honoring the victims of the Taylor-Neylan sister's case...*

Fiona's jaw set. They connected nothing to him, or Porter & Ashburn, publicly, yet they left an unpleasant taste in her mouth. And she doubted the case just closed would be their last interaction with them.

Chad appeared on screen, standing before a sea of microphones. He wore a tailored suit and had a wide, charming smile. American flags flanked him.

"Today," he began, "Porter & Ashburn is proud to announce the Neylan-Taylor Memorial Scholarship Fund at Yale University. It will support young women in pursuing justice, ethics, and public service. The legacy Bridget and Lisa devoted their lives to at our legal firm."

Fiona leaned forward slightly. Her mouth dry.

"The FBI absolved our firm in the tragic crimes that unfolded," Chad continued. "We cooperated fully with the FBI, which cleared us of any wrongdoing. We immediately severed ties with Transition AI when Marshall Hays's dealings came to light. It was a betrayal. But it was not ours." The camera panned to a reporter asking about Everett Taylor.

"I cannot speak to the actions of others," Chad said smoothly. "But I commend Esq. George Shaw and his investigators at O'Brien & Galloway Investigations for their timely contribution of evidence in clearing Mr. Taylor's name. Most of the information Bridget and Lisa exposed while working at our firm. Without them, the truth might never have surfaced."

Fiona stared at the screen, every syllable digging deeper.

"I did not know Bridget and Lisa were still investigating after we assigned an internal review when they first informed us of what they found," Chad said. "Had I known, I would've insisted they stop. It was simply too dangerous for junior partners to pursue an investigation; only law enforcement should have, because of the danger."

He offered a last look at the camera. With just the proper hint of sadness and resolve.

"We mourn their sacrifice. And I promise to honor it. In Washington, and beyond."

The screen faded to commercials.

Fiona muted the TV. He somehow turned it into their firm being the hero of the story.

She pressed her thumb hard into the seam of her coffee mug and gritted her teeth.

They spun it. They spun everything. Fiona stared at the screen. The spin. Major Buck warned her and Curtis about.
Bridget and Lisa's deaths, and they'd already minted a scholarship out of it.
Marshall Hays? In the wind. Joe Bell, conveniently dead. Reid Cavanaugh's name buried in layers of deniability. And Chad? Clean as a pressed suit. The perfect candidate.
Of course, they would protect him. Groom him. Make sure no dirt ever touched the golden boy. And yet the Ashburns, especially Chad, had come out with a shine like gold. And there wasn't a damn thing she could do about it.

Not yet, of course; it could be a rogue faction within Porter & Ashburn. How Reid Cavanaugh walked away with his position and reputation intact burned deeper than she cared to admit.

Buck had advised her. Keep quiet. The intelligence community needed information, and time needed silence. Project SILO had unearthed too many threads, and most were not ready to be pulled. They wanted them to believe they had never discovered the use and extent of SILO in the human trafficking business. He reminded her that the organization thought they had retrieved the external drives with evidence to convict them. Only Buck's division and the PI firm knew about Reid's connection to any of the shell companies.

And Chad? Buck wasn't sure he even knew anything about what went on at his father Edward's legal firm.

"Edward or someone else powerful in rarefied air is protecting him," Buck informed her. "Shielding him from the rot, grooming him for the big leagues, making sure no dirt can touch him."

Fiona understood how the criminal world functioned and knew how they used that strategy well. Keep the upper members clean, untouched, so that the organization survives. Let someone else do the dirty work, take the fall, do the time.

She pulled a photo from her desk drawer: Lila, Bridget, and Lisa. Not posed, just laughing over takeout boxes at the cabin, now a burned-out hollow, only a cracked foundation and a few blackened pieces of wood in its place.

Fiona stared at it for a long moment; thumb pressed to the edge. Then she tucked it away. Looking at the picture on her desk, a picture of her husband, Matt, with her and Josh a month before he died. She would keep her word. She would find out what happened to Lila and discover who murdered her husband. A silent vow. Sighed and picked up her coffee cup. The last of her coffee had gone cold, the taste bitter.

She dumped it in the sink, watching the creamy liquid spiral until it vanished down the drain. Thought about the strange string of numbers from the burner phone Everett originally gave them, she put Josh on trying to figure it out, sighed then. She turned back to her desk. Sighed and hoped for the refurbishment of their new headquarters to get done soon. Then refocused.

Time to get back to work.

PLATINUM OAK PUBLISHING

Platinum Oak Publishing was founded with one clear purpose: to champion independent authors who treat writing as a craft worthy of rigor, discipline, and excellence.

We believe that independent publishing should never mean compromised quality. In an industry flooded with rushed releases and disposable stories, Platinum Oak stands apart by partnering exclusively with serious authors — those who labor over every sentence, who revise with honesty and precision, and who refuse to cut corners on research, character depth, or narrative integrity.

ABOUT THE AUTHOR

Raina Wolfe

She grew up as an Air Force military brat and later married into the Army, experiences that took her across the United States and around the world. Her diverse path includes working for a petroleum geologist in Ventura, California, commercial salmon fishing on Alaska's Kenai Peninsula, and handling horses as a stable hand at two prestigious Oregon stables—an adventure that eventually led her to own land in Colorado.

She has served as armed and unarmed security with Pinkerton, worked as a civilian telephone operator for the American Military in Mannheim and also the University of Maryland in Mannheim, Germany, and earned her Criminal Justice degree while working full time. After receiving her police POST certification, she served as a police officer, gaining firsthand insight into investigations, procedure, and the human cost of crime that now fuels her writing.

A lifelong story writer, Raina decided to write professionally after a serious injury forced her to reassess her path. She is the author of the Dark Horizons series—hard-edged investigative thrillers rooted in realism and moral complexity. When she's not writing, she lives on thirty-six acres on Colorado's eastern plains with her family, her dogs Sadie and Lily, and three homes that keep life lively. She is the proud mother of two grown daughters and grandmother to bright, inquisitive grandkids, who still laugh at her online gaming adventures in Guild Wars 2.

www.ingramcontent.com/pod-product-compliance
Lightning Source LLC
LaVergne TN
LVHW100501110826
845146LV00002B/481

* 9 7 9 8 9 9 4 7 6 3 6 2 9 *